THE INFORMATION

By the same author

FICTION
The Rachel Papers
Dead Babies
Success
Other People: A Mystery Story
Money
Einstein's Monsters
London Fields
Time's Arrow

JOURNALISM
Invasion of the Space Invaders
The Moronic Inferno
Visiting Mrs. Nabokov

THE INFORMATION

by MARTIN AMIS

Harmony Books
New York

Published by Harmony Books, a division of Crown Publishers, Inc., 201 East 50th
Street, New York, New York 10022. Member of the Crown Publishing Group.

Random House, Inc. New York, Toronto, London, Sydney, Auckland

HARMONY and colophon are trademarks of Crown Publishers, Inc.

Manufactured in the United States of America

Design by Rick Pracher

Library of Congress Cataloging-in-Publication Data
Amis, Martin.
The information / by Martin Amis.—1st ed.
p.   cm.
I. Title.
PR6051.M515   1995
823'.914—DC20   94-44512
CIP

ISBN 0-517-58516-2
10 9 8 7 6 5 4 3 2 1
First Edition

To Louis and Jacob

And to the memory of
Lucy Partington
(1952–1973)

PART ONE

Cities at night, I feel, contain men who cry in their sleep and then say Nothing. It's nothing. Just sad dreams. Or something like that . . . Swing low in your weep ship, with your tear scans and your sob probes, and you would mark them. Women—and they can be wives, lovers, gaunt muses, fat nurses, obsessions, devourers, exes, nemeses—will wake and turn to these men and ask, with female need-to-know, "What is it?" And the men say, "Nothing. No it isn't anything really. Just sad dreams."

Just sad dreams. Yeah: oh sure. Just sad dreams. Or something like that.

Richard Tull was crying in his sleep. The woman beside him, his wife, Gina, woke and turned. She moved up on him from behind and laid hands on his pale and straining shoulders. There was a professionalism in her blinks and frowns and whispers: like the person at the poolside, trained in first aid; like the figure surging in on the blood-smeared macadam, a striding Christ of mouth-to-mouth. She was a woman. She knew so much more about tears than he did. She didn't know about Swift's juvenilia, or Wordsworth's senilia, or how Cressida had variously fared at the hands of Boccaccio, of Chaucer, of Robert Henryson, of Shakespeare; she didn't know Proust. But she knew tears. Gina had tears cold.

"What is it?" she said.

Richard raised a bent arm to his brow. The sniff he gave was complicated, orchestral. And when he sighed you could hear the distant seagulls falling through his lungs.

"Nothing. It isn't anything. Just sad dreams."

Or something like that.

3

After a while she too sighed and turned over, away from him.

There in the night their bed had the towelly smell of marriage.

He awoke at six, as usual. He needed no alarm clock. He was already comprehensively alarmed. Richard Tull felt tired, and not just underslept. Local tiredness was up there above him—the kind of tiredness that sleep might lighten—but there was something else up there over and above it. And beneath it. That greater tiredness was not so local. It was the tiredness of time lived, with its days and days. It was the tiredness of gravity—gravity, which wants you down there in the center of the earth. That greater tiredness was here to stay: and get heavier. No nap or cuppa would ever lighten it. Richard couldn't remember crying in the night. Now his eyes were dry and open. He was in a terrible state—that of consciousness. Some while ago in his life he had lost the knack of choosing what to think about. He slid out of bed in the mornings just to find some peace. He slid out of bed in the mornings just to get a little rest. He was forty tomorrow, and reviewed books.

In the small square kitchen, which stoically awaited him, Richard engaged the electric kettle. Then he went next door and looked in on the boys. Dawn visits to their room had been known to comfort him after nights such as the one he had just experienced, with all its unwelcome information. His twin sons in their twin beds. Marius and Marcus were not identical twins. And they weren't fraternal twins either, Richard often said (unfairly, perhaps), in the sense that they showed little brotherly feeling. But that's all they were, brothers, born at the same time. It was possible, theoretically (and, Richard surmised, their mother being Gina, also practically) that Marcus and Marius had different fathers. They didn't look alike, especially, and were strikingly dissimilar in all their talents and proclivities. Not even their birthdays were content to be identical: a sanguinary summer midnight had interposed itself between the two boys and their (again) very distinctive parturitional styles, Marius, the elder, subjecting the delivery room to a systematic and intelligent stare, its negative judgment suspended by decency and disgust, whereas Marcus just clucked and sighed to himself complacently, and seemed to pat himself down, as if after a successful journey through freak weather. Now in the dawn, through the window and through the rain, the streets of London looked like the insides of an old plug. Richard contemplated his sons, their motive bodies reluctantly arrested in sleep, and reef-knotted to their bedware, and he thought, as an artist might: but the young sleep in another country, at once very dangerous and out of harm's way, perennially humid with innocuous libido—there are neutral eagles out on the windowsill, waiting, offering protection and threat.

Sometimes Richard did think and feel like an artist. He was an artist when he saw fire, even a match head (he was in his study now, lighting his first cigarette): an instinct in him acknowledged its elemental status. He was an artist when he saw society: it never crossed his mind that society had to be like this, had any right, had any business being like this. A car in the street. Why? Why *cars*? This is what an artist has to be: harassed to the point of insanity or stupefaction by first principles. The difficulty began when he sat down to write. The difficulty, really, began even earlier. Richard looked at his watch and thought: I can't call him yet. Or rather: Can't call him yet. For the interior monologue now waives the initial personal pronoun, in deference to Joyce. He'll still be in bed, not like the boys and their abandonment, but lying there personably, and smugly sleeping. For *him*, either there would be no information, or the information, such as it was, would all be good.

For an hour (it was the new system) he worked on his latest novel, deliberately but provisionally entitled *Untitled*. Richard Tull wasn't much of a hero. Yet there was something heroic about this early hour of flinching, flickering labor, the pencil sharpener, the Wite-Out, the vines outside the open window sallowing not with autumn but with nicotine. In the drawers of his desk or interleaved by now with the bills and summonses on the lower shelves on his bookcases, and even on the floor of the car (the terrible red Maestro), swilling around among the Ribena cartons and the dead tennis balls, lay other novels, all of them firmly entitled *Unpublished*. And stacked against him in the future, he knew, were yet further novels, successively entitled *Unfinished*, *Unwritten*, *Unattempted*, and, eventually, *Unconceived*.

Now came the boys—in what you would call a flurry if it didn't go on so long and involve so much inanely grooved detail, with Richard like the venerable though tacitly alcoholic pilot in the cockpit of the frayed shuttle: his clipboard, his nine-page checklist, his revving hangover—socks, sums, cereal, reading book, shaved carrot, face wash, teeth brush. Gina appeared in the middle of this and drank a cup of tea standing by the sink . . . Though the children were of course partly mysterious to Richard, thank God, he knew their childish repertoire and he knew the flavor of their hidden lives. But Gina he knew less and less about. Little Marco, for instance, believed that the sea was the creation of a rabbit who lived in a racing car. This you could discuss. Richard didn't know what Gina believed. He knew less and less about her private cosmogony.

There she stood, in light lipstick and light pancake and light woolen suit, holding her teacup in joined palms. Other working girls whose beds Richard had shared used to get up at around eleven at night to interface themselves for the other world. Gina did it all in twenty minutes. Her body threw no difficulties in her way: the wash-and-go drip-dry hair, the candid orbits that needed only the mildest of emphasis, the salmony tongue, the ten-second bowel movement, the body that all clothes loved. Gina worked two days a week, sometimes three. What she did, in public relations, seemed to him much more mysterious than what he did, or failed to do, in the study next door. Like the sun, now, her face forbade any direct address of the eyes, though of course the sun glares crazily everywhere at once and doesn't mind who is looking at it. Richard's dressing gown bent round him as he fastened Marius's shirt buttons with his eaten fingertips.

"Can you fasten it?" said Marius.

"Do you want a cup of tea making?" said Gina, surprisingly.

"Knock knock," said Marco.

Richard said, in order, "I am fastening it. No thanks, I'm okay. Who's there?"

"You," said Marco.

"No, *fasten* it. Come on, Daddy!" said Marius.

Richard said, "You who? You don't mean *fasten* it. You mean do it faster. I'm trying."

"Are they ready?" said Gina.

"Who are you calling! Knock knock," said Marco.

"I think so. Who's there?"

"What about macks?"

"Boo."

"They don't need macks, do they?"

"Mine aren't going out in that without macks."

"*Boo*," said Marco.

"Are you taking them in?"

"Boo who? Yeah, I thought so."

"Why are you crying!"

"Look at you. You aren't even dressed yet."

"I'll get dressed now."

"Why are you crying!"

"It's ten to nine. I'll take them."

"No, I'll take them."

"Daddy! Why are you *crying*?"

"What? I'm not."

"In the night you were," said Gina.

"Was I?" said Richard.

Still in his dressing gown, and barefoot, Richard followed his family out into the passage and down the four flights of stairs. They soon out-speeded him. By the time he rounded the final half-landing the front door was opening—was closing—and with a whip of its tail the flurry of their life had gone.

Richard picked up his *Times* and his low-quality mail (so brown, so unwelcome, so slowly moving through the city). He sifted and then thrashed his way into the newspaper until he found Today's Birthdays. There it stood. There was even a picture of him, cheek to cheek with his wife: Lady Demeter.

At eleven o'clock Richard Tull dialed the number. He felt the hastening of excitement when Gwyn Barry himself picked up the telephone.

"Hello?"

Richard exhaled and said measuredly, ". . . You fucking old *wreck*."

Gwyn paused. Then the elements came together in his laugh, which was gradual and indulgent and even quite genuine. "Richard," he said.

"Don't laugh like that. You'll pull a muscle. You'll break your neck. Forty years old. I saw your obit in *The Times*."

"Listen, are you coming to this thing?"

"I am, but I don't think you'd better. Sit tight, by the fire. With a rug on your lap. And an old-boy pill with your hot drink."

"Yes, all right. Enough," said Gwyn. "Are you coming to this thing?"

"Yeah, I suppose so. Why don't I come to you around twelve-thirty and we'll get a cab."

"Twelve-thirty. Good."

"You fucking old *wreck*."

Richard sobbed briefly and then paid a long and consternated visit to the bathroom mirror. His mind was his own and he accepted full respon-sibility for it, whatever it did or might do. But his *body*. The rest of the morning he spent backing his way into the first sentence of a seven-hundred-word piece about a seven-hundred-page book about Warwick Deeping. Like the twins, Richard and Gwyn Barry were only a day apart in time. Richard would be forty tomorrow. The information would not be carried by *The Times: The Times*, the newspaper of record. Only one celebrity lived at 49E Calchalk Street; and she wasn't famous. Gina was a *genetic* celebrity. She was beautiful, every inch, and she didn't change. She got older, but she didn't change. In the gallery of the old photographs she was always the same, staring out, while everyone else seemed disgracefully protean, kaftaned Messiahs, sideburned Zapatas. He sometimes wished she wasn't: wasn't beautiful. In his present travail. Her brother and sister were ordinary. Her dead dad had been ordinary. Her mother was still around for the time being, fat and falling apart and still mountainously pretty somehow, in a bed somewhere.

We are agreed—come *on*: we are agreed—about beauty in the flesh. Consensus is possible here. And in the mathematics of the universe, beauty helps tell us whether things are false or true. We can quickly agree about beauty, in the heavens and in the flesh. But not everywhere. Not, for instance, on the page.

In the van, Scozzy looked at 13 and said,

"Morrie goes to the doctor, right?"

"Right," said 13.

13 was eighteen and he was black. His real name was Bently. Scozzy was thirty-one, and he was white. His real name was Steve Cousins.

Scozzy said, "Morrie tells the doc, he says, 'I can't raise it with my wife. My wife Queenie. I can't raise it with Queenie.' "

Hearing this, 13 did something that white people have stopped really doing. He grinned. White people used to do it, years ago. "Yeah," said 13 expectantly. Morrie, Queenie, he thought: all Jews is it.

Scozzy said, "The doc goes, 'Unlucky. Listen. We got these pills in from Sweden. The latest gear. Not cheap. Like a *carpet* a pill. Okay?' "

13 nodded. "Or whatever," he said.

They were sitting in the orange van, drinking cans of Ting: pineapple-grapefruit crush. 13's fat dog Giro sat erectly between them on the hand-brake section, keeping still but panting as if in great lust.

" 'Take one of them and you'll have a stiffy for four hours. A bonk with a capital O.' Morrie goes home, right?" Scozzy paused and then said thoughtfully, "Morrie rings up the doc and he's like, 'I just took one of them pills but guess what.' "

13 turned and frowned at Scozzy.

" 'Queenie's gone shopping! Won't be back for four hours!' The doc says, 'This is serious, mate. Is there anybody else indoors?' Morrie says, 'Yeah. The au pair.' The doc says, 'What she like?' 'Eighteen with big tits.' So the doc goes, 'Okay. Stay calm. You'll have to do it with the au pair. Tell her it's an emergency. Medical matter.' "

"Medical matter whatever," murmured 13.

" 'Ooh I don't know,' says Morrie. 'I mean a *carpet* a pill? Seems like an awful waste. I can get a stiffy with the au pair anyway.' "

There was silence.

Giro gulped and started panting again.

13 leaned back in his seat. Grin and frown now contested for the suzerainty of his face. The grin won. "Yeah," said 13. "Do it on the carpet is it."

". . . What fucking carpet?"

"You said carpet."

"When?"

"Pill on the carpet."

"Jesus Christ," said Scozzy. "The pills *cost* a carpet. Each."

13 looked mildly unhappy. A mere nothing. It would pass.

"A *carpet.* Jesus. You know: half a stretch."

Nothing—a mere nothing.

"*Fucking* hell. A stretch is six months. A carpet is half a stretch. Three hundred quid."

It had passed. 13 grinned weakly.

Scozzy said, "You're the one who's always in fucking prison."

With fright-movie suddenness (Giro stopped panting) Richard Tull appeared in the left foreground of the van's glass screen and fixed them with a wince before reeling on by. Giro gulped, and started panting again.

"Woe," said Scozzy.

"The man," 13 said simply.

"He's not the man. The man's the other one. He's his mate." Scozzy nodded and smiled and shook his head with all these things coming together: he loved it. "And Crash does his wife."

"The man," said 13. "Of TV fame." 13 frowned, and added, "I never seen him on the telly."

Steve Cousins said, "You just watch fucking Sky."

Richard rang the bell on Holland Park and, momentarily haggard in his bow tie, presented himself to the security camera—which jerked round affrontedly at him in its compact gantry above the door. He also made mental preparations. The state Richard sought was one of disparity readiness. And he never found it. Gwyn's setup always flattened him. He was like the chinless cadet in the nuclear submarine, small-talking with one of the guys as he untwirled the bolt (routine check) on the torpedo bay—and was instantly floored by a frothing phallus of seawater. Deep down out there, with many atmospheres. The pressure of all that Gwyn had.

To take a heftily looming instance, the house itself. Its mass and scope, its particular reach and sweep he knew well: for a year he had gone to school in an identical building across the street. The school, a cosmopolitan crammer, which was dead now, like Richard's father, who had scrimped to send him there, used to accommodate a staff of twenty-five and over two hundred pupils—an ecology of estrogen and testosterone, bumfluff, flares, fights, fancyings, first loves. That tiered rotating world was vanished. But now in a place of the same measurements, the same volume, lived Gwyn and Demeter Barry. Oh yeah. And the help . . . Richard moved his head around as if to relieve neck pain. The camera continued to stare at him incredulously. He tried to stare back at it, with mad pride. Richard wasn't guilty of covetousness, funnily enough. In the shops he seldom saw anything that looked much fun to buy. He liked the space but he didn't want the stuff you put in it. Still, everything had been so much nicer, he thought, in the old days, when Gwyn was poor.

Allowed entry, Richard was shown upstairs, not of course by Demeter (who at this hour would be unguessably elsewhere down the great passages), nor by a maid (though there were maids, called things like Ming and Atrocia, shipped here in crates from São Paolo, from Vientiane), nor by any representative of the home-improvement community (and they were always about, the knighted architect, the overalled stiff with a mouthful of nails): Richard was shown upstairs by a new type of auxiliary, an American coed or sophomore or grad student, whose straightness of hair, whose strictness of mouth, whose brown-eyed and black-browed intelligence was saying that whatever else Gwyn might be he was now an *operation*, all fax and Xerox and preselect. In the hall Richard saw beneath the broad mirror a shelf so infested with cardboard or even plywood invitations . . . He thought of the van outside, a month of tabloids wedged between dash and windscreen. And the two guys within, one white, one black, and the fat German Shepherd, more like a bear than a dog, with its scarf of tongue.

Gwyn Barry was nearing the climax of a combined interview and photo session. Richard entered the room and crossed it in a diagonal with one hand effacingly raised, and sat on a stool, and picked up a magazine. Gwyn was on the window seat, in his archaeologist's suit, also with archaeologist's aura of outdoor living, rugged inquiry, suntan. He filled his small lineaments neatly, just as his hair filled the lineaments (only a rumor, for now) of male-pattern recession. Gwyn's hair was actually gray, but bright gray: not the English gray of eelskin and wet slates; nor yet the gray that comes about through tiredness of pigment, and dryness. Bright gray hair—the hair (Richard thought) of an obvious charlatan. Richard himself, by the way, was going bald too, but anarchically. No steady shrinkage, with the flesh stealing crownwards like rising water; with him, hair loss happened in spasms, in hanks and handfuls. Visits to the barber were now as fearful and apparently hopeless as visits to the bank manager, or the agent—or the garage, in the tomato-red Maestro.

"Have you any thoughts," the interviewer was saying, "on turning forty?"

"Happy birthday," said Richard.

"Thanks. It's just a number," said Gwyn. "Like any other."

The room—Gwyn's study, his library, his lab—was very bad. When in this room it was Richard's policy to stare like a hypnotist into Gwyn's greedy green eyes, for fear of what he might otherwise confront. He didn't really mind the furniture, the remoteness of the ceiling, the good proportion of the three front windows. He *really* didn't mind the central space-platform of floppy discs and X-ray lasers. What he minded were Gwyn's books: Gwyn's books, which multiplied or ramified so crazily now. Look on the desk, look on the table, and what do you find? The lambent horror of Gwyn in Spanish (sashed with quotes and reprint updates) or an American book-club or supermarket paperback, or something in Hebrew or Mandarin or cuneiform or pictogram that seemed blameless enough but had no reason to be there if it wasn't one of Gwyn's. And then Gallimard and Mondadori and Livro Aberto and Zsolnay and Uitgeverij Contact and Kawade Shobo and Magveto Konyvkiado. In the past Richard had enjoyed several opportunities to snoop around Gwyn's study—his desk, his papers. Are snoopers snooping on their own pain? Probably. I expect you get many young girls who. You will be delighted to hear that the air tickets will be. The judges reached their decision in less than. These terms are, we feel, exceptionally. I am beginning to be translating your. Here is a photograph of the inside of my. Richard stopped flipping through the magazine on his lap (he had come to an interview with Gwyn Barry), and stood, and surveyed the bookshelves. They were fiercely alphabetized. Richard's bookshelves weren't alphabetized. He never had time to alphabetize them. He was always too busy—looking for books he couldn't find. He had books heaped under tables, under beds. Books heaped on windowsills so they closed out the sky.

Interviewer and interviewee were winding up some guff about the deceptive simplicity of the interviewee's prose style. Unlike the interviewer, the photographer was a woman, a girl, black-clad, Nordic, leggy—how she crouched and teetered for her images of Gwyn! Richard looked on with a frowsy sigh. Being photographed, as an activity, was in itself clearly not worth envying. What was enviable, and unbelievable, was that Gwyn should be worth photographing. What *happened* inside the much-photographed face—what happened to the head within? The Yanomano or the Ukuki were surely onto something. One shot wouldn't do it, but the constant snatch of the camera's mouth—it would take your reality, in the end. Yes, probably, the more you were photographed, the thinner it went for your inner life. Being photographed was dead time for the soul. Can the head think, while it does the same half smile under the same light frown? If this was all true, then Richard's soul was in great shape. No one photographed him anymore, not even Gina. When the photographs came back from the chemist's, after an increasingly infrequent Tull holiday, Richard was never there: Marius, Marco, Gina, some peasant or lifeguard or donkey—and Richard's elbow or earlobe on the edge of the frame, on the edge of life and love . . . Now the interviewer said, "A lot of people think that, because you're the figure you now are, that the next step is politics. What do you . . . Do you . . . ?"

"Politics," said Gwyn. "Gosh. Well I can't say I've given it that much thought. Thus far. Let's say I wouldn't want to rule it out. As yet."

"You sound like a politician already, Gwyn."

This was Richard. The remark went down well—because, as is often pointed out, we are all of us in need of a good laugh. Or any kind of laugh at all. The need is evidently desperate. Richard dropped his head and turned away. No, that really wasn't the kind of thing he wanted to be saying. Ever. But Gwyn's world was partly public. And Richard's world was dangerously and increasingly private. And some of us are slaves in our own lives.

"I think writing'll do me," said Gwyn. "They're not incompatible, though, are they? Novelist and politician are both concerned with human potential."

"This would be Labour, of course."

"Obviously."

"Of course."

"Of course."

Of course, thought Richard. Yeah: of course Gwyn was Labour. It was obvious. Obvious not from the ripply cornices twenty feet above their heads, not from the brass lamps or the military plumpness of the leather-topped desk. Obvious because Gwyn was what he was, a writer, in England, at the end of the twentieth century. There was nothing else for such a person to be. Richard was Labour, equally obviously. It often seemed to him, moving in the circles he moved in and reading what he read, that everyone in England was Labour, except the government. Gwyn was the son of a Welsh schoolteacher (his subject? Gym. He taught gym). Now he was middle class and Labour. Richard was the son of a son of a Home Counties landowner. Now he was middle class and Labour. All writers, all book people, were Labour, which was one of the reasons why they got on so well, why they didn't keep suing each other and beating each other up. Not like America, where spavined Alabaman must mingle with Virginian nabob, where tormented Lithuanian must extend his hand to the seven-foot Cape Codder with those true-blue eyes. By the way, Richard didn't mind Gwyn being rich and Labour. Richard didn't mind Gwyn being rich. It was important to establish the nature of the antipathy (to free it from distractions), before everything gets really awful, all ripped and torn. *He made me hit my kid*, thought Richard. *He made me—with my wife* . . . Rich and Labour: that was okay. Having always been poor was a good preparation for being rich. Better than having always been rich. Let the socialist drink champagne. At least he was new to it. Anyway, who cared? Richard had even been a member of the Communist Party, in his early twenties—for all the fucking good *that* did him.

"Thank you very much," said the interviewer, in a tone of mild surprise. For a moment he hesitated and stared desolately at his tape recorder, but then nodded and got to his feet. Now the photographer's presence started to gather and expand—her height, her health.

"If I could just have *three minutes* over in the corner there."

"I don't pose," said Gwyn. "The deal was you snap away while we talked. But no posing."

"Three minutes. Please. Two minutes. The light's so perfect there."

Gwyn acquiesced. He acquiesced, Richard thought, in the manner of someone who had similarly acquiesced many times before, conscious both of his magnanimity and of its limits. The well and all its sweet water would surely one day run dry.

"Who's coming to this thing?" Gwyn called, from beyond, as the photographer's trussed and pouch-swathed figure interposed itself between the two men.

"Not sure." Richard named some names. "Thanks for coming along. On your birthday and everything."

But now without turning to him the photographer with frantic fingers was making quelling gestures behind her back and saying,

"Good: I'm getting something. I'm getting something. Higher. Stay. That's very good. That's very good. That's beautiful."

On the way out they encountered Lady Demeter Barry in the hall. She was twenty-nine, and had the abstracted and disorganized air you might expect from somebody who was related to the Queen. Like Gina Tull, she had no connection with literature other than marriage to one of its supposed practitioners.

"Got a lesson, love?" said Gwyn, moving up close.

Richard waited. "My dear Demi," he then said, giving a brief stiff bow before kissing her on either cheek.

The orange van was still out there—the soiled orange van, with its soiled white trim, and its soiled cream curtains fringing the windows side and back. Steve Cousins sat there, alone but for Giro, having sent 13 off for more Tings.

A monkey. A pony. Cockle and hen: ten. Why the animal imagery for proletarian money? Lady Godiva: fiver. Then the back slang. Rouf, nevis: sounds stupid. A *carpet* stood for three (and its multiples). And six was *half a stretch*, and a *stretch* was twelve, and a *double carpet* was thirty-three, and sixty-six was a . . . Jesus. That was type talk, and prison talk, and you shouldn't use it. And Steve had never *gone* to prison. He had never gone to prison, being (as many lawyers on many occasions had wearily reminded many courtrooms) of stainless record . . . At this juncture Steve was reading a magazine called *Police Review* but he also had a book on the dash: *Crowds and Power*, by Elias Canetti. Funnily enough, in Steve's circle (and Steve's circle was elliptical and eccentric), reading books like *Crowds and Power* was tantamount to a proclamation that you *ha*d gone to prison—and for a very long time. Beware the convict with his Camus and his Kierkegaard, his *Critique of Pure Reason*, his *Four Quartets* . . .

Steve. Steve Cousins. Scozz.

Scozz? Scozz had dyed hair, worn spiky—the color of syrup or even treacle; but the roots were black (sedimentary dye from a slightly earlier phase). His hair resembled damp ripe hay that had undergone reckless chemical enrichment. Where the colors merged they looked like the creases between a smoker's teeth. Scozzy didn't smoke. You don't smoke: what you do is stay fit and healthy. His face was long, despite the absence of chin (his chin was about the same size as the Adam's apple on which it perched); and in certain lights his features seemed to consist of shifting planes and lenses, like a suspect's face "pixelated" for the TV screen: smeared, and done in squares; blurred, and done in boxes. Scozzy wore two wire-thin silver rings in either ear. His pre-violence stare featured the usual bulged eyes—but the lips also widened and parted in avidity and amusement and recognition. Not tall, not stocky: he surprised people when he took off his shirt, revealing himself like an anatomical demonstration. He excelled at surprise. In fights and frightenings, the surprise was always inordinate. Because Steve didn't stop. When I start, I don't stop. I don't stop. He was the kind of criminal who knew what *recidivist* meant. He was good. He had the ism.

Unsmilingly Scozzy rotated his neck muscles as 13 slid the door open and climbed back inside. Giro, lying further back now in his huge fur coat, sighed hotly in sleep.

13 said, "He come out?"

"Both did. Hopped in a cab. Account."

"Size of that fucking gaff."

Scozzy turned to him, and exhaled, and said indulgently, "Oh, Thirt. Thirt, mate. What do you think we're here for? Think we come to screw it? Run round the house nicking stuff and fucking everything up?"

13 smiled with lowered head. He *had* had something of the sort in mind.

"Get a life. Get a century."

"Hey."

"Hold up."

They watched.

"The wife," said Scozzy, with conviction. "Off to her lesson."

"Big girl," said 13. "Yat," he added, with admiration.

Yeah: Lady Demeter certainly looked like a brother's dream pull: blonde, rich, stacked. But she wasn't Steve's type. No human woman was. No, nor man, neither.

13 reached for the ignition and looked up expectantly but Steve's slow blink was enough to tell him they were going nowhere for now. With Scozzy, you were always doing much less than you thought you'd be doing. Much less, then much more.

"Crash said she was a big girl."

Steve spoke neutrally. Come to think of it: "The Queen's got big tits. Oi. These ain't Tings. They Lilts!"

"Pineapple-grapefruit crush," said 13 petulantly. "Jesus. Same difference."

An hour into lunch in this fish restaurant for rich old men and something extraordinary was about to happen. Nothing from the outside world. It was just that Richard was on the verge of passionate speech. Yes: passionate speech.

You don't think that's extraordinary? Oh, but it is. Try and think of the last time you did it. And I don't just mean "Well I think it's absolutely disgraceful" or "You're the one who brought it up in the first place" or "Get straight back into your room and get into bed." I'm talking speech: passionate speech. *Speeches* hardly ever happen. We hardly ever give them or hear them. See how bad we are at it. "Marius! Marco! The pair of you—are a pair!" See how we fuck it up. We salivate and iterate. Women can do it, or they get further, but when the chance of tears presents itself they usually take it. Not having this option, men just shut up. They are all *esprit d'escalier*. Men are spirits on the staircase, wishing they'd said, wishing they'd said . . . Before he spoke, there in the buttoned plush, Richard hurriedly wondered whether this had been a natural resource of men and women—passionate speech—before 1700 or whenever Eliot said it was, before thought and feeling got dissociated. The sensibility of men was evidently much more dissociated than the sensibility of women. Maybe, for women, it just never happened. Compared to men, women were Metaphysicals, Donnes and Marvells of brain and heart.

So, his passionate speech. Passionate speech, which unrolls, with thoughts and feelings dramatized in words. Passionate speech, which is almost always a bad move.

How can we explain this? After all, Richard was here to impress people. He wanted a job.

Was it the place? A semicircular banquette, full of food and drink and smoke—and, beyond, little bunkers full of old men patiently jawing their way through the money extorted by their forebears?

Was it the company? Financier, male columnist, female columnist, publisher, newspaper diarist, newspaper profilist, photographer, captain of industry, Shadow Minister for the Arts, Gwyn Barry?

Was it the alcohol provided and consumed? Actually Richard had been very good, managing to get through a Virgin Mary and a lite beer before his pre-lunch whisky. Then a ton of wine. But before that, while everyone was still milling around, he had gone to the pub across the road with Rory Plantagenet—the newspaper diarist. Richard and Rory sometimes described one another as schoolfriends, which is to say that they had been at the same school at the same time. The school was Riddington House—well known to be the least good public school in the British Isles. For some years now Richard had been selling Rory literary gossip. How much that advance had been. Who would win that prize. Occasionally, and more and more often, he sold him gossip about literary divorces, infidelities, bankruptcies, detoxifications, diseases. Rory paid for the information, and always for all the drinks, as a kind of tip. He paid for the gen and the gin, the shrugs, the cheap jokes. Richard didn't like doing this. But he needed the money. While he did it, he felt as if he was wearing a cheap new shirt—one from which he had failed to remove the packager's pins.

Was it the provocation? The provocation, some might think, turned out to be considerable. It was sufficient, in any case.

London weather was also bound to play its part: a hot noon gloom. Like night falling on the interior of the church, the lunchers hovered and gathered . . .

Gwyn Barry had his photograph taken. The financier—Sebby—had his photograph taken. Gwyn Barry was photographed with the financier. The publisher was photographed with Gwyn Barry and the captain of industry. The captain of industry was photographed with the Shadow Minister of the Arts and Gwyn Barry. Two speeches were given, read from pieces of paper—neither of them passionate. The captain of industry, whose wife was interested in literature more than enough for both of them (Gwyn often dined there, Richard knew), gave a speech in praise of Gwyn Barry on this, his fortieth birthday. That took about ninety seconds. Then the financier gave a speech during which Richard smoked three cigarettes and stared tearfully at his empty glass. So the financier was trying to get something back for his money. It wasn't just going to be a free meal with a bit of slurred shop over coffee. The financier spoke about the kind of literary magazine he would like to be associated with— the kind of magazine he was prepared to be the financier of. Not so much like magazine A. Not so much like magazine B. More like magazine C (defunct) or magazine D (published in New York). Gwyn Barry was then asked about the kind of magazine *he* would like to be associated with (the kind that had high standards). Ditto the captain of industry, the Shadow Minister for the Arts, the female columnist, the male columnist. Rory Plantagenet was not consulted. Neither was the photographer, who was leaving anyway. Neither, depressingly, was Richard Tull, who was struggling to remain under the impression that he was being groomed for the editorship. The only questions that came his way were about technical matters—print runs, break-even junctures, and the like.

Would there be any point, the financier, Sebby, was saying (and his public popularity owed a great deal to this bandied diminutive: never mind, for now, all the fellow sharks and vultures he had left shivering over their visual display units), would there be any point in getting some market research under way? Richard?

"What, reader profile stuff?" He had no idea what to say. He said, "Age? Sex? I don't know."

"I thought we might press a questionnaire on, say . . . students reading English at London? Something of that kind?"

"To see if they like high standards?"

"Targeting," said the male columnist, who was about twenty-eight and experimentally bearded, with a school-dinner look about him. The column the male columnist wrote was sociopolitical. "Come on, this isn't America. Where the magazine market is completely balkanized. Where, you know, they have magazines," he said, already looking round the table to garner any smiles that might soon be cropping up, "for the twice-divorced South Moluccan scuba diver."

"Still, there are more predictable preferences," said the publisher. "Women's magazines are read by women. And men . . ."

There was a silence. To fill it, Richard said, "Has anyone ever really established whether men prefer to read men? Whether women prefer to read women?"

"Oh please. What is this?" said the female columnist. "We're not talking about motorbikes or knitting patterns. We're talking about *literature* for God's sake."

Even when he was in familiar company (his immediate family, for instance) it sometimes seemed to Richard that those gathered in the room were not quite authentic selves—that they had gone away and then come back not quite right, half remade or reborn by some blasphemous, backhanded, and above all inexpensive process. In a circus, in a funhouse. All flaky and carny. Not quite themselves. Himself very much included.

He said, "Is this without interest? Nabokov said he was frankly homosexual in his literary tastes. I don't think men and women write and read in exactly the same way. They go at it differently."

"And I suppose," she said, "that there are *racial* differences too?"

He didn't answer. For a moment Richard looked worryingly short-necked. He was in fact coping with a digestive matter, or at least he was sitting tight until the digestive matter resolved itself one way or the other.

"I can't believe I'm hearing this. I thought we came here today to talk about *art*. What's the matter with you? Are you drunk?"

Richard turned his senses on her. The woman: gruff, sizable, stately handsome; and always barging through to her share of the truth. Richard knew the type—because literature knew the type. Like the smug boiler in the Pritchett story, the Labour politician, up North, proud of her brusqueness and her good big bum. The column the female columnist wrote wasn't specifically about being a woman. But the photograph above it somehow needed to have long hair and makeup—for it all to hang together.

The Shadow Minister for the Arts said, "Isn't this what literature is meant to be about? Transcending human difference?"

"Hear hear," said the female columnist. "Me? I don't give a damn whether people are male, female, black, white, pink, puce or polka-dotted."

"And that's why you're no good."

"Steady there," said Sebby. And then he added, as if the very appellation refreshed him: "Gwyn."

Everyone turned to him in silence. Gwyn was staring at his coffee spoon with a fascinated frown. He replaced it in its saucer and looked up, his face clearing, his green eyes brightening.

Gwyn said slowly, "I find I never think in terms of men. In terms of women. I find I always think in terms of . . . *people.*"

There was an immediate burble of approbation: Gwyn, it seemed, had douched the entire company in common sense and plain humanity. Richard had to raise his voice, which meant that his cough kicked in— but he went ahead with his passionate speech.

It was the little rapt pause before the word *people: that* was what did it.

"A very *low-level* remark, if I may say so. Hey, Gwyn. You know what you remind me of. A quiz in a color magazine—you know, Are You Cut Out To Be a *Teacher?* Final question: Would you rather teach (a) history, or (b) geography, or (c) . . . *children.* Well, you don't get a choice about teaching children. But there is a choice, and a difference, between history and geography. It must make you feel nice and young to say that being a man means nothing and being a woman means nothing and what matters is being a . . . *person.* How about being a *spider,* Gwyn. Let's imagine you're a *spider.* You're a spider, and you've just had your first serious date. You're limping away from that now, and you're looking over your shoulder, and there's your girlfriend, eating one of your legs like it was a chicken drumstick. What would you say? I know. You'd say: I find I never think in terms of male spiders or in terms of female spiders. I find I always think in terms of . . . *spiders.*"

Richard sank back, rhythmically sighing or whinnying with all that this had cost him. He didn't have the will to look up, to look up into that unanimity of downward revision. So he stared at the tarnished table-cloth, and saw only the rising—no, the plunging—seahorses that lived behind his eyes.

That evening it was six o'clock by the time Richard got back to Calchalk Street. As he entered (the front door led straight into the sitting room), a crabbed, metallic voice was saying something like,

"Sinistor cannot now be opposed in the completion of his evil plan. Our only hope is to confront Terrortron."

The twins did not look up from the television. Neither did Lizzete, the muscular but very young black girl who collected them from school on Gina's workdays and then watched television with them until Richard returned, or staggered out of his study. She herself wore a school uniform. Lizzete's new boyfriend, on the other hand, got busily to his feet and nodded repeatedly and with his gym-shoed foot tapped Lizzete's muscular calf until she introduced him as Teen or Tine. Short for Tino? Itself short for Martino, Valentino? A well-sprung youth with a core of softness in the kind of black face that would become finely lined rather than sleekly smooth in early middle age. Richard was gratified that his children felt at ease with and even envied black people. When he had met his first black person, the six-year-old Richard, despite much prepping and coaching and bribing, had burst into tears.

"Hi boys . . ."

Side by side on the sofa, with that low, committed gaze, Marius and Marco went on looking at the television, where great slanting hulking cartoon robots fluidly transformed themselves into planes and cars and rockets, like icons in a new socialism of machines.

"Sinistor, prepare to meet your doom. Do not think that Horrortroid's cohorts can avail you now."

Richard said, "Who christens these characters? How did Horrortroid's parents know he was going to be horrible? How did Sinistor's parents know Sinistor was going to be sinister?"

"They make up their own names, Daddy," said Marius.

Now Gina was coming through the door, in her suit, in her street pancake. The boys glanced up, and glanced at each other; the room prepared itself for the transfer of power. Richard, with his bow tie askew, was staring at his wife with unusual attention. Her eyes, set in bruised loops of darkness, like badger, like burglar; her nose, a caligulan quarter-circle; her mouth, wide but not full. He was thinking that perhaps all loved faces cover and outreach the visible spectrum—white of tooth, black of brow. Red and violet: the mouth infrared, the eyes ultraviolet. Gina, for her part, was giving Richard her standard stare: she was looking at him as if he had gone mad a long time ago.

They moved into the kitchen for a moment while Lizzete was gathering her things—her bag, her blazer. Gina said,

"Have you got five quid on you? Did you get the job?"

"No. But I have got five quid on me."

Her chest rose in its white shirt. She exhaled. "Bad luck," she said.

"He wasn't ever going to offer me the editorship. For a while it looked like he was going to offer me a job driving a van. Or selling ad space."

"What are you looking so happy about?"

Richard wanted to kiss her. But he wasn't in a position to kiss her. And had not been for some time.

"I'm him," Marius was saying, meaning some robot, the leader of the robot fraternity which stood there potently glittering behind the credits.

"No *I'm* him," said Marco.

"No you're *him*," said Marius, meaning some other robot.

"No *you're* him. I'm *him*."

"Christ," said Richard, "why can't you *both* be him?"

And three seconds later Marius's teeth were stuck fast in Marco's back.

Tensely followed by Lizzete, 13 strode the length of lampless Calchalk Street and hoisted himself up into the soiled orange van. He did not immediately slide the door shut after him. Indeed, a single trainer still dangled with pale allure from the brink of the dark cab.

"That's it?" said Lizzete.

13 just smiled at her.

"That's it?"

"Look, I'll take you down the Paradox."

"When?"

"They won't let you in. Thursday."

She pointed a finger at him. "Thursday," she said.

Left in peace, 13 made a move with his hand in the gloom for the last of the Lilts. He pulled off the tab and thirstily tasted the blood-heat crush. There was a book on the seat too. 13 creased his face at it: *Crowds and Power.* As soon as Lizzete walked away 13's face changed. From that of a cheerful and possibly quite feckless but basically decent black kid, more or less as seen on TV: to the realer face, and a look of unhappy calculation. He was glad he had seen Gina: the wife. At least it was something to tell fucking Adolf. Adolf was Scozzy. Adolf was one of the names Scozzy had that he didn't know about. Others included Psycho and Minder. We all have names we don't know about. For instance, if you have a girlfriend as well as a wife, then your girlfriend will have a name for you that you won't want to hear, a name your girlfriend uses with her girl-friends and her other boyfriends. We all have names we don't know about and don't want to hear.

Now 13 gave a puzzled sigh. He couldn't figure out what was coming down—which wasn't unusual, come to think of it, when you were work-ing for Adolf. There was nothing there anyway apart from the video.

Scozzy was elsewhere. He wouldn't have been along at that time in the evening in any case; but Scozzy was elsewhere. With far from the best intentions, Scozzy had gone to the hospital to visit an associate. The associate, Kirk, had been savaged, rather seriously, by his own pit bull, Beef. Beef had survived the mishap. Kirk had not had Beef put down. Beef lived on, at Kirk's brother's, Lee's, grimly awaiting Kirk's recovery and return. Forgive and forget, said Kirk. Put it behind you. Kirk argued that he had brought it on himself, plainly overreacting, there in the little kitchen, to Arsenal's embittering defeat, away goals counting double in the event of a draw, at the hands of Dynamo Kiev.

13 adjusted his demeanor to drive to St. Mary's to fetch Scozzy, and then, noticing the time, readjusted it to go home for his tea.

Shame about that. The black kid cannot just be a black kid anymore. Nobody can just be somebody anymore. Pity about that.

Take Richard. This was one of Gina's workdays, so it fell to him to do the boys. The following acts he performed selfconsciously conscientiously (or the other way round): bath, snack, book, fresh water for their jug, Marco's medicines, more book, the two dotlike fluoride pills pressed into their moist mouths, kiss. He kissed the boys as often as he could. His knowledge told him that boys should be hugged and kissed by their fathers—that what fucked men up was not being hugged and kissed by their fathers. Richard had not been hugged and kissed by his father. So he told himself to regard his relationship with his sons as purely sexual. He hugged and kissed them every chance he got. Gina did the same, but she hugged and kissed them because she physically wanted and needed to.

When the boys were done Gina came down in her nightdress and cooked him a lamb chop and ate a bowl of rustic cereal and then went to bed. While they ate, Gina read a travel brochure, in its entirety, and Richard read the first seven pages of *Robert Southey: Gentleman Poet*, his next book up for review.

Later, heading for his study, where he intended to drink scotch and smoke dope for a couple of hours, and examine his new destiny, he heard an italicized whisper through the half-open door of the boxroom that the boys shared (and were rapidly outgrowing): *Daddy*. He looked in. Marius.

"What do you want now?"

"Daddy? Daddy: what would you rather be? An Autobot or a Decepticon?"

Richard leaned his head against the doorjamb. The twins were being particularly knowing and apposite that night—the twins, with their subtle life, their weave of themes. Earlier in the bathroom Marco had raised a characteristically crooked finger at a daddy-longlegs on the water pipe. A daddy-longlegs so long-legged that it was almost tripping over itself and made you think of some valiant and tragic sports day for the disabled, all the three-legged races, all the sacks, all the eggs and spoons, all the speeches so nervously prepared and kindly meant. "Daddy? Is that Spiderman?" Daddy with his long legs bent over the bath had answered, "It looks more to me like Spiderspider." . . . Now Richard said to Marius,

"Autobot or Decepticon. A good question. Like many of your questions. And guess what. I think I've finally made up my mind."

"Which?"

"No more Autobot. All Decepticon."

"Me too."

"Hush now."

Richard sat at his desk in the dark. He rolled and lit; he poured and sipped. Richard was obliged to drink heavily when he smoked dope—to fight the paranoia. To combat the incredible paranoia. On dope he sometimes thought that all the televisions of Calchalk Street were softly crackling about Richard Tull: news flashes about his most recent failures; panel discussions about his obscurity, his neglect. Now he drank and smoked and he was neither happy nor sad.

The really good bit with Gwyn had happened afterwards, in the cab. Half past three, and the light outside, the sky, was the same as the driver's tinted windscreen, the upper half all charcoal and oil, the lower leadenly glowing. Richard pulled the side window down to validate this, and of course the glass surged slowly up again, interposing its own medium. Here perhaps was the only way to see London truly, winging low over it, in a cab, in darkness-at-noon July. London traffic lights are the brightest in the world, beneath their meshed glass: the anger of their red, the jaundice of their amber, the jealousy of their green.

The profile beside him was keeping quiet so Richard said boldly, "Could you believe that woman? You know—she really thinks she's *authentic*. Whereas . . ." He paused. Whereas to him she had seemed horrifically otherwise. "Unmarried, I assume. She reeked of spinst."

Gwyn turned to him.

"Spinst. Spinst. Like unmarried men reek of batch."

Gwyn turned away again. He shook his head—sadly. You can't say such things. And not just for public reasons. Richard deduced (perhaps wrongly, perhaps over-elaborately) that Gwyn meant something like: You can't say such things because the whole area has been seen to be contaminated—contaminated by men who really do hate women.

(Maybe he had come up with a bad example: with the spiders. People would assume he thought women *were* spiders. Or that he only hated *women* spiders.) Anyway Richard went ahead and said,

"Great gusts of spinst. A miasma of spinst."

Gwyn waved a hand at him.

"I can describe it for you if you like. Imagine a Wembley of rain-damaged makeup. Or a—"

"Would you pull in at the corner here please?"

No, it was nothing. Gwyn was just buying an evening paper from the boy. Jesus, the light through the open door looked like the end of London, the end of everything; its guttering glow was livid now, and something you wouldn't want to touch, like the human-hued legs of pigeons beneath their dirty overcoats.

The cab resumed its endless journey, its journey of hurry up and wait, hurry up and wait. Gwyn opened his paper and turned to the Diary and eventually said,

"Well there's nothing about it here."

Richard was staring at him. "Nothing about what?"

"About the lunch. Your little outburst."

Richard stared harder. "Relieved about that, are you?"

Gwyn spoke with restraint. He said: "It's quite a while since anybody talked to me like that."

"Is it? Well this time you won't have so long to wait. Because somebody's going to talk to you like that again right away. That's the lunchtime edition. You think the guy just phones it on to the newsstands? It's lucky no one knows how fucking thick you really are. What a fucking dunce you really are. That *would* be a scoop."

"Nothing about the job offer, either," said Gwyn, his bright eyes still scanning the page.

"There wasn't any job offer."

"Yes there was. While you were off on one of your visits to the toilet. I turned it down of course. I mean, as if *I* . . ."

The cab pulled up. As Richard hunched forward he said, "One last thing. *Why* can't I talk about spinst?"

"Because people will start avoiding you."

Now the first drop of rain grayly kissed him on one of his bald spots as he climbed out of the cab and into the shoplit dungeon of Marylebone High Street. Richard went on up to the offices of the Tantalus Press.

Round about here, in time, the emotions lose lucidity and definition, and become qualified by something bodily. Something coarse and coarse-haired in the fury, something rancid and pulmonary in the grief, something toxic and drop-toothed in the hate . . . Richard put his thoughts in delivery order, as a writer might: stuff to be *got in*. And at the same time he experienced one of those uncovenanted expansions that every artist knows, when, almost audibly to the inner ear, things swivel and realign (the cube comes good), and all is clear. You don't do this: your talent does it. He sat up. His state was one of equilibrium, neither pleasant nor unpleasant in itself, but steady. He gave a sudden nod. Then and there it crystallized: the task. A literary endeavor, a quest, an exaltation—one to which he could sternly commit all his passion and his power.

He was going to fuck Gwyn up.

Outside there hung the crescent moon. It looked like Punch. But where was Judy?

Fly a mile east in our weep ship to the spires of Holland Park, the aerials, the house, the layered roof, the burglar alarms, the first-floor window, thick with reflections, looming over the still garden. This is the window to the master bedroom, where the master sleeps. I'm not going in there—not yet. So I don't know what his bed smells of, and I don't know if he cries in the night.

As Richard does.

Why do the men cry? Because of fights and feats and marathon preferment, because they want their mothers, because they are blind in time, because of all the hard-ons they have to whistle up out of the thin blue yonder, because of all that men have done. Because they can't be happy or sad anymore—only smashed or nuts. And because they don't know how to do it when they're awake.

And then there is the information, which comes at night.

The next day it was *his* turn: Richard turned forty. Turned is right. Like a half-cooked steak, like a wired cop, like an old leaf, like milk, Richard turned. And nothing changed. He was still a wreck.

Just because he wore bright bow ties and fancy waistcoats didn't mean he wasn't falling apart. Just because he slept in paisley pajamas didn't mean he wasn't cracking up. Those bow ties and waistcoats were cratered with stains and burns. Those paisley pajamas were always drenched in sweat.

Who's who?

At twenty-eight, living off book reviews and social security, pale and thin and interestingly dissolute, most typically to be seen wearing a collarless white shirt and jeans tucked into misshapen brown boots—looking like the kind of ex-public-schoolboy who, perhaps, did some drug-impaired carpentering or gardening for the good and the great—with his fiery politics and his riveting love affairs in which he was usually the crueller, Richard Tull published his first novel, *Aforethought*, in Britain and America. If you homogenized all the reviews (still kept, somewhere, in a withered envelope), allowing for many grades of generosity and IQ, then the verdict on *Aforethought* was as follows: nobody understood it, or even finished it, but, equally, nobody was sure it was shit. Richard flourished. He stopped getting social security. He appeared on "Better Read": the three critics in their breakfast nook, Richard behind a desk with an unseen Gauloise fuming in his trembling hand—he looked as though his trousers were on fire. Three years later, by which time he had become books and arts editor of a little magazine called *The Little Magazine* (little then, and littler now), Richard published his second novel, *Dreams Don't Mean Anything*, in Britain but not in America. His third novel wasn't published anywhere. Neither was his fourth. Neither was his fifth. In those three brief sentences we adumbrate a Mahabharata of pain. He had plenty of offers for his sixth because, by that time, during a period of cretinous urges and lurches, he had started responding to the kind of advertisements that plainly came out with it and said, WE WILL PUBLISH YOUR BOOK and AUTHORS WANTED (or was it NEEDED?) BY LONDON PUBLISHER. Of course, these publishers, crying out for words on paper like pining dogs under a plangent moon, weren't regular publishers. You paid them, for example. And, perhaps more importantly, no one ever read you. Richard stayed with it and ended up going to see a Mr. Cohen in Marylebone High Street. He came out of there, his sixth novel still unplaced, but with a new job, that of Special Director of the Tantalus Press, where he went on to work about a day a week, soliciting and marking up illiterate novels, total-recall autobiographies in which no one ever went anywhere or did anything, collections of primitive verse, very long laments for dead relatives (and pets and plants), crackpot scientific treatises and, increasingly, it seemed to him, "found" dramatic monologues about manic depression and schizophrenia. *Aforethought* and *Dreams Don't Mean Anything* still existed somewhere, on the windowsills of seaside boardinghouses, on the shelves of hospital libraries, at the bottom of tea chests in storage, going for ten pee in cardboard boxes at provincial book fairs . . . Like the lady who was of course still there between the mortar board and the prosthetic legs (and what a moving acceptance speech she gave), like the laughing athlete who, after that mishap in the car park, awoke to find himself running a network of charities from his padded rack, Richard had to see whether the experience of disappointment was going to make him bitter or better. And it made him bitter. He was sorry: there was nothing he could do about it. He wasn't up to better. Richard continued to review books. He was very good at book reviewing. When he reviewed a book, it stayed reviewed. Otherwise he was an ex-novelist (or not ex so much as void or phantom), the Literary Editor of *The Little Magazine*, and a Special Director of the Tantalus Press.

Bitter is manageable. Look how we all manage it. But worse happened, and the real trouble began. It was a viscous autumn, and Richard had stopped dating girls (he was married now), and Gina was expecting not just one baby but two, and the rejection slips were coming in on novel number four, *Invisible Worms* (does it merit these italics, having never been born?), and his overdraft practically trepanned him every time he dared think about it: imagine, then, Richard's delight when his oldest and stupidest friend, Gwyn Barry, announced that his first novel, *Summertown*, had just been accepted by a leading London house. Because he at least partly understood that the things you hate most always have to go ahead and happen, Richard was ready for this—or was expecting it, anyway. He had long been an amused confidant of Gwyn's literary aspirations, and had chortled his way through *Summertown*—plus a couple of its abandoned predecessors—in earlier drafts. *Summertown*? *Summertown* was about Oxford, where the two writers had met; where they had shared, first, a set of rooms in the mighty hideousness of Keble College and, later, a rude flatlet off the Woodstock Road, in Summertown, twenty years ago. Twenty years, thought Richard, forty today: Oh, where had they all *gone*? Gwyn's first novel was no less autobiographical than most first novels. Richard was in it, clumsily and perfunctorily disguised (still the promiscuous communist with his poetry and his ponytail), but affectionately and even romantically rendered. The Gwyn figure, who narrated, was wan and Welsh, the sort of character who, according to novelistic convention, quietly does all the noticing—whereas reality usually sees to it that the perspiring mute is just a perspiring mute, with nothing to contribute. Still, the Gwyn figure, Richard conceded, was the book's only strength: an authentic dud, a dud insider, who brought back hard news from the dud world. The rest of it was the purest trex: fantastically pedestrian. It tried to be "touching"; but the only touching thing about *Summertown* was that it *thought* it was a novel. On publication, it met with modest sales and (Richard again) disgracefully unmalicious reviews. The following year a small paperback edition limped along for a month or two . . . We might have said that Richard was tasting fresh failure, except that failure is never fresh, and always stale, and weakly fizzes, like old yogurt, with his sixth novel when Gwyn sent him bound proofs of his second, entitled *Amelior.* If Richard had chortled his way through *Summertown*, he cackled and yodeled his way through *Amelior:* its cuteness, its blandness, its naively pompous semicolons, its freedom from humor and incident, its hand-me-down imagery, the almost endearing transparency of its little color schemes, its Tinkertoy symmetries . . . What was it "about," *Amelior*? It wasn't autobiographical; it was about a group of fair-minded young people who, in an unnamed country, strove to establish a rural community. And they succeeded. And then it ended. Not worth writing in the first place, the finished book was, in Richard's view, a ridiculous failure. He was impatient for publication day.

With this mention of patience, or its opposite, I think we might switch for a moment to the point of view of Richard's twin sons—to the point of view of Marius, and of Marco. There was in Richard a fatherly latitude or laxity that the boys would, I believe, agree to call *patience.* Richard wasn't the one who went on at them about duties and dress codes and, above all, toy tidying—Gina had to do all that. Richard didn't scream or storm or spank. Gina had to do all that. On the contrary, with Richard in sole charge, they could gorge themselves on ice cream and packets of Wotsits and watch TV for hour after hour and wreck all the furniture, while he sat slumped over his desk in his mysterious study. But then Daddy's patience changed . . . *Amelior* had been out for about a month. No stir had been caused by it, and therefore no particular pall had fallen over the Tull maisonette. The reviews, while hardly the pyrotechnic display of sarcasm and contempt for which Richard hoped, had nonetheless been laudably condescending and unanimous and brief. With any luck, Gwyn was finished. It was a Sunday morning. To the boys this meant a near-eternity of unmonitored delectation, followed by an outing to Dogshit Park or better (the zoo or the museum, with one or other tranced and speechless parent) and at least two hired tapes of cartoons, because even Gina was TV-patient on Sunday nights, after a weekend in their company, and was often in bed before they were.

So. Daddy in the kitchen, enjoying a late breakfast. The twins, their legs further slenderized by the baggy bermudas they both sported, were to be found on the sitting room carpet, Marius ably constructing sca- and space-faring vessels with plastic stickle-bricks, Marco more dreamily occupied: with the twined cords of the telephone and angle lamp, which shared the low round table by the fireplace, Marco was ensnaring and entwining various animal figurines, here a stegosaurus, there a piglet, with a transformation on his mind, thus arranging things—how did the fable end?—so that the lion might lie down with the lamb . . . The boys heard a loud bedraggled wail from across the passage. This sound, its register of pain or grief, was unconnectable with their father or anyone else they knew, so perhaps some stranger or creature—? Marco sat back, thus tugging at his pickle of duckling and velociraptor, and the little table slewed; his eyes had time to widen before it fell, had time to glaze with tears of contrition and preemption before Richard came into the room. On patient days he might have said, "Now what have we here?" or, "This is a sorry pickle," or, more simply (and more likely), "Jesus Christ." But not this Sunday morning. Instead, Richard strode forward and with a single swoop of his open hand dealt Marco the heaviest blow he had ever felt. Marius, sitting utterly still, noticed how the air in the room went on rolling, like the heaving surface of the swimming pool even after the children had all climbed out.

Twenty years from now, this incident would be something the twins can lie back and tell their psychiatrists about—the day their father's patience went away. And never returned, not fully, not in its original form. But they would never know what really happened that Sunday morning, the chaotic wail, the fiercely crenellated lips, the rocking boy on the sitting room floor. Gina might have pieced it together, because things changed there too, and never changed back again. What happened that Sunday morning was this: Gwyn Barry's *Amelior* entered the best-seller list, at number nine.

But before he did anything else, before he did anything grand or ambitious like pressing on with *Untitled* or rewriting his review of *Robert Southey: Gentleman Poet* or getting started on fucking Gwyn up (and he had, he thought, a good opening move), Richard was supposed to take the vacuum cleaner in. That's right. He had to take the vacuum cleaner in. Before he did this, he sat down in the kitchen and ate a fruit yogurt so rubbery with additives that it reminded him in texture of one of his so-called hard-ons . . . Proposing the errand to him, inviting him to take the vacuum cleaner in, Gina had used the words *nip* and *pop*: "Could you nip round to the electrician and pop the Hoover in," she had said. But Richard's nipping and popping days were definitely over. He reached out and opened the door of the airing cupboard. The vacuum cleaner lay coiled there, like an alien pet belonging to the Dallek of the boiler. He stared at it for about a minute. Then his eyes closed slowly.

The visit to the electrician's would additionally involve him in a visit to the bathroom (to shave: he was by now far too mired internally to let the world see him with his surface unclean; he too much resembled the figure he knew he would eventually become: the terrible old man in a callbox, with a suitcase, wanting something very badly—cash, work, shelter, information, a cigarette). In the bathroom mirror, of course, he would be reduced to two dimensions, so the bathroom mirror was no place to go if what you wanted was depth. And he didn't want depth. *By a certain age, everyone has the face they deserve.* Like *the eyes are the window to the soul.* Good fun to say, good fun even to believe, when you're eighteen, when you're thirty-two.

Looking in the mirror now, on the morning of his fortieth birthday, Richard felt that *no one* deserved the face he had. No one in the history of the planet. There was nothing on the planet it was that bad to do. What happened? What have you *done*, man? His hair, scattered over his crown in assorted folds and clumps, looked as though it had just concluded a course of prolonged (and futile) chemotherapy. Then the eyes, each of them perched on its little blood-rimmed beer gut. If the eyes were the window to the soul, then the window was a windscreen, after a transcontinental drive; and his cough sounded like a wiper on the dry glass. These days he smoked and drank largely to solace himself for what drinking and smoking had done to him—but smoking and drinking had done a lot to him, so he drank and smoked a lot. He experimented, furthermore, with pretty well any other drug he could get his hands on. His teeth were all chipped pottery and prewar jet glue. At each given moment, whatever he was doing, at least two of his limbs were immovably numb. Up and down his body there were whispered rumors of pain. In fact, physically, at all times, he felt epiphanically tragic. His doctor had died four years ago ("Unfortunately I am terminally ill."); and that, in Richard's mature opinion, was definitely that. He had a large and lucent lump on the back of his neck. This he treated himself, by the following means: he kept his hair long to keep it hidden. If you went up to Richard Tull and told him he was in Denial, he would deny it. But not hotly.

None of this altered the fact that he had to take the vacuum cleaner in. He *had* to take it in, because even Richard (who was, of course, being a man and everything, a fabulous slob) could tell that the quality of life, at 49E Calchalk Street, had dramatically declined without it. In his study the feathery ubiquity of dust made him suspect, quite wrongly for once, that he was due another liver attack. And additional considerations obtained, like Marco's life-threatening allergies, which also had to be factored in.

By the time he had grappled the vacuum cleaner out of its sentry box Richard had long been weeping with self-pity and rage. He was getting good at crying. If women were right, then you needed to cry about three or four times a day. Women cried at the oddest times: when they won beauty contests, for instance (and when they lost them too, probably: later on). If Richard won a beauty contest—would he cry? Can we see him there, on stage, with his bouquet, his swimsuit and his sash, and with all his mother coming into his eyes?

By the time he got the vacuum cleaner out of the apartment and onto the stairs Richard was wondering if he had ever suffered so. This, surely, is how we account for the darkness and the helpless melancholy of twentieth-century literature. These writers, these dreamers and seekers, stood huddled like shivering foundlings on the cliffs of a strange new world: one with no servants in it. On the stairs and landings there were bikes leaning everywhere, and also shackled to the walls—and to the ceiling. He lived in a beehive of bikers.

By the time he got the vacuum cleaner down into the hall Richard was sure that Samuel Beckett, at some vulnerable time in his life, had been obliged to take a vacuum cleaner in. Céline, too, and perhaps Kafka—if they had vacuum cleaners then. Richard gave himself a loud breather while he looked through his mail. His mail he no longer feared. The worst was over. Why should a man fear his mail, when, not long ago, he had received a solicitor's letter from his own solicitor? When, rather less recently, in response to a request for more freelance work, he had been summarily fired, through the post, by his own literary agent? When he was being sued (for advances paid on unwritten books) by both his ex-publishers? Most of the time, though, his mail was just junk. Once, in the street, on an agitated April afternoon, on his way back from lunch with some travel editor in some transient trattoria, he had seen a city cyclone of junk mail—leaflike leaflets, flying flyers, circling circulars— and had nodded, and thought: me, my life. And a lot of the time he got no mail at all. Now, on the morning of this his fortieth birthday, he received one small check and two large bills—and a brown envelope, hand-delivered (no address, no stamp), featuring his own name in tortured block capitals, with the accurate but unfamiliar addendum, "M.A. (Oxon)." He put it in his pocket, and once more shouldered his load.

Calchalk Street was to be found off Ladbroke Grove, a good half-mile beyond Westway. For a time it looked as though Calchalk Street was going up in the world. Richard and Gina had formed part of the influx of new money, more than half a decade ago, soon after their marriage, along with several other youngish couples whom they would see and smile at in the corner shop, in the coin-op launderette. For a while, that spring, under the apple blossom, Calchalk Street was a wholesome jingle of progress music, with a tap-tap here and a bang-bang there—there were skips and scaffolds, and orange pyramids of builders' sand. Then all the couples moved back out again, except Richard and Gina. Offered gentrification, Calchalk Street had said—no thanks. Instead it reassumed a postwar identity of rationing and rent books. Offered color, it stayed monochrome; even the Asians and West Indians who lived there had somehow become Saxonized—they loped and leered, they peed, veed, queued, effed and blinded, just like the locals. Calchalk Street had a terrible pub, the Adam and Eve (the scene, for Richard, of many a quivering glassful), and a terrible sub post office, outside which, at eight o'clock every weekday morning, a queue of Hildas and Gildas, of Nobbies and Noddies, desperately coalesced, clutching forms. There were Irish families crammed into basements, and pregnant housewives chain-smoking on the stoops, and bendy old men in flares and parched gym-shoes drinking tinned beer under the warm breath of the coin-op. They even had whores, up there on the corner—a little troupe of them. Richard moved past these young women, thinking, as he always thought: You're shitting me. In parkas, in windbreakers, grim, ruddy, they presented themselves as socioeconomic functionaries. For money they kept the lid on men in cars.

A vacuum cleaner is designed to cruise grandly round a carpet. It is not designed to be toted through a wet London Wednesday, with the traffic trailing its capes of mist. Painfully hampered, cruelly encumbered, Richard staggered on, the brown base under his arm as heavy as a soaked log, the T-shaped adjunct in his free hand, the tartan flex-tube round his neck like a fat scarf, and then the plug, freed from its broken catchlet, incensingly adangle between his legs. The "freshness and moral vivacity," the "bravely unfashionable optimism" and the "unembarrassed belief in human perfectibility" for which *Amelior* was now being retrospectively praised—all this would presumably get even better when its successor appeared, now that Gwyn Barry never had to take the vacuum cleaner in. Richard crossed Ladbroke Grove with his head down, not looking and not caring. The plug and cord snarled his ankles like a hurled bolero. The tartan tube clutched his neck in a pythonic embrace.

Once in the shop he let the whole contraption crash to the counter, on which he then leaned for a while with his head in his arms. When he looked up again a young man was standing over him and readying a foolscap document. Richard croaked his way through MAKE, MODEL, REGISTRATION NUMBER. At length they came to TYPE OF MALFUNCTION, and the young man said,

"What's wrong with it?"

"How would I know? It cuts out all the time and it makes this screeching sound and the bag leaks all the crap out of the back."

The young man considered Richard, and this information. His stare and his biro returned to the relevant rectangle. The biro hovered there unhappily. He looked up for a moment—time enough for onerous eye contact. He looked down. The biro itself now struck you as gnawed, cracked and capless, and paranoid, conscious of its disadvantage. Eventually, under TYPE OF MALFUNCTION, the young man wrote NOT WORKING.

"Yeah," said Richard. "That ought to cover it."

Beyond them, in the street outside, the old divisions of class and then race were giving way to the new divisions: good shoes versus bad shoes, good eyes as opposed to bad eyes (eyes that were clear, at one extreme, ranged against eyes that were far fierier than any Tabasco), different preparedness for the forms that urban life was currently taking, here and now. The young man looked at Richard with pain and with pre-weakened hostility. He had gone on working here much longer than he should have gone on working here, and so his eyes were as dim and marginal as the lights of a car left on all night and well into the next day. What divided the two of them, in the shop, was words—which were the universal (at least on this planet); the young man could look at Richard and be pretty sure there were more where *they* came from. Display fixtures were tacked to the wall, decorative or labor-saving, white cones and spheres. Beyond, in the back, in a valved heap like the wet city, lay all the stuff that wasn't working and would never work again: the unrecompleted, the undescribed.

On his way home he looked in at the Adam and Eve. Seated in the corner with a pint of bitter and a packet of Wotsits, the birthday boy slipped the brown envelope out of his pocket: Richard Tull, M.A. (Oxon). At Oxford (to hear Richard tell it), Gwyn had worked round the clock for his middle second, whereas Richard had taken a formal first without ever lifting a pen . . . He removed a single sheet of paper that might have been torn from a child's exercise book: blue-lined, softly creased, suggesting much effort, and little progress. The letter had been heavily corrected by another hand, but it still said,

> Dear Richard You are the writer of a "novel." Aforethought. Congratulations! Hows it done. First, you get the topic. Next you package it. Then, comes the hipe.
>
> I am thinking of becoming "an author." Snap. Shake. If you would like to meet and discuss these issues over a few "jars" feel free to give me a bell.
>
> Yours DARKO

Well-known writers get this kind of letter every other day. But Richard was not a well-known writer, and he got this kind of letter every other year (and they were normally about book reviewing anyway— though he did receive the odd scrawled note from hospitals and mental institutions where his novels were found in the libraries or on the book trolleys and stirred strange responses in depressives and amputees and other patients whose minds were disorganized by drugs). So Richard looked at this letter rather harder than a well-known writer would have done. And his scrutiny was rewarded: in the lower left-hand corner of the half-filled sheet, almost hidden by the fringe of the rip, it said, TPO. Richard turned the page over.

> I know the wierd girl, Belladonna. Shes the one they all wan't. Jesus what a looker. You'r mate Gwyn Barry, is in love with her of TV fame.

On the whole, this sounded like excellent news. Richard finished his drink. What he was looking at here might turn out to be a serviceable plan B. Though as it happened he was feeling exceptionally upbeat about plan A. Richard, in fact, was full of hope.

When he got back he made two telephone calls. The first telephone call was to Anstice, his forty-four-year-old secretary at *The Little Maga-zine*. He talked to her for an hour, as he did every day, not about *The Lit-tle Magazine* and not because he wanted to, but in case she killed herself or told Gina that he had slept with her, once, about a year ago. The sec-ond telephone call was to Gwyn. Richard wanted to confirm their fort-nightly snooker game. But Gwyn couldn't make it. The reason he (nauseatingly) offered was that he had spent too many evenings, just recently, "away from my lady." Gwyn, incidentally, wasn't just famous for being a novelist. He was also famous for being happily married. The pre-vious spring a TV producer with a lot of time on his hands had cobbled together a series called "The Seven Vital Virtues." Gwyn had picked Uxoriousness. The program won wide praise, and two repeats, as an example of British charm. It was an hour long. It showed things like Gwyn helping Demi in the garden, and bringing Demi tea, and sitting there gazing at Demi in childish absorption while she talked on the tele-phone and absentmindedly rearranged lunch dates.

The weather wasn't great but it was still meant to be summer. Something had gone wrong with summer. But this is England—and that's nothing new.

Consider. The four seasons are meant to correspond to the four prin-cipal literary genres. That is to say, summer, autumn, winter and spring are meant to correspond (and here I list them hierarchically) to tragedy, romance, comedy and satire. Close this book for a second and see if you can work it out: which season corresponds to which genre.

It's obvious, really. Once you've got comedy and tragedy right, the others follow.

Summer: romance. Journeys, quests, magic, talking animals, damsels in distress.

Autumn: tragedy. Isolation and decline, fatal flaws and falls, the throes of heroes.

Winter: satire. Anti-utopias, inverted worlds, the embrace of the tun-dra: the embrace of wintry thoughts.

Spring: comedy. Weddings, apple blossom, maypoles, no more mis-understandings—away with the old, on with the new.

We keep waiting for something to go wrong with the seasons. But something has already gone wrong with the genres. They have all bled into one another. Decorum is no longer observed.

Lady Demeter Barry had a driving instructor called Gary.

And 13 had an older brother called Crash.

They were the same person.

Crash was his street name. It wasn't his real name, and it wasn't his professional name, even more obviously: for Crash was a driving instructor. His real name was Gary.

It is still not altogether clear how Gary came to be called Crash. Street names are by no means always descriptive, or even counter-descriptive. Among 13's acquaintances—among his brothers—there were several entirely nondescript personages with names like Big Cool and Lightning and Here-Behold. For instance, 13 had a little cousin called Ian whose street name was Emu. E stood for Ian; and Ian liked music: hence Emu. Brill. EMU was what Ian assiduously spray-canned all over the bridges and ramparts of West London, in between the more elaborate injunctions and imprecations and invocations like TOOL UP ZIMBABWE and FUCK THE POLICE and SONS OF THUNDER. Or take another cousin of 13's: Link. Link was called Link not, as one might readily assume, because of his fantastically rudimentary facial features, but as a preferred alternative to Chains, a name that commemorated a certain Carnival riot during which Link had cleared an entire high-rise stairwell of police, with only these two four-foot lengths of humming, spark-spattering steel. Chains were what Link spent the following eighteen months in, which is probably why it was Link that stuck.

Who knew? Crash might have been called Crash because he was very big and made a lot of noise when he fell over. Crash might have been called Crash because of the predictable rhythm of his personal finances: the thing that always happened after the fortnightly boom of his paycheck. Most probably, though, Crash was called Crash because of his long-abandoned habit of sleeping in other people's houses: on couches, floorboards, in bathtubs . . . A relative newcomer to the scene might intelligibly suppose that Crash was called Crash because of what kept happening to him in the cars at the driving school. Close my eyes and I see Crash presiding with arms unhappily folded over a ten-acre breaker's yard of totaled Metros. Or, by modest extension, one might assume that Crash was called Crash because of what kept happening to his students in *their* cars within days of passing the test. And their cars were burnished and German, with cruise control and the digitalized speedo: for the school was a fashionable one, and all the women asked for Crash—though not by that name.

Among his students was Lady Demeter Barry.

So: Steve Cousins in the dark interior of the office at the end of the mews with a book on his lap (he always had a book with him: today it was *On Aggression* by Konrad Lorenz), looking out. And Crash on the cob-

bles among the burning roofs of cars, looking in. Neither knew if their
eyes had met through this fierce division of light. Steve put his book
aside. Crash bade farewell to another student, a rich teenage boy with
the good build and a space-ranger short back and sides and Mekon cra-
nium of the future.

"Crash mate," said Scozzy.

"Scozzy," said Crash.

Crash went to get the coffees from the perc. Like many young men in
the neighborhood, Crash had once worked for Scozzy, as a salesman of
cocaine. This fact defined the current protocol. Black Crash now stood
bunched over the coffee nook, big, not fat, just big, and not hopelessly
enormous either, by no means, not like some with the same black magnitude, whose mothers must have watched them grow with steadily dimin-
ishing pride. Scozzy experienced regret. Crash could have been useful. It
was a real pisser that he wasn't more like his little brother 13, who was
basically very dishonest—who was effortlessly dishonest.

"Forgot how you like it," he called.

And Steve told him: "Black. Two sugars."

The two men settled on the low sofa. The luminous track suit that
Crash wore (none of that gear for Scozz: no warmup stuff, no fucking
sweats) was well outshone by the heavy life that wavered from his face.
Like 13 he talked London, but there were memories of Africa in him,
like the great event of the nose, which resembled the back of a black
bullfrog squatting on his face, and the token dreadlocks, done in little
sprigs at right-angles from the head. Not real dreadlocks, of course; real
dreadlocks remained religiously unwashed and ended up looking like a
length of giant fag ash. His eyes were bright—even the blood in them
was bright. Famously big on white flip, as if he was doing research: bedroom with a revolving door. Steve looked at Crash and thought there
was no way in the world he was *related* to a trog like Link. And Steve
knew, further, that in any evolutionary illustration charting the course
from Link to Crash, he himself (Scozzy with his flared genes) would not
be on Crash's right but somewhere in the middle.

"Tits?" began Crash when Scozz got the ball rolling. "A man need a
rope and a pickax. And better take you climbing boots."

"She's racked," said Steve, not without grimness.

"Like them fucking things in the—freak vegetables. Marrows or
whatever. When they overdone it on the injections."

Steve flexed his neck. "Big tits is one thing," he said. "But you don't
want them all over the gaff."

"She hitch them up. I tell you, she leaning backward like . . . prop in the tug-of-war." Crash laughed quietly, in admiration. "She don't want to fall over. All that lot come tumbling down on top of her."

In different company, Crash might have spent a contented half hour in similar vein before changing the subject—before moving on, say, to how Lady Demeter Barry was built from the waist down. But now he was suddenly wondering what he was doing here—talking tits with Scozzy. You didn't want to be doing that, not with him, not with this fucking neuro. You definitely didn't want to be doing that . . . Crash saw that Steve's sloped chin was puckering as his mouth hardened into a beak; dissatisfaction was also expressing itself through heat in the eyes. Reflexively, and in the present case not even mildly indignantly, Crash checked the air for a white-black interaction—our women: all this. He came up with nothing in particular. Maybe Scozz was just getting to the point. At the end of the day, whatever happened, Crash was going to give 13 a smack. He waited. He was at a disadvantage, of course. Because nobody, but nobody, knew about Steve's strange taste in tits.

Now Steve told Crash what he wanted him to do, framed as a series of suggestions. Crash looked elsewhere. Fellow instructors, students (the office was filling up as the hour turned), those girls behind the desk to the side: they would have found it unbelievable, seeing the two men on the sofa, that the black man feared the white, that the big man feared the small. But he did fear him. Many times he had seen Scozzy go about his work, in pubs, in car parks. And Scozzy didn't stop. When he started, he didn't stop. In such contexts, too, the big man was traditionally wary of the small, because the small man always made the first move. And then there was Scozzy and words.

"She's a happily married woman," Crash heard himself saying. "On TV as such."

"Listen. Driving instructors. Spend all day looking at parted legs. Seat belt on all right, darling? Allow *me*. And you. This is the brothers' time, son. You got latitude." Steve's breath moved closer, its flavor incredibly man-made, like the new breath of a fleet car. "Out there in the little Metro. Some rich flip sits herself down on your courting finger. And if she so much as blinks, you go: 'Raciss!' Don't bother you the other way though, does it." The breath came nearer still. The breath was just another weapon. "When they're down there, doing it for democracy. Or anthropology. Or some other reason. Enjoy it, mate. While it lasts. Reparations—that's the *ting*. Yat. Slave trade is it."

Crash turned away from this for a moment. As it happened he had his own image of the slave trade, which he carried around with him in his head. This image was of a contained volume of absolute darkness; its sound effects were dull human hooting and the creak of boards at sea. He turned back. He was going to *smear* 13. Crash didn't drink as a rule but sometimes, when the pressure built too big, he got a bottle of scotch—he didn't give a fuck—and drank the whole thing. Not often. But sometimes, to sort out the stress, he got a bottle of scotch and threw away the top. (He didn't give a fuck.) Now Crash swallowed and said musingly,

"Got to eat bland for a day or two. Gut's all sour."

"You don't have to *do* nothing, Crash, mate. All I want's information. Advice: cut out the perfume. You reek of cheap ponce. You smell like a fucking minicab."

Yeah that's right, thought Crash. Scozzy was bad news, all bad news, terrible information from start to finish, like a catastrophic telecast that kept going on for hour after hour.

"This is it."

Demeter Barry was punctual: the stroke of noon. She came out of the sunshine and in through the glass door with her head lowered so that she seemed to be peeping upward and at an angle. The first thing you noticed about her from the waist up, actually, was the central line of her gray silk blouse: it was not quite sheer or true, wavering on the way down and missing her belt buckle, which was itself, perhaps, imperfectly justified.

"Hi Gary," she said.

"And how are you this morning," said Crash in the deeper and more priestly and African tones he used for the driving instruction of white women. He turned to Scozzy, who picked up his book, and nodded, and extended his hand and said: "Steve Cousins."

As he walked down the mews Steve realized that this was the closest he had ever come to saying something he often came very close to saying: "Steve Cousins," he had almost said: "Barnardo Boy."

As one might say "Sound Recordist" or "Political Analyst" or "Poet and Essayist."

Of course, he could have said "wild boy," which was also true.

"What's your agent scene at the moment?" asked Gwyn Barry. "Have you got one?"

Gwyn and Richard were at the Westway Health and Fitness Center, surrounded by thirty or forty etiolated drunks: playing snooker. In the ferrety light of pool halls everywhere. Gwyn himself had had several beers, and Richard, naturally, was completely smashed. Eighteen tables, all in use, eighteen lucent pyramids over the green troughs and the bright bone balls; and then the multicolored competitors, Spanish, West Indian, South American, Pacific Rim—and the no-color Brits, indistinguishable, it seemed, from the great genies of cigarette smoke that moved between the tables like the ghosts of referees ... England *was* changing. Twenty years ago Richard and Gwyn or their equivalents could never have gone to a snooker hall—Gwyn in his chinos and cashmere turtleneck, Richard in his (accidentally appropriate) waistcoat and lopsided bow tie. They would have stood outside, blowing into cupped hands, smelling the bacon grease, and scanned the stubbornly just-literate lettering on the basement placard, and moved aside for the donkey-jacketed and zoot-suited cueists weaving through the dead and wounded on their way down the crackling stone steps. Gwyn and Richard might have got in. But they wouldn't have got out. In those days the Englishmen all had names like Cooper and Baker and Weaver, and they beat you up. Now they all had names like Shop and Shirt and Car, and you could go anywhere you liked.

"Why do you ask?"

"The thing is I've moved. I'm with Gal now."

"So I've read."

"You remember Gal."

"Of course I remember Gal."

Richard reassumed his cueing posture, chin at table height, upper body bent or slumped over the side cushion. You were not supposed to talk while playing snooker—except about snooker. Richard had had to insist on this. Too many times, or so Richard felt, he would be lining up a frame-clinching sitter, and Gwyn would start telling him about the Italian TV crew he was expecting the next morning or the surprising figure offered for his Saudi translation rights, and Richard would find that he had somehow shoveled the cue ball onto the adjacent table ... Two weeks after the event, he was still reading Rory Plantagenet's diary columns, hoping for a long piece about how Richard Tull had humiliated Gwyn Barry in front of the Shadow Minister for the Arts. Instead, that morning, he had found a long piece about how Gwyn Barry had switched agents, controversially taking his custom from Harley, Dexter, Fielding to Gal Aplanalp.

"She's already got me a *huge* deal on my next one."

"You haven't finished your next one."

"Yeah, but they like to do these things earlier now. It's a campaign. It's like a war out there. World rights."

"Get more drinks."

"So who are you with now? What's your position with agents?"

"More drinks," said Richard, whose position with agents went like this. He had started out under the wing of Harley, Dexter, Fielding, who had signed him up as a twenty-five-year-old, pre-*Aforethought*, on the strength of his eye-catchingly vicious reviews of new fiction and poetry. Richard stayed with Harley, Dexter, Fielding for his first two novels and then fired them after his third was rejected by every publisher in the land, including John Bernard Flaherty Dunbar Ltd., Hocus Pocus Books, and the Carrion Press. He then transferred his talents to Dermott, Jenkins, Wyatt, who fired *him* after his fourth novel met an identical fate. Next, Richard went solo, and dealt personally with all submissions and negotiations on novel number five: that is to say, he photocopied and packaged it so many times that he felt like a publisher himself—or a printer, printing *samizdat* in a free country. As yet he had no plans for his sixth novel: *Untitled*. And he needed plans. He badly needed plans.

"I haven't got an agent," he said.

"You know, Gal's a big fan of yours."

"You mean she has pleasant memories of me? Or that she liked my stuff."

"Both. She liked your stuff."

All the reds were gone. Only the eight balls remained on the table: the black and the brown, the pink and the blue, the green and the yellow; the lone red; and of course the white. Both of them were so lousy at snooker that it would be misleading to claim that Richard was better at it than Gwyn. But he always won. In this area, as in one or two others, he understood that there was a beginning, a middle and an end. He understood that there was an endgame. And it was in the endgame that Gwyn showed his only wisps of talent: a certain Celt-Iberian canniness, a certain sideburned cunning. Careful now.

"She told me to tell you to expect her call."

"It's a pretty cheesy list though isn't it—Gal's?" said Richard, who found that he was blushing and almost fainting as he lowered his head over the drinks table: blushing bloodier than the pink, bloodier than the red. "Isn't it all rock stars and cookbooks? And how-to?"

"She's taking it upmarket. More literary. She's got quite a few novelists."

"Yeah but they're all famous for being something else. Famous mountaineers. Comedians. Newscasters." Richard nodded to himself. The newscaster, he had read, was not only famous for being a newscaster and for being a novelist. He was also famous (at present) for something else: for getting fantastically beaten up, the other night, in a mews off Kensington High Street. "And politicians," he said.

"It's the right move, I think. She'll go in a bit harder for me. Because of her list. Because I'm prestigious."

"Because you're what?" But then Richard paused and just said, "Of course you wouldn't know what prestigious means. Or meant. Deceptive. As is prestidigitation. Conjuring."

"When was the last time you saw Gal? She was a nice-looking kid but now she's . . . she really . . . She's really . . ."

Richard looked on, not at all sympathetically, as Gwyn's mind blundered about, searching for a way of saying what he wanted to say. What he wanted to say, presumably (Richard had heard this from others, and believed it), was that Gal Aplanalp was mercilessly beautiful. Gwyn stood there with his concessionary shrugs and frowns, beset by reasons for not saying what he wanted to say. Which he couldn't do without seeming invidious or impolitic, disrespectful both to Gal and to those less well favored. And so on.

"I hear she's very lucky in her looks," Richard said. "Wait a minute. *You're* famous for being something else too."

"Am I? What?"

"Happily married. Uxorious."

"Oh that."

Gwyn sneaked home on the black, but it was a dead frame anyway, and Richard didn't hate that too much, having prevailed 3–1. On their way out, moving side by side down the passage with their slender cue cases, like musicians or executioners, they passed an exercise room where, by the way, Steve Cousins had given karate lessons for six months, six years ago, to the juveniles of West Ten. The arrangement ended because all the parents complained and because Steve couldn't bring himself to punctuate his discourse with enough religious shit about restraint and self-control and the *empty hand*.

"Have you ever come across a girl called Belladonna?"

"I don't think so," said Gwyn. "And I think I'd remember, with that name."

"Still. People are always changing their names, aren't they. These days."

They parted on Ladbroke Grove beneath the elevated underground: that patch of London owned by bums and drunks, exemplary in its way—the model anti-city; here the pavement, even the road, wore a coat of damp beer (in various manifestations) which sucked on your shoes as you hastened past. Crouching men with upturned fucked-up faces . . . It made Richard think of Pandaemonium and the convocation of rebel angels—hurled like lightning headlong over the crystal battlements of heaven, falling and falling into penal fire and the deep world of darkness. Then their defiant council. He liked Moloc best: *My sentence is for open war.* But he felt Beelzebub was more on the money: contrivance, slow revenge, seduction—the undermining of innocence and Eden.

My sentence is for open war ... That *sentence* was awfully good. When writers hate, it all comes down to something very simple. His word against mine.

This whole thing is a crisis. The whole mess is a crisis of the middle years.

Every father knows the loathed park and playground in the unmoving air of Sunday morning (every mother knows it Friday evening, Tuesday afternoon—every other time), the slides and seesaws and climbing-frames like a pictogram of inanity. The fathers on the edges of benches, or strolling, or bending and peering: this is their watch. They exchange slow nods of resignation and hear the wall of childish sound from which no sense is detachable: its twangs and pops and whipcracks.

I was there in the fog. The fog was sorry about it—the fog was wretched about the whole thing. Like the fathers the fog had nowhere else to go. Ancient and stupid, but equipped with new chemical elements and contributions, the fog loomed and idled, hoping it wasn't in the way.

Here I found a reversal of the more familiar protocol: no adult was allowed into the playground unless accompanied by a child. The playground was therefore maniac-free, murderer-free. You were not a murderer. Your child was the living guarantee that you were not a murderer.

A little boy approached me—not one of my own. And he made a sign. Keeping a humorous distance, he made a sign: the two forefingers in the shape of a T. Deaf-and-dumb kid, I thought, and felt my face widen with the unsurprised tolerance I automatically wanted it to have. My look was so tolerant it didn't even *look* tolerant: just open. T. Wasn't that deaf-and-dumb for *the*? Wait. He was doing another one now, and another. Wasn't the circle, the O, deaf-and-dumb for *nothing*? I found that my head was intensely inclined toward him, that I was suddenly braced for revelation, frowning, essaying, as if the boy could tell me something I really might need to know.

Because I know so little. Because I need information from any source. "Tom," he said. "It's my name."

And I made the signs—the M, the A—with my strange and twisted fingers, thinking: how can I ever play the omniscient, the all-knowing, when I don't know *anything*? When I can't read childish capitals in the apologetic fog.

I wrote those words five years ago, when I was Richard's age. Even then I knew that Richard didn't look as bad as he thought he looked. Not yet. If he did, then someone, surely, a woman or a child—Gina, Demi, Anstice, Lizzete, Marius, Marco—would take his hand and lead him to somewhere nice and soft and white, kindly whispering to his gasps for breath. Intimations of monstrousness are common, are perhaps universal, in early middle age. But when Richard looked in the mirror he was looking for something that was no longer there.

It might help if we knew where we lived. Each of us, after all, has the same address. Every child has memorized it. It goes something like.

> This or That Number,
> This or That Street,
> This or That Conurbation,
> This or That County,
> This or That Country,
> This or That Continent,
> This or That Hemisphere,
> The Earth,
> The Superior Planets,
> The Solar System,
> Nr. Alpha Centauri,
> The Orion Spur,
> The Milky Way,
> The Local Group,
> The Local Cluster,
> The Local Supercluster,
> The Universe,
> *This* Universe. The One Containing:
> The Local Supercluster,
> The Local Cluster,
> And So On. All the Way Back To:
> This or That Street,
> And This or That Number.

It might help if we knew where we were going, and how fast.

> The Earth revolves at half a kilometer per second.
> The Earth orbits the Sun at thirty kilometers per second.
> The Sun orbits the center of the Milky Way at 300 kilometers per second.

The Milky Way is traveling in the general direction of Virgo at 300 kilometers per second.

Astronomically, everything is always getting further away from everything else.

It might help if we knew what we were made of, how we keep going and what we will return to.

Everything before your eyes—the paper and the ink, these words, and your eyes themselves—was made in stars: in stars that explode when they die.

More proximately we are warmed and hatched and raised by a steady-state H-bomb, our yellow dwarf: a second-generation star on the main sequence.

When we die, our bodies will eventually go back where they came from: to a dying star, our own, five billion years from now, some time around the year 5,000,001,995.

It might help if we knew all this. It might help if we felt all this.

Absolutely unquestionably, the universe is high style.

And what are we?

Flat-earthers. Richard's opening move, in his plan to ruin Gwyn's life, was not calculated to be in itself decisive, or even dramatic. On the other hand it did demand from Richard a great deal of trouble and expense—and internal wear. All these phone calls and stunned crosstown journeys and talentless grapplings with brown paper and string. Whether Richard had any talent for fictional prose remained arguable, perhaps; but he was definitely no good at all with brown paper and string. Nonetheless, he was decided. He even raised his chin for a moment in simple heroism. His nostrils widened. Richard Tull had resolved to send Gwyn Barry a copy of the Sunday *New York Times*. With a note. And that was all.

He was quite clear about it in his own mind . . .

"Daddy? Are you bold?"

"I sometimes like to think so, yes, Marco."

"Will you always be bold?"

"Despite the ills that await life's balm, Marco, though made weak by time and fate, but strong in will, to strive, to seek—"

"Have you always been bold? How did you get bold?"

Richard closed his eyes. He dropped his pen on to the desktop and said, "You mean *bald*. Go elsewhere, Marco."

The child remained. He went on gazing at his father's hair. "Have you got male-*pattern* boldness?"

"I suppose so. I suppose that's the kind I've got."

"When did you start to be bold?"

"Go elsewhere, Marco. Go and play in the traffic. I'm trying to work."

He was quite clear about it in his own mind . . . Richard sat at his desk; he had just put *Untitled* away for the morning, after completing an hysterically fluent passage of tautly leashed prose, and was now assembling his notes (which were widely dispersed) for a review of *The Soul's Dark Cottage: A Life of Edmund Waller*. Even Richard's book-reviewing career, unusually, described a tidy downward curve, like the bedside graph of an open-and-shut moribund. He had started off with fiction and poetry; then fiction; then American fiction (his specialty and passion). Things began going wrong when they steered him on to *South American fiction*: an interminable succession, it seemed, of flowery thousand-pagers about sheep-dips or coconut shies. Then biographies.

Then more biographies. Like most young reviewers, Richard had come in hard. But instead of getting softer, more catholic, more forgiving (heading toward elderly impartiality and, beyond that, journey's end: a gurgling stupor of satisfaction with everything written), Richard had just got harder. There were personal reasons for this, of course, which everyone eventually sensed. As a reviewer he wrote forcefully—he had an individual voice and an individual memory. But he subscribed to the view of the Critic as Bouncer. Only geniuses were allowed in Richard's speakeasy. And the real trouble with all those novels he was sent was that they were *published*. And his weren't . . . Richard leaned back: he was achieving the difficult feat of taking his own pulse while continuing to bite his nails. His smaller son Marco, who had failed Gina's dawn fitness test and was taking another day off school, remained at his father's side, balancing a rubber troll or goblin on various roughly horizontal surfaces: Richard's forearm, Richard's shoulder, one or other of Richard's bald spots. And from outside through the shivery window came the sound of fiercely propelled metal as it ground against stone, shearing into the sore calcified struts and buttresses with sadistic persistence: the house, the street, the whole city, taking it deep in the root canal.

For instance, it had to be *The New York Times*. The *Los Angeles Times* was even bigger, Richard knew, but in his judgment Gwyn wasn't quite nuts enough for the *Los Angeles Times*. Still, he was surely nuts enough for *The New York Times*. Richard would have staked his sanity on it. If Gwyn wasn't nuts enough for *The New York Times*, then Richard was losing his grip. Now he reached for his jacket, hooked over the chair and dug out the bent checkbook on which he hoped he might have written a few words about *The Soul's Dark Cottage: A Life of Edmund Waller*. He had: *shops his mates to avoid axe p. 536ff.* The checkbook joined his other notes, loosely gathered on the heaped desk: a credit-card slip, a torn envelope, an empty matchbook. His desk was so horrendously burdened that his telephone often stopped ringing before he found it—or, quite possibly, before he even heard it.

The plan was this: Richard would send Gwyn Barry a copy of the Sunday *New York Times*, the whole thing, that forest-razing suitcase of smeared print, accompanied by a typed note that would read, in its entirety,

Dear Gwyn,
    Something in here to interest you. The price of fame!
                                                    Yours ever,
                                                    John

There would of course be no indication where this interesting some-thing might be found. Sitting back, sitting back in the alphabet soup of his study, Richard imagined Gwyn opening the package, frowning at the note, looking first, with a slight smile, at the Book Review, then, rather less equably, at the Arts and Leisure, then . . .

"Marco, what's the point of doing that?"

Either Marco didn't hear or he didn't understand. He said: "Wot?" There is of course this difficulty of rendering childish speech. But how do you get round it? Marco didn't say "What?" He said "Wot?"—defi-nitely a humbler and shorter word, and entirely unaspirated.

"Balancing that toy on my arm," said Richard. "Why? What for?"

"Does it bolla you?"

"Yes."

"Does *that* bolla you?" he asked, balancing the toy on Richard's head.

"Yes."

"Does *that* bolla you?" he asked, balancing the toy on Richard's shoulder.

"They all bother me." Edmund Waller bothers me. "How'm I sup-posed to do this review?"

He wanted Marco elsewhere so that he could call Anstice and smoke a cigarette with his head out the window and generally get on with fucking Gwyn up. *Edmund Waller was born in. Go, lovely Rose! Tell her, that wastes her time and me . . .* Basically, now that the guilt had evaporated, the Anstice thing was just a bottomless drag. He spent all this time talking to her in case she killed herself. *A consummate air-sniffer and seat-warmer (and mediocrity), Edmund.* But he *wanted* her to kill herself. Conversely, killing yourself demanded energy, which Anstice didn't normally have. In an energetic state, she might do other things too, like ringing up Gina. *A fairweather Royalist, an expedient Republican, and a mercenary bridegroom.* Although he had gone to bed with Anstice, he hadn't made love to her—but she didn't seem to realize this. *Waller's Plot was in itself a fiasco. Yet it provided him with the chance to betray all his.* How bad would it be anyway, if Gina found out? As it happened, Richard assumed and even hoped that Gina was having an affair herself: for pressing reasons that will soon become clear. *Small is the worth of beauty from the light retired . . .* Writers don't lead shapely lives. Shape they give to the lives of others: accountants, maniacs. *Whereas Edmund Waller. While Waller. Although. Despite the fact that. Whilst Waller . . .*

What *was* it with *whilst*? A scrupulous archaism—like the standard book review. Like the standard book. It was not the words themselves that were prim and sprightly polite, but their configurations, which answered to various old-time rhythms of thought. Where were the new rhythms—were there any out there yet? Richard sometimes fancied that his fiction was looking for the new rhythms. Gwyn sure as hell wasn't looking for them. Gwyn's style played a simple tune: the eyes that bulged over the pennywhistle were all bright and clear and artless. Richard pulled open the top drawer of his desk and consulted his recent fan letter: from Darko, confidant of the weird girl Belladonna. The worn page with its marked lines of swimming-pool blue, the fingerprints, the sweat, the epidermal avidity: here perhaps were the new rhythms.

Marco didn't want to be left alone so in the end Richard took him down to the stoop where he could at least get through some cigarettes in his company. The summer air of London was such that he might as well have blown the fagsmoke into Marco's face, or split the pack with him. Marco had asthma. He had another difficulty too. Richard didn't think about it that much. The five percent of his mind that was occupied by Marco (and this was capable of big expansions when Marco was sick or sad) had convinced itself that five percent would do: Marco was an okay little boy, with a quirk. It was called a learning disability and it had to do with repeated category mistakes. If you told Marco why the chicken crossed the road, Marco would ask you what the chicken did next. Where did it go? What was its name? Was it a boy or a girl? Did it have a husband—and, perhaps, a brood of chicks? How many?

Wait. Richard's face veered up with an animal snarl. Jesus: that fucking guy. Twice every weekday, at irregular hours, a big man in a big car drove down Calchalk Street at sixty miles an hour. What was his *hurry*? Who could want him anywhere sooner than he was going to get there already? He had his jacket on a hook. He had a wide-pored vest beneath his sleek white shirt. He had an outscrolled underlip and a fat nose and fair brows and lashes, like a cool new pig they'd knocked up in a lab somewhere. Richard got to his feet to watch the man rip by: an animal hating another animal. He comes here twice a day, thought Richard. He comes here twice a day, trying to kill my kids.

When the air settled again Richard sat down and lit another cigarette . . . If, in bringing about Gwyn's destruction—if there was time for art, then it would be much more satisfying to use contemporary forces, to awaken and array them, against his life. Ladbroke Grove and the Portobello Road and their daily flailing and groping and needing. If you could hydroelectrify the energies of the street and point them in the path you chose. A big project. Easier, and cheaper, just to find whoever did this kind of thing, and pay him money to knock Gwyn's block off. Meanwhile, there was Belladonna to be activated. Meanwhile, there was the Sunday *New York Times*.

By now Marco was stretched out on the stoop, his right ear on his right bicep, his free hand toying with troll, with goblin. Richard sat there, smoking. Nicotine is a relaxant. Cigarettes are for the unrelaxed.

We are the unrelaxed.

13 was in the van, waiting, which was how he spent much of his time. In one hand he held the scruff of Giro's coat; in the other, a consoling can of Ting.

13? 13 was in bits. The activities of the night before had involved him in a 120-minute, 120-mile-an-hour Indianapolis down the wrong way of the M20 in a stolen GTi with five blue-and-whites up his pipe. So? Okay. When you're doing the driving yourself: you take what comes. But when the bloke behind the wheel is only twelve years old, and out of his bonce on Wite-Out solvent . . . Through the windscreen, on which an ultra-light rain had left a kind of fur or plush or bumfluff, 13's stare addressed the city hospital library: St. Something's. He saw himself mummified in bandages with just his hair spike sticking out. Sad!

Steve Cousins was within. He walked fast, his mack-tails and belt-ends whipping up the air in his wake. The bends of his hat's brim answered to his rostral face and the slant of its asymmetries. A traffic light of blood marked the trailing mack. On the ground floor now, heading for the hospital: there was a book he expected to find and intended to steal.

He had just been to visit Kirk, upstairs. There Scozzy sat, after passing on the propitiatory speedway mags, and there Kirk lay, in the little room to himself, his face a Scalextric of stitches, when the door opens. It's Kirk's brother: Lee. With a big crackling hamper in his arms. Lee goes, "Fortnum's and Mason's," parks the hamper on the end of the bed—and unclasps it. And this horrible head pops up. Beef the pit bull! Kirk spreads out his arms with tears in his eyes: "Beef boy. He's smiling! See that? He's that pleased to see me!"

Jesus. That fucking dog was all over him like a video nasty. And you can't call them off. You can't call them off. Like me in that respect. Call me off? You can't call me off. The owner, the trainer, he can't call them off: that's what's meant to be so good about them: you can't call them off. Kirk can't call Beef off: it's got his mouth between its teeth. Anyway, Lee pounds it on the neck about fifteen times with a full Lucozade bottle, and the drip-stand comes crashing down, and by the time they drag Beef off and kick the shit out of it and cram it back in the hamper, there's five nurses in there saying what's this little lot. Scozzy and Lee were sitting on the hamper lid—Beef beneath, going out of its nut. "Nothing!" said Kirk. "Me stitches come undone!" They were talking about calling the police or whatever and Steve didn't fucking need that. Slipped away. With Kirk still slobbering something to Lee about putting English mustard in its grub, mornings and last thing, to keep Beef tasty.

13 saw him coming and climbed out of the van: oof. When you spent half your life waiting, when you spent half your life lurking and loitering, you got this stiffness sometimes and your limbs went dead.

"What's that you got?" said 13.

Scozzy held it up for him.

"Afterthought," said 13.

"*Aforethought,*" said Scozzy.

"By the man."

"No. Not by the man. By his mate."

"Or whatever."

Steve was still in a lenient mood, after his recent success. He had beaten up the man from the Ten O'clock News: and, the next night, it was *on* the Ten O'clock News! You do a newscaster, and they do you a newscast about it. Now that's the way the world's *supposed* to be run.

"Holland Park," announced Scozzy.

"Can't."

"Why?"

"Due in court is it."

"Jesus," said Scozzy.

The heat was stiffling, read Richard. He sighed, and lit a cigarette.

> The heat was stiffling. Moodly he looked out of his bedroom window. Yes, the day was far too hot to be sleepy. The time had come. He *had* to chose.

Richard wasn't reading this in a speculative spirit. He was marking it up for the printer. He said,

"Now there's a first sentence that seizes you by the lapels. *The heat was stiffling.*"

Balfour Cohen came and looked over Richard's shoulder. He smiled understandingly and said, "Ah yes. That's his second novel."

"Did we publish his first?"

"We did."

"How did that start? Let's think. *It was biterly cold.*"

Balfour smiled understandingly. "It's probably a pretty good yarn."

Richard read on:

> He *had* to chose. To win, to suceed, would be incredulous. But to fail, to loose, would be contemptuous!

"What I don't understand," said Richard, "is what these people have against dictionaries. Maybe they don't even know they can't spell."

As he said this he found he was sweating, and even crying. Another thing he didn't understand was why he had to correct the spelling. I mean, why bother? Who cared? No one was ever going to read this stuff, except the author, and the author's mum.

"I'm amazed he spelt the title right."

"What is the title?" asked Balfour.

"*Another Gift from Genius.* By Alexander P. O'Boye. That's assuming he spelt his name right. What was his first one called?"

"One moment." Balfour tapped his keys. "*A Gift from Genius,*" he said.

"Jesus. How old is he?"

"Guess," said Balfour.

"Nine," said Richard.

"Actually he's in his late sixties."

"Pitiful, isn't it? What's the matter with him? I mean is he *insane*?"

"Many of our authors are retired. This is one of the services we perform. They have to have something to do."

Or something to be, thought Richard. Sitting in the pub all day with a dog on your lap would be more creative, and more dignified, than nine-to-fiving it on the illiterate delusion. He glanced sideways. It was possible that Balfour regarded Alexander P. O'Boye as one of the flowers of his list. He was always more hushed and pious when it came to the fiction and the poetry. In any case it was Richard who was now Fiction and Poetry Editor at the Tantalus Press. He didn't have to do what Balfour did, which was mark up the biographies of pet goldfish and prize gherkins, the thousand-page treatises that supposedly whipped the carpet out from under Freud and Marx and Einstein, the revisionist histories of disbanded regiments and twilit trade-union outposts, the nonfictional explorations of remote planets, and all the other screams for help.

"One should remind oneself," said Balfour, as he said every week, "that James Joyce initially favored private publication." Then he added: "Proust, too, by the way."

"But that was . . . Wasn't that just a maneuver? To avoid a homosexuality scandal," said Richard carefully. "Advice from Gide. Before Proust went to Gallimard."

"Nabokov," suggested Balfour.

"Yeah but that was just a book of love poems. When he was a schoolboy."

"Nevertheless. Philip Larkin. And of course James Joyce."

Balfour was always doing this. Richard expected to learn that Shakespeare got his big break with a vanity publisher; that Homer responded to some ad whining for fresh trex. The Tantalus Press, it went without saying, was not a springboard to literary eminence. The Tantalus Press was a springboard to more of the same: to *Another Gift from Genius.* "Private" publishing was not organized crime exactly, but it had close links with prostitution. The Tantalus Press was the brothel. Balfour was the madam. Richard helped the madam out. Their writers paid *them* . . . And a writer ought to be able to claim that he had never paid for it—never in his life.

"What have you got?" said Richard.

"Second World War. It looks rather controversial."

"The myth of the six million?"

"He goes further. He argues that the concentration camps were run by Jews and that the prisoners were all Aryan Germans."

"Come on, Balfour. You're not taking that."

Had he been around for the Holocaust in which all four of his grandparents were enslaved and then murdered, Balfour would have been dead half a dozen times over. Pink triangle, yellow star: it would have been a complicated badge he wore, in his last days. Racially subhuman (Jewish), sexually perverted (homosexual), mentally unsound (schizophrenic), physically deformed (clubfooted) and politically deviant (Communist). He was also a vanity publisher; he was also entirely uncynical. Furthermore—and as it were disinterestedly—Cohen was a serious collector of anti-Semitic propaganda. Look at him. There never was a gentler face, Richard thought: the bald brown head, the seashell undulations of his temples, the all-forgiving orbits of his hot brown eyes. Balfour was an erratically generous Jew who also got into weird states about money. When they all ate lunch together, in some caff, or sandwich nook, Balfour would either quietly pick up the bill or ask for exactly calibrated contributions—and then grab everyone's money and seem about to bolt for the door. He would talk in a loud and irrelevant voice, and then simmer down, slowly. It was atavistic, Richard felt: Balfour had been on the road for two thousand years. Curiously, Richard also felt that Balfour loved him but wanted to destroy him . . . He had another hobby which Richard suspected was also a sideline: faking modern first editions. In his casual employ were several little hermits and other little maniacs who, overnight, could knock up astounding facsimiles of a *Sons and Lovers,* a *Brighton Rock,* a *Handful of Dust.*

"It's not my business to question an author's views or his findings."

"Findings? They're not findings. He didn't find them. They found him. Go on, Balfour. Destroy it unread."

The downstairs office of the Tantalus Press was communal: eleven people worked there, arranging things like *translations*. Richard wasn't yet clear how it went. Translations of *this* crap, into French, say? Or translations of *French* crap, into more of *this* crap? Anyway Richard sat ensconced upstairs, with the boss. Their office was comfortable, even tasteful, but diligently unluxurious (Balfour enjoyed saying, as an ordinary publisher would not enjoy saying, that his operation was non-profit-making), and you were allowed to smoke in it. A Communist could hardly forbid smoking. As well as Communists, sick people, the racially inferior—the unnecessary mouths, the life unworthy of life—the German state killed malingerers, troublemakers, shirkers and grumblers. But not smokers. Richard might have faced the ultimate penalty for grumbling (and for much else), but not for smoking. Hitler disapproved of smoking. Stalin didn't, apparently. When the Russians were repatriating the wanderers of Europe, when the war was over, every itinerant under their care was granted an astonishingly—almost an unsmokably—generous allowance of tobacco: even children, even babies. Balfour paid Richard very generously for his one day a week.

"I think we might have found a rather promising poet. Rather striking, for a first collection."

"Sling it over . . . Good name. Keith Horridge. *Very* good name," said Richard.

Who was aware that if he worked here two days a week instead of one he would be finished, humanly, within a year. Richard's novels might have been unreadable, but they were novels. Braced at first by the Saharas and Gobis of talentlessness which hourly confronted him, he now knew this stuff for what it was. It wasn't bad literature. It was anti-literature. Propaganda, aimed at the self. Richard's novels might have been unreadable, but they were novels. Whereas the finished typescripts, printouts and flabby exercise books that lay around him here just hadn't made it out of some more primitive form: diary, dreamjournal, dialectic. As in a ward for the half-born, Richard heard these creatures' cries, and felt their unviewable spasms, convulsed in an earlier version of being. They were like tragic babies; they were like pornography. They shouldn't be looked at. They really shouldn't be looked at.

Balfour said with infinite circumspection, "And how is your—how is your latest?"

"Nearly done." And he didn't go on to add—because he couldn't see that far ahead, because men can't see further than the next fight or fuck—that his latest might be his last. Not just couldn't see: couldn't look. That couldn't be looked at either.

"If for any reason you don't find a home for it, I would of course be proud to publish it under the Tantalus imprint."

Richard could see himself ending his days with Balfour. This presentiment was becoming more and more common—habitual, reflexive. Ending his days with Balfour, with Anstice, with R. C. Squires, that bus conductress, that postman, that meter maid. Richard the haggard and neurotic ex-prettyboy, in an airless pool of batch or spinst, sparing and unpredictable with his sexual favors, vain, hideous and sullen, and a miserable pedant about his China tea.

"I know you would, Balfour."

"We could do it on subscription. Make a list. Starting with your friends."

"Thanks. Thanks. But it's got to take its chances. It's got to sink or swim."

Sink or swim in what? In the universal.

The ancients used to think that the stars—all of them—lay just beyond Saturn. Go beyond Saturn, and you would encounter the slipstream of the Milky Way. And that would be that. It isn't the case. Go beyond Saturn, a long way beyond Saturn (more than doubling the distance of your journey from the Earth), and you will encounter Uranus. Go another thousand million miles and you will encounter Neptune, the last of the gas giants. Keep going and what do you get? You get Pluto.

Unlike the other gas giants, unlike the failed sun of Jupiter, Uranus has no internal heat source; it is tilted at a right angle—eight degrees more than a right angle, in fact, so its rotation is retrograde; it has black rings, and fifteen known satellites.

Neptune boasts its Great Dark Spot, its 700-mph winds, and, among its eight satellites, glamourous Triton: moon-sized, with geysers of nitrogen, and pink snow. Neptune has rings. One of its minor satellites, Galatea, is a ring-stabilizer—or a "ring-shepherd," as they are called.

Now Pluto. One must never mock the afflicted, of course, but Pluto really *is* an awful little piece of shit. Jupiter didn't make it as a star; Pluto didn't even make it as a planet. Tenuous atmosphere, a crust of ice (300 miles deep), and then rock. Pluto's mass is about a fifth of the mass of our moon, and *its* moon, Charon (another toilet), is half as small again. There are no rings, so Charon is no shepherd: he is a ferryman, ferrying the dead to Pluto's underworld. The orbit of Charon matches the rotation of Pluto, so this terrible little pair, this terrible little pair of two-bob planetesimals are "locked." Depending on which hemisphere of Pluto you were on, Charon would either be permanently immobile or permanently invisible. Wherever you were on Pluto, you could stare at the sun. It would sometimes seem cruciform, like the brandished sword of god. But it wouldn't warm you and it wouldn't give you life.

The ancients also used to think of the stars as *fixed*: eternal and immutable. Human beings found such a notion hard to abandon, and it persisted well beyond Copernicus and Galileo. This is why they had so much difficulty with *novas* (what we would now think of as *supernovas*). This is why they had so much difficulty with "new stars."

Take this thing about Gwyn and carpentry. If you really want a terrible time (thought Richard, who was having a terrible time—that night, in his study), take this thing about Gwyn and carpentry.

In an interview Gwyn said, or was quoted as saying, that he always likened the craft of fiction to the craft of *carpentry*.

"You are chipping away, planing, sanding, until everything is smooth and everything fits. Above all, the construction has to *work*. The carpenter knows that what he makes has to be functional. It has to be *honest*."

Q: "Do you actually do any carpentry or work with your hands?"

"Yes. I have a kind of workshop area where I potter about. I find it very therapeutic."

The next time Richard saw him (this was some months ago), Richard said, "What's all this bullshit about you and carpentry? Do you do any carpentry?"

"No," said Gwyn.

"It's a worthless metaphor for writing anyway. They have nothing in common."

"Sounds good, though. It makes writing more accessible to people who work with their hands."

"Why do you want to make writing more accessible to people who work with their hands?"

A couple of weeks later Gwyn took Richard down to his basement to show him how the wine cellar was coming along. Richard noticed a workbench under the stairs. There was a vise, a plane, a saw, even a spirit level. There were also several blocks of wood which someone had perfunctorily savaged with chisel and mallet.

"So you *do* do carpentry."

"No. I just got worried that some interviewer might ask to see the place where I did carpentry. Look. I even bought this handmade stool so I could say I made it."

"Good thinking."

"I even cut my hand."

"How? Doing carpentry?"

"No. Messing around with that chisel to make it look like I did carpentry."

"Fucking up that chair to make it look like you made it."

"Exactly."

It was midnight. Richard sloped out of his study and went to the kitchen in search of something to drink. Anything alcoholic would do. He experienced a thud of surprise, from temple to temple, when instead of the usual striplit void he confronted his wife. Gina was not a large woman, but the mass of her presence was dramatically augmented by the lateness of the hour. And by marriage, and by other things. He looked at her with his infidel's eyes. Her oxblood hair was up and back; her face was moist with half-assimilated night cream; her towel dressing gown revealed a triangle of bath-rouged throat. With abrupt panic Richard realized what had happened to her, what she had done: Gina had become a grownup. And Richard hadn't. Following the pattern of his generation (or its bohemian wing), Richard was going to go on looking the same until he died. Looking worse and worse, of course, but looking the same. Was it the kids, was it the job, was it the lover she must surely have by now (in her shoes, in her marriage—if Richard was married to Richard, *he'd* have one)? He couldn't object on grounds of ethics or equity. Because writing is infidelity. Because all writing is infidelity. She still looked good, she still looked sexual, she even still looked (you had to hand it to her) . . . dirty. But Gina had made a definite move toward the other side.

"I was thinking we might have a progress report," she said. "It's been a year."

"What has?"

"To the day." She looked at her watch. "To the hour."

Relief and recognition came together: "Oh yeah." He had thought this might have something to do with their *marriage*. "I got you," he said.

He remembered. A close and polluted summer night, crying out for thunder, just like this one. A late emergence from his study in search of drink, just like this one. A dressing-gowned and surprise-value manifestation from Gina, just like this one. There were probably one or two differences. The kitchen might have felt a little brighter. There might have been more toys about. Gina might have looked a day or two younger, back then, and definitely un-grown-up. And Richard might have looked a bit less like shit than he looked now.

That time, a year ago, he had had a very bad week: the debut of Gwyn Barry in the bestseller list; the striking of Marco; Anstice; and something else.

This time he had had a very bad year.

"I remember."

He remembered. A year ago to the hour, and Gina saying,

"How many hours a day do you spend on your novels?"

"What? Spend?" said Richard, who had his whole head in the drinks cupboard. "I don't know. Varies."

"You usually do it first thing, don't you. Except Sundays. How many hours, on average? Two? Three?"

Richard realized what this reminded him of, distantly: being interviewed. There she sat across the table with her pencil and her notebook and her green tea. Pretty soon she would be asking him if he relied, for his material, on actual experience or on the crucible of the imagination, how he selected his subjects and themes, and whether or not he used a word processor. Well, maybe; but first she asked:

"How much money have they earned you? Your novels. In your life."

He sat down. Richard wanted to take this sitting down. The calculation didn't occupy him for very long. There were only three figures to be added together. He told her what they amounted to.

"Give us a minute," she said.

Richard watched. Her pencil slid and softly scraped, then seemed to hover in thought, then softly scraped again.

"And you've been at it for how long?" she murmured to herself: good at sums. "Right. Your novels earn you about sixty pee an hour. A cleaning lady would expect to make seven or eight times that. From your novels you get a fiver a day. Or thirty quid a week. Or fifteen hundred a year. That means every time you buy a gram of coke—which is what?"

He didn't know she knew about the coke. "Hardly ever."

"How much is coke? Seventy? Every time you buy a gram of coke . . . that's more than a hundred man-hours. About six weeks' work."

While Gina gave him, in monotonous declarative sentences, a précis of their financial situation, like something offered to test his powers of mental arithmetic, Richard stared at the tabletop and thought of the first time he had seen her: behind a tabletop, counting money, in a literary setting.

"Now," she said. "When was the last time you received actual payment for your novels?"

"Eight years ago. So I give them up, right?"

"Well it does look like the one to go."

There followed a minute's silence—perhaps to mark the passing of Richard's fiction. Richard spent it exploring his own numbness, whose density impressed him. There were surf sounds in his ear. Emotion recollected in tranquillity, said Wordsworth, describing or defining the creative act. To Richard, as he wrote, it felt more like emotion invented in tranquillity. But here was emotion. In his room across the hall, Marco was pleading in his sleep. They could hear him—pleading with his nightmares.

She said, "You could review more books."

"I can't review more books." There on the table lay a slablike biography of Fanny Burney. Richard had to write two thousand words about it for a famously low-paying literary monthly, by next Friday. "I already review about a book a day. I can't review more. There aren't enough books. I do them all."

"What about all this *non*-fiction you keep agreeing to write? What about that Siberia trip?"

"I'm not going."

"I don't like to say this, because at least it's regular, but you could give up *The Little Magazine*."

"It's only a day a week."

"But then you spend forever writing those 'middles.' For nothing."

"It's part of the job. The literary editor has always written the middles." And he thought of their names, in a wedge, like an honors board: Eric Henley, R. C. Squires, B. F. Mayhew, Roland Davenport. They all wrote the middles. Richard Tull. Surely you remember R. C. Squires's controversial attack on the Movement poets? R. C. Squires was still alive, unbelievably. Richard kept seeing him, in Red Lion Street, in the callbox, staring with terrible and illegible purpose at the crowded entrance of the language school. Or flapping around on his hands and knees in the passage behind the Merry Old Soul.

"For nothing," said Gina.

"Yeah that's right."

"No one reads *The Little Magazine*."

"Yeah that's right."

One of Richard's recent "middles" was about writers' wives—a typology of writers' wives. The pin was a biography of Hemingway, who, Richard argued, had married one of each. (Stoutly or fogeyishly resistant to clever headlines, Richard in this case submitted to the inevitable "For Whom the Bells Toll.") How did they go? The Muse, the Rival, the Soulmate, the Drudge, the Judge . . . Of course there were many, many others, Peer Wives like Mary Shelley, and Victim Wives like Emily Tennyson, and Virgin Saints like Jane Carlyle, and a great multitude of

Fat Nurses like Fanny Stevenson . . . What type was Demeter Barry? What type was Gina Tull? Transcendence-Supplier, Great Distractor, Mind-Emptier in the act of love. Anyway it didn't matter. Gina was deciding to absent herself from the company. She wasn't leaving Richard, not yet. But she was ceasing to be a writer's wife.

"You can't give up the Tantalus thing, which is pretty decent as well as regular. You tell me. You could give up smoking and drinking and drugs. And clothes. It's not that you spend. You don't earn."

"I can't give up novels."

"Why not?"

Because . . . because then he would be left with experience, with untranslated and unmediated experience. Because then he would be left with life.

"Because then I'd just have this." The kitchen—the blue plastic tub filled with the boys' white pants and vests, the stiff black handbag on the chair with its upturned mouth open wanting to be fed, the bowls and spoons and mats laid out on the table for the morning and the eight-pack of cereal boxes in its cellophane: all this became the figure for what he meant. "Days. Life," he added.

And this was a disastrous word to say to a woman—to women, who bear life, who bring it into the world, screaming, and so will never let it come second to anything.

Her eyes, her breasts, her throat, showing him his mistake, all became infused. "The possible alternative," said Gina, "is I go full time. Except Fridays of course." She told him what they would pay her: a chastening sum. "That'd mean you getting the twins up every morning and getting them down every night. The weekends we share. You shop. You clean. And you cook."

"I can't cook."

"I can't either . . . That way," she said, "you'll be getting plenty of life. And we'll see what you've got left for the other thing."

There was a third alternative, Richard reckoned. He could fuck her twice a night forever and take no more shit. And have no money. Oh sure: do it that way. He looked at her face, its flesh lightly glazed in preparation for sleep; and her throat, with its weathered complexities of raisin and rose. She was his sexual obsession. And he had married her.

"I tell you what," she said. "How close are you to finishing the one that's on the go now?"

Richard creased his face. One of the many troubles with his novels was that they didn't really get finished. They just stopped. *Untitled* was already very long. "Hard to tell. Say a year."

Her head went back. This was steep. But she took in breath and said, "Okay. You've got a year's grace. Finish that and we'll see if it makes any money. I think we can hold on. Financially I mean. I'll do what I have to do. I'll manage. You've got a year."

He nodded. He supposed it was just. He wanted to thank her. His mouth was dry.

"A year. I won't say a word."

"A year," Gina now resumed. "And I haven't said a word. Have I. I've been as good as my word. What about you?"

Nasty repetition that, he thought: word. But it remained true enough. She had kept her promise. And he had forgotten all about it. Or he'd tried. They had held on, financially, though even the most perfunctory calculation told Richard that they were falling short by two or three book reviews a week. Marco was still in his boxroom, and still remonstrating with his nightmares.

"What's your progress been? Is it finished?"

"Virtually," he said. This wasn't quite true. *Untitled* wasn't finished exactly, but it was certainly unbelievably long. "A week or two away."

"And what are your plans for it?"

"I was thinking," said Richard. "There are these minor earnings from my novels that we didn't include. It all adds up, you know."

"What all adds up?"

"Things like PLR." He checked. Gina was staring at him with a new order of incredulity. "Public Lending Right," he went on. "Money from libraries. It all adds up."

"I know PLR. With all the forms. How much did you get that time? The time you spent the whole weekend lying down behind the couch. What was it? Thirty-three pee?"

"Eighty-*nine* pee," said Richard sternly.

". . . Well, that's a big help!"

There was a silence during which he steadily lowered his gaze to the floor. He thought of the time when his PLR check had burst into the three figures: £104.07. That was when he had two novels in print and it was still the case that nobody was sure they were shit.

"I think I've got an agent. Gwyn's agent. Gal Aplanalp."

Gina took this in. "Her," she said. "Have you signed up?"

"Not yet. Maybe soon."

"Hey this is really going to *happen* you know. You don't care about money and that's a nice quality but I *do* and life is going to change."

"I know. I know."

". . . What's it called anyway? Your new one."

"*Untitled.*"

"When will it be?"

"No it's *called Untitled.*"

"You mean you can't even think what to call it?"

"No. It's *called Untitled.*"

"How can it be *called Untitled*?"

"It just is. Because I say so."

"Well that's a bloody stupid name for it. You know, you might be a lot happier, without them. It might help with the other thing too. It might be a big relief. Gwyn and everything, that's a whole other story." Gina sighed, with distaste. She had never liked Gwyn much even in the old days, when he was with Gilda—and they were *all* poor. "Demi says it's *frightening* the way the money comes in. And she's rich! I don't know if you still really believe in it. Your novels. Because you never . . . Because what you . . . Ah I'm sorry, Richard. I'm so sorry."

Because you never found an audience—you never found the universal or anything like it. Because what you come up with in there, in your study, is of no general interest. End of story. Yes: this is the end of your story.

"Marry your sexual obsession," Richard had once been told. By a writer. Marry your sexual obsession: the one you kept going back to, the one you never quite got to the end of: marry *her*. Richard was interviewing, was profiling, this writer, so it more or less followed that he was neither famous nor popular. His obscurity, in fact, was the only celebrated thing about him (let's call him Mr. X): if everything went through okay, he had a chance of becoming a monument of neglect, like a Powys. How many Powyses *were* there? Two? Three? Nine? Your sexual obsession, he kept saying: marry *her*. Not the beauty, not the brains. Mr. X dwelt in a two-up-two-down back-to-back, in Portsmouth. The stuff he wrote was hieratic and recondite, but all he could talk about was sex. And sexual obsession. There they sat, at lunchtime, in the dockside pub, over their untouched seafood platters, with Mr. X sweating into his mack. Don't marry the droll brain surgeon. Don't marry the dreaming stunner who works in famine relief. Marry the town pump. Marry the one who does it for a drag on your cigarette. Richard felt his shoulders locking. By this point he had readied himself to face a full nervous breakdown of sexual hatred—a complete unraveling, an instantaneous putrefaction of bitterness and disgust. But it never quite happened. Marry the one who made you hardest. Marry *her*. She'll bore you blind, but so will the brain surgeon, so will the dreaming stunner, in time . . . Dropping the writer off after lunch in the minicab, Richard hoped for a glimpse of his wife. Hoped for a chance to wonder what *she* was: rocket scientist? hysterical goer? The woman staring suspiciously down the damp dark passage, her small head half lost in the sprouty collar of her housecoat, didn't look like an hysterical goer. She looked more like a rocket scientist; and one whose best work was long behind her. And another thing: whatever life choice Mr. X had gone ahead and made, Mrs. X didn't strike you as too happy about it either, contemplating her husband's return, it seemed to Richard, with infinite weariness. He was forgotten now anyway, or reforgotten, silent, out of print. He never even made it into Neglect . . . Some of us, most of us, all of us, are staggering through our span with half a headful of tips and pointers we've listened to (or overheard). Use Cold Water To Soak The Pot After Making Scrambled Eggs. When Filling A Hot Water Bottle, Keep The Neck Of The Hot Water Bottle At Right Angles. Unless The Kettle Boiling Be, Filling The Teapot Spoils The Tea. Starve a cold, feed a fever. Banks do most of their business after three o'clock. Richard married his sexual obsession. He just did what he did.

Except in one important respect, the love life enjoyed by Richard and Gina, over the past year, remained as rich and full as it had ever been. There was still that sense of anticipation when nightdress and pajama conjoined, last thing, and, at weekends, when they stirred, and at other stolen moments, such as they were, with two little boys in the house. Gina was a healthy young woman. Richard was in the prime of life. After nine years together, their amorous dealings were, if anything, even more inflexibly committed to variety and innovation than at any point in their past. The only real difference, I suppose you'd have to concede, was that Richard, nowadays, was impotent. Chronically and acutely impotent. Apart from that, though, things were just as they were before.

He was impotent with her every other night and, at weekends, in the mornings too—when those boys of his gave him half a chance! (The patter of tiny feet; the stubborn and inexpert worrying of the doorknob; the hoarse command from the bedroom met by puzzled whispers, puzzled withdrawal; the mind-filling silence before the sickening impact or collision—the scream, the wail.) Sometimes, when the Tulls' schedules conspired, he would be lazily impotent with her in the afternoons. Nor did the bedroom mark the boundary of their erotic play. In the last month alone, he had been impotent with her on the stairs, on the sofa in the sitting room and on the kitchen table. Once, after a party outside Oxford, he had been impotent with her right there on the backseat of the Maestro. Two nights later they got drunk, or rather Gina got drunk, because

Richard was already drunk, and on their return from Pizza Express stole into the communal garden, using their key, and Richard was impotent with her in a sylvan setting. Impotent in a sylvan setting, under some dumb blonde of a willow, with Diana above them, her face half-averted, feeling wounded or betrayed, and higher, much higher, the winking starlets of the Milky Way.

It got so bad that Richard talked—and even thought—about giving up drinking: he even talked—but didn't think—about giving up smoking. He knew, though, that his troubles were dully and intricately and altogether essentially literary, and that nothing would ease them except readers or revenge. So he didn't do anything, apart from taking up Valium and cocaine.

"It's hard on you. It's like an ultimatum," said Gina in the dark.

Richard said nothing.

"You're tired. And you've got a lot on your mind."

Richard said nothing.

Gwyn's dove-gray house in the innocent morning; Demi's house at dawn. And our vigil, and an even more extraordinary one, in its way. That of Steve Cousins: Barnardo boy.

Scozz seeing it not from the van but through the treated glass of his Cosworth (tinted windows, whitewalls, low racing skirt). Seeing it not as an architectural or even a real-estate phenomenon but as a patchwork of weaknesses. Bits of it seemed to flash and beep at him in outline—to flash and beep in his robot vision. Security-wise the first-floor terrace was a fucking joke. But given his choice Scozzy would probably gain entry by the front door. Using the Sli-Mo. Not that he'd be wanting to bring anything out of there except the information.

Take the opposite vantage. There are the windows to the master bedroom. The glass trembles lightly. Who can go in there—the intruder, the informer, the private dick? Richard Tull wants to go in there. Not corporeally, not in person. He wants to do to Gwyn what Gwyn has done to him. He wants to assassinate his sleep. He wants to inform the sleeping man; an I for an I.

But I'm not going in there. I'm not going in there, not yet. I'm just not going.

It was quite clear to everyone that Gwyn and Demeter Barry had the perfect marriage. You only had to look at them to see that this was a match made in heaven.

They held hands all the time (they were "inseparable"). He called her *love* all the time. She gave him kisses on the cheek all the time. They were the fond, they were the ideal—they were the dream. Even Richard had to admit it: it was absolutely nauseating. Social diarists like Rory Plantagenet noted their practice, at parties and functions, of releasing each other "lingeringly" as the dynamics of the convivium urged them apart. Gwyn was known to fall into a reverie when his wife was several partygoers from his side: "Just gazing," he would say, when roused, "at my lady." (Richard, if he happened to be present and nearby, would similarly drift into a brown study: the sledgehammer in the alleyway, the poked chisel on the dark basement steps . . .) Literary interviewers and profilists marked how Gwyn's face would "light up" when Demeter parted the double doors of the drawing room, bearing a tea tray on which Gwyn's favorite Chocolate Olivers were infallibly arrayed. (Reading this, Richard would light up too. Through the sigh of his cigarette smoke he would see the sidling berk with his tire tool, the jagged neck of the smashed beer bottle.) In "The Seven Vital Virtues, 4: Uxoriousness" the Barrys were lensed as they strolled past the squirrels and mazelets and mantled pools of Holland Park, with arms interlocked and fingers interwoven; then, too, you saw the author's wife frowning interestedly over the author's shoulder as the author smiled and murmured at his desktop display screen; next you copped them at their "local" French restaurant, during the dessert course, feeding each other dripping spoonfuls of goopy ice cream. Gwyn spoke to camera about the need for a constant exchange of presents—"little things, but always a little bit too expensive." (Richard, gagging weakly at the TV, would also be pushing the boat out on this one: the hired fist, the chartered army boot.) She was rich. But so was he now. He was intelligent. And now she was too. Her father, with his stick, in the coach-torn grounds of the stately; *his* father, the trunked Taff on the sluiced duckboards. Love melds. Blood meets brains, in High Bohemia. Just look at the clippings file. "I think the world of her"—Gwyn. "I simply feel incredibly lucky"—Demi.

Gwyn: "She's the best thing that ever happened to me." Demi: "People ask me what it's like being married to a genius, and I say it's completely brilliant."

And there was Richard, jackknifed over his sickbag, searching for assassins in the Yellow Pages . . .

He rang the London offices of *The New York Times*. They *did* keep a copy of the Sunday paper, and Richard was free to come in there to consult or admire it; but he couldn't take it away. They told him, rather, to go to International Dispatches in North Islington. With his mack and his hangover and his book (a biography of William Davenant, Shakespeare's bastard: six hundred words by early next week), he embarked at Ladbroke Grove, changed at Paddington and Oxford Circus, and rode in the slatted light to Islington, whose streets he paced for fifty-five minutes, wringing his hands, until he stumbled upon a lone old man, walled in with information, a crofter in a cottage thatched with *Frankfurter Zeitung*s and *El Paise*s and *India Today*s and many other journals daubed in exclamatory Farsi or Sanskrit. The old man told him that he no longer stocked the Sunday *New York Times*; only the daily. Pressure of space. Richard came home again. Half a week later, when he had calmed down, he rang the London offices of the *The New York Times*: they told him to ring the distributors in Cheapside. He did so. They told him that such copies of the Sunday *New York Times* as came their way were subscription copies, though occasionally—true—there was a spare . . . Richard used all his charm on the young woman at the other end of the line. But the trouble was that he didn't have any charm, not any longer, and she told him he would just have to turn up on Monday morning on the off chance, like anybody else.

So began his weekly journeys to the warehouse in Cheapside, where they would typically pass him round from portakabin to van mouth to storage room and back again, before sending him on his way—to *The Little Magazine*, in fact, where in the dawn he would start subbing the book reviews over a papercupful of tomato soup. As well as a very bad reality, that papercupful of tomato soup was always a very bad sign . . . It was on his fifth visit that Richard revealed, to the assistant manager's intense sneer of puzzlement, that he didn't necessarily want a copy of *that week's* Sunday *New York Times. Any* Sunday *New York Times* would do. In full contrition Richard followed the assistant manager to another storage room, one never seen before, where any number of Sunday *New York Times*es were lavishly and promiscuously heaped, along with countless Sunday *Boston Globe*s, Sunday *San Francisco*

THE INFORMATION / 67

*Chronicle*s, and so on. Richard listed faintly on his feet. In the fever and vertigo he felt there was now an element of everyday incomprehension—at the sadness and grayness and dampness and deadness of disregarded newsprint; and at human profligacy and clamor. Christ, can't everyone *shut up*. Anyway, he cracked, and went for size. That day he came home with the outrageous bulk of the Sunday *Los Angeles Times* carefully cradled in his arms. It wasn't just bigger than the Sunday *New York Times*. It was *much* bigger.

Brown paper and a ball of string took about a week each to purchase and assemble. Then Richard was ready to move. That day he picked through the corpses of his old typewriters until he found one that was capable of saying, "Dear Gwyn, Something to interest you here. The price of fame! Yours ever, John."

On his desk lay another letter, smudged, crumpled: second-class. Nothing much gets affected by the second-class mail. You don't expect your life to be changed by the second-class mail. This letter said:

Dear Richard,
So then? No reply from the man. Well you said it, Dreams don't mean Anything. Gwyn Barry loves Belladonna, and Darko love's Belladonna but who does Belladonna love. She is deadly.
What about that "jar."

Yours, DARKO

How would you *find out* about a marriage? How would you find out? Because all marriages are inscrutable. I can tell you everything there is to know about the marriage of the Tulls (I can even tell you what their sheets smell of: they smell of marriage); but I don't know anything, yet, about the marriage of the Barrys. A close scrutiny of "The Seven Vital Virtues, 4: Uxoriousness" would disclose, perhaps, that Demeter was less happy about everything than Gwyn—or less happy about being happy on TV. But how would you find out? Richard, at his desk, fondling Darko's letter, fondling Demi in his thoughts, had a couple of ideas. Steve Cousins, in his Cosworth, had a couple of ideas too. But he was far more practical. Scozz was going to *find out*—he was going to find out something or other. And he was going to do it today: right now. First he had to fetch 13.

When he at last emerged, coming out between the pillars and walking solemnly down the steps of Marylebone Magistrates' Court, 13 had the proud, moistened, middle-distance stare of a man who believes himself to have been gravely and perhaps insupportably traduced. He always looked like this on his way out of court, unless, for one reason or another, he'd got off. As Steve proceeded in the Cosworth down Edgware Road, in a series of short bursts and long waits, he glanced at 13's profiled face: too youthful, too rounded, for the stunned and bitter glaze it wore.

"What you get?"

"Six months suspended."

"And?"

13 sighed and belatedly fastened his seatbelt. "Fines."

Steve nodded. 13 drew in breath: he was about to give voice—and in the high style. His intention, plainly, was to speak not just for himself but for all men and women, in all places, in all times—to remind the human heart of what it had once known and had now long forgotten.

"The titheads," 13 began, "is like a gang. The Old Bill," he went on, "is like a gang. Hired by the government. When did it happen? It happened when they upped they pay—1980 or whatever. They saying: it's gonna get rough. Unemployment is it. Riots or whatever. You keep a lid on it and we pay you extra. Where's the money come from? No worries. We'll *fine* the fuckers."

"Who've you been talking to?"

"No one. Common sense."

Although he sounded amused or at least indulgent, Steve was in fact displeased. He kept trying to harden his voice and make his face go all blocked and reptilian—but it wasn't quite happening. Why? Coz Scozz was losing it? Or the old forms, the old rhythms, were just giving out . . . The reason for Steve's displeasure was as follows: 13 had kept him waiting. For ten minutes. They'd had words. "Where *you* been?" "Looking for the Coke machine. Fancied a Coke." "You spend half your fucking life in there. You know there's no *Coke* machine." 13 just shrugged and said, "Fancied a Coke." Yeah: leaving his mentor and patron on a double yellow and on a block much frequented by people in uniform, under the shadow of a municipal construct which was really just a massive doorway. The stuff in Latin on the portals, it said: This Is the Way to Other Places . . .

"Know how much it costs to keep a bloke in nick for a week?"

"Go on then."

13 told him. Jesus: like fucking Claridge's. And for that world, with its slops and slop-outs, its stalled testosterone. Labor-intensive: all those retarded parkies in their reeking serge. Security was expensive, and got more expensive quicker than other things. Super-inflationary, like weaponry and medical equipment. Though you'd think, with security,

that some counterforce would bring prices down eventually, what with the incredible demand.

13 turned to him and said, "Know what they should do with all that fucking money?"

"Go on then."

"Buy you a mortgage. Buy you a mortgage. All that money locking you up where all you do is learn more of the same. Watching TV about antiques is it. Buy you a mortgage. You got your own house you stay indoors out of trouble."

Until now 13's social analysis had found, in Steve Cousins, a reasonably sympathetic listener. There were lags of ninety who saw crime that way too: as guerrilla work in the class war. But 13 was leaving him here.

"Not much of a deterrent though, is it, Thirt?" said Scozzy. "What kind of message is that sending? Don't break into a house. Or else we'll buy you a house."

13 brooded for a traffic light or two. Then he said: "What they don't get is rich people *like* being robbed."

"Yeah? Why's that then?"

"Insurance! They in it together is it. Can't see what all the fucking fuss's about. They get it all back plus more and the insurance ups the premiums on the poor people. Simple as."

Passing Speakers' Corner and entering Park Lane, Steve had the rare and transient pleasure of engaging third gear. He glanced sideways. He changed down. In the days when he'd played squash regularly, and tried tennis out for a while, Steve had given a lot of thought to the question of where the power came from, on the shot: wrist or arm? Take a cloth serviette. You can throw that into somebody's face as hard as you like and it's nothing: just a powderpuff. But with a good flick of the wrist you can bloody their nose or blacken their eye. As he pulled away from the lights by the Dorchester, Scozzy changed from first to second and with a flick of the wrist gave his passenger four knuckles right across the cheekbone. 13's head smacked into the side window and then bounced back again.

"Jesus. What was that for?"

"Never keep me waiting. Never do it, mate. Never."

13 sat there blinking and feeling his cheek. This was all he fucking needed. He was going to get beaten up tonight by Crash and Rooster-Booster anyway, as it was. To mark his appearance in court. 13 said, "That really hurt, man."

Of course you'd never get a meter. So 13 could just drive round Berkeley Square as fast as he dared for as long as it took while Steve went to pay his call on Mrs. V.

"See? All in the wrist, that," said Steve. "All in the wrist."

Anita Verulam's basement office was, as usual, a two-room altar of middle class and Middle Eastern gratitude and praise. Cellophaned bouquets, professionally gift-wrapped boxes of chocolates and bottles of champagne, various hampers and caskets: all these were offerings from the opulent households which Mrs. Verulam supplied with maids, cooks, chars, nannies, nurses, drivers, gardeners, hewers of wood and drawers of water, batmen, bondmen, gentlemen's gentlemen—and anyone else who came under the heading of *help*. In the saunas and restaurants and department-store coffee shops of West London the name of Mrs. Verulam was mouthed in sacred whispers by wealthy housewives, all of them, by now, crack delegators, their homes thrumming empires of monosyllabic vassalage. Had these ladies been a little bit crazier, and a lot richer, they might have built "shrines" to Mrs. Verulam, in attics, in disused guest rooms. The help she dealt in was exclusively foreign. Foreign help was actually helpful, foreign cleaning ladies could actually clean: they knew how you did it. Whereas the cleaning gene had long absented itself from the indigenous DNA. This was unfortunate, if you took the long view at the big picture. Cleaning, in planetary terms, and unlike other sectors, held wonderful promise. Cleaning was obviously going to be huge. Lady Demeter Barry had never set eyes on Mrs. Verulam, but on the telephone she poured her heart out to her three times a week.

Steve said, "Did you take a look in the file for us?" *Us* came naturally: it was less culpable somehow.

The cigarette in her mouth wagged up and down as she said, "When were they married exactly?"

He gave the month and the year.

"It seems to have got steadily choppier. A whole stream of walkouts." Mrs. Verulam was a fifty-year-old widow in a pink two-piece suit; when Mr. Verulam was alive she had walked with address into a certain kind of drawing room—Paris, Barcelona, Frankfurt, Milan. "It's not Lady Demeter. No complaints there." Her voice was warmly emphysemic, but her eyes were hooded and cold. Often during their encounters here Mrs. Verulam talked on, holding the telephone at arm's length while a baffled female larynx, a marooned existence, wailed or pleaded into the air, as if seized at the throat by her painted fingers. "It's him they don't like. No children," she added pitilessly.

"Do you think he uh . . .?"

"My little Spanish ladies and Portuguese ladies are sometimes *very* religious. They'll walk out on a couple if they think the rhythm method is being used. And of course Demeter's Catholic, isn't she? The other thing about these little ladies is that they're astonishingly discreet. Even to me. What we need," she said, re-consulting the folder, "is a Filipino. Or a *Colombian.*"

Steve nodded approvingly. He understood. Filipinos, Colombians: you could lean on them with threats of deportation. You know: Been here long, have we, Charito?

"Mm, lots. Ah, Ancilla. Good. I'll talk to Ancilla and let you know."

"Appreciate it, Mrs. V. How's our friend Nigel?"

"Yes, thank you for that, Steve."

"I had a word with him."

"Good as gold now. Quiet as a mouse after ten o'clock."

"Yeah, well. I had a quiet word with him."

They looked at each other. Mrs. Verulam was a modern person, and routinely traded in information; and if it had ever struck her as odd or unprofessional it struck her that way no longer. She too was childless. There was an affinity between the Barnardo boy and Anita Verulam. Because the family was one thing and they were the other.

On the way out Steve wondered if Mrs. V. had any idea just how *loud* it had been—his quiet word with Nigel. Nigel was a rich hippy who lived in the flat above Mrs. Verulam's best friend, another widow, called Aramintha. It was once Nigel's habit to play classical music, mostly Mahler, at full volume, well into the small hours. Aramintha tried everything. She asked Nigel nicely; she asked him not so nicely; she got the landlord to ask him; she got the police to ask him; she asked Nigel nicely again. All of Aramintha's entreaties were to no avail. Until Steve smashed his door down at three in the morning and went in there with Clasford and T, and kicked fucking Nigel out of bed and dragged him across the fucking floor by his fucking hair and put his fucking head on the . . . What *did* they do? Oh yeah. Jammed his head between the amp and the CD player while they shattered them with baseball bats. And Steve cracked his fucking elbow into Nigel's fucking mouth and told him, at full volume—*no noise after ten.* Good as gold now, and very polite on the stairs. It wasn't the first time Scozzy had helped out Mrs. V. She had a few bob and liked the sort of young man who gave trouble.

He climbed into the Cosworth, next to 13, and said, "Warlock."

At four-fifteen Lizzete showed up with Marius, who wore a green sash athwart his burgundy blazer to commemorate some extraordinary achievement in art or football, and Richard was relieved of Marco and all further duties. He went upstairs. Upstairs consisted of his and Gina's cramped bedroom, plus a little stall in the corner with a shower and a can in it. He undressed and redressed quickly, although there was plenty of time, and as if he felt cold suddenly, although the room was warm. Richard had had a more than averagely bad afternoon. After three he realized that his book-review roster was all out of synch. He was obliged to free his mind of *The Soul's Dark Cottage: A Life of Edmund Waller* and *The Unfortunate Lover: William Davenant, Shakespeare's Bastard* and hastily reacquaint it with *Robert Southey: Gentleman Poet*, on which he was meant to write seven hundred words in the next seventy minutes. He achieved this while also smoking fifteen cigarettes with his head more or less out of the window and while also conducting some kind of conversation with Marco, who, that day, was being especially clinging and garrulous and ill. The last sentence took him a quarter of an hour and caused him to draw blood on his bitten fingertips . . . Richard had to do the room over before he found a pair of white shorts; he had to upend the laundry basket and shake it out onto the bathroom tiles before he found a pair of white socks, which cracked and creaked to his touch. It didn't strike him then, even though Gina was in his thoughts, as she would be, in their bedroom: it didn't quite strike him then that everything was getting less clear, less bright—even the universe of his laundry, over which Gina presided with decreasing gravity, like a divinity insufficiently prayed to, who no longer felt gripped by the force of the covenant, who no longer felt gripped by belief. If Gina was cheating on him, then she would be cheating on him on Fridays. Friday was consecrated as Gina's day to herself: no one was allowed in the flat, without warning, until teatime, when the boys came home from school. This was their agreement—of a year's standing. Richard went to the Tantalus Press or *The Little Magazine* or the Adam and Eve. But for a while he didn't go anywhere, and lurked outside, watching. Gina would regularly glance out of the window and see cigarette smoke wafting from the off-white Prelude, as it then was, before that car collapsed and they bought the tomato-red Maestro.

Richard went downstairs in his shorts. He felt cold and it looked like rain. "Go for it Daddy," said Marius. "Just do it."

He stood outside waiting for the biker sent to collect his review. Who was prompt. Here he came, complacently speeding through the torment of his brutish raspberry, his black body cocked with the biker's spurious urgency, as if what he was doing was so clearly more important than what you were doing. Was it his crash helmet that went on fizzing and squawking at him, like a fat old earphone? Biker and book reviewer bawled "Cheers" at each other and did the thing with the clipboard and the ballpoint, these two eyesore deviants, the biker in his city scuba gear, the book reviewer with bare legs beneath the cold skirt of his raincoat. Book reviewers would be around for a while, but bikers would soon be gone, or would all switch to pizzas and baked potatoes—casualties of the fax.

At the Warlock Sports Center he parked the dusty Maestro next to Gwyn's new Swedish sedan, which was still gulping and chirruping, Richard noticed, as its computer ticked off the final security checks. Then, abruptly without intelligence, the car seemed to settle back into its silent, sullen crouch, and its sullen vigil. Leaving the Maestro unlocked (it contained nothing but banana skins and the fading carbons of dead novels), Richard strode through the car park and its exemplary diversity of stilled traffic, like an illustration of all you might meet on the contemporary road with its contraflow and intercool: hearse, heap, dragster, dump truck, duchess wagon, cripple-bubble. He duly sighted Gwyn, strolling, with slowly swinging sports bag, along the brink of the bowling green, where sainted figures in white shirts and white hair archaically bent and straightened on the shallow yellow lawn. The protective affection that a nice person is expected to feel when observing another nice person who is innocent of this scrutiny—such affection, Richard found, was not absent in the present case so much as inverted or curdled: his face was all glints and snickers, and he felt briefly godlike, and exhaustingly ever-hostile. Just then, over the black slope of the tudoresque clubhouse, a loose flock of city birds reared up like a join-the-dots puzzle of a human face or fist . . . The gap between the two men closed. Richard broke into an ankle-lancing trot and was no more than a racket's reach from Gwyn's shoulders when, with a blat of the side door, they exchanged the late-summer air for the dense breath of the clubhouse.

All men are faced with this. But wait . . . First we have to get past the hatch of the booking office and the sexual indifference of the pretty girl who worked there, then the notice boards with their leagues and ladders (dotted with multicolored drawing-pins and one dying, throbbing wasp), then the aggressive levity of the Warlock manager, John Punt. "Gwyn," said Richard, as they stepped on into the clubhouse proper and the greater bar. And? There it lay: the pub of life. Eighty or ninety souls, in knots and echelons; and here came the familiar moment, a dip in the sound, a gulp, a swallow and a selection of profiles turning full face, as if on a rap sheet. All men are eternally confronted by this: other men, in blocs and sets. Equipped with an act, all men are confronted by an audience which might cheer or jeer or stay silent or yawn rancorously or just walk out—their verdict on your life performance. As Richard remembered, he and Gwyn used to be equally unpopular here at the Warlock, never directly addressed, quietly sneered at. As Gwyn, with his pewtery hair, his body as tall as his sports bag was long, moved past the low tables to the tag board there were cries and croaks of greeting, of "Still scribbling?" and "Sold a million yet?" The acceptance world. As if Gwyn was suddenly visible now, adjudged not to have been wasting his time; TV had democratized him, and made him available for transference to the masses; the life performance was seen to be worthy of sagacious applause. Whereas Richard, as a figure, was still entirely alien. For one thing, nobody could bear his habit, while on court, of shouting *shit* in French.

"I won't be much good to you today," said Gwyn (they had ten minutes to kill). "What with this Profundity thing."

"What with this what?"

"Profundity thing. Haven't you heard about it? It's a literary stipend, awarded every year. Administered out of Boston. Called a Profundity Requital."

"Don't tell me," said Richard cautiously. "Some loo-paper heiress. Looking for a tony way of dodging tax."

"Far from it. They're already calling it the mini-Nobel. The money's ridiculous. And you get it every year. For life."

"And?"

"I'm told I'm on the shortlist."

John Punt, his face scalded and broad-pored from the sun-ray lamp, often referred to the Warlock as a *dinosaur*. By which he meant: no Jacuzzis, no parasols, no quiche counter, no broccoli juice. Instead: unhealthy fare served all day long, smoking allowed and even encouraged, continuous and competitive drinking and strict non-exclusivity. Anyone could join the Warlock, cheaply and right away. Within the outer bar was an inner bar, an antiworld where many men and few women sat in arcs staring at hands of cards or kwik crosswords or architect's drawings or lawyers' briefs or escape routes, where bankruptcies and bereavements were entrained by a twingeing shake or nod of some great ruined head, and where, at this moment, behind a mephitic banquette of cigarette smoke, his back turned, Steve Cousins sat talking the higher shop with three bronzed pocked mug shots: the most exalted villainspeak (no detail, just first principles) about getting back what you put in and this being life and this being *it* . . . Gwyn and Richard stood between the two arenas, in a latticed passage that was also an amusement arcade: golf video, Bingomatic, Poker Draw, and, of course, the Knowledge Machine. Instead of a jukebox there stood a black upright piano on which, after lunch, drowsy criminals would occasionally interpret some tremulous ballad. The clubhouse acoustics had a funny tilt to them; voices sounded warped or one-way, as many mouths nuzzled the necks of cellular telephones; many an ear was plugged with Walkman or hearing aid, nursing its individual tinnitus.

"A Profundity Requital," said Richard pensively. "Well. We know one thing."

"What's that?"

"You're not going to get it."

Gwyn, who was wrong, flexed his forehead and said, "A million people can't be wrong."

Richard, who was also wrong, said, "A million people are *always* wrong. Let's play."

Anyone who shared the common belief that the decline of British tennis was a result of the game's bourgeois, garden-party associations would have felt generally braced and corrected, at the Warlock Sports Center, to hear the ragged snarls and howls, the piercing obscenities and barbaric phonemes which made the wired courts seem like cages housing slaves or articulate animals in permanent mutiny against their confinement, their lash-counts, their lousy food. On the other hand, anyone watching Gwyn and Richard as they prepared to play would at once agree that Richard's clear superiority owed everything to being middle class. Gwyn was encased in a new track suit that looked as though it had been designed and marketed that morning; its salient feature was a steadily contoured bagginess, a spacesuit or wind-bubble effect, reminding Richard of the twins' salopetts and the padded boiler beneath the stairs. Richard himself, more subtly, and more horribly, for once, in a way, was dressed in wrinkly khaki shorts and, crucially, an off-white top—which was old, which wasn't modern, which glowed with its prewar sour-milk light (numb and humble now, against the burnished ease of the T-shirt), the light of longjohn seams, old surgical tape, old field hospitals, old triage. Even his shoes were intolerably antique: beige, canvas, intended to enfold the thoughtless trudge of explorer or humorless imperialist. You expected him to carry a wooden racket in a wooden press and a plastic shagbag full of bald balls pried free from the under-gardener's lawnmower.

Through the window of one of the Warlock's games rooms (not in use at present: after six it became a grot of darts) Steve Cousins watched the two novelists begin their game and wondered what they'd be like at *his* sport. In other words he was wondering what they'd be like at fighting—or, even more simply, what they'd be like to beat up. This involved him in pseudo-sexual considerations, because, yes, the truism is true, and fighting *is* like fucking (proximity alone sees to that, plus various texture tests and heft assessments you wouldn't otherwise be making); and, while we're at it, the truism is true, and the criminal *is* like an artist (though not for the reasons usually given, which merely depend on immaturity and the condition of self-employment): the criminal resembles the artist in his pretension, his incompetence, and his self-pity. So, for a moment, Scozzy watched Gwyn and Richard like an animal—an articulate animal. The wild were humans who were animals while still being human. So their minds contained a meteorology of good/bad, warm/cold, tastes fresh/tastes old, and, concerning humans, he is kind/he is cruel, he is familiar/he is new, he is controllable/he is uncontrollable. He is strong/he is weak. Looking at Richard and Gwyn, Steve couldn't honestly say that either of them would give him any bother.

The match began. He watched. And not with an untutored eye. Like many *faces* he had spent a significant fraction of his life in sports clubs and leisure centers; such people had a lot of leisure, a lot of time to kill, this being the polar opposite, in their universe, to *time*, as served, in an institution. Steve could see the hateful remains of Richard's antique technique, its middle-class severity: the shoveled forehand, the backhand with its heavily lingering slice. Look: you could see his socks had a pink tinge to them. The dull blush of the family wash. Two kids: twins. He could play a bit, Richard. Though the love-handled midriff was well prolapsed, it did turn to shape the shot; though the legs were hairless and meatless, they did bend. As for Twinkletoes on the other side of the net, in his designer rainbow gear: as for Tinkerbell there, flitting around with her wand . . . What you had here was one man playing all the tennis, up against a maneuverable little hacker taking the pace off everything, always obvious, never contrary, with no instinct to second-guess or wrong-foot. Steve was scandalized by Gwyn's lack of guile.

So why all the temper—from Richard's end? No way in the fucking world was he going to lose to this guy. Dear oh dear: the swearing, the racket abuse. The way he wiped visible deposits of tea or nicotine from the corners of his scum-storing mouth. Hang on. Some old bat from the mansion flats was sticking its head out of the window:

"Less of that language, Richard!"

"Sorry!"

Must do it a lot: she even knew his name! He must be famous for it, his language. Round these parts anyway. Round Court 4 anyway. Now here's something interesting. Nice angle on his approach shot (Richard), taking Twinkletoes way out of court—crashing, indeed, into the side wire. Oof. But he managed to get it back somehow: an apologetic plop over the net. And as Gwyn comes haring back for this lost cause, instead of just smacking the ball into the wide-open spaces Richard tries to slide it in behind him, down the line. And puts it out.

What was that Richard said, bent over the net post? "Oh Jesus. Nda! Piece of *shit*."

What was that Gwyn said, standing in the tram lines? "Richard, you're a gilder of lilies."

Gilda, thought Steve. Lily. Lil: means tit. But he understood. Like over-egging the pudding. Gilders of lilies. Now. Steve's *intention* . . . In common with all the very worst elements at the club, Steve wasn't a Tennis Member of the Warlock, nor was he a Squash Member or a Bowls Member: he was a *Social* Member of the Warlock. So it was with quiet confidence that he strolled upstairs with his glass of Isotonic, to the darts room, which was empty and stood tensed in its unnatural shadows, the windows all smeared with light-excluding cream paint or paste. This gloom and silence and sudden solitude made him momentarily uncertain about who he was or might be. Low-level unreality attacks didn't necessarily disquiet him—because they didn't *feel* unreal. They felt appropriate. Steve expected them, saying to himself, after all, there's no one quite like me. Yet. And it wasn't a delusion of uniqueness, not quite. He just believed he was the first of many. Many Scozzys were out there waiting to happen. I am a time traveler. I come from the future.

Steve's intention was to be unforgettable. Gwyn, or Richard, or maybe both, would not forget him. And that was a promise. Gilders of lilies. You don't get too many of them, he said to himself as he silently closed the window: not in my line of work. I'm the only one.

"Played," said Gwyn.

"Thanks," said Richard. "Tough."

They shook hands at the net. Tennis was the only time they ever touched. Games were the only reason they ever met. It had become clear about six months ago that Richard was no longer capable of getting through a dinner in Gwyn's company without disgracing himself. Though Gina and Demi still met up sometimes.

"I'm improving," said Gwyn.

"No you're not."

"I'll get there."

"No you won't."

Using the net as a guide rail or a walking-frame, Richard reached his chair. He sat down suddenly and at once assumed a posture of tranced or drunken meditation. Gwyn remained standing—under the shadow of the mansion flats, from which the detailed noises of DIY scraped and whined against the air: drill, plane, sander.

"I don't know what it was today," said Gwyn. "Couldn't get my head right. Couldn't find the desire. It's this Profundity thing. Ridiculous really," said Gwyn, who still pronounced "really" *reely*. "It's not even announced till the spring."

"Oh I get it. Nothing to do with technique or talent or timing or anything. You just couldn't be fucked."

"Yes, well I was all over the bloody shop today. Couldn't get my backhand working."

Richard was enjoying his breather—and *breather* was definitely the word he wanted. "You haven't got a backhand. It's just a wound in your side. It's just an absence. Like an amputee's memory of a vanished limb. You haven't got a forehand either. Or a volley. Or an overhead. *That's* the trouble with your game. You haven't got any shots. You're a dog on the court. Yeah. A little Welsh retriever."

He put a cigarette in his mouth and, as a matter of silent routine, offered one to Gwyn, who said,

"Just couldn't concentrate. No thanks."

Richard looked at him.

"I packed it in."

"You *what*?"

"I stopped. Three days ago. Cold. That's it. You just make the life choice."

Richard lit up and inhaled needfully. He gazed at his cigarette. He didn't really want to smoke it. He wanted to eat it. This move of Gwyn's was a heavy blow. Almost the only thing he still liked about Gwyn was that Gwyn still smoked. Of course, Gwyn had never smoked seriously. Just a pack a day. Not like Richard with his carton-eons, his suede lungs, his kippered wisteria . . . Richard was reminded of another inexpiable exchange he'd had with Gwyn, on the same court, on the same green chair, under the same gut-colored sky and the same summer moon. A year ago, when *Amelior* was taking off and all the other stuff was coming down, Gwyn turned to him, courtside, and said abruptly: "I'm getting married." Richard replied, at once, "Good. About time." And he meant it. He was as they say "genuinely pleased." Pleasure came to him in the form of voluptuous relief. Yes, good. About time Gwyn shackled himself for ever to that speechless pit-pony, Gilda: his teenhood sweetheart, invisible Gilda. Even now Richard could close his eyes and see her small shape in a dozen different bedsits and flatlets, her averted face damp with steam as she served up yet another bowl of spaghetti, her pale hair and sore and coldly upper lip, her (or maybe his) functional underwear on a curved string above the fibrous white tubes of the gas fire, her phobic humility, her unpoetic sadness, her lumpy, childish emerald-green over- coat that came from another time and another place. "Great. I bet Gilda's thrilled. Is Gilda thrilled?" Gilda was good. Richard didn't fancy her. He didn't even want to fuck her *once*. So we must imagine his moodswing when Gwyn paused and said, "No. Not so's you'd notice. No, I think we can say that Gilda is definitely not overly chuffed. Because I'm not marrying *her*." Gwyn wasn't marrying Gilda Paul. He was marrying Lady Demeter de Rougemount, a celebrated knockout of limitless fortune and imperial blood whom Richard knew and admired and had recently taken to thinking about every time he came. "There it is," said Gwyn. Richard failed to offer his congratulations. He stalked off, ostensibly to locate and solace Gilda. In fact he just drove away in his Maestro and parked it somewhere and sat in it sobbing and swearing and smoking cigarettes.

"You bastard," said Richard. "I thought we were in this together."

"Three days ago. Hark at you gasping away. Couple of years I'll be having you six-love, six-love."

"What's it like?"

Richard had *imagined* giving up smoking; and he naturally assumed that man knew no hotter hell. Nowadays he had long quit thinking about quitting. Before the children were born he sometimes thought that he might very well give up smoking when he became a father. But the boys seemed to have immortalized his bond with cigarettes. This bond with cigarettes—this living relationship with death. Paradoxically, he no longer wanted to give up smoking: what he wanted to do was take up smoking. Not so much to fill the little gaps between cigarettes with cig- arettes (there wouldn't be time, anyway) or to smoke two cigarettes at once. It was more that he felt the desire to smoke a cigarette even when he was smoking a cigarette. The need was and wasn't being met.

"Actually it's a funny thing," said Gwyn. "I gave up three days ago, right? And guess what?"

Richard said long-sufferingly, "You haven't wanted one since."

"Exactly. Well, you know. Time. The future."

"You've thought about it, and you'd rather live for ever."

"Isn't that what we scribble away for, Richard? Immortality? Anyway, I think my duty to literature is plain."

One more male ordeal awaited them: the changing room. The chang- ing room had the usual hooks and benches and too few coat hangers, and steamy mirrors for men to lean backwards and comb their hair at, if they had any, and much effortlessly evaporating male sweat (stalled in this process, and forming a furtive mist which slowed the air) together with competing colognes and scalp gels and armpit honeyers. There was also a shower stall full of pulsating backsides and soused and swinging Johnsons which of course forbade inspection: you don't look. Gwyn's new affectation of staring at things with childlike wonder remained unexercised in the changing room. You don't look, but as a man you mentally register yourself, with inevitable and ageless regret (it would have been *so* nice, presumably, to have had a big one) . . . Naked, Richard watched Gwyn, naked, and vigorously toweling his humid bush. Richard was excited: Gwyn was *unquestionably* nuts enough for the Sunday *Los Angeles Times*.

They walked back through the bar, which gave them time to start sweating again, and out into the late afternoon. Richard said carefully,

"You were saying? About immortality?"

"Well, I don't want to sound pretentious . . ."

"Speak as your heart tells you."

"Milton called it the last infirmity of noble minds. And—and someone said of Donne when he was dying that immortality, the desire for immortality, was rooted in the very nature of man."

"Walton," said Richard. He was doubly impressed: Gwyn had even been *reading* about immortality.

"So you know. You're bound to have such thoughts. To flesh out the skeleton of time."

"I have been looking again," said Richard, even more carefully, "at *Amelior* . . ."

The unspoken wisdom between them was as follows. The unspoken wisdom was that Richard, while taking a hearty and uncomplicated pleasure in Gwyn's success, reserved the right to keep it clear that he thought Gwyn's stuff was shit (more particularly, *Summertown*, the first novel, was forgivable shit, whereas *Amelior* was unforgivable shit). Oh yeah: and that Gwyn's success was rather amusingly—no, in fact completely hilariously—accidental. And transitory. Above all transitory. If not in real time then, failing that, certainly in literary time. Enthusiasm for Gwyn's work, Richard felt sure, would cool quicker than his corpse. Or else the universe was a joke. And a contemptible joke. So, yes, Gwyn knew that Richard entertained certain doubts about his work.

"First time through," he went on, "as you know, I didn't really think it came off. Something bland and wishful. Even ingratiating. And programmatic. An insufficient density of elements. But . . ." Richard glanced up (they had reached their cars). No question that Gwyn had been patiently waiting for that *but*. "But second time through it all came together. What threw me was its sheer originality. When we started out I think we both hoped to take the novel somewhere new. I thought the way forward was with style. And complexity. But you saw that it was all to do with subject." He glanced up again. Gwyn's expression—briefly interrupted to acknowledge the greeting of a passerby, then stolidly reassumed—was one of dignified unsurprise. Richard felt all his caution disappear with a shriek. "A new world," he went on, "mapped out and reified. Not the city but the garden. Not more neurosis but fresh clarity. That took its own kind of courage," he said, still weirdly capable of meeting Gwyn's eye, "—to forge a new art of the brave."

Slowly Gwyn held out his hand. "Thanks, man."

Jesus, thought Richard. Which of us is going nuts faster? "No," he said. "Thank *you*."

"Before I forget, Gal Aplanalp is off to L.A. any minute, so you'd better give her a call. Tomorrow. Morning."

And then they parted in the car park, under the afternoon moon.

Out there, in the universe, the kilometer definitely has it over the mile. If the universe likes roundness, which it seems to do.

The speed of light is 186,282 mps, but it is very close to 300,000 kps. One light-hour is 670,000,000 miles, but it is very close to 1,000,000,000 kilometers.

Similarly, one Astronomical Unit, or the average distance between the earth and the sun, center to center, is 92,950,000 miles, but it is very close to 15,000,000 kilometers.

Is this arbitrary anyway? Is this *anthropic*? In a million millennia, the sun will be bigger. It will feel nearer. In a million millennia, if you are still reading me, you can check these words against personal experience, because the polar ice caps have melted and Norway enjoys the climate of North Africa.

Later still, the oceans will be boiling. The human story, or at any rate the terrestrial story, will be coming to an end. I don't honestly expect you to be reading me then.

In the meantime, though, the kilometer definitely has it over the mile.

"When entering a main road from a side road, you come to a halt, look left and right," said Crash in his deepest and stateliest tones, "and wait until you see a car coming."

"Really?" said Demeter Barry.

"You engage first gear. When the car come good and close—you pull out in front of it."

"I see."

"And then you slow down to a crawl. And stick you elbow out the window."

"Really."

"Unless of course he try to overtake."

"Then what?"

"Then of course you speed up."

The thrashed Metro lurked in a dead-ended sidestreet off Golbourne Road. Beneath its roof rack of ads and L-signs Demeter sat strapped into the front passenger seat, while Crash was wedged behind the wheel. As he spoke he made intently carving gestures with his hands.

"Allow me to demonstrate. Here, let's—seatbelt on okay? There we go."

It was true—what Steve Cousins said. Driving instruction was sustained by a deep scholarship of lechery, in common with many other callings in which men were obliged to serve unattended women: plumbing, policing, clothes vending (particularly shoes). Consider the milkman, and milkman lore. How Eros must have wept at his disappearance from the English streets ... Take it from Crash: contrary pulses to do with male-female authority—plus this cool new fear rich chicks had about seeming racist or snobbish—bred a helpful confusion. Even the window-cleaner, a door-to-door artist with his tramplike rags and plastic pail, his dramatic windowsill clearances, his perched and watchful form on the other side of the glass, the new light he let flow into the living space: even the window-cleaner was the cause of rearrangements, of domestic reconsiderations ... Probably a pamphlet as long as the *Highway Code* could be written on, say, the Use of the Seatbelt in the Promotion of Instructor-Student Bodily Contact; also Seat-Elevation Adjustment, the Pardonability of Tactile Reassurance During and After the Emergency Stop, the Gearstick as Symbol or Totem.

"And the bottom line being?" said Crash invitingly.

"What?" asked Demeter.

"I'm asking you."

"Um. I don't know."

"*To impress your personality on the road.* I say it again. Your purpose when driving is not to arrive at your destination safely or quickly. Your purpose when driving is ... ?"

"To impress your personality on the road."

"Exactly. *To show who own the road.*"

Boldly Crash fired the Metro and approached the junction, indicating left. The street was clear, and uncannily remained so, for twenty seconds, for forty, for sixty, for more. And this was London, where there was no shortage of cars. This was a modern city, where cars were in endless supply, where there were cars, cars, cars, as far as the eye could see. They went on waiting. Crash craned his neck. A sizable segment of Demi's allotted hour had already been consumed by their vigil.

"Neutron bomb is it."

They went on waiting. At last a smudged white van appeared, from the right. You could always eventually rely, in London, on a smudged white van: it looked as though it had been scrabbled at by the sooty fingers of huge children. Here it came, over the bridge beneath the bristling council block, and advancing with steady purpose. The van was upon them— the van was practically past them—when Crash pounced out in front of it.

First, the great sinus effort of the brakes; then brutal honk of horn and (Demi half-turned) the incensed strobe of headlights. Crash now sat back, humming, and steadily quenched the Metro's speed, the van whinnying and jostling in its wake, trying to pass, to climb on top of, to leapfrog over. Glancing at Demeter, Crash lowered the side window and stuck an exaggerated length of elbow out of it.

"Now," he instructed, "for the irrational burst of speed."

And Demeter was duly pressed back into her seat as Crash's slablike trainer hit the floor.

Twenty minutes later the Metro stood double-parked on the All Saints Road, parallel with Portobello, before the hulk of the old Adonis. Crash was explaining that the techniques he had just demonstrated, and other mysteries to which he might soon introduce her, lay in the realm of advanced motoring; of such skills, Crash gently hinted, Demi could only dream of one day becoming mistress.

"But the same principle always apply. You show who own the road."

With a nod or two and a quiet clearing of the throat Crash fell into a high-minded silence. His thoughts lay, perhaps, in that land where advanced motorists, with many a veer and screech and pile-up, deployed their expertise. Or maybe he was pondering his very recent misadventure: the smudged white van, it had transpired at the next traffic lights, contained three uniformed policemen.

"Probably get off," mused Crash, who ought to know, "with a DWD."

"I'm sorry?"

"Driving Without Due."

"Sorry?" said Demi. And she sounded it: sorry she asked.

"Driving Without Due Care and Attention," Crash elaborated.

"But you *weren't*. I'll be your witness. You were driving with *incredible* care. Everything you did was—"

Crash waved a great hand: it was not given to all, this grasp of the higher motoring mysteries. It was definitely not given to the police . . . His devout but wounded gaze turned to the façade of the old Adonis. The All Saints Road, with its new poster galleries and tapas bars, had changed dramatically even in Crash's adult lifetime. But not so long ago (Crash nodded to himself) the old Adonis had loomed over perhaps the busiest and certainly the noisiest drug corner in West London: "a symbolic location," to quote *Police Review*. It was a drive-by, All Saints and Lancaster: the cars came and slowed, all night, and the shaved black heads bobbed up to the unwinding windows. The Adonis, the old superpub with its sticky chandeliers and sodden carpet, its contrapuntal rock videos and the thick bank of dole-quaffing fruit machines, was the natural fulcrum of the play. And there you found the reverse apartheid of the drug economy, with the whites, in their frothing melee of malt beer, keeping the given distance from the sober but hot-faced brothers, who tended their Lucozades and Ribenas on the streetside bar. The Adonis. Its colonial symmetry and gaiety—where were they now? Effaced, abashed, behind planks and mesh wire. But if you (Crash grunted as he eased his neck round further), but if you . . . that bit there. A low door, to the side and down a step or two, and the guy within, watching and glinting. If you listened you could faintly hear the modest monotony of the music and—yeah—the sound of glasses clashing or cracking. So: the old Adonis refuse to die. It had found, in the eaves and runnels, a diminished and secondary existence: but continuation, all the same. Demi, who was watching Crash, saw a look of pleased indulgence show in his eyes. She didn't know, either, about the deep association between Adonis and rebirth, of his shared identity with Orpheus, and with Christ, who represented a power that could bring the dead souls back, as Orpheus had failed to do.

"Bastards," said Demi.

Crash smiled. She meant the police. "You don't want to go in there," he said.

"The Adonis?"

"That a *bad* pub."

He went on smiling; there was even a quiet complicit gurgle somewhere in the back of his throat. The light was failing but here were the bleach and ivory of his teeth. She laughed musically and said,

"I know all about the Adonis."

"You never!"

So. Then it comes out. Crash was mainly relieved, but he also felt promoted, and flattered, of course, in many tender points of head and heart. Up until now, with Demi, he could think of no investigative move to make, other than sexual harassment. Where you would find out something, whatever the downside: where you would get information. And he just couldn't do that. He just couldn't do that. Now, though, before he put the Metro into gear, he leaned over and into the costly universe of her blondness and Englishness and kissed the side of her pale mouth. No, this was all right. This was calm. This was good.

Later, back at his flat in Keith Grove, down Shepherd's Bush way, after the gym and his big debrief with fucking Adolf, Crash reclined on his futon in thong underpants with his hands clasped behind his head. Yat. On the raised screen: the football match he'd taped. He watched its progress with full terror and pity, and with extreme fluctuations of blink rate, reserving a specialist's compassion for the fates of both goalkeepers, for it was in this position that he himself turned out, twice a week, for the church and for the pub. "Early ball!" said Crash. "Ah, unlucky." The way her lips gave just enough to be more than very polite. No tongues or whatever. "Keeper's! Played, keeper." Would be treating her with respect, same as before. "Turn! Shielded." But that little suggestion of give: it made its own suggestion. Telling him something he wouldn't ever tell Scozz. "Man on! Good release." That here was *another* woman—oh, Jesus, there were so many—who was loved maybe. "Header. Shot! Saved, keeper." But not enough or not in the right way. "First time! Yes! *Finish*!"

The match ended with the right result, but Crash was feeling right no longer: upset in himself. Slowly and angrily he donned his black track suit and jogged down to Pressures. It was called Thresher's, but Crash called it Pressures. On the way back up Keith Grove he realized what it was: him, in the fruit-juice bar, saying to Scozzy, and *laughing*: "Oh yeah She's definitely Experienced." 13: that *bad* kid.

He closed the door of his flat behind him and opened the bottle of scotch and threw away the top. He didn't give a fuck.

Before he delivered it, but after he had wrapped it, Richard was struck by an unpleasant thought: what if there *was* something to interest Gwyn Barry in this particular issue of the Sunday *Los Angeles Times*? An eight-page symposium on his work, for example. Or a whole Gwyn Barry Section. As in the UK, *Amelior* had first been a flop, then a sleeper, and finally a smash in the United States. Brought to Richard's attention not by Gwyn but by a patriotic item in a London newspaper, this fact inflicted a wound that still out-throbbed all others: out-throbbed the gouges and gashes visited on him by the book's apparent popularity everywhere else on earth, which he got to hear about piecemeal, from

Gwyn's offhand grumbles: this importunate Argentinian journalist or camera crew, that interminable questionnaire from Taiwan. But *America.* Come *on* . . . Richard lit a cigarette. Could it be that Gwyn had stumbled on the universal, that voice which speaks to and for the human soul? No. Gwyn had stumbled on the LCD.

Now Marco entered the room. As he faithfully took up position at his father's side, Richard dragged on his cigarette and then flicked it out of the window. "I like Daddy," sang Marco, his voice discreetly lowered, "he lives with me . . ." Ever since that day when Richard hit Marco across the head because *Amelior* had entered the best-seller list at number nine (and that was just the beginning: in comparison, the chartbusters of Francophile fatsoes, of gimp cosmologists, it seemed to Richard, came and went like mayflies), the child had fallen in love with his father, helplessly, as if, that day, instead of hitting Marco across the ear Richard had poured something into it. "I love you," the child often said. There was also this song Marco had made up, remarkable, really, for how little information it got across (and for its dud *rime riche*):

> I like Daddy.
> He lives with me.
> I like him.
> And he likes me.

Though perhaps, under the new demographics, this was all stunning news. In the cities of England the children were singing:

> I don't like Daddy.
> He doesn't live with me.
> I don't like him.
> And he doesn't like me.

Technically, too, Marco's song or poem would certainly be deemed to cut the mustard at the Tantalus Press, where Richard had spent a sorrowful afternoon. This song made up by Marco: his father had been very pleased to hear it, on the whole, the first couple of hundred times. Gina sang no such song . . . Richard didn't like to think that Marco's marathon display of emotion might have fear as its spur. He didn't like to think that Marco knew his father was losing his mind and was trying, through his presence and example, to help him tether it. He had apologized, for the blow, many times. The only thing Marco ever said in reply was that we all had our bad days.

Richard was having a relatively good day. He had called the offices of Gal Aplanalp and Gal Aplanalp had called him back within minutes— from the airplane that was taking her to Los Angeles. She was returning, however, frivolously soon. Or so it seemed to Richard. His passion was the American novel. He had never been to America. Which about summed him up. Probably as a result of his conversation with Gal, *Untitled* was making a great leap forward. It had what its two immediate predecessors had not had: the sure prospect of a reader. Gina didn't read him. He didn't expect her to: fanatically difficult modern prose wasn't her thing. Even when she tried to read his published novels she always said that his stuff gave her a headache.

"Sling your . . . Get your . . . Bung your finger in there. Your thumb. Now keep it there while I make the knot but take it *out* when I . . . Good."

"Helping Daddy, in whatever he does. Each day."

He laughed—a quieter version of his trapped, guttural, lockjawed laugh. "Go somewhere else now," he said. "Find Marius. I'll give you both a quid if you do."

It was seven o'clock in the evening. A space on his desk had not been cleared for the package containing the *Los Angeles Times*, but there it was anyway, reasonably symmetrical, massive, anomalous, like a UFO on a slum rooftop. Richard weakly supposed that he had better glance through its contents, prior to delivery. It would demand incredible deftness, true, but if he could urge the thing out while preserving at least the general shape of the wrapping . . . He picked at the master-knot (so recently and securely fastened, over Marco's crimson thumbtip); he worried the folds and flaps of the creased brown paper: and in the end he just wrenched it all apart. The boys in the next room—they heard his savage cries but hardly registered them, so familiar was their timbre. Perhaps Daddy had misplaced his pencil sharpener, or dropped a paper clip? Because Richard's relationship with the physical world of things, always very poor, had deteriorated sharply. Christ, the dumb insolence of inanimate objects! He could never understand what was *in it* for inanimate objects, behaving as they did. What was *in it* for the doorknob that hooked your jacket pocket as you passed? What was *in it* for the jacket pocket?

With care and dread, Richard inspected Book World (all the reviews, plus Briefly Noted, We're Talking About . . ., All Booked Up and Information Please), Arts and Entertainments (in case something of Gwyn's had been harrowingly translated to screen or stage), the main Magazine (including Fresh Faces and Bedside Reading) and the Week in Review (the Gwyn Barry phenomenon). In a more relaxed spirit he thoroughly skimmed the Style Section, the Update Section, the Flair Section, the Briefing Section, the Poise Section, the Now Section and the You Section. Next, feeling laughably rigorous and vastly vindicated, he checked the Op-Ed page of the News (I) section: multiculturalism? the redefined syllabus? whither publishing? The Business Section, the Personals Section and the Appointments Section: none detained him long. The Lawnmower pullout and the Curtain Rail supplement—these he scathingly ignored.

At midnight Richard was coming to the conclusion that the last five hours had been divertingly and rewardingly spent. He didn't doubt that Gwyn was nuts enough to read the whole thing at least twice, maybe three times, maybe four—maybe more. Maybe Gwyn would just go on reading it *forever*. Richard imagined his friend, a few years from now, mumbling his way through the recipes and the crossword clues and the golf results—his unwashed clothes, his mugs of instant coffee. There he was, rubbing his eyes as he reached yet again for the Deckchair Section . . . And here was another thing: if Gwyn Barry was such a big cheese, you wouldn't know it from the Sunday *Los Angeles Times*.

Using a kilometer of string and about four rolls of cellotape, Richard bandaged his package together. It was ready to go. Over a cognac he began to contemplate the fateful, the exalted challenge of delivery.

Every other day on the cover of my newspaper there is a photograph of a murdered child.

Murdered by a pale loner, murdered by sectarians or separatists, murdered by a burping businessman encased in a ton of metal, murdered by other children. Hard work, this last, for the watchful and uninnocent eye. Feel your unwelcome sweat as you move among them now, on traffic islands, in shop doorways—the new children.

Of the perpetrator or perpetrators the mother or the father of the dead will often say, *I have no words for them.* Something like, *Words cannot express what I feel for them.* Something like, *As for those who did this, I have no words for them.* Or, *There are no words for them.*

By which I take them to mean: words are inadequate and also inappropriate. You cannot find the right words—so don't look for them. Don't look.

And I agree. I am with the father, with the mother. As for those who did this, I have no words.

The information is telling me—the information is telling me to stop saying *hi* and to start saying *bye.*

Where I live there's a yellow dwarf I keep seeing, out on the streets with their shops and bus stops. She is young and yellow and less than four feet tall with characteristically compacted limbs (the arms tucked inwards as if in pugilistic readiness, the legs like castors), half-Asian, half-Caribbean, pale-eyebrowed, white-lashed; her hair is an animal orange, its filaments electrically charged. She is young. She will get older, but not taller . . . For the first instant, whenever we exchange glances, she looks up at me and her chin stiffens in *defiance.* Mistrust, and everything else, but above all *defiance.* More recently, as these glances now tend to prolong themselves, her face develops, away from defiance; defiance is discarded as unnecessary (though it has been necessary, so many times). Not quite smiling or nodding, we acknowledge one another.

A yellow dwarf is a terrible thing to be called, probably because—more pertinently—it is a terrible thing to be. A terrible thing. Poor, poor yellow dwarf. I would like her to know that yellow dwarves are *good.* I owe my life to a yellow dwarf, as do we all—the one up there: the sun.

The yellow dwarf is not exotic. Yellow dwarves are not exotic. They're among the most exemplary phenomena in the universe. A quasar, now—

a galaxy the size of a solar system clustered round some quantum monstrosity or cryptogram and barreling out of observable space at a hundred thousand miles a second: that's exotic.

I will never be able to meet the eye of the yellow dwarf up there. Its stare will never soften; its defiance will always be absolute.

She is ordinary, in the big picture. Who will ever tell her? She is ordinary. Not like the other stars of the street. Not like the red giant flailing and falling under the overpass, not like the black hole behind the basement window, not like the pulsar on the roundabout in the deserted playground.

Richard Tull, with his own consignment of strictly local concerns, stood forty stories above the city. He had an authentically frightening hangover and he was in the offices of Gal Aplanalp. Not just above the city, but above the City, within hearing range of Bow Bells, perhaps (when will you pay me?). This was no cockneyland of barrowboys and winkles. Large-scale and cathartic construction work was taking place all around him: jumpsuits, hardhats, trenches, cranes, breeze-blocks in skip-sized packages. A hot-blue magnesium light shone upward through the morning haze. Richard thought of the backyard his study overlooked, where builders were always fucking around, year in year out. To him, builders meant destruction. Bumcrack cowboys, knee-deep in pointlessness and slime, and raising nothing but hell.

The walls of the offices of literary agents, in Richard's wide and unhappy experience, tended to be furnished with books. Here he was surrounded by posters—posters of authors whom Gal already represented. He was surrounded by well-known novelists; but they were novelists who were well known for something else. Well known for newscasting, cliff-scaling, acting, cooking, dress-designing, javelin-throwing, and being related to the Queen. None of them was well known for book reviewing. There was Gwyn, of course. Many of the authors Richard failed to recognize. He cross-checked with the brochures attractively fanned out on the coffee table. So this dope with the ponytail . . . wrote biographies of rock stars. His large corpus consisted entirely of rock-star surnames followed by exclamation marks. Each title caused Richard's head to jolt in regrettable counterpoint to the pulse of his headache. He imagined . . . *Davenant! Deeping! Bottrell! Myers!*

Gal entered. Richard turned. He hadn't seen her for ten years. When Gal was seventeen and over here for a summer doing odd jobs for publishers, Richard and Gwyn had taken her up and shown her around: the

bowling alley in Shaftesbury Avenue, the Irish pubs beneath Piccadilly
Circus; once (yes) they had taken her boating, in Hyde Park. They liked
her. She had a talent for warmth, he remembered; she kissed your cheek
at odd moments. Who else does that? Oh yeah: Marco. A buxom tomboy,
American, seventeen: it sounds like just what you want. But Richard
wasn't up for it. He seemed to want something more complicated: he
liked—or kept going out with—dark and violent depressives who never
ate anything and never got the curse. And Gwyn wasn't up for it: he had
Gilda. And no doubt Gal wasn't up for it either. And anyway the young
men had reached a silent understanding: they were young enough themselves to think that Gal Aplanalp was too young to be touched.

They shook hands, and embraced, which was her idea (Gal's lips went
"mwa" into the whiskers of his right ear). Then she said the thing he
least wanted to hear. She said,

"Well let's take a look at you."

Richard stood there at arm's length.

"Are you . . .? You look—you look rather, I don't know, you look
a bit . . ."

"Old," said Richard. "The adjective—or is it the com*ple*ment—you
are searching for is *old.* "

The numerous symptoms of his hangover included a strong reluc-
tance to meet any human eye. But Richard told himself to be mad and
proud (and what a wag his head gave on that *complement*): he went on
standing there, proud and mad and unpublished, the palely bleeding ruin
of Richard Tull. It could be that his hangover wasn't really that bad, war-
ranting no more, perhaps, than half a week of sepulchral suffering, in the
fetal position, behind drawn blinds.

"Coffee? It's good. We send out for it."

"That would be very nice."

They talked for a while about the old days. Yes, how much better
things had been, in the old days, when Gwyn was poor, his bedsit
cramped, his girlfriend rough, his career quite prospectless. In the old
days Gwyn was just a failed book reviewer (Richard's designation) and
publisher's skivvy. During the summer of Gal's stay Gwyn had been
preparing A-level guides to various sections of *The Canterbury Tales.*
They weren't even books, or pamphlets. They were sold in *packets* . . .
Now that Gal was out of his force field Richard was free to contemplate
her. And he nodded his head; he conceded. Not just young, not just
healthy and symmetrical. Somebody who worked in the marketing of
face creams or bath oils would give Gal a high beauty rating. These were
looks you could actually sell things with. These were looks that men and

women alike admired. It had all come together, the skin, the bones, the coiled black hair. Also the body: that too. When she shifted in her chair the upper half of her torso rearranged itself a beat late, with a certain ordered heaviness. Richard supposed she was turned out in accordance with the cutting edge of female-professional thinking and praxis. She was pitilessly businesslike from head to foot; but the foot wore an ankle bracelet and a spikey heel. When they greeted one another, Richard would have liked to be able to say something like "I've been potholing for a month" or "I got shot in the head last week." Yet it was Gal who had spent the last two nights on the red-eye—over America, over the Atlantic. All Richard had done was sit at his desk.

The coffee came. They paused. They began.

First, the necessarily depressing issue of Richard's *curriculum vitae*. Attached to her clipboard she had a printout on him; she had information. Gal made notes and said "Mm-hm." Her manner suggested, encouragingly, that she was no stranger to the stalled career; Richard began to believe that she routinely dealt with greater prodigies of obscurity and pauperism—with seedier duds, with louder flops.

"What's this biography of Denton Welch?" she said, and frowned accusingly at her clipboard.

"I never did it. It fell through."

"And of R. C. Squires?"

"R. C. Squires. A literary editor of *The Little Magazine*."

"Which little magazine?"

"*The Little Magazine*. The one I'm literary editor of. An interesting life. He was in Berlin in the thirties and in Spain during the Civil War." Respectively whoring in the Kurfürstendamm and playing ping-pong in Sitges, as Richard had learned, after a month of desultory research. "May I smoke?"

"What about this travel book? The Siberia trip."

"I'm not going."

"The Siberian *lepers* . . ."

"I'm not going."

"What's this? *The History of Increasing Humiliation*. Nonfiction, right?"

Richard crossed his legs and then recrossed them. This was a book he still wanted to write: one day. He said, as he had said before, "It would be a book accounting for the decline in the status and virtue of literary protagonists. First gods, then demigods, then kings, then great warriors, great lovers, then burghers and merchants and vicars and doctors and lawyers. Then social realism: you. Then irony: me. Then maniacs and murderers, tramps, mobs, rabble, flotsam, vermin."

She was looking at him. "And what would account for it?"

He sighed. "The history of astronomy. The history of astronomy is the history of increasing humiliation. First the geocentric universe, then the heliocentric universe. Then the eccentric universe—the one we're living in. Every century we get smaller. Kant figured it all out, sitting in his armchair. What's the phrase? The principle of terrestrial mediocrity."

". . . Big book."

"Big book. Small world. Big universe."

"What is the status of all these projects?"

"The status of all these projects," said Richard, "is that I've taken advances on them and not written them."

"Hell with that," she said, and now the exchange started speeding up. "They write it off."

"The new novel. What's it about."

"Modern consciousness."

"Is it as difficult as your other novels?"

"More difficult. Much more difficult."

"You didn't think you might change tack?"

"And write a Western?"

"What's it called?"

"*Untitled*. Its title is *Untitled*."

"We'll soon fix that."

"We will not fix that."

"I reread *Dreams Are Hard to Find* and I—"

"*Dreams Don't Mean Anything*."

"Don't *say* that. You're too easily discouraged."

"Point *one*," said Richard. He fell silent. He was applying the brake. In fact he *had* written a Western. He had tried to write a Western. His Western had petered out after a couple of pages of banging shutters, of hurrying tumbleweeds . . . "Point one. The title of my book is *Dreams Don't Mean Anything*. Point two. It—what I mean is dreams don't *signify* anything. Not exactly. Point three. I am not 'easily discouraged.' It has been difficult getting me discouraged. It has been arduous."

"Can I have a drag?"

He held the cigarette out to her butt-first. She met it not with her fingers—she met it with her lips. So Richard was mollified by a glimpse of star-bright brassiere, against Persian flesh. Gal inhaled expertly, and sat back. She liked to smoke; she used artificial sweeteners in her espresso. Her hand, he noticed, was no less plump than it was ten years ago. A hand he had held, avuncularly, many times. Gal had a flaw. A predisposition. Weight wanted her. Fat wanted her. The desk she sat at was organized, but there was something in her that wasn't organized, not quite . . . Beyond was the window: in this frame of gray sky the cranes were like T-squares on a drawing board. The paper the architect was using was soiled and smudged. Too much rubbing out and starting again, with soiled eraser. Graphic cancellations, and the grains of the rubber shading the air, brushed and nudged by the hovering pinkie. A good idea, when imagining London, when imagining cities, to go back to the drawing board.

"I want to represent you," she said.

"Thank you," he said.

"Now. Writers need definition. The public can only keep in mind one thing per writer. Like a signature. Drunk, young, mad, fat, sick: you know. It's better if you pick it rather than letting them pick it. Ever thought about the young-fogey thing? The young fart. You wear a bow tie and a waistcoat. Would you smoke a pipe?"

"Well I would, probably," said Richard, stretching his neck, "if somebody offered me one. With tobacco in it and a match. Listen. I'm too old to be a young fart. I'm an old fart." Flatulence, as it happened, was on Richard's mind. That morning, while shaving, he had geared himself, expecting the usual pungent blare. And all he heard was a terrible little *click*. "Aren't we forgetting that I've got to get published first?"

"Oh I think I can call in some favors. Then we'll get everything working together. Your fiction is your fiction. I won't fuck with you creatively but we've got to get something else to play it off against. Your journalism needs a gee-up. It's too bad you review all over the place. You should have a column. Think about it."

"Don't mind me asking this. I gather you're very good at what you do. Do you find your appearance helps?"

"Absolutely. How about . . . how about doing a long in-depth piece about what it's like to be a very successful novelist?"

Richard waited.

"You know: what's it *really like*. People are very interested in writers. Successful ones. More interested in the writers than the writing. In the writers' lives. For some reason. You and I both know they mainly sit at home all day."

Richard waited.

"So how about this piece. I'll sell it in America. Everywhere."

"The one about what it's like being an incredibly successful writer?"

"Day by day. What's it like. What's it really *like*."

Richard went back to waiting.

". . . Gwyn's new novel is published in the States in March. Here it'll be May. He's doing the eight-city tour. New York, Washington, Miami, Chicago, Denver, Los Angeles, Boston, New York again. You go with him. I'll set it up."

"Whose idea is this?"

"Mine. I'm sure he'll be delighted to have you along. Those tours are a sentence. Go on. Do it. You're smiling. Do it. It'll show everybody how unenvious you are."

"Is that my signature? Unenvious?"

He said he would have to think about it (untrue: he was going), and they shook hands without the hug this time, like professionals. In the tube train to Soho and the offices of *The Little Magazine* Richard considered his signature: what marked him out. Because we all needed them now, signatures, signatures, even the guy sitting opposite: his was the pair of pink diaper pins he wore through his nose . . . Richard couldn't come up with anything good. Except—this. He had never been to America. And he would tell you that quite frankly, raising his pentimento eyebrows and tensing his upper lip with a certain laconic pride.

I quite agree. What an asshole.

Gal's right. Nothing ever happens to novelists. Except—this.

They are born. They get sick, they get well, they hang around the inkwell. They leave home, with their stuff in a hired van. They learn to drive, unlike poets (poets don't drive. Never trust a poet who can drive. Never trust a poet at the wheel. If he *can* drive, distrust the poems). They get married in registry offices. They have children in hospitals—the ordinary miracle. Their parents die—the ordinary disaster. They get divorced or they don't. Their children leave home, learn to drive, get married, have children. They grow old. So nothing ever happens to them, except the universal.

With so many literary biographies down him, Richard knew this perfectly well. Confirmation came seasonally, every April and September, when he sneered his way through the color supplements and met the novelists' tremulous stares—sitting on their sofas or their garden benches. And doing fuck-all.

Although they don't or can't drive, poets get around more. William Davenant certainly took his chances: "He got a terrible clap of a black handsome wench that lay in Axe-yard . . . which cost him his nose." And Johnson's *Life of Savage*—bastardy, adultery, the fatal tavern brawl, the sentence of execution—describes a savage life: it reads like a revenger's tragedy that really happened. In mitigation, it should be said that an asshole is not the same thing as an arsehole. An Atlantic divides them. We are all assholes some of the time, but an arsehole is an arsehole *all* of the time. What *was* Richard? He was a revenger, in what was probably intended to be a comedy.

When Gwyn said, of the Profundity Requital, that the money was "ridiculous," Richard took him to mean that the money was derisory. But it wasn't derisory. It was ridiculous. And you got it *every year.*

Richard, unsurprisingly, was to be found at his desk, on which, along with pp. 1–432 of *Untitled* and many sloping stacks of assorted trex, three items were prominently displayed: a minutes-style letter from Gal Aplanalp; a bourgeois tabloid, staked open on the Rory Plantagenet page; and a third scrawled note from "Darko"—Belladonna's backer or abettor. Richard was making a connection.

He reread:

> To recap: the itinerary is New York, Washington, Miami, Chicago, Denver, Los Angeles, Boston, New York.

Denver. Why Denver? He reread:

> ... awarded annually, in perpetuity. The three judges are Lucy Cabretti, the Washington-based feminist critic, poet and novelist, Elsa Oughton, who lives and works in Boston, and Stanwyck Mills, author and Sue and Ron L. Summerdale Professor of Law at the University of Denver.

Richard sat back, nodding. He reread:

> Whats the secret. Come on. Or is it all just the hipe. Belladonna is good at secrets. She can get any thing out of anyone, that one. Thats' why Gwyn Loves Belladonna. Its not too late for that "jar."

What interested Richard here, naturally, was the bit about Gwyn loving Belladonna. Even in Darko's world—with its sense of futile toil—*love* might mean something. It might mean vulnerability. *Gwyn Loves Belladonna* would look pretty interesting even if you saw it carved on the trunk of a lumpen evergreen in Dogshit Park or smeared in spray paint on the gray flank of the flyover. But given who Gwyn was and whoever the hell Belladonna might be: this was a matter of broad—of tabloid—interest. *Gwyn Loves Belladonna* would look even better as a headline, positioned directly beneath the compromised and epicene features of Rory Plantagenet. Undermining or destroying Gwyn's marriage seemed broadly attractive but also clumsily wide of the mark, just as a physical attack on his person would surely never rise above the gruesomely approximate. Richard didn't want to single out Gwyn's *life*, which came a poor second to what he really hated. Still, if he had to make do with Gwyn's marriage, he would make do with Gwyn's marriage. If he had to make do with Gwyn's life, he would make do with Gwyn's life.

"Hello. Is Darko there please? Sure. Yes, this is uh, Richard Tull." Richard was Richard's name and there was nothing you could do to it: Rich and Richie were out for obvious reasons, and he had never liked Rick, and bad things had happened to Dick. "No, I'll wait . . . Darko? Hi. This is Richard Tull."

There was a silence. Then the voice said, "Who?"

"Richard Tull. The writer."

". . . What's the name again?"

"Christ. You're Darko, right? You wrote to me. Three times. Richard *Tull.*"

"Got it. Got it. Sorry uh, Richard. I'm half asleep."

"I know the feeling."

"Still in a daze. I got to get myself sorted out," said the voice, as if suddenly and worriedly considering something more long-term.

"Happens to the best of us."

". . . Anyway: what you want?"

"What do *I* want? I want to hang up. But let's go another half-mile. I want to have a word with this girl you mentioned. Belladonna."

"She can't come to the phone."

"No, not now."

"Belladonna, she does what she fucking well likes. Yep. She pleases herself, I reckon."

"Why don't the three of us get together some time?"

". . . Nothing simpler."

When that was over he rang Anstice and did his hour with her. When that was over, he went to the boys' room and fished Marco out from under his GI Joes and clothed him. Sitting on the twin bed, he looked out of the window and saw the lightest swirl of thinning cloud, way out there, like a wiped table in the last few seconds before it dries . . .

The day was heating up and so in the end he took Marco out into it, into Dogshit and into park culture, which is something to see. Queueing at the snack stall with all the other weight problems and skin conditions, among the multiple single mothers in crayon-color beachwear, the splat and splotch of English skin, beneath treated hair, and all the sticky children each needing its tin of drink, Richard watched the joggers pounding the outer track in scissoring shellsuits of magenta, turquoise, of lime or sherwood green. Marco stood there with his upper teeth warily bared to the press of sense data.

With their papercupfuls of Slushpuppy, they walked past the flat-roofed park toilets where a boy younger than Marco had recently been raped while his mother tapped her foot on this same patch of asphalt. One man and his dog went by the other way, man as thin as a fuse, dog as cocked and spherical as a rocket. The sloping green was mud, churned and studded, beige and dun, half soil, half shit. On the bench, Marco faced the prospect with the candid bewilderment of his gaze, turning and lifting his head, every few seconds, to his father's stunned profile. The boy might have looked at the hospital smokestacks, and then at the loners, the ranters, the post-pub staggerers, all those born to be the haunters of parks, and then looked again at his father, with the six or seven immediate difficulties pulling on the skin around his eyes, each with its own nervous tic, and wondered what the difference was.

For Richard was thinking, if thinking is quite the word we want (and we now do the usual business of extracting those thoughts from the furious and unceasing babble that surrounds and drowns them): you cannot demonstrate, prove, establish—you cannot know if a book is good. A sentence, a line, a phrase: nobody knows. The literary philosophers of Cambridge spent a century saying otherwise, and said nothing. Is "When all at once I saw a crowd" worse than "Thoughts that do often lie too deep for tears"? (Yes. But it was the better line that contained the identifiable flaw: that *do*, brought in to make up the numbers.) I. A. Richards reanatomized the human mind so that it might be capable of such divination. William Empson offered a quantity theory of value, of what was ambiguous, what was complex, and therefore *good*. Leavis said that while you can't judge literature, you can judge life, so for the purposes of judgment life and literature are the same! But life and literature were not the same. Ask Richard. Ask Demi or Gina. (Ask Scozzy, Crash, Link, 13.) Ask the man with the rocket dog. Ask the rocket dog . . . Gwyn was no good. Clearly, but not demonstrably. Richard's neck did an 8 of pain. So: a sandwich man on Oxford Street (GWYN BARRY IS NO GOOD), a tub-thumper under the arrow of Eros ("Gwyn Barry is no good!"), a frontier preacher in the wind and rain of Ongar, Upminster, Stanmore, Morden, spreading the word: that Gwyn was no good. Speakers' Corner (men on inverted milk crates, looking like schoolmasters but quietly madder than any rat)—Speakers' Corner was no longer to be found on the south side of Marble Arch. It was now to be found on all the other corners: every corner of London Town. Thus the voices raised and reedy, Natural Law, cosmopolitan finance, Moral Rearmament, an

American angel called Moroni, the infernal nature of electricity; and Richard Tull, deploying apt quotation and close reading, proving beyond any reasonable doubt to his three or four strangely attentive listeners that Gwyn Barry was no good.

In the local sublunary sphere, your taste in literature was like your taste in sex: there was nothing you could *do* about it. Once, in bed, fifteen years ago, someone had asked him, "What's your favorite?" He told her. His favorite turned out to be her favorite too. So it all worked out. Gwyn, or *Amelior*, was *everybody's* favorite. Or nobody's aversion. *Amelior* was something like the missionary position plus simultaneous orgasm. Whereas Richard's stuff, Richard's prose, was clearly minority-interest to a disgusting degree: if the police ever found out about it, Richard's stuff would be instantly illegalized—if, that is, the police could bring themselves to *believe* there were people around who went in for anything so contorted and laborious . . . Richard had married his sexual obsession. His sexual obsession she had now ceased to be. Gina had been supplanted, as his sexual obsession, by every other woman on earth between the ages of twelve and sixty. The park—Dogshit Park—pullulated with his sexual obsessions. These hopeless clamorings, he knew (from books), were just the final or penultimate yodels of his DNA: of his selfish genes, craving propagation before they died. It was to do with getting old, he knew. But it made him feel like a prototypical adolescent: a reeking gloom of zits and tit mags. He wanted everyone. He wanted anyone. Richard wanted Gina but his body and his mind were not permitting it. How long could this go on? I will arise—I will arise . . .

Marco finished his Slushpuppy, and then finished Richard's (whose skull ached to the crushed ice). Hand in hand they did their tour of the urban pastoral, the sward beneath the heavenly luminary, its human figures brightly half-clad at rest and play. How did people ever get the idea that *white skin* was any good at all, let alone the best? White skin was so obviously the worst: carved from the purest trex. Walking here, he felt the pluralism and the pretty promiscuity and, for now, the freedom from group hostilities. If they were here, these hostilities, then Richard didn't smell their hormones; he was white and middle-class and Labour and he was growing old. It sometimes seemed that he had spent his whole life avoiding getting beaten up (teds, mods, rockers, skinheads, punks, blacks) but his land was gangland no longer: violence would come, if it came, from the individual, from left field, denuded of motive. The urban pastoral was all left field. There was no right field. And violence wouldn't come for Richard. It would come for Marco.

The northern gates were chained shut so Richard unsurely, quiveringly, scaled the spikes and then hoisted Marco over. To their left, to their left field, itself spike-cordoned, lay the cleanest patch of grass in all Dogshit, the showpiece of the park (staunch those tears of pride). This of course was the dog toilet, where the dogs were meant to shit, and never did.

There was much speculation about where Gwyn Barry would "go" after *Amelior*—in literary circles, anyway, wherever those may be. (In literary circles, which are, perhaps, themselves a polite fiction.) There was certainly much speculation at 49E Calchalk Street. In what "direction" would Gwyn now "turn"? Humbly local, abjectly autobiographical, *Summertown* was a prentice work. *Amelior* was a freak best-seller. Then what? The question was soon answered, at least to Richard's satisfaction: the day after he delivered the *Los Angeles Times*, Richard received, also by special messenger, a sample first chapter of novel number three. It came in a green pouch designed to resemble an expensive rucksack; in addition it featured a picture of Gwyn and some quotes, not from the critics but from the balance sheets. Richard tore the thing open and examined its contents with a spartan sigh. Jesus Christ. Gwyn's third novel was called *Amelior Regained*. Not *Summertown Regained*, you notice. Oh no. *Amelior Regained*. And why did they need to regain it? They never even lost it.

In *Amelior* itself twelve youngish human beings forgathered in an unnamed and perhaps imaginary but certainly very temperate hinterland some time in the near future. No holocaust or meteorite or convulsing dystopia brought them there. They just showed up. To find a better way . . . Every racial group was represented, the usual rainbow plus a couple of superexotic extras—an Eskimo, an Amerindian, even a taciturn Aborigine. Each of them boasted a serious but non-disfiguring affliction: Piotr had hemophilia, Conchita endometriosis, Sachine colitis, Eagle Woman diabetes. Of this twelve, naturally, six were men and six were women; but the sexual characteristics were deliberately hazed. The women were broad-shouldered and thin-hipped. The men tended to be comfortably plump. In the place called Amelior, where they had come to dwell, there was no beauty, no humor and no incident; there was no hate and there was no love.

And that was all. Richard would tell you that that was all: honestly. Apart from a very great deal of talk about agriculture, horticulture, jurisprudence, religion (not advised), astrology, hut-construction and diet. When he first read *Amelior* Richard kept forgetting what he was doing and kept turning abstractedly to the back flap and the biographical note, expecting to see something like Despite mutism and blindness, or Although diagnosed with Down's syndrome, or Shrugging off the effects of a full lobotomy . . . *Amelior* would only be remarkable if Gwyn had written it with his foot. Why was *Amelior* so popular? Who knew? Gwyn didn't do it. The world did it.

All that week, as he sat on the can each morning, Richard read a few more pages of Gwyn's teaser—accurately so called. The first chapter of *Amelior Regained* consisted of a discussion between one of the men and one of the women, in a forest, about social justice. In other words, here was some Narnian waterbaby or other and some titless Hobbit or other, with her foot on a log, talking freedom. The only real departure came in the prose. While it was pretty simple stuff, *Amelior* every now and then attempted a night-school literary cadence. *Amelior Regained* was barbarically plain. Richard kept looking at the back flap. It just said that Gwyn lived in London, not Borneo, and that his wife's dad was the Earl of Rieveaulx.

It was Sunday afternoon, and Richard was going over there, as he sometimes did on Sunday afternoon.

Down on Calchalk Street he climbed into the Maestro with a sense of prospective novelty. Six nights earlier, at 3:30 A.M., as he drove back from Holland Park Avenue after delivering the *Los Angeles Times* to Gwyn's doorstep, Richard had been successfully charged with drunken driving. This was not a complicated case. He had in fact crashed the car into a police station. Others of us might find so thorough a solecism embarrassing, but Richard was pleased about that part of it because at least it speeded the whole thing up. No hanging around while they radioed in for the Breathalyzer. No being asked to accompany them to the police station . . . Nor for the moment did he particularly regret being so bounteously far over the limit. At least he couldn't remember anything— except the sudden contrast: there you are comfortably driving along, a little lost, perhaps, and with your left hand over your left eye; then the next thing you know you're bouncing up the steps to the police station. And smashing into its half-glass doors. As he drove, now, down Ladbroke Grove toward Holland Park, feeling self-consciously sober and clandestine, Richard remembered what he said, when the three rozzers came crunching out to greet him. No, this was not a complicated case. He rolled down the window and said, "I'm very sorry, Officer, but the thing is I'm incredibly drunk." That, too, got things moving. His appearance in court was scheduled for late November. And the car looked no worse (though it certainly smelled worse, for some reason). And at least it hadn't happened on the way there. "What were you doing, driving around at all hours?" said Gina. Richard gave her a three-quarters profile and said, "Oh. You know. Thinking about things. The new book. And what it might be like. Not being a writer . . ." Yeah, it would be tough, not being a writer. He wouldn't be able to spin Gina any more lines like that one . . .

In the octagonal library, seated on a French armchair, Gwyn Barry *frowned down* at the chessboard. Frowned down at it, as if some gangly photographer had just said, "Could you like *frown down* at it? Like you're really concentrating?" Actually there were no photographers present. Only Richard, who, seated opposite, and playing black, made a move, N(QB5)-K6 in the old notation, N(c4)-e5 in the new, and let his peripheral vision feast on the Sunday *Los Angeles Times*, which lay on a nearby sofa in encouraging disarray. The room was tall and narrow, something of a miniature folly; it felt like the chamber of a beautiful gun or antique missile—the six facets of inlaid bookcases, and then the two facing windows, like blanks. Now Richard gave Gwyn's hair an exasperated glance (so thick, so uniform, so accurately barbered—the hair of a video vicar) before his eyes returned, in brief innocence, to the board. He was a pawn up.

"Do you take the *Los Angeles Times*?" he said wonderingly.

Gwyn seemed to lose the tempo, or the opposition: he paused awkwardly before replying. Richard's last move was of the kind that presents the adversary with a strictly local, and eventually soluble, problem. An adequate—a more than adequate—response was available. Richard had seen it as his fingers retreated from the piece. Gwyn would see it, too, in time.

"No," said Gwyn. "Some stupid bugger sent it to me."

"Why?"

"With a note saying, 'Something here to interest you.' No page number, mind. No marks or anything. And look at it. It's like a bloody knapsack."

"How ridiculous. Who?"

"I don't know. Signed 'John.' Big help that is. I know loads of people called John."

"I always thought it must be quite handy being called John."

"Why?"

"You can tell when you're going nuts."

"Sorry? I don't follow."

"I mean, a real sign of megalomania, when a John starts thinking that 'John' will do. 'Hi. It's John.' Or: 'Yours ever, John.' So what? *Everybody's* called John."

Gwyn found and made the best reply. The move was not just expedient; it had the accidental effect of clarifying White's position. Richard nodded and shuddered to himself. He had forced Gwyn into making a good move: this seemed to happen more and more frequently, as if Richard was somehow out of time, as if Gwyn was playing in the new notation while Richard toiled along in the old.

Richard said, ". . . Gwyn. That's Welsh for John, isn't it?"

"No. Euan. That's Welsh for John."

"Spelt?"

"E, u, a, n."

"How definitively base," said Richard.

He looked down at the sixty-four squares—at this playing field of free intelligence. Oh yeah? So the intelligence was free, then, was it? Well it didn't *feel* free. The chess set before them on the glass table happened to be the most beautiful that Richard had ever used, or ever seen. For some reason he had neglected to ask how Gwyn acquired it, and anxiously assumed it was an heirloom of Demi's. For surely Gwyn, left to his own devices (his taste, and many thousands of pounds) would have come up with something rather different, in which the pieces consisted of thirty-two more or less identical slabs of quartz/onyx/osmium; or else were wincingly florid and detailed—the Windsor castles, the knights with rearing forelegs and full horse-brass, the practically life-sized bishops with crooks and pointy hats and filigreed Bibles. No. The set was in the austere Staunton measure, the chessmen delightfully solid and firmly moored on their felt (even the pawns were as heavy as Derringers), and the board of such proportion that you did indeed feel like a warrior prince on a hilltop, dispatching your riders with their scrolled messages, and pointing through the morning mist, telescope raised. And not a drop of blood being shed. That's how the valley had looked two minutes ago: Field of the Cloth of Gold. Now it resembled some sanguinary disgrace from a disease-rich era, all pressed men, all rabble, the drunken cripples reeling, the lopped tramps twitching and retching in the ditch. Richard was now staring at what any reasonable player would recognize as a lost position. But he would not lose. He had never lost to Gwyn. It used to be that Richard was better at *everything*: chess, snooker, tennis, but also art, love, even money. How casually Richard would pick up the check, sometimes, at Burger King. How thoroughly, and with how many spare magnitudes, did Gina outshine Gilda. How good *Dreams Don't Mean*

Anything had looked, in hard covers, when placed beside the weakly glowing wallet of Gwyn's crib-notes to *The Maunciple's Tale* . . .

They exchanged knights.

"So what did you do? I suppose you could have just chucked the whole thing out . . . The *Los Angeles Times*. What's the matter with you?"

In formulating this last question Richard had lightly stressed the personal pronoun. For Gwyn was doing something he did more and more often these days, something that brimmed Richard's neck with mumps of hatred. Gwyn was inspecting an object—in the present case, the black knight—as if he had never seen it before. With infant wonder in his widened eyes. Richard really couldn't sit there: opposite somebody pretending to be innocent. Maybe Gwyn had got hold of some novel, by a woman, about a poet, and thought that this was how dreamers and seekers were meant to behave. Another possible explanation was what Richard called the Maggot Theory. According to the Maggot Theory, Gwyn had a maggot in his brain, and every frown, every pout, every pose was directly attributable to the maggot's meanderings and its maulings and above all its meals. Watching Gwyn now, Richard felt the Maggot Theory gaining ground.

"It's a chessman," said Richard. "It's a knight. It's black. It's made of wood. It looks like a horse."

"No," said Gwyn dreamily, placing the piece with his other captures, "I found the thing in the end."

"Found what?"

Gwyn looked up. "The thing about me. The thing that was meant to interest me in the *L.A. Times*."

Richard ducked back to the board.

"My glance just fell on it. Luckily. Look at it. I could have been slaving through that thing all bloody week."

"Now this calls for some serious thought," said Richard in a higher and frailer register. "Around from the king side," he said. Behind him a door opened. "And see what we can find," he continued, "on the queen side."

Demi was entering, or crossing: the library lay between the two drawing rooms. She moved past them with reverent stealth, actually tiptoeing for the central few strides, with knees naively raised. Big, blond, unsatirical, but not quite the other thing either (unburnished, unrefined), Demi performed her tiptoe without ease and without talent. Like the not-so-natural parent, playing a children's game. Richard thought of the flash accountant he had unnecessarily and very temporarily hired, after the American sale of *Aforethought*: how, during the appointment at his place, he had made a show of jovially chasing his daughter from the room, with jangle of keys and coins, with knees raised, past the modern first editions and the texts of tax . . . Demi paused at the far door.

"Brrr," she said.

"Hi Demi."

"It's not very warm in here."

Gwyn turned her way, his eyes bulging uxoriously. To Richard he looked like a clairvoyant who, as a matter of policy, was keen to demystify his profession.

"Why not put a cardy on, love?"

"Brrr," said Demi.

Richard got his head down and, with infinite grief, started working to a different plan.

PART *TWO*

There was the street, as midnight neared, after the rain, glossy, with a noirish wet-downed look. And there was the canal, sickly hued even in the dark, turbid, caustic, like a Chinese medicine of ferocious efficacy. The season was about to change.

Between road and water, Richard sat slumped over a Zombie in the Canal Creperie. He wore a deceptively cheerful red bow tie; he wore a deceptively opulent paisley waistcoat; he wore his hair long at the back to cover that strange and frightening lump on his neck; and he wore dark glasses, behind which the boiling beer-guts of his eye sacs now itched and seeped. Darko had said, on the telephone, that he and Belladonna would meet him here at eleven. It was 12:05. Now a young man sat down opposite in Richard's booth and flattened a book out on the table. His face was ectomorphic and asymmetrical and preoccupied. This wasn't Darko. This wasn't Belladonna.

Richard endeavored to persuade himself that he had good cause for celebration. That morning he had personally delivered the completed text of *Untitled* to the offices of Gal Aplanalp. Over the last twelve days, applying himself with great clarity and focus, Richard had worked almost unprecedentedly hard: reading the *Los Angeles Times*. No, he didn't get Gwyn's copy off him ("Are you finished with that?"), nor did he crouch each midnight by the Barry dustbins waiting for the significantly bulky ten-gallon bag. He considered such stratagems. But instead he went and bought another one right away, incurring the familiar inconvenience and expense, down in Cheapside. This second copy of the *Los Angeles Times* he had just pummeled into a dustbin, en route to the Canal Creperie. He found what he was looking for.

Books, Arts, Entertainment, The Week in Review, Real Estate, Sports. It seemed that he knew the whole thing backwards anyway. Poise, Style, Flair. He read everything from the cookery column to the crossword clues. *Could* it be that there was a special way of preparing egg and chips in the mode of Gwyn Barry? *Was* it possible to contrive a crossword clue out of that vilely vowelless forename, that curt and surly surname (NY wry grab—wait—*agitated* by British novelist? 4,5)? When Richard walked the streets with all his fingertips on his forehead he was saying to himself, am I one? am I two? am I worse? am I better? At night, as he prepared to enter the forests of sleep and temptation, things looked like two things: the ironing board was a deck chair and the mirror was a standing pool. He was being *informed*—the information came at night, to inhume him. Jump-leads of agony: for all this time, jump-leads of agony went from Holland Park to Calchalk Street. What was it? A flux tube, an electric whip with scorpion sting. And now it seemed that the Grove itself was a league-long knout or sjambok, made of London, thoughtlessly wielded by Gwyn Barry and danced to, howling and sweating, by Richard Tull.

Thoughtlessly? It did of course occur to Richard, as he sat in his study scanning the college hockey results or the wheat futures, as he abandoned Barcaloungers, say, and started rereading the weather forecast, that he had been rumbled and finessed—that the *Los Angeles Times* was guilelessly and even winsomely Gwyn-free. But he was basically convinced that Gwyn wouldn't need to pull a flanker on him. The world would do it. Late in the evening of the tenth day he found it. Page eleven, column three: the personals page, in the Classified Section, under "Miscellaneous." It went like this:

"Stephanie." Pet Adoptions. Rottweiler 1 yr. Gentle girl. Plus free hamster given with purchase of cage.
Summertown. Wanted. First ed. of novel by Gwyn Barry.
Swap-Meet Garage Yard Sale. All welc.

He waved to the waitress. No, not another Zombie, thank you; he would try a Tarantula. The young man sitting opposite with his scalene face and his shoulders hunched over his book in the posture of a professional bicyclist—the young man took the opportunity to order a club soda. The waitress lingered, making notes.

The waitresses were less young and pretty than they used to be; but then the Canal Creperie was less young and pretty than it used to be—was now, in fact, the resort of insomniac boozers prepared to pay for, and sit quite near to, the platefuls of food which the law obliged them to order with their drinks. On the table, untouched, there stood a basket of sauce-glued nachos, and heavily cooling tortilla, as inert as an organ on a medical tray. Richard's waitress reappeared with his Tarantula. She looked right through him as he thanked her. Before, girls looked at him and showed interest or no interest. Then, for a while, they looked past him. Now they looked through him. Richard felt a generalized regret, mild, chronic, secretive—like, say, the pang of the domestic tutor with his chaste crush on the family four-year-old who, for once, says her good-nights without favoring him with the usual glance and smile, and he must sniff bravely, and tell himself that children ought to be allowed their childish concerns, and go on talking with the grownups about Aristophanes or Afghanistan . . . They used to look past him. Now they looked through him. Because he no longer snagged on their DNA. Because he was over on the other side, and partly invisible, like all the ghosts who walked there.

Suddenly the young man sank back; he raised his book to chin height and held it aloft like a hand of cards. Richard jolted. The book was *Dreams Don't Mean Anything*. Its author was Richard Tull. There, on the top corner of the back cover, above the bubbles and sequins of its artwork (the effect intended, and not achieved, was one of jazzy icono-clasm), perched a passport-size photograph: Richard Tull at twenty-eight. How clean he looked. How extraordinarily clean.

Richard blushed, and his eyes sought something else to stare at— other photographs, framed and hung, of grinning or glowering movie stars: examples, like the loaf-shaped paper-napkin dispensers and the fluted sugar-pours and the podgy old jukebox, of the eminently exportable culture to which the Canal Creperie had dedicated itself. There were even a couple of American writers up there on the wall, their faces scored by epic wryness, epic celebrity . . . A week after *Aforethought* was published Richard had seen a beamingly intelligent youth frowning and smiling over a copy of the book—on the Underground, at Earl's Court, where Richard then lived. He'd considered saying something. A tap on the shoulder, maybe. A raised thumb. A wink. But he had thought: stay cool. It's my first book. This is obviously going to happen all the time. Get used to it . . . It never happened again, of course. Until now.

"Do you want me to sign that for you?"

The book was lowered. The face was hereby revealed. Its asymme-tries resolved themselves into a smile. The smile was not, in Richard's opinion, a good smile, but it did disclose surprisingly and even sinisterly good teeth. The lower set, in particular, was almost feline in its acuity and depthlessness. Richard's lower teeth were like a rank of men in macks on a stadium terrace, tugged into this or that position by the groans of the crowd.

"Sorry?"

"Do you want me to sign that for you?" He leaned across and tapped the back cover. He removed his dark glasses, but not for long. He smiled gauntly.

The young man did the thing of dividing his stare between photo and face until he said, "Who would have oddsed it? Small world. Steve Cousins."

Richard took the hand that was flexed out to him like a shot card. He felt the rare and uneasy luxury of letting his own name go unannounced. Also he asked himself, with what seemed to be abnormal pertinence, whether he was about to get beaten up. His nuts-and-violence radar used to be good, when he was soberer, and less nuts himself.

Steve said, "I think I saw you one time down the Warlock."

"The Warlock: sure. Are you a player?"

"Not tennis. Not tennis. I always thought tennis was an effeminate game. No offense meant."

"None taken," said Richard sincerely. His impulse now was to flip his wallet onto the table and produce the photographs of his two boys.

"Squash is my game. *Squash.* But I don't play down there. I'm not even a Squash Member. I'm a Social Member."

Everybody knew about the Social Members of the Warlock. They didn't go down there for the tennis or the squash or the bowls. They went down there because they *liked* it.

"Well, I'm injured," said Richard. "Tennis elbow." This was true. Lift a racket? He could hardly lift a cigarette.

His interlocutor nodded: such was life. He was still holding the (closed) book out in front of him; it seemed inevitable, now, that he would have to say something about it. The anxiety this gave rise to led Steve Cousins to consider a rather serious change of plan: from plan A to plan B or plan V, plan O, plan X. To activate plan X he even reached into his pocket for the eyedrop bottle. This was plan X: lace his drink with lysergic acid and then, the minute he started looking nauseous or talking stupid about the funny lights, take him outside, for some air, down the walkway near the water, and kick his teeth out one by one. Scozz paused. Plan A regained its substance. It was like the glow that came up on a stage set. With a soft gulp of effort he said,

"I'm an autodidact."

Yes, listen, thought Richard: he can even say *autodidact* . . . He waved to the waitress. No, not another Tarantula, thank you: he would try a Rattlesnake. Actually Richard was undergoing a series of realizations. Which was just as well. He realized that the young man was not a type. Not an original, maybe; but not a type. He also realized (for the first time) that autodidacts are always in pain. The fear of ignorance is a violent fear; it is atavistic; fear of the unknown is the same as fear of the dark. And finally Richard thought: but, I'm nuts too! Don't be steamrollered: show your own quiddity in the field where the mad contend.

"I got a First at Oxford," said Richard. "Autodidact—that's a tough call. You're always playing catch-up, and it's never wholly that you love learning. It's always for yourself."

This turned out to be a good move of Richard's. It didn't calm the young man, but it made him more cautious. He weighed *Dreams Don't Mean Anything* in his hand and held it out at arm's length, to assess it, to see it in perspective, with parallax. "Interesting," he said.

"Interesting how?"

"You shouldn't smoke, you know."

"Oh really? Why ever not?"

"Toxins. Bad for your health."

Richard took the cigarette out of his mouth and said, "Christ, I know *that* about it. It says on the fucking packet that it kills you."

"You know what? I found it . . . very readable. It's a page-turner."

That proved it. It was clinically impossible that this guy was playing with a full deck. Richard knew very well that nobody found him readable. Everybody found him *un*readable. And all agreed that *Dreams Don't Mean Anything* was even more unreadable than *Aforethought*.

"I read *Aforethought* too. Raced through that one as well."

It hadn't occurred to Richard that these admissions were bluff or hoax. Nor did it seriously occur to him now. And he was right: the young man was telling the truth. But he said because he wanted to cover himself,

"What big thing happens exactly halfway through *Aforethought*?"

"It goes into the—into italics."

"What happens just before the end?"

"It goes back again," said Steve, opening the book and gazing down "fondly," so to speak, at the copyright page (because the modern person isn't always well served by the old adverbs), which also bore, beneath a thick film of polyethylene, the borrowing card of the hospital library he had stolen it from. Not the hospital library from which he had stolen *Aforethought*: the library of the hospital to which Kirk had been transferred, after his second savaging by Beef. With tears in his eyes (and blood-soaked bandages all over his mouth) Kirk told Scozz that Lee was going to have Beef put down. Now Kirk wanted Scozz to go over and do Lee! Scozzy said, "Don't talk fucking stupid." Yet Kirk swore that Beef's death would not pass unavenged . . . If literary courtesy compelled him to have the author sign his own book, then Scozzy had an answer ready. *Dreams Don't Mean Anything* was in very good condition: as new. The wonky-hipped old dears, the wraiths in towel robes awaiting the results of tests, the stoical criminals on the mend from line-of-work spankings and stripings—none of them, apparently had sought solace or diversion in the pages of *Dreams Don't Mean Anything* . . .

"At the Warlock. You play with the other writer."

"Gwyn."

"Gwyn Barry. Best-seller."

"That's him."

"Numero uno. Beyond meteoric. Quite an achievement."

"Yes, it is. Quite an achievement. When what you write is *unadulterated shit.*"

"Total crock."

"The purest trex."

"Complete crap."

Richard looked at him. The eyes lit but narrowed. The bent slot of the mouth. A violent maniac who hated Gwyn's stuff. Why weren't there any more where he came from?

"With the junkie wife."

"Demi? Demeter?"

"Who has a distinct liking for—for our colored brethren."

"Oh come on."

"Do you or do you not know how it goes? First off: she was a classic coke rat. In and out of those deluxe dryout joints. NA. All this. A big blond Lady who likes black stuff. You think that don't get around?"

"When was this? Why *didn't* it get around?"

"See, it's *face.* It's *face.* You're lying on a floor somewhere, right? All blissed out. The reason you're feeling so good is that Lance or whoever has just come in with the white bag and helped you pump it up your nose. And there's this great big solemn schwartzer staring down at you and holding out his hand the way they do." He held out his hand the way they do, with palm slowly upturned. "Everyone else, okay, they're half out of it, but not Lance, who touches nothing stronger than Lilt. You telling me she's going to say no to Lance? 'No thanks, mate'? With the political pressure on her? Half them pushers are only in it for the flip."

"The what?"

"The skirt. The women."

Making it clear, making it entirely clear, how the young man felt about flip: how he felt about women. Often accused of this sin himself (though never by his wife), and largely innocent of it, in his view (in his view he was just candidly and averagely semi-fucked-up, along the usual male lines), Richard could spot genuine woman-hatred at twenty paces. It was something in the eyes or something in the mouth. The mouth, which would soon be thickly salivating as it began the joke about the skunk and the knickers. Again Richard cautioned himself. The young man contained sexual complication. But he wasn't a type. And his mouth wasn't going to start telling the joke.

"Her dad's the Earl of . . ."

"Rieveaulx," said Richard, supplying the simple duosyllable—and intercepting (he imagined) the young man's Polack tonguetwister.

"Big connections. With the so-called press barons. He kept it quiet. This was five years ago. Drug orgies with schwartzers. The Queen's twentieth cousin twice removed. You couldn't keep it quiet now."

"Fascinating," said Richard, who, at this stage, was sleepily considering the lunch he might soon arrange with Rory Plantagenet.

Steve had straightened up. He was looking shrewdly at the copyright page of *Dreams Don't Mean Anything*: there, opposite the pristine borrowing form. If Richard offered to sign it (which, as it happened, he never got round to) Steve would say that he'd fished it out of a cardboard box on the Portobello Road and paid thirty pee for it. He didn't know about literary pride, about literary face: not yet.

"I see—I see it was published . . . way back. What? You uh . . ."

"This very morning I delivered the new one. Breaking a long silence, as they say."

"Yeah? What's it called?"

Richard readied himself. "*Untitled.*"

"Nice. Here's to it. Cheers."

"Cheers. All this with Demi." He was thinking: Demi doesn't drink. He was thinking of Demi at dinner, covering her empty wineglass with her hand. "That's all over now. I mean look. There she is. Happily married."

"My arse. Public relations that is. Don't want to believe everything you see on TV."

"How do you know all this?"

"You remember a Mrs. Shields? Cooks for them. Or did."

"Yeah," said Richard, with slow emphasis but without commitment. "That's my brother's mum."

". . . *Your* mum."

"Half brother."

"Same dad," said Richard, who unfortunately chose this moment to look at his watch. If he had gone on looking across the table he would have known for sure that the young man didn't have a half brother. Or a mum. Or a dad.

"She said she'd never seen a newlywed cry so much."

"And why would that be?"

"She wants kids: Catholic. And he won't have them."

Richard sipped his Rattlesnake with some wariness. He was wondering how good at walking he was going to turn out to be, when the time came. There was still a pretty good guy in here, he reckoned. But his voice was slipping from baritone to bass; and he knew the signs. He said,

"What do you do?"

"You've forgotten my name, haven't you? You've forgotten it."

"Yes. Come to think of it. I've completely forgotten it."

Again the hand was flexed out towards him, tense, vertical—the shot card.

"Steve Cousins. What do I do? Well I could say 'this and that.' As some do. 'Me? Ah you know. This and that.' You know. 'Bit of this. Bit of that.' Thing is I'm in a more fluid thing now. I don't need to interact now, financially. Semiretired if you like. My main activities now are what you'd call recreational."

For a moment they studied each other: quid pro quo. To Richard (who was "pixelated," and thoroughly, in the old sense), Steve looked like a white-and-gray chessboard: like a forensic suspect on TV, his face smeared into squares. To Steve (who was Sunday-best sober, as always), Richard looked like an artistic two-dimensionalization of himself, hollow, wavery, approximate and rendered with minimum talent: the work of a court portraitist. Richard was a witness. Richard was a character witness.

"So?" said Richard. He sipped and waited.

And Scozzy shrugged and said, "I fuck people up."

Richard turned in his seat. He felt that this called for another Rattlesnake.

The Little Magazine now lived in Soho, where it had only recently arrived and would not long remain. *The Little Magazine* had seen better days. The offices of *The Little Magazine* were little offices, and the rent was overdue.

The Little Magazine was born and raised in a five-story Georgian town house next to the Soane Museum in Lincoln's Inn Fields (1935–1961). Dusty decanters, hammocklike sofas, broad dining tables strewn with books and learned journals: here a handsome philanderer in canvas trousers bashing out an attack on Heinrich Schliemann ("*The Iliad* as war *reportage*? *The Odyssey* as ordnance survey cum captain's log? Balderdash!"); there a trembling scholar with his eleven thousand words on Housman's prosody ("and the triumphant rehabilitation of the trochee"). From the swards of Lincoln's Inn *The Little Magazine*—increasingly nomadic and downwardly mobile—had made its way to Fenchurch Street, to Holborn, to Pimlico, to Islington, to King's Cross (1961–1979). It slept in attics, in spare rooms, it dossed down on the floors of friends; it was always seeking cheaper lodgings. There used to be something reassuringly Edwardian, something defiantly scapegrace, in these compulsive changes of address (1979–1983). No longer.

The Little Magazine, for many years now, had lurked and lurched across town with the ruddily averted face of bum or bag lady. Evicted often and forcibly from this or that blighted flatlet, it sometimes lingered in the dark behind the beaten door like a reeking squatter in his vest. The money was running out. The money was always running out. Its identity—the only thing it had plenty of—was patrician; its owner and editor, despite the desperate squalor of his surroundings, always wore a monocle and took frequent pinches of snuff. Prodigiously inefficient and self-pitying, *The Little Magazine* drained money from anyone who went anywhere near it. Push your way past its hardboard door, in your silk hat and cashmere overcoat, and after a couple of weeks you too would be sleeping rough. On the other hand *The Little Magazine* really did stand for something. It really did stand for something, in this briskly materialistic age. It stood for not paying people. And when it did pay people, it paid them little and it paid them late. Printers, landlords, taxmen, milkmen, contributors, staff: it paid them next to nothing and always at the very end of the eleventh hour. No one knew what happened to the "contributions"—the minor loans, the royal ransoms—which *The Little Magazine* impartially processed: the dole-checks and dowries, the nest-eggs, the five-generation brewing fortunes. Some magazines were success stories, but *this* magazine was a sob story: even Richard Tull, after a year of unremunerated labor in its offices, found himself writing out a check for a thousand pounds, made payable to the monocled threnodist in the editor's chair . . . Richard edited the back half. He often edited the front half too. Every other Monday he went in and did the books. Every other Friday he went in and did the arts. All the rest of the time, it seemed, he spent writing the "middles"—unpaid, of course, and also unsigned, although "everybody" (in fact a select company) was supposed to know he had written them.

Today was Friday. Here came Richard. Umbrella, bow tie, portly biography wedged into the armpit, cigarette. He paused, on Frith Street, as he approached the triptych of doorways which *The Little Magazine* shared with a travel agent and a shop that sold clothes to the very tall and the very fat—he paused, and looked down. He looked down because the tramp he was stepping over (who intently ate dog food from the can with a plastic spoon) bore a close resemblance to his opera critic. So close that Richard even said, "Hugo?" But the tramp wasn't Hugo. Or Hugo wasn't the tramp. Not yet: not this week. Richard went inside and was relieved to see Hugo lying facedown on the stairs to the first-floor office. He stepped over Hugo and paused again in a marveling attempt to identify the source of the seal-house or dolphinarium sound effects (the hooting and squeal-ing, the egregious belly-flops) which issued from the half-landing toilet. It was his ballet critic: Cosmo. Then he entered the literary department. His secretary came forward and helped him off with his mack.

"Thank you. Well, Anstice?"

Anstice, with her head dipped, told him what he needed to be told. He didn't need to be told about the opera critic or the ballet critic—or the radio critic, who stood nearby with his head out the window, rubbing his eyes and panting rhythmically, or the art critic who sat at the books table weeping into his drenched hands. Richard asked about the film critic, who, very ominously, had slipped out some hours ago for a packet of cig-arettes. But he was pleased to hear that the theater critic, who was writ-ing the lead review that fortnight, was emplaced in his usual nook farther up the stairs. Very shortly Richard went to see how he was doing. There Bruno sat at his little table, his bearded face immersed, as usual, in his typewriter keys. Richard reached out for a firm handful of his crackling hair, and tugged: thus he saw that Bruno, before losing consciousness, had very nearly completed the first word of his piece. What he had writ-ten, so far, was "Chehko." And Richard happened to know that Bruno's subject that fortnight was a new production of *The Three Sisters*. He regained the literary department in time to see the film critic mount the stairs in such a fury of dissimulated torpor that he would surely have hurled himself into the far wall beyond Anstice's desk. But the kneeling figure of the ballet critic was there to check his stride. Richard stepped over them and went to the editor's office on the floor above, which he always hid in when the editor wasn't hiding in it.

What he wanted to know was this. Why had he received no word from Gal Aplanalp? Why wasn't the telephone bouncing on its cradle? Where was the long, favorable and riveted critique of *Untitled*? And how high were Steve Cousins's rates? Richard wondered what was stopping him from just going ahead and ringing Gal Aplanalp. Pride, he supposed; and a sense of his own artistic worth. So he lit a cigarette and went ahead and called Gal Aplanalp.

"It's all going forward," she said. "In fact it's placed."

She was referring, of course, not to his novel but to his projected five thousand–word profile of Gwyn Barry, which had inspired broad and competitive interest. Gal named a sum of money which exactly corresponded to Richard's annual salary at *The Little Magazine*. After a silence he said,

"What about my book?"

"I know. I've cleared the weekend for it. I'm taking it home tonight. Gwyn says it's remarkable."

"Gwyn hasn't read it."

"Oh," said Gal Aplanalp.

Having said good-bye and hung up, Richard managed to apply himself to some constructive work. Ringing round various publishers, he identified and called in three books for review. One was by Lucy Cabretti. One was by Elsa Oughton. One was by Professor Stanwyck Mills. These authors, we might remember, were the judges of the Profundity Requital. Ringing round various contributors, Richard then entrained three favorable notices. We must trust him on this. He had his reasons. Richard was about to get up and go and find her when Anstice slowly put her head round the door. Her face blinked at him.

"Is there anything I should be worrying about, Anstice?"

"Oh no. I expect we shall soldier through."

"Cosmo seems much improved. So does Hugo."

"You know, I really respect Hugo for the way he's getting to grips with it. No, it's Theo."

"Oh?"

By a long-established anomaly, the last page of the books (it was the batched fiction review) was put to bed on the same day as the arts. Now you expected no trouble whatever on the batched fiction review. It was *The Little Magazine*'s plum job, often squabbled and feebly brawled over: he who wrote the batched fiction review ended up with perhaps a dozen new hardbacks to sell to the man in Chancery Lane. Richard wanted to write the batched fiction review. Even the editor wanted to write it.

Anstice said, "He wants to know if he can fax it in."

"He hasn't got a fax. *We* haven't got a fax."

"That's what I told him."

"Well tell him to get out of bed and get dressed and get on the bus and bring it in. Like he always does."

"He sounded a bit . . ."

"No doubt he did." Richard told her that if she could bear it—and if indeed Theo had written it—she should simply phone him up and have him slur it in. Before she went he said, "How are you?"

"Pretty well, really. For a ruined woman. One roughly used and then cast aside. R. C. Squires was in here."

"How horrible. Is he coming back?"

"I don't know. Will I be seeing you later?"

"Of course, Anstice," he said.

She left. She left slowly, her presence reluctantly receding from him. When it was there no longer his head dropped suddenly like a weight. It hung, at right angles to the sheen of his paisley waistcoat. Having dropped about forty-five degrees . . . Which is a lot, on some scales, by some reckonings. For example, Barnard's Star, as it is called, crosses 10.3 seconds of arc per year. This is a quarter of the Jupiter pinpoint—about a sixth of a degree: per year. Yet no other heavenly body shows so great a proper motion. This is why it is called the Runaway Star . . . And just by dropping his head like that Richard was changing his temporal relationship with the quasars by thousands and thousands of years. He really was. Because the quasars are so far away and getting farther away so fast. This is to put Richard's difficulties in context. The context of the universe.

Eleven hours later he was emplaced with Anstice in the Book and Bible. The paper had been put to bed. To put to bed was what you did with children—whereas grownups *took* each other there.

Crooned at and lullabied, given snacks and glasses of water, its fears assuaged, *The Little Magazine* had been put to bed. Bruno, the theater critic, had finished his major piece on *The Three Sisters*. Unfortunately it proved to be only thirty words long. The opera critic, Hugo, had failed to write anything at all, despite spending the afternoon in a sinkful of iced water and despite engaging, with Anstice, in a program of deep-breathing exercises which reminded Richard of the classes he had attended with Gina: the adults sitting around on the floor and gazing up at teacher like the children they would shortly bear. Otto, the radio critic, finished his piece and then tore it up and threw it out the window. Several heads slewed round, at first in dismay and then in hard suspicion, when Inigo, the film critic, said through his tears that he was betraying his poetry by writing for money. You mean someone around here was getting *money*? Towards dusk it looked for a while as though Richard and Anstice would be faced with another Black Friday. This was the occasion on which all seven arts writers—grouped about the place in varying postures of weary contemplation—had produced not a syllable between them. And Richard had hurled together a ragged quilt of house ads, overmatter, crosswords and killed chess columns.

"Inigo was amazing," said Anstice, finishing her white wine.

"Inigo was incredible," said Richard, finishing his scotch.

Inigo was also lying on the carpet at their feet. A man of great and curdled abilities, as they all were, kind of, Inigo had written 7,500 largely coherent words about a Bulgarian cartoon—the only thing he had seen, or remembered seeing, over the past two weeks.

Piously Anstice dipped her head. Richard stared, as he often stared, at the center-parting of her hair. Here, it seemed, two opposing forces met and with bristling difficulty contended. Oh dear, oh my: those people you see on streetcorners, when their hair is not just bad but wrong, too obviously comprising individual and uncoordinated strands, not just curled but bent, twisty, and propagating at all the wrong angles. Anstice's hair grew with futile force; here was the ponytail, as weighty as old navy rope, reaching to the gathered lap of her smock. Her hair looked never-washed, Rasta-like. She lifted her head and smiled at him slowly with that flicker of apologetic tenderness.

"Last one?" he said.

When he came back from the bar he thought Anstice might be turned to the wall and staring at the backs of her own eyes and singing scraps of songs—the crazed ditties, perhaps, of the ruined Ophelia. Not much less ominously, Anstice had her face over the table; her nose was perhaps an inch from its surface. Without stirring she said, as he sat,

"The time has come for us to tell Gina. Or else why go on? It's all right. We'll do it together. We'll tell Gina *everything*."

Richard thought he would probably end up with Anstice. He thought he would probably end up with Anstice. Would they marry? No. It was on his way out of her flat that morning, a year ago, that he had coined the word *spinst*. There was just no avoiding it. This is *spinst*, pal, he said to himself. We're talking *spinst* here. And I do mean *spinst*. He meant the blast-wave of spinst that he had walked into on arrival. He meant the mantle of spinst he had walked away with, as if he was wearing her clothes, her sheets, her towels, her hair. It was the smell of clothes not taken to the dry cleaners for many years; it was the smell of rain-dam-aged ceilings; but above all it was the smell of neglect. Richard knew about neglect and understood neglect. But neglect in the physical sense? These days he kept thinking he smelled of *batch*. Of old pajamas and slippers and cardigans and pipe cleaners. But I can't, he kept saying. I can't smell of batch. I'm married. In his study, with a biography on his lap, sniffing at his own shoulder, and then looking up suddenly, and frowning, and waving a hand to adduce his fastidious wife, his sweet-smelling children, whom he still had. And then it wasn't long before he saw himself alone, and with his single worn suitcase mounting the damp stairs to Anstice's. Spinst and Batch would come together, in eternal head-to-head. Batch and Spinst, in timeless morris.

"Bloody hell," said Gina. "Have you seen *this*?"

Richard looked up long enough to make sure that *this* wasn't a ten-page letter from Anstice and then looked down again at *Love in a Maze: A Life of James Shirley.* Gina was reading an extensive account, in her tabloid, of a series of murders, somewhere in America. Nearby on the passage floor the twins were playing quietly and even tenderly with their violent toys. Saturday morning, at the Tulls'.

The trouble with getting Gwyn beaten up . . . Richard strove to be more specific. The trouble with getting Gwyn catapulted into his seventies was this: Gwyn would never know that it was Richard who had cata-pulted him there. Only a moron, true, would have failed to *suspect* (uneasily) that it was Richard who was responsible for the *Los Angeles Times*. But Gwyn *was* a moron: according to Richard. And you couldn't expect a moron—particularly a moron who was upside down in a dustbin or groping for consciousness in Intensive Care—to suspect that Richard was responsible for Steve Cousins. No, the whole thing lacked justice: artistic justice. Richard found himself increasingly drawn to another quest or project, something more classical, something simpler, something nobler. He was going to seduce Gwyn's wife.

"Why?" said Gina. "I just can't . . . Ooh."

His head, today, was full of women, as it always was, but not just the opposite sex. Genuine individuals—there was Gina, there was Anstice, there was Demeter. There was also Gal Aplanalp: lying on her bed and clad in her ankle bracelet, curled up with *Untitled*, and lightly frowning with amused admiration. There was also Gilda: Gilda Paul . . . When Gwyn took up with Demi, he ended it with Gilda, his teenhood sweet-heart, and with some dispatch: he ended it the next morning. One moment Gilda was living with a little Welsh scrivener with two dud novels under his belt, plus a stack of A-Level Guides; the next, she was being helped on to a train by the cult author of a surprise best-seller, at Euston, with her cracked plastic suitcase and her podgy green overcoat, heading for Swansea and a full nervous breakdown. At that stage Richard was already in need of a good-looking reason for hating his oldest friend, and Gilda's collapse, at first, seemed like a breath of fresh air. To strengthen his case, morally, he even traveled, with the flat smile of the deeply inconvenienced, to the cliffside hospital in Mumbles and sat for an hour with Gilda's dank white hand in his, while one TV spoke English and another TV spoke Welsh, in a room whose light seemed to come from the brick-red tea and the orange-brown biscuits, and peopled by women, none of them old, whose favorite food (how did this notion come to him, over the fumes of the bloody tea?)—whose favorite food was *brains*. Richard still wrote to Gilda. His letters tended to coincide with some fresh coup of Gwyn's, or with some new gobbet of praise that made mention of his humanity or—better—his compassion. Rather regrettably, perhaps, Richard sent her a print interview in which Gwyn mentioned Gilda and characterized their parting as "amicable." Only occasionally did he suggest that the true story was something that the public—or Rory Plantagenet—deserved to learn. Richard was pleased that Gwyn had never been to see Gilda. Richard hoped he never would. Richard didn't really care about Gilda, of course. Richard really cared about Demi.

"I mean . . . *why*?" said Gina. "Ooh, if I had my way."

He looked up. Gina's hand was at her throat. An hour ago, his lips had been where that hand was now. And it hadn't worked out . . . Richard's stare returned to the index of *Love in a Maze: A Life of James Shirley. The Maid's Revenge, The Traitor, Love's Cruelty, The Lady of Pleasure, The Imposture, Love in a Maze.* While contemplating the seduction of Lady Demeter, Richard had no mustache he could twirl, no barrelly chortles he could summon: the Jacobean boudoir creeper had a big advantage over Richard. You couldn't imagine, say, Lovelace holding his shoes by their buckles as he limped from the bedroom in tears. You couldn't imagine Heathcliff propped up in the four-poster, with a forearm resting limply on his brow, telling Catherine how anxious and overworked he must be. Things seemed to start loosening up after 1850. Bounderby, in *Hard Times*: an obvious no-show merchant. And as for Casaubon, in *Middlemarch*, as for Casaubon and poor Dorothea: it must have been like trying to get a raw oyster into a parking meter. Acute and chronic impotence, Richard knew, was no kind of springboard for a seduction operation. But he had information on her now, which always meant the vulnerable, the hidden, the intimate, the shame-steeped. It panned out. And he couldn't be accused of trying to deceive Gwyn. Because there wasn't any point in it unless he got caught.

"Words," said Gina, "—words fail me. *Why*? Won't someone tell me."

Slowly sliding from his chair, Richard took up position behind her. The center pages of Gina's tabloid described the trial, and conviction, of a child-murderer in Washington State. There was a photograph. You could see him. He stood there in his prison fatigues, his eyes introspectively recessed, his upper lip exaggeratedly cupid's bow, the shape of a gull coming right at you. "I'm sorry! I'm sorry!" shouted one of his victims, according to witnesses: a little boy, stabbed to death by an adult stranger in the neighborhood playground. The little boy's brother was also stabbed to death. He didn't say anything. There was also a third and much younger child whom the murderer kept for several days, beforehand.

Gina said, "Look at the face on that horrible queer."

Marius entered the kitchen and, without ceremony, presented his parents with the contention that he "looked like shit" in his school photograph. The school photograph was produced and exhibited. Marius *didn't* look like shit.

"You *don't* look like shit," said Richard authoritatively. He felt he knew all there was to know about looking like shit. "You look good."

"I think that's so awful," said Gina, "the little boy saying 'I'm sorry, I'm sorry' like that."

The young swear more now, and the old swear more now. This is perhaps the only area in which your parents can shock you as much as your children. The middle-aged swear more too, of course, in reflexive protest against their failing powers.

"I'm sorry! I'm sorry!" cried the little boy to the adult stranger in the neighborhood playground. The little boy's brother was also stabbed to death. He didn't shout, "I'm sorry! I'm sorry!" He was older and maybe he knew something that his little brother didn't know.

Among its many recent demotions, *motive* has lost its place in the old law enforcement triumvirate: means, motive, opportunity. Means, motive, opportunity has been replaced by witnesses, confession, physical evidence. A contemporary investigator will tell you that he hardly ever thinks about motive. It's no help. He's sorry, but it's no help. Fuck the why, he'll say. Look at the how, which will give you the who. But fuck the why.

"I'm sorry! I'm sorry!" cried the little boy. He thought he had offended and angered his murderer in some way, without meaning to. He thought that that was the why. The little boy was searching for motivation, in the contemporary playground. Don't look. You won't find it, because it's gone. I'm sorry. I'm sorry.

A square of city rather than a city square, it branched out like an inbred slum family whose common name was Wroxhall. Wroxhall Road, then Wroxhall Street. Wroxhall Terrace, then Wroxhall Gardens. Then Court, Lane, Close, Place, Row, Way. Drive, then Park, then Walk. Richard locked the Maestro, whose days were numbered, and turned to confront a landscape out of one of his own novels—if you could speak of landscape, or of *locus*, or of anywhere at all, in a prose so diagonal and mood-warped. Actually this is as good a time as any to do what Gal Aplanalp is doing and take a quick look at Richard's stuff—while the author stumbles, swearing, from Avenue to Crescent to Mews, in search of Darko, and of Belladonna.

Essentially Richard was a marooned modernist. If prompted, Gwyn Barry would probably agree with Herman Melville: that the art lay in pleasing the readers. Modernism was a brief divagation into difficulty; but Richard was still out there, in difficulty. He didn't want to please the readers. He wanted to stretch them until they twanged. *Aforethought* was first person, *Dreams Don't Mean Anything* strictly localized third; both nameless, the I and the he were author surrogates and the novels comprised their more or less uninterrupted and indistinguishable *monologues interieurs*. *Untitled*, with its octuple time scheme and its rotating crew of sixteen unreliable narrators, sounded like a departure, but it wasn't. As before, all you had was a voice. This was the basket that contained all the eggs. And the voice was urban, erotic and erudite . . . Although his prose was talented, he wasn't trying to write talent novels. He was trying to write genius novels, like Joyce. Joyce was the best yet at genius novels, and even he was a drag about half the time. Richard, arguably, was a drag *all* the time. If you had to settle on a one-word description of his stuff then you would almost certainly make do with *unreadable*. *Untitled*, for now, remained unread, but no one had ever willingly finished its predecessors. Richard was too proud and too lazy and—in a way—too clever and too nuts to write talent novels. For instance, the thought of getting a character out of the house and across town to somewhere else made him go vague with exhaustion . . .

He reached a corner. Wroxhall *Parade*? Across the road was a wired children's playground populated not by children (note the silence) but by menacingly sober old drunks, behind seesaw, behind jungle-gym, between swings and roundabouts. Would New York be like this? On his way here Richard had noticed all the speed bumps. Sleeping policemen were the only kind of policemen you would find in such a land, a land of stay-away and no-go. Richard walked past yet another scorched mattress. Revelation would come, hereabouts, in the form of the mattress-fire . . . Richard continued to write about this world but he hadn't actually walked around in it for six or seven years. All he did, nowadays, with this world, was drive through it, in the vermilion Maestro.

As he made towards the given address, and identified it, he paused and turned and gave his surroundings one last dutiful sweep of the eyes. The pale wire, the brutalist hairdos of the lopped trees. Poverty said the same thing, century after century, but in different kinds of sentences. The sentences spoken by what confronted him here would be short sentences, rich in nothing but solecism and profanity. Now how did this tie in with the mangled syllogism, arrived at ten hours earlier over a cup of tea and a stupefied cigarette, following the usual failure with Gina. Going something like:

A. Gwyn's trex was loved by the world; his trex was universal.
B. The world loved trex; the world was trex.
C. Better *use* the world, in that case; better have Gwyn picked on by something his own size . . .

No need for Richard to knock himself out, humping the *Los Angeles Times* all over town. Or seeking the hospitality of the pages of *The Little Magazine* for that gory "middle" he was forever rehearsing in his mind. Literature couldn't do it. The world could fucking do it . . . As Richard climbed the steps, the supposedly superseded notion of paying money to get Gwyn beaten up returned to him with all the freshness of discovery.

As promised, the front door was unlatched ("I guarantee it," Darko had said). Steadying himself in the hall Richard heard the sound of a sander or a plane-saw: a plane-saw whining for its plane-saw mummy. It was the noise of dental pain: it was the noise of pain. *The weak link is you*, Steve Cousins had said, in the Canal Creperie. If we do this, he had said, the weak link is you. If someone leaned on you—you'd break. People don't know pain and fear, he had said. *I* know pain and fear. Pain and fear are my friends. I'm watertight. The weak link is you . . . Richard had always thought that he knew pain and fear; but he didn't—not yet. Pain and fear were waiting for him, as they waited for everyone. A whole hospice of pain and fear, patiently waiting.

He knocked on the first inner door he came to. Darko opened it. A Transylvanian confrontation, just for a second: Darko's eyes were redder than his red hair, redder than the Maestro. He looked Richard up and down, and said, as if identifying him by name, "Charisma bypass." Very soon they were standing in a room roughly the size of a tennis court and filled with furniture that might have come from anywhere or even everywhere: from the SCRs of provincial sociology departments, from business hotels, from schoolrooms, from barracks.

Turning, Richard said boldly, "Where are you from, Darko? Originally."

"From the place I still call Yugoslavia."

Darko was standing in the middle of the room's kitchen district and staring down at some kind of foodstuff splayed on a plate. Now he looked up, and smiled. Long upper lip with a feathery mustache on it; long upper gum, also gingery in hue.

"Are you Serb or Croat? Out of interest."

"I don't accept that distinction."

"Yes. Well. There isn't any ethnic distinction, is there. Just religion. Nothing visible." On the mantelpiece Richard thought he saw a devotional knickknack or icon, lit from within by a bulb the shape of a closed tulip; it was the Virgin Mary (he sensed), but travestied, with joke breasts outthrust like the figure of a redoubtable maiden on a ship's prow. "Isn't there some big deal about the sequence of making the sign of the cross? In the war, in the world war, Croat soldiers rounded up children and got them to make the sign of the cross. To see which way they did it. To see if they lived or died."

This was obviously news to Darko: fresh information. Richard tried to relax himself with the following thought: that nowadays, in a sense, you could know more about a stranger than the stranger knew about himself. Recently he had involved himself in an argument on his doorstep with a proselytizing Mormon (soon to be sent on his way with a taunt) who had never heard of Moroni: Moroni, the nineteenth-century American angel, the Messiah of the wild-goose chase in whose name the bearded ranter trudged from house to house. Big clue, that: Moroni. Moron with an *i* on the end of it. Moronic without the *c*.

Darko said, "I believe that everyone is a human being."

"I buy that too. Belladonna, I take it, is a human being. I mean I assume she exists. Where is she?"

"Getting dressed. Getting undressed. What's the diff? Now what do I do with this cholesterol bomb?"

He gestured at the dish and what it contained. The dish glowed back up at him like the palette of a busy artist: some modern primitive who worked in pastels.

"Bung it in the fucking MW," Darko decided.

MW equaled microwave. That was good. The word had fewer syllables than its abbreviation. Especially good, especially self-defeating, because the microwave was a device intended to cheat time. Anyway Darko had already heated it, and was already eating it—his mango pizza or pomegranate rissole—with both hands . . . On a video he'd hired and admired, Richard remembered the motorist hero referring to his FWD, or four-wheel drive. One might add that there are certain frolicsome cosmologists who refer to "the WYSIWYG universe," or "What You See Is What You

Get." To be fair, this isn't an abbreviation but an acronym. They don't actually stand there and say Double-U-Why-Ess-Eye-Double-U-Why-Gee. They stand there and say *Wysiwig*. Those assholes. Whom we ask to do the job of wondering how we're here. The WYSIWYG universe is the one in which *dark matter*, the overarching shadow comprising perhaps 97 percent of universal mass, remains unexotic, the usual proton-neutron-electron arrangement, just planets, possibly, bigger than Jupiter but not big enough to shine, "massive compact halo objects," known (what is it with these guys?) as MACHOS. What *is* it with these guys? The "free lunch" universe. The "designer" universe. The "charisma bypass" universe? Sending their minds back eighteen billion years, they reach for catchphrases that were getting old eighteen months ago.

"Will Belladonna be joining us? And tell me more," said Richard, making sure there was plenty of amusement in his tone, "about her thing with Gwyn Barry."

Darko held up a finger while he finished a demanding mouthful, one that involved much tongue work on all four sets of molars. At last he said, "Who?"

"Belladonna."

"You mean Diva. She's called Diva now. Now I don't know Diva mega-well."

"Is that right."

"With men, everywhere you look there's Divagate."

No, not *divagate*: Divagate. Like Watergate, etcetera.

"A lot going on," Richard suggested. "More than meets the eye."

"She gives good girlrock, I reckon. Yep."

Richard went on standing there.

"Oh yeh," said Darko with resignation. "Diva's wild for the wild thing."

"Have you known her mega-long? Where is she, for instance?"

Darko excused himself and left the room through a door beyond the kitchen. When he came back he looked at Richard suddenly and said, "Who are you?"

"Richard. Who are you?"

"Ranko."

"You mean Darko."

"Darko is my twin brother. He's Croat. I'm Serb. We look the same but we've got nothing in common."

"Well you both eat pizza. You've still got a bit of it hanging from your mustache."

The man stood there neutrally, continuing to clean his teeth with his tongue. "She's getting up," he said. "Me I'm off out."

Richard was alone in the room he should never have entered for only five or six turbulent seconds, while one door closed and another opened. If you could have micro-monitored this time frame you would have found: fear of injury, disease and murder, fear of the dark that was now descending, fear of poverty, of poor rooms, fear of Gina and her swelling irises; despair for the stranded self and its timidly humming blood; and, among all these fears and hates, the sense of relief, of clarity and surety a man feels, at the prospect of temptation, when he knows he has washed his cock before leaving the house. He took one smeared glance at Diva as she came slanting into the room and thought: hopeless. He's safe. I'm safe. Not deadly nightshade. Just poison ivy. We're all safe.

"Hi."

"Hi."

"Richard," she said.

"Diva."

She turned a full circle and looked up at him, saying, "Belladonna. That's me."

Richard surveyed her, now (he felt), with a census-taker's detachment. No doubt she would have laughed in his face to hear him say so (she was probably a goth or a grrrl or a bombo: I haven't yet read the Saturday newspapers, he thought, with a self-fortifying swallow, but Belladonna was a punk. That is to say, she had gone at herself as if to obliterate the natural gifts. Her mascara she wore like a burglar's eye-mask; her lipstick was approximate and sanguinary, her black hair spiked and lopped and asymmetrical, like the pruned trees outside the window. Punk was physical democracy. And it said: let's all be ugly together. This notion held a lot of automatic appeal for Richard—for Richard, who would not mind being poor if no one was rich, who would not mind looking rough if no one looked smooth, who would not mind being old if no one was young. He certainly didn't mind being nuts, though, however many were sane; in fact he was really enjoying it, and believed it was the only good thing that had happened to him for years. She was very young and very small and very brown. With effective perversity she wore her underwear as over-wear: floppy pink knickers over the black cycling pants; tight white bra emblazoning the black T-shirt. Her voice was London. Richard could not place her, ethnically. He thought she probably came from some island.

She said, "You're not like I imagined you."

"Really?" This was a novel idea: that anyone imagined him. He said lightly, "You mean I'm different from my book reviews?"

Belladonna looked for somewhere to sit down, and selected the sofa.

"You're not as I imagined you either."

"Yeah?"

"You're so young. I don't know. You don't seem to be Gwyn's type."

"He's like . . . in love with me."

With a defiant shake or twitch of the head. On the word *love*.

"Is he now?" said Richard as he sat beside her. She was gazing down at her clasped hands: anchorectic Belladonna. He found himself entertaining the reckless hope that she was already pregnant. "And how do you feel about that?"

"Pleased, obviously. Proud. I know he's married or whatever."

"Are you . . .? I mean has this been going on long?"

She smiled secretively. "You know what my thing is? Read my lips." *My thing*, she said silently, *is my mouth*.

"Your mouth."

"That's what they call me: The Gob. The Mush. Ever since I was little I had this *mouth*." *My thing is my mouth. I'm famous for my mouth*.

"You're still little," said Richard.

Here, he thought, we had the second punk principle. Everyone their own artist. Everyone their own legend. That guy's thing is to have a kilo of old newspapers glued to his hair, that girl's to wear a clothespeg through her cheek. Belladonna's thing was her mouth. Richard felt the contradiction (or would later feel it: he was busy now), because the talent was still no-talent, still idly particular, with no claim on the universal. It picked on a contradiction of Richard's. He wouldn't mind having no genius, if no one else had any? No, not true. He did want people to have it, genius; he wanted it to be out there.

Come and look, Belladonna mouthed. *Look closely*. She leaned back and adjusted the head of the angle-poise lamp, as if she was her own dentist. Richard—a consultant, a second opinion—bent himself nearer. *I've never had a filling*, he saw her say, her lower lip answering, as in a dance, to the movement of the tongue. Her teeth were indeed pitilessly perfect. *Look how long my tongue is* . . . Belladonna's mouth: Richard almost had his nose in it. And he knew he would never feel the same way about women's mouths again, how internal they were, how red and pink and white and wet. Yes, that was right: like a lateral and platonically perfect pubis, containing thirty-two teeth. There was no confusion here. He knew where the teeth were and where they weren't. Before he sat back he let her breath register on him and he found its taste was sweet, but sweet like a medicine, not like a fruit.

"There are tricks I can do with it."

Her tongue appeared and arched up and settled its straining sting on the tip of her nose. Then it withdrew, and the mouth smiled, and said, "Or this." Now the lips distended and scrolled away from one another. They said, "Blackface." The teeth and gums within looked distant, like a mouth within a mouth. Reconstituted, the mouth mouthed, *Take my hand.*

He obeyed her. It was a normal hand, too, but he could hardly connect it with Belladonna, who was, as she said, as her mouth said, just a mouth.

Which said "Watch" as the free hand approached it and then disappeared into it, wrist-deep.

Richard turned away, in search of his identity. All he could find was some very worn old stuff. "You want to be careful," he said, "who you show that to."

"I am." Her whole face was looking at him with indulgent reproach. *I am.*

When she switched off the lamp Richard realized that the room had been smoothly and silently invaded by the adulterous light of dusk; the light that lovers know, intimate and isolating and flatteringly amber. In this particular spasm of his spousal evolution, adultery was a red-light district, and the red just meant danger. He had been in wrong rooms before. He had been in wrong rooms before, but they tended to be better appointed than the one in which he now lurked. The circumambient red was the red of Darko's gums, closing on the *fruit vert.* A year ago, with Anstice, he had shed his clothes in one of these wrong rooms. What saved him from technical adultery, on that occasion, was a mysterious inner strength, something mysterious even to himself (though he knew a whole lot more about it now): impotence . . . What starts to go, around now, he had decided, is not necessarily the hard-on but the *sensation* of the hard-on. And with the loss of that sensation (the hurting blood) goes the loss of the belief, the loss of the transcendence and, very soon afterwards (before you know it, in fact), the loss of the hard-on. Such as it was. In its stead, the little death, the little death of ruined powers, of dud magic. Anyway, sensation informed him that impotence would not save him now, if it came to it. Some other dynamic would be obliged to intercede. The most likely candidate, at present, was premature ejaculation. He thought: I'm here because I'm scared of dying. *I didn't do it. Death did.*

His life, his whole life, was approaching its third-act climax. There would be two acts to follow. The fourth act (conventionally a quiet act). And then the fifth. What genre did his life belong to? That was the question. It wasn't pastoral. It wasn't epic. In fact, it was comedy. Or anti-comedy, which is a certain kind of comedy, a more modern kind of comedy. Comedy used to be about young couples overcoming difficulties and then getting married. Comedy wasn't about that now. Romance, which used to be about knights and wizards and enchantment, was now about young couples getting married—romance, supermarket romance. Comedy was about other things now.

"There's a test I do on boys," she said. Richard showing interest, she continued, "Just tell me. I'll go out of the room and then come back in again and do whatever you want."

"How do you mean?"

"It's simple. Just tell me and I'll do it."

"What kind of thing?"

"Whatever. Your favorite."

"My favorite what?"

"Don't be shy. You know: any little thing. Your favorite."

"Say I don't have a favorite."

"Everyone has a favorite. They're funny, these little things, sometimes. It tells you so much about someone."

"Yeah, but what *kind* of thing?"

"Anything!"

Abruptly the room reminded Richard of the classroom in the crammer he had attended years ago, on Gwyn's street. Mostly it was the dimensions, he supposed, and the room's intransigently undomestic feel. Perhaps, too, the sense he had then, at eighteen, that he was being graded here for the rest of his life; that information about himself, welcome or unwelcome, was on its way, and getting nearer.

"Do you like doing this test on boys?"

"Yeah I really want to know it about people. What their favorite is."

"Because . . ."

"It tells you so much. About them."

"How many times have you uh, run this test on boys?"

She shrugged expressively—but not enlighteningly. Two or three times? Two or three times a day? Richard thought that there probably wasn't much point in trying to read her manner. Not much point in assigning adverbs to it, and so on (proudly, indignantly, flusteredly). As was the case with Steve Cousins, Belladonna had her feelings and reactions and affectations, but they played to a different and newer rhythm whose beat he didn't know.

"Give me an example. What was Darko's favorite?"

"*Darko*," said Belladonna (proudly, indignantly, flusteredly).

". . . Okay. What's the most usual favorite? What do they usually want you to do?"

"Well, *usually* . . ." She paused—fondly, you might say. Her eyes opened wide, in all innocence. "*Usually* they ask me to go out of the room," she said, "and then come back in nude, and then do a little dance. And then like suck their cocks."

The room gained another magnitude of dark. Who else but lovers—and solitary depressives—would sit in light like this and make no move for the switch?

"I always think it's the trick I show them with my hand. That makes them choose that. So go on. What's your favorite?"

But Richard asked, "What was Gwyn's favorite?"

"Gwyn." And here the adverbs would say thoughtfully, wistfully, tenderly. She turned to him, her face still lowered in shadow. Her clothes, as you might expect, emphasized what she liked most about herself and her body, what she was best pleased with, not a body part (in her case) but a certain rotational quality in the waist and hips. She squirmed and smiled and said, "You know I've never actually 'met' Gwyn Barry."

Richard stood up. He was leaving. He was pretty sure he was leaving. "So you don't know him," he said, "mega-well."

"He loves me."

"You mean you think he loves you."

"It's the way he like looks at me."

"When does he look at you?"

"When he's on TV."

"Do a lot of people on TV look at you?"

"No. Only Gwyn," said Belladonna, staring straight ahead, as if conducting a conversation with Richard's trousers. Then she tipped her head back. "You think I'm all mouth, don't you," she said, and let it half-smile and pout and quiver. "I'm not. I'm not. What's your favorite? I want to know."

"Why?"

"So we can make Gwyn jealous."

And Richard was gone.

Gal Aplanalp didn't call.

"Gal Aplanalp is on the phone to me two hours a day," said Gwyn. "Foreign rights. She does it all herself. Alexander used to just give them away. But Gal gets decent bread even from the East Europeans. Gal's great. So much vivacity. So much exuberance. So much love of life."

It seemed to Richard that the maggot that lived in Gwyn's brain had got itself stuck in a corner or a U-bend between the two frontal hemispheres, causing its host to go on standing there (perhaps indefinitely) making faces of chaste and twinkly approval. The two men were in the outer bar of the Warlock, leaning on the quiz machine, or the Knowledge, as it was called hereabouts, even by the cab drivers, for whom the Knowledge had meant crouching for a year on a kid-sized moped with a clipboard up on the handlebars. Gwyn and Richard were not here to play tennis. They were here to play snooker (the Portobello Health and Fitness Center was closed for remodernization). This meant they had to wait for a table. At length, Gwyn's maggot freed its wiggling back leg. His face cleared, and then frowned, watchfully. He was wearing a new tweed jacket; the material was yellowish and tufty, like a lightly chewed corncob.

"Thanks for the first chapter of the new one," said Richard. "Mouthwatering. Is it all like that, more or less?"

"More or less. If it ain't broke, don't fix it—that's what I always say. Proofs will be ready next month. You'll get one."

"I can't wait."

A gum-chewing teenage girl in a hot-pink catsuit walked past, heading for the stairs and the aerobics room. They watched her go.

"Do you wonder," said Gwyn, "do you ever wonder, as you get older, about changing sexuality?"

"What the next batch is like?"

"Because that's progressing at the same rate as everything else. It's all speeded up. They're different now."

"Probably."

"But different in what way? My impression is . . . and this is only from the letters I get, mind . . . my impression is that they're more pornographic. More specialized."

"What letters do you get?"

"There's usually a photograph. And a broad hint at a certain—speciality."

Richard realized that he had always found Gwyn erotically inscrutable. Who cared, when Gwyn was with Gilda? Not for the first time he wondered if—thanks to an impossibly humiliating complication—he was queer for Gwyn in some way. He thought about it. Richard didn't want to kiss Gwyn. It was surely inconceivable that Gwyn wanted to kiss *him*. Anyway, it wasn't going to happen, was it. And Richard didn't really care why he was doing what he was doing.

"Demi's young."

"Not *that* young."

And Richard felt power slowly absent itself from him as Gwyn said,

"She didn't really grow up in the sexual swim. Not sheltered, exactly. Between you and me, she's been around. Not that she remembers that much about it. This was in her cocaine phase. You know. Upper-class girls all have a cocaine phase. When they're born their dads put their names down for the smart dryout clinics. She's even been—she's even had several lovers of West Indian origin."

"You astonish me."

"I'm proud to say it. Good for her! But she's hardly your thoroughly modern miss. Now take fellatio. My impression was, years ago, that some girls did it and some didn't. Or they were like Gilda, and did it on your birthday. Well I bet they all do it now. It's not whether they do it. It's how they do it."

It was like a game when you lost the rhythm of dominance, and you never moved freely but always in reply. Richard said, "There's this girl who wants to meet you."

"Attractive?"

"Extraordinary mouth. She wants to ask you a question."

"What's my favorite color?"

"No. What's your favorite."

Richard then found himself giving Gwyn a gavel-to-gavel account of his experience with Belladonna. As he did so he thought: what was I *playing at* in there? Belladonna was barely seventeen, and out of her mind. Common sense demanded that he should have made her take her clothes off, at least, and do a little dance. Ever since that crepuscular encounter Richard had been adding to the large number of outrageous novelties that were, he discovered (now he came to think about it), his favorite. There was one favorite in particular: the kind of sexual intercourse that involved not an exchange of bodily fluids so much as a full transfer.

"Well," said Gwyn. "Send her over."

"What *is* your favorite?"

"No, no. I just want to fill out the picture. Why knock yourself out for a hamburger when your wife serves chateaubriand every night."

Yes, thought Richard, who had heard this line before: but a hamburger is sometimes just what you fancy. And do you really want chateaubriand every night?

"I would never—I mean, what I have with my lady is just . . ." Gwyn fell silent. The maggot kicked in for a while, as he shook his head with his eyes closed and then nodded his head with his eyes open. "We were making love this afternoon. No. It must have been last night. No. It was *yesterday* afternoon. Or this morning. Anyway. That's not important. We were making love and I was kidding her about one of her West Indian lovers. And she looked up at me and said, 'Darling. Believe—' Ah. Here she is!"

He broke off and greeted his wife as if—as if what? As if this was 1945, and he hadn't seen her since 1939. When that was over Demi regained her balance and stood there, with a change of clothes in her shopping bag, smiling weakly at Richard, who moved forward to kiss her, in his turn.

Gwyn said, "When are you two going to get together? For your in-depth chat about yours truly. It's the least I can do to fix you two up. In exchange for the 'sexy young fan' that Richard is bringing over for me. Come on, Demi—get up those stairs. We don't want any extra inches, do we love."

When Demi had gone on up for her class Gwyn spent the last few minutes filling Richard in on his European deals for *Amelior Regained*. While doing this he used several slang synonyms for the denomination of one thousand. Richard had noticed that as soon as any novelist clawed his way past three figures he immediately started trying out the word *grand*. He himself would never do this. He would never do this, even if he got the chance. It was a disgraceful capitulation to the here and now—to the secular, to the mortal. Why would you want to sound like a tycoon or a gangster? Whatever you were going to get, you weren't going to get it in *your* time. That was the gamble. That was the shot . . . Anyway, and more locally, Richard was feeling so poor these days that he switched off his windscreen wipers every time he drove under a bridge.

"So I said, 'Take the fifteen large from the Portuguese but subtract the dime on the audio deal. What's a K?' I said it," said Gwyn, steadying himself, "I said it just to get *Gal* out of my hair."

During the last couple of minutes of their wait, the maggot got itself stuck again, or ravenously burst into a whole new chamber, condemning Gwyn, in any case, to a series of imperious scowls and glares . . .

They went on up. Richard won 3–2 on the final black. His concentration was poor.

There are other ways of doing it, the young man had said. *Botulism—in his sandwich. Or send a woman at him. Like an antibody. Work on him psychologically. Fear. Doesn't have to be straight physical damage.*

Still, there's something about *straight physical damage . . .*

Same for everybody. Unlike the other stuff. It's simple.

Richard lay, with Marco, on the balding but still conspicuously elegant chaise longue; the child's cheek rested on his reverberating chest as he read aloud from the pages of *The Jungle Book*; he read uncommonly well . . . *Damage is simple.* As he read, Richard was discovering, rather to his surprise, just how much he admired simplicity. Not simplicity in fictional prose—but elsewhere. That which is universal is often simple. Scientific beauty (and beauty, here, was a sound indicator of truth) was often simple. He didn't want to hear any brusque or unfeeling remarks about simplicity.

So, talking hypothetically, Richard had said, *if I wanted someone fucked up . . .*

And the wild boy had said, *You'd come to me.*

He read on: the bit about Shere Khan's imminent approach and the wolf's affecting admonitions. He read on, until he noticed that Marco's immobility had long passed beyond raptness, noticed, too, the broad patch of drool on his shirt. Marco was asleep. Groaning at the use of many strange muscles, Richard slid out from underneath him and then stared down at his sleeping face: open-mouthed, sweat-slicked—the face of a desperate little doggy. A domestic doggy, one accustomed to being at home. Prodded awake, Marco mumbled of orangutans . . . Orangutan meant *wild man*. Mowgli was a wild boy, raised by wolves. Even Marco, to his pain, dreamed wildly, and went in his sleep to where the wild things were.

Another day. Another day off school. Having clothed him so heavily that the child could hardly move, let alone walk (he looked like a sports logo: a racetrack blimp), Richard took Marco to Dogshit, for some air. The green world, in autumn, in fall. So the wild boy, the young man, was the green man: in modern dress. *You'd come to me.* That was really the high point of the evening. Thereafter Richard had to sit there listening to literary criticism: Steve Cousins's assessment of *Amelior*.

Marco took his hand. As they walked, under a midterm daytime moon, like a mask flattened at the brow and sharpened at the chin, like a shield raised against arrows, Richard was remembering, how, in the

Canal Creperie, between Rattlesnakes, he had reached for his food punnet and felt the lateness of the hour when the nacho clung to its sauce like a stirring-stick left too long in the paint, and the young man had said, "It's a sham, it's a *sham*. Sweetness and light? Out there? Jesus. Where's my violin. I know the wilds. I *ran* wild, mate. For years. Just me. *Out* there. For years." Steve Cousins: foundling of a new-age community? Or a borstal boy on the lam? It didn't become clear. What became clear was that Steve Cousins had read *The Wild Boy of Aveyron* (so indeed had Richard), and reread it, and *mis*read it; and that he saw himself, somehow, as a contemporary update of that frazzled and swarthy mute—two centuries on. Richard sighed. He sighed then and he sighed now, with Marco's hand in his. Still, with his own confusions, Richard could certainly imagine disliking a book so much that you decided to *do* something, you decided to sort this shit out, by banning it or burning it or by getting hold of its author and beating him up. Not so strange, in a world where novelists needed bodyguards, hideouts, freedom railways. "When you feel you're ready," the young man said, out on the street, "activate me."

"Look!" said Marco.

Perhaps the urban pastoral was all left field. There was no right field. And now came a moment when London seemed to configure itself for the observing eye, and grossly, like a demonstration. Richard and his son were passing the toilets; again, one of its two pathways was cordoned off by orange crime-scene tape. How playfully the tape wriggled in the breeze: Marco yearned out towards it, the kiddie crime-scene tape! In attendance stood two police officers, protecting and preserving their crime scene. Richard moved through the loose talk of the loose clump of mums and heard their choric song: a little girl, this time; in the summer it had been a little boy, and the crime-scene tape had played on the other path. Heading west now, towards the exit, father and child passed a benchful of mid-teens snorting and giggling to something pornographic on their boombox. Not just a hot lyric either, but straight audio Adult: a man-woman duet, snarling-carnal. While snorting and giggling, one pale youth was also managing to taunt his dog *and* eat crisps, all at the same time. Congratulations: here was the culture, and he was living it, to the full. Ten feet away a boy and girl dressed in black were standing in a formal embrace like arrested dancers on the green floor. Richard recognized them, with a give in the back of the knees, as he ducked on by. Darko, and Belladonna. They had about them an air of isolation that made him think—that made him think of the Siberian lepers and also, unconnectedly, wildly, of the awfulness of unforeseen consequences . . .

"Look!" said Marco, as he rested on the bench by the gate.

High in the thin blue east, on an angled collision course, two airplanes climbed towards their shared apex—like needles, with the twin strands of white thread trailing from their eyes. They passed: no contact. Briefly, though (for the sky hates straight lines and soon destroys their definition), the two white slipstreams formed a leaning cross: leaning backward, away from the earth. Something was over, over on the other side.

"Terryterry," said Terry. "That what it all come down to. Every man want to be cock of the walk. All the Indians want to be chief. That what it all come down to: terryterry."

"Yeah mate," said Steve Cousins, and turned to his other guest—Richard.

"What *I* want," said Richard, and it was all right to do this, because Scozzy was conducting two conversations at once, and could probably conduct many more, as many as necessary, like a chess master giving a simultaneous display, "is a free sample. Well, not free. We could come to an agreement on that."

"You want me to let him have a slap."

". . . Yeah," said Richard. "More than a slap. More like a—"

"Yeah well, that's what we call a slap. It's more than a slap." Steve turned to Terry and said, "Listen, I *got* my territory. And it ain't on the fucking street." From under his hat he looked from Terry to Richard and back again, and back again, inviting the two men to contemplate each other. His sparse but uniform eyebrows were genially raised. And above the gray band the hat's slopes were indented in direct answer to the cheekbones beneath and their famished angularity. He turned to Terry and said, "Ah. Star! See the way how me vex!"

Like most London faces, Steve could do a pretty good Yardie accent. He had even read the novel called *Yardie*—as had most Yardies. But Terry wasn't a Yardie. Terry, as Richard had been apprised beforehand, through the bleats and squawks of Steve's mobile phone, was a Quacko: the next lot. Richard was sitting in on this meet "as an observer": good material. And that was exactly how he felt. He was an onlooker, but he was shorn of point of view.

Terry said, "Some of my boys—they totally rootless. Debt mean nutting to them. Normal to them. Debt is they way of life."

"Jesus, I spend my life with all these speech impediments. The schwartzers *I* know all say *roofless* and *def* and *nuffing*." Like when we were going to do Nigel, thought Steve. I tell Clasford, He's a fuckin hippy. And Clasford says, A nippy. And I say, Nah—a hippy. And Clasford says, An ippy? Jesus.

"They all want the big car and the chain round the troat as big as you fist. Gold taps. Diamonds in the ear and the teet."

Steve turned to Richard and said, "When do you want this to happen?"

"Soon. This week."

"Okay. I'll give you a freebie. A teaser. And we'll get a schwartzer. Clasford. Nice, that. It works out. You know: Demi. You all right? Try the bacon sandwich."

The three men sat in what Scozzy had referred to as a *spieler*: a private (i.e., illegal) gambling club, way up the Edgware Road. You reached the back room through a low-morale beauty parlor and a half-flight of stairs. The ambiance was one of entrenched and hallowed old-firm London villainy: Jesster's was the resort of senior felons, of various career sons of bitches, and it was no small thing to be here among them. But if you didn't know any of this you could look around Jesster's and mistake the place for the lounge of an indulgent granny, with the teapot on the counter in its tasseled cozy, the antique fruit machine which would certainly respond to no current coin, the pictures on the walls of soldiers and fox hunters and the four or five old stiffs at the card table, playing not poker or even brag or pontoon but some strictly indigenous whist-derivative called Swizzle. Steve Cousins had a nice word for old men: he called them *results*. And Richard quite liked *flips* or *flip*: for girls. Otherwise, Steve contented himself with a smattering of rhyming slang—and Richard had written off rhyming slang long ago. The only ones that were any good were *jekylls* (for trousers, via Jekyll and Hides-strides) and *syrup* (for wig, via syrup of figs). And there was something almost poetically crass about *boat* (for face, via boat race. What boat? What race?) It was midmorning. Jesster's seemed wholly innocuous. Richard, whose internal alarm system was not what it ought to be, felt quite at home.

"Terry mate," said Steve, applying himself to his concentration. He stared without blinking into Terry's face, which was in fact a kind of deep yellow, like the seam of an aging banana, but darkened by its innumerable impurities—pocks, brown speckles, black freckles. "I'm having no trouble understanding you. You want my thing, right. You want my *ting*."

"Yeh. They want you thing. The helt."

Steve Cousins liked to think of himself as a criminals' criminal. Every day he pulled off the crime of the century. They didn't have to be complicated or successful crimes, because he didn't mean *this* century. He meant the next one. Steve's thing was sweet—and it made money, unlike his other crimes, which were largely recreational (administering concussive beatings, for instance, to people whose drinks he had spiked with mind-expanding drugs). Steve's thing was: he sold cocaine and heroin to health clubs. No steroids or any of that buff stuff or sex-change shit. Coke and Smack. Frequenters of health clubs were by definition overinterested in the body and often wanted to push it in both directions. All the way to detox, in some cases. Steve was proud of his thing, easy, safe, regular; but the point was that it came from left field. It was cute. It was cute, feeding a bushel of heroin to some stinking jock, a pinhead in a singlet under a crane of weights . . .

"Say you just changing you supplier," Terry suggested.

"You guys. You fucking guys. Where's it all leading, mate? You Quacks. I mean, when slicing up each other's kids and grans is what you *start* with. That's dinosaur stuff. It's all paperwork now. That's how far we've come. From pickaxes—to paperwork."

Richard was wondering about the relationship between the history of modern crime and the history of modern armaments—or of modern literature. Gang A was in a garage polishing its knives. And Gang B showed up with handguns. And that was that until Gang C showed up with shotguns. And then Gang D showed up with machineguns. Old firms, then new firms, then Yardies, then Quackos. Gang Z. In the outer world, out there, the escalation ladder ended with—or pointed up towards—nuclear weapons. But the Quackos sounded more like Chaos Theory. That was the Quacks: tooled-up chaos. And the same with literature, getting heavier and heavier, until it was all over and you arrived at *paperwork*. You arrived at *Amelior*.

"We reach an understanding."

"Yeah I know about these understandings. I give you all my money."

"Any message for my people?" said Terry as he got to his feet.

"If I wanted to send them a message, you know what I'd do?"

Terry's top lip curled up in appreciative anticipation.

"Send you home in three different minicabs."

They laughed. They laughed on, with willed raucousness. Then Steve turned to Richard and they worked out how they'd do it.

Half an hour later, as they were about to leave, Richard said, "I just want to see what it's like. Violence. It might not be . . . It might not be appropriate."

"Okay. We give him a slap. See how it goes down. Looking further down the road. Just thinking. Has he got any powerful friends?"

"One or two." Richard named the financier—Sebby.

"That one's connected," said Steve. "He's the fucking *army*."

"Yeah, but Gwyn's a moron. He'll never work anything out."

Now Steve said, "None of my business. You got your reasons. Nothing to do with me. I respect that. None of my business."

Richard thought he saw where all these disclaimers were leading. He could open up a little now, or he could consign Steve Cousins to the merely menial.

"It's to do with your uh, literary . . ."

"No no." He hadn't thought of anything to say but it came out awful quick: "Son of a bitch fucked my wife."

"Piece of shit," said Scozzy.

Gal Aplanalp called.

"I'm sorry about the delay," she said. She was sitting at her desk.

"That's all right," said Richard. He, too, was sitting at his desk.

Gal always tried to be as straight as possible with her clients. She told Richard the plain truth. The weekend before last she had taken *Untitled* home with her, as promised. Like an old-style literary agent she had a light supper and settled down on the chaise longue, wearing a dressing gown and reading glasses. Halfway through page four, an acute migraine—and she never suffered from migraines, or even headaches—sent her crashing into the bathroom pill shelves. She still had a bruise where she'd barked her forehead against the mirror. She slept well enough that night, and got up early. On page seven the migraine returned.

"How unfortunate," said Richard.

"I'm afraid it's kind of missed its slot with me now." Gal had a seven-hundred–page family-saga novel written by a slimming expert to read and place by the end of the week. "I'm giving it to Cressida, my assistant. She's damn smart—don't worry. I'll have a report for you in the next four or five days."

Among the tacks and paper clips and unpublished novels on Richard's desk stood a jug of tapwater—tapwater boiled and then chilled (Gina showed him how). This was his new health kick: drinking water all the time, not instead of but on top of the usual quarts of coffee, the wriggling jolts of scotch, the cleansing beers. Drinking water all the time assisted him in the massive task of daily rehydration. Drinking water all the time didn't cost anything. And it didn't actually hurt.

Richard pushed the jug aside and sat there with his hand on his brow.

Midnight, and the orange van was parked on the corner of Wroxhall Parade.

13 sat at the wheel. He was alone—alone but for Giro, twitching in nightmare on his tartan rug. 13 wore his characteristically scandalized expression: evidence of yet another visit to Marylebone Magistrates'

Court. They'd done him for breaching the peace. On Ladbroke Grove. On a Saturday night. And it was just a laugh: they were just having a laugh with all the milk bottles. *Empty* milk bottles. Could you believe it. Breaching the peace? On Ladbroke Grove? On a Saturday night? *What fucking peace?*

Shaking his head, 13 stared at the numbered door. Steve was within, sorting it with Darko, and with Belladonna.

The sentence, which, strangely and arrestingly, was non-value-free, said: *And the good boy and the bad boy went into the forest.*

"Okay," said Richard—dressing-gowned, breakfastless: a little heap of nuclear waste. It was eight in the morning. Gina and Marius were eating their rustic cereal, in the kitchen, across the passage. Richard felt like a coal miner coming off night shift, dully gray except where he sparkled with cold motes of sweat. "Okay. Now what's the first word."

Marco addressed his frown to the page.

"Okay. What's the first letter?"

". . . A," said Marco. A short *a*. As in *cat*.

"A . . .?"

"Muh."

"Try again."

". . . Nuh."

"Good."

". . . Buh."

"Try again."

". . . Duh."

"Good. Which spells . . .?" Richard waited. "Which spells . . .?" Richard waited. And then he stopped waiting and said, "*And.*"

They were now staring at the fortress of word number two.

"Tuh," said Marco. Later, he said, "Huh." Later still he said, "É."

"Well, Marco?"

"Het," said Marco.

"Jesus," said Richard.

Actually, he was wondering how the little boy could bear being on his lap. Couldn't he hear the tuneless blues that was always playing in his father's head? As quite often happened Marco's pajamaed presence (his innocently silky writhings) had provided Richard with an erection. This used to cause him disquiet, and struck him as something he had better shut up about. But, again, he was enough of an artist to have faith in the universality of his own responses. He asked around among the dads and found that it was so. It was general—universal. It still struck him as essentially perverse. When you thought of all the other occasions which cried out for hard-ons that never came. And here you not only didn't need one. You didn't even want one.

So they somehow got through *good* (qood, yood, goob), and did *and* again, and *the* again, and *bad* (dad, dab, bab), and toiled their way (*boy* was all right, for some reason) past *went* and eventually *into*, and staggered towards the penultimate *the*. Marco stared at the *the* word for perhaps a minute and a half. At that point Richard got out from underneath him. That was it: you could forget *forest*. Forests . . . forests, which in Dante and Spenser and Virgil and Milton symbolize the temptations of life. Good boy and bad boy go there. Enchanted glades or drear woods, places of complication or places where complication falls away—but places where you *will be tested*. Richard wondered whether Gwyn, in the course of his experiments in childishness and childish amazement, ever read like Marco read: one letter every twenty seconds. How had Gwyn developed this habit? Perhaps it came on him automatically: say at mag-got mealtimes. Or perhaps he just thought it was good for business. He did it for interviewers, who obediently and admiringly described the phenomenon. Gwyn falling silent midsentence and picking up an orange from the bowl and staring at it. Gwyn pausing in the street as he leaves the restaurant, transfixed by a toyshop window. And you *especially* can't do that any more, because the orange is designed by a spook in a labcoat, and the toyshop is no shrine of wonder but a synchronized thrash of tar-geters and marketers . . . Gwyn, incensingly, had gone off, still in one piece, on a ten-day promotional tour of *Italy*, where, he informed Richard, a relaunched *Amelior* was "on fire." The only real progress Richard could claim to have made was that he had successfully commis-sioned, received, subbed, and duly shepherded into print a favorable review of *Double Dating* by the Washington-based feminist critic Lucy Cabretti in *The Little Magazine*.

Marco slipped off his lap. and Richard tossed the kiddie book over his shoulder. For a moment his eye fell on the latest biography they'd sent at him: it was the size of a Harlem boombox. Richard rubbed his brow. The night before he had dreamed about some clubhouse in the Arctic, where women were eaten as if in a cafeteria, and where old Nazis hobnobbed with drugged monsters . . .

Heavily and dutifully, Richard moved up the stairs, to shower and dress—to put clothes on, to stand bent in the little cubicle while water fell. One glance in the mirror here, upon rising—the bruised scars beneath his eyes, his hair standing on end in terror—had caused him to scrap, or at least shelve, his immediate plan: seducing a lightly sun-kissed

Demeter Barry. Had also caused him to think, to whisper: Where have I come from? Where have I *been*? Not in the land of sleep, not sleep as it used to be, but some other testing ground, some other forest. The forests of *Comus* and *The Faerie Queene*? No. More like the forests that the wild boy must have known: the clearing, the picnic facility no sooner erected than rotten and ruined, the contemporary leavings and peelings, the rain, and all around the trees patiently dripping, in chemical lamentation. The bedcovers had as usual been pulled back, by Gina. Richard stood there naked, looking at the bared sheet, its crenellations, its damp glow. Every morning we leave more in the bed: certainty, vigor, past loves. And hair, and skin: dead cells. This ancient detritus was nonetheless one move ahead of you, making its own humorless arrangements to rejoin the cosmos.

Richard shaved. A fly, a London fly, was bumping and weakly buzzing around in the small and steamy cubicle; London flies are a definite type—they are fat, and slow, and, come October, they are the living dead. Richard shaved. He noticed that his bristles were getting bristlier, more ornery. But wait a minute, he thought: I *am* young. I still get spots, blackheads, whiteheads, and, yes, even the mirror-splatting bigboys of yore (often his face felt like one big bigboy). I still think about sex all the time, and beat off whenever I get the chance. I still stare at my own reflection. This is the journey we all make, from Narcissus to Philoctetes—Philoctetes, whose wound smelled so bad. Richard flinched, as if he'd cut himself. With Gina, he realized, he was now in the condition of sexual hiding. He couldn't even hug her anymore, because hugs led to kisses, and kisses led—kisses led to the little death. The poets were wrong when they said that sex was like dying. What *he* had, and kept on having, was the little death. How did Gina spend her Fridays? He had stopped snooping on her. He had lost the right to inquire. Christ, and there was that fat fuck of a fly, buzzing and weakly bumping around between his legs. Bristly and obese and hopeless, having outlived its season. When Gina watched frightening films she put her hands over her ears. Not over her eyes—over her ears. Richard didn't want to think about it. Where could he put his hands?

For the moment he fingered the lump on the back of his neck. Just a cyst, no doubt: he was a pretty cysty kind of guy. Telling himself not to worry about it, Richard decided that he had made tangible progress with his hypochondria. He no longer suffered from the periodic panics of early middle age, where a twinge here or a sting there made you suspect, for a while, that you had this or that fatal disease. Coping with his daily aches and pains, he no longer suspected that he had cancer or muscular dystrophy or Ebola or Lassa Fever or rat-borne hantavirus or toxic-shock syndrome or antibiotic-resistant staphylococcus. Or gangrene or leprosy. Nowadays he was sure he had them all.

That morning there had been some idle prattle between Mr. and Mrs. Tull—would they never learn?—about the possibility of Marco taking a day off home and paying a visit to that fabled location, school. After all his temperature was barely into the low hundreds; he had woken just twice during the night, and then for no more than an hour each time. Only one of his ears was aching. Only one of his eyes was actually gummed shut with conjunctivitis (the other wasn't nearly so bad and even had the odd patch of white in it). At around eight-thirty, though, in an interval between coughing fits, Marco succeeded in throwing up his breakfast and could be heard crying for help from the bathroom as Gina went off with Marius (perfectly yet insouciantly uniformed, with up-to-date homework pouch, junior tennis racket and football kit bag festooned with rosettes). Richard would have Marco until four-thirty. Then Lizzete came, when her own schoolday was done. They paid her extra if she played hooky, and money was tight.

He wondered about Marius. That morning the senior twin had approached him and said, "Daddy? You're taking too much quack." Marius often neglected to sound his *r*s. So he must have meant *crack*.

Feral: that's what the wild boy was. That was what Steve Cousins was. And Richard could defend *feral*: it had to put up with a lot of dismissive talk (which it didn't like—which it didn't like *one bit*) from those who claimed that it was just a fashionable synonym for *wild* or *untamed*. Ooh, it *hated* it when anybody said that. Because *feral* derived not only from *ferus* (wild) but also from *ferox* (fierce). Now, something wild need not be fierce, may even be gentle. And the lion can lie down with the lamb. The lion can and must lie down with the lamb.

People who look at dictionaries all day keep seeing words at the top of the page—words they don't like seeing. Syzygy, crapulent, posterity, smegma, toiletry, dystopia, dentrifrice, bastinado, *ferae naturae*.

Two old ladies who lived in Calchalk Street did strange things for money. Old ladies, who wore the ovine uniform of the good.

One of these old ladies was called Agnes Trounce. She didn't just look old: she looked middle class and reliable and comfortably off. She had that benignly pleading expression of the diplomatically elderly in a youthful culture. Normally you could meet an old lady on a dark night—with equanimity. But you wouldn't want to meet this old lady, any time, when she was doing her strange thing for money.

The target is driving along. Without a care in the world, as they say. Although of course no one old enough to drive is without a care in the world. No one old enough to drive a trike is without a care in the world. Everyone is right up there at the very brink of their pain limit. That was one of the reasons why it was so easy to hurt people: they were never ready. More pain? Nobody needed that. Nobody thought they could possibly have room for any more, until it came.

Anyway, the target is driving along, feeling relatively happy, immeasurably happier, certainly, than he is going to feel in about ninety seconds. These moments will in retrospect appear golden-age, prelapsarian. So that's right: he doesn't have a care in the world. Intense and lasting cares are arriving, brought to him by Agnes Trounce. For many years, also, he will look back on this interval as the last time that his powers of concentration were any good.

So that's right: the target is driving along without a care in the world. He may be whistling. Perhaps he is listening to music; and because he is driving some of his mind is just plugged into the city . . . He reaches the end of the side street and slows as he approaches the traffic lights that guard a main road. It is evening and the bloodbath of sunset is daubed over the rooftops. No, it is darker, and on its way to being a dark night. In front of him before the red light is a wood-framed Morris Minor, gentlest of cars. The red light spells arterial warning; then red-amber; then green. And the Morris Minor backs into him—and stalls.

Mrs. Agnes Trounce, a widow, sixty-eight years of age in a little-old-lady hat and a gray-white shawl (nice touch), climbs flusteredly from her car and turns the target with her eyes benign and pleading. He climbs out too. Well, these things happen. But you'd be surprised how impatient, how non-understanding, people can be in such circumstances. None of this "Dear oh dear—well, not to worry!" It's "What are you doing on the road anyway, you fucking old cow?" And this makes things easier for Agnes Trounce. Because then the two young men, big lads, who have been lying low in the back of the Morris suddenly extend their bodies into the street. Then it's "You rammed my mum!" Or, if you were using black talent, "You rammed my gran!" And so on. "That's my mum you're fucking swearing at!" Or "That's my gran you're calling a fucking old cow!" Agnes Trounce gets back into her woody Morris and drives away. And in the other car the target's head, by this time, is jerking and crunching around between the door and the doorframe. It was just a motoring dispute that got out of hand and you know how people are about their cars.

The other old lady who lived on Calchalk Street was seventy-two and weighed three hundred pounds and provided sexual relief over the telephone. She was called Margaret Limb. Her voice was hoarse and weathered but also high-pitched and musical, even maidenly, what with all that weight pressing down on it. The siren song of Margaret Limb could lure leaden businessmen out of humid hotel rooms on dark nights. An endless narrative of fat, she lay on a sofa doing the concise crossword and talking dirty. On the other end of the line, men arched and shivered to her tune.

Which old lady would you rather meet, on a dark night?

Now here is something very sad to think about.

The sun will die prematurely, in the prime of life, cut down at the age of fifty-three! One can imagine a few phrases from the obituaries. After a long struggle. Its brilliant career. This tragic loss. The world will seem a duller . . .

Looking on the bright side, though (and Satan, when he visited it, found the sun "beyond all description bright"), we mean *solar* years here, not terrestrial years. A solar year is the time it takes for the sun to complete an orbit of the Milky Way. And this is a good long while. For example, one solar week ago, man came stumbling out of the African rainforests. Herbiverous, bipedal—erect but by no means sapient. Four solar months ago, dinosaurs ruled the earth. One solar minute ago, we enjoyed the Renaissance. Having recently celebrated its twenty-fifth birthday, the sun will be with us for many solar years to come.

But it won't make old bones. Predictably, somehow (don't we see this every day?), the great decline will be presaged by increasingly hypermanic activity (look out of the window, at the twanging joggers), by a frantic reassertion of once-infinite but now-vanishing powers. The doomed despot wants to leave nothing behind: its policy, then, is scorched Earth.

First will come the solar winds. It is not given to human beings to imagine the power of the solar winds. But we can make a start by trying to think of an ultimate hurricane consisting of heavy objects—things like trucks and houses and battleships.

During its life on the main sequence, the sun was never accused of being small or cold. Everyone knows that the sun is big and hot. Being big and hot is what it's always been so good at. Now, therefore, it gets even bigger and even hotter. It leaves the main sequence. The yellow dwarf becomes a red giant.

At this stage we give the sun about eighteen (solar) months—two years, at the most. In necrotic rage Chronos consumed its young. Now it retreats and shrinks and curls up and dies, a white dwarf, like all dead things, crystalline and embittered and entombed.

It would seem that the universe is thirty billion light years across and every inch of it would kill us if we went there. This is the position of the universe with regard to human life.

"The History of Increasing Humiliation, dear sirs, proceeds apace." "Please don't fret. I have got dear Denton out of Repton and into the Goldsmith. He didn't live very long anyway, so completion is more or less in sight." "Gentlemen: Worry not! The ice and cobalt blue of Siberia loom ever nearer." In the haystack of Richard's desktop (he couldn't find the needle), among its schemes and dreams and stonewallings, its ashtrays, coffee cups, dead felt-tipped pens and empty staplers, were traces and deposits of other books: books he hadn't told Gal Aplanalp about; books commissioned yet unfinished, or unbegun. These included a critical biography of Lascelles Abercrombie, a book about literary salons, a book about homosexuality in early twentieth-century English literature with special reference to Wilfred Owen, a study of table manners in fiction, his half of a picture book about landscaping (his half was meant to be a 25,000-word meditation on Andrew Marvell's "The Garden"), and a critical biography of Shackerley Marmion . . . Richard definitely wasn't going to Siberia. But then again, all the other books felt like Siberia: they felt laughably inimical. There were leper colonies, in Siberia. Richard had read about them for a week. To think of the Siberian lepers made him feel cold—it wasn't the weather but the isolation. The Siberian lepers, with all their pathos and disgrace; and lost in time, too, because nobody went near their world and so nobody changed it, and there it was, preserved in ice. What drew him to the Siberian lepers? Why did he feel like one? Siberia wasn't all like that; it wasn't all quarantine and gulag, wasn't all bitter ends. Siberia had bears, and even tigers.

He reread the impatient and quietly menacing letter from the publishers—about Siberia and Richard's wanderings there.

"They're *kidding.* Fuck it, I'm just not going."

"You said a swear": this was Marco, who now half-entered the study, supporting himself against the doorway in a leaning embrace.

"I'm not going, Marco. They can't make Daddy go."

"Who?"

"Birthstone Books."

"Where?"

"Siberia."

Marco took this in. After all it was, for him, a perfectly average conversation. His face framed itself to say something nice—something, perhaps, about not wanting Daddy to go anywhere; but he just ducked shyly. That's where I'll end up, he thought. After Gina goes, and after Anstice has wearied of me. Among the Siberia lepers will I dwell. He imagined he would cut quite a dash, there in the colony, and would be entitled and even expected to go around sneering at those less fortunate than himself, at least to start with, until he too succumbed.

Kirk was out of hospital and Steve went around to see him: as you do.

They sat together, watching a video, Steve in his mack, Kirk on the couch, with a blanket. His face still looking like a pizza: heavy on the pepperoni. Kirk: his lieutenant. Organized the muscle.

It was a normal video they sat staring at. Cops and robbers. Or FBI and serial murderers. Steve had watched so much pornography, and so little else, that he had some mental trouble, watching normal videos. Whenever you got a man and a woman alone in a room, or an elevator, or a police car—Steve couldn't understand why they didn't start ripping each other's clothes off. What was the matter with them? Steve's glazed eyes strayed. Up on the book nook, above the TV console, was Kirk's modest collection of erotica: megaboobs from the boondocks. Steve knew all about Kirk's visions of eros: 200 pounds of nude blonde—on a trampoline.

"This it?" said Steve, meaning Kirk's general condition and immediate career plans.

Kirk droopily waved a hand at him.

"Beef?" said Steve.

"Beef," said Kirk, dropping his quilted face—with its onion rings, its anchovies.

See? Still pining. Beef had been put down by Kirk's brother Lee—after its third attack on Lee's daughter. Next came Kirk's retaliatory attack on Lee. And Kirk's brief rehospitalization.

"Kirk mate. You ain't going anywhere, are you?" said Steve, getting to his feet. "Give my love to your mum."

No one had as yet written a novel called *Quacko*. And for good reason. This novel would have no beginning, no middle and no end—and no punctuation. This novel would be all over the fucking gaff.

There wasn't going to be a novel called *Quacko* and there wasn't going to be any drugs war—or *drogs whah* (rhymes with *ma*), as Terryterry called it. Drugs war? Get real. "Get real," Steve Cousins would sometimes murmur, when he saw women, in pornography, who hadn't had their breasts surgically enhanced. "Get real. Get a life," he would murmur, seeing the unfixed tits, scarless on the underhang. "Jesus. Get a life." And now that was what *he* had to do. He had to get a life. *Taking* a life: he knew how you did that. Some old guy in some old hut somewhere, in the fucking rain . . . The planet definitely lacked a person, down to Scozz. Taking a life and getting one were very different activities. But they weren't opposites, Steve Cousins felt.

Like a musician who can jam all night the love-life with legs is constantly improvising on anything that comes its way. So the Tulls, Richard and Gina (those veterans of sexual make-do and catch-can), as they faced this new challenge, looked to their powers of extemporization. After each display, after each proof of his impotence, it was into his *excuses* that Richard poured his creative powers. Nor did Gina's talent for the humane go untested by all these let-outs and loopholes, because, after all, she had to lie there and listen to them, nudging him here, prompting him there (yes, there . . . Ouuu, yes there!).

In the early weeks—they were still all shy and green, finding their way—they explored the theme of *tiredness*; and then they reexplored it. As in "Just tired, I suppose" and "I suppose it's just tiredness" and "You're just tired" and "It must be tiredness" and "I suppose I'm very tired" and "You must be very tired" and "So tired." There they lay together, yawning and rubbing their eyes, night after night, working their way through the thesaurus of fatigue: bushed, whacked, shattered, knackered, zonked, zapped, pooped . . . As excuses went, tiredness was clearly a goer, amazingly versatile and athletic; but tiredness couldn't be expected to soldier on indefinitely. Before very long, tiredness made a natural transition to the sister theme of *overwork*, and then struck out for the light and space of *pressure, stress* and *anxiety*.

Of course they could now afford to look back on all this with a certain wry amusement. At their timorousness, their inhibition. That was in the past. These days, how boldly Richard reached, how broadly he roamed, for his excuses! Poor circulation, unhappy childhood, midlife crisis, ozone depletion, unpaid bills, overpopulation; how eloquent he was as he frowned his way through Marco's learning disability or the new damp patch on the sitting room ceiling. (Sometimes she liked it purely physical: upset stomach, bruised knee, tennis elbow, bad back.) There were disappointments, naturally. *Book reviewing*, for instance, never got off the ground, despite the clear appeal of stuff like *deadlines* and *sub-editorial deletions* and *late payment*. Richard didn't know why, but he couldn't quite bring himself to blame his plight on Fanny Burney or Thomas Chatterton or Leigh Hunt. On the other hand, *artistic frustration*, and more par-

ticularly the strains associated with *Untitled*, proved to be almost embar-
rassingly fruitful. Gina really bought that shit—or could *sound* as if she
did. Best of all, unquestionably (no contest), was *the death of the novel*, not
as a cause of general concern (Gina wouldn't mind if the novel died) but
as it related to Richard personally. The End of Fiction, the foreclosure of
Richard's art, the casting of his staff into the cold waters: because they
couldn't afford it. *That* worked. Not for the first time, and not insincerely,
Richard pitied life's straightmen, its civilians, its one-dimensioners, all
non-artists everywhere, who couldn't use art as an excuse. In any event,
all that was behind him now. He didn't need to make excuses anymore.
Because he didn't go near her. And she didn't go near him.

So Richard was now where he imagined he very much wanted to be:
on the sofa of the big front room near the corner of Wroxhall Parade, in
illicit evening light. Not only that: Belladonna was at his side, and she
was also, in a certain sense, already *more* than in the nude. When he went
to bed with Anstice that time Richard somehow persuaded himself that
he was doing it "for Gina"—for his marriage, for his rattled virility. And
that turned out real good, didn't it? With Belladonna, the internal argument was considerably more challenging (and harder to follow). If
Richard succeeded in sleeping with her, then many benefits would of
course be passed on to Gina, who would reap them in the marital bed, at
her sated leisure. Besides, it wasn't his fault—it was death's fault. Every
sensitive man was allowed a midlife crisis: when you found out for sure
that you were going to die, then you ought to have one. If you don't have
a midlife crisis, then *that's* a midlife crisis. Finally, Richard's presence in
this room was just one more move in the great game of Gwyn's ruin. He
was here for the information. He had it all worked out.

Belladonna was at his side. Neither of them had spoken for three or
four minutes. Richard told himself that this shared silence, maintained
over a period of three or four minutes (that deracinating eternity), was
clear proof of how relaxed they must be. Her face was half-averted.
Soft-skinned and luminous, she smoked, with concentration, with self-
communing ardor.

"I've been thinking," said Richard, with a faint and fussy smile, "about
my 'favorite.' "

That wasn't really true. Richard's favorite, by now, would have taken
eight hours to summarize, let alone perform. He was glad the room was
getting darker, because that meant he could look at her without unavoid-
able and intrinsic lechery. For Belladonna wore a printed body-stocking
which bodied forth—the body: the naked female body. Unlike the nipples, which were pink and rubbery, the kind of nipples a plumber might

need a bag of in his kit, the pubic triangle, Richard judged, was quite tastefully rendered: an economic delta of dark brushstrokes. She was definitely younger than him. He was a modernist. She was the thing that came next.

"What favorite?"

"My favorite."

"Your favorite what?"

"You know. Like you were saying that time. The thing that tells you so much about someone. The thing that everyone has. A favorite."

She turned to him: a cartoon of nudity. There was no indignation in her voice—only puzzlement. "A favorite what?"

"Like you said. Do a little dance and—"

"I don't do that any more."

"Ah. What *do* you do?"

"I only do *my* favorite."

"Which is?"

"Everything."

"Everything?"

Belladonna stared into space and said zestlessly, "You do me and then I do you. Then straight, then cowgirl, then doggy. Then there's all the other stuff. How long have you got?"

Richard didn't look at his watch. And he didn't ask himself how old he was: because the answer was ninety-five. These rhythms, these rhythms of thought—he just didn't know these rhythms, and that was that. His voice cracked straight into near-senility as he said, "I ought to be home in half an hour."

"That's no good. I'd need that long just to get started." She reached down for her handbag. Another cigarette? No. She handed him a sheet of paper (a printout, a coded damage report: curlicues of computer graphics, marked here and there with a yellow highlighting pen), and said, "My blood test. You said you were going to take me round to Gwyn's."

All in good time, my dear. "And so I shall. And so I shall." He stood up. Richard used to think that young girls, these days, might like old men for reasons of hygiene. They could look at the old man's wife and think: Well, *she's* still walking. Well, *he* was still walking. But only just. He said, "I have to insist, I think, that you . . ." He swayed, and steadied himself on the sofa's arm. "I'll have to insist that you tell me all about it. And that you'll ask him about *his* favorite."

"Okay, Richard. I guarantee it."

He stood on the corner of Wroxhall Parade. Across the way in the chained playground some large and muffled figure creaked alone and pleasurelessly on the pendulum of the swing; it stopped, and then started again, in a slower but no less desperate rhythm . . . The night before Richard had dreamed that he was having an unhappy love affair with his own son Marius. "Let's not do it any more," Marius had said. And Richard had said, "Yes—let's not." And Marius had said, "Because Daddy, if you do, it means you're inadequant."

Inadequant. Ah, innit *sweet*.

Gal Aplanalp called.

She said at the outset that she had an unfortunate coincidence to report.

Richard sat there, waiting. He felt far from resilient. His right ear still throbbed from its recent hour with Anstice. And then Gwyn, newly returned, had phoned in a knuckle-whitening celebration of Italian warmth, generosity, erudition and discernment—and Italian willingness to buy a novel called *Amelior* in record numbers.

"Tell me about it," said Richard.

On Tuesday, Gal explained, her assistant, Cressida, had stayed at home to apply herself to *Untitled*. So Cressida didn't go to work on Tuesday. And Cressida didn't go to work on Wednesday either, or on Thursday. Why was this? Because halfway through Tuesday morning, and halfway through the anomalously brief first chapter of *Untitled*, Cressida had suffered an attack of diplopia or double vision—of sufficient severity for her GP to suspect a case of (you'll like this) "vascular embarrassment" or even, quite possibly, an organic lesion of the central nervous system. Cressida? Cressida was fine. On light duties, and taking plenty of rest.

"What I'm going to do now is fire off a copy to Toby Middlebrook at Quadrant. He has the right kind of taste and the right kind of list. Both Cressida and I—we agree that *Untitled* is obviously a challenging and highly ambitious novel."

"How far did she get? Cressida."

Gal always tried to be as straight as possible with her clients. She told him: page nine.

He said good-bye. He hung up. He cleared a space for his elbows and sat there for a while with his head in his hands.

"Piece of shit," said Steve Cousins (to himself, and to the old man who was taking ten minutes to cross the road: the zebra stretched before him like a track event). He turned off Floral Grove and entered Newland Crescent. When they get like that they're better off dead. Number sixty-eight: he pulled up. This was Terry's house—the Quack. Scozzy wasn't looking for Terry himself. Home, out Wimbledon way, was clearly the last place you'd look for Terry. He'd be in a club somewhere, or fucking up some deal in some Quacko go-down, or under a jukebox of black flips in that flat he had above the casino in Queensway. See those blokes doing dope: ropes of smoke coming out of their noses like their skulls were on fire.

Two children, two little girls wearing flower dresses and kinky up-pointing braids were playing in the garden of the detached pebbledash: swing, climbing frame, slide. Under thrashing trees. Such a scene struck no chord in Steve's past. Watch out, girls: here comes mum. Cooking in a track suit, with her face in the steam. Now she's calling out the kitchen window. Be there in a minute . . . Steve was in his Cosworth with its low racing skirt. He swiveled his neck: 13, asleep on the back seat. What did *he* do last night? Stole a double-decker and went to Scotland and back. The triangles of Steve's face—the equilateral, the isosceles, the scalene—stirred and recomposed themselves.

"I deplore gratuitous violence," Steve used to say. Which was untrue, which was well known to be untrue. One of his nicknames was Gratuitous.

"Jesus," said 13.

Steve turned: gone back to sleep again . . . Richard Tull intelligent? Steve knew wholesalers who were just down from Oxbridge or wherever. Twenty-two, twenty-three, and they had a chain of command that covered five thousand miles, with Afghani army captains, Japanese diplomats, and British customs officers all on their payroll. *That* was intelligent. That was *organized*. With drugs, with supplying, you tended to go on and on until you exploded like a tick full of blood. And big time was just a big drag. Considering the business he was in, it was prudent to have your midlife crisis at the age of twenty-nine. Now what? He had money. But he couldn't see himself taking the usual route. Running a bar in Tenerife. Flogging San Migs and scotch eggs and screening FedExed videos of "Match of the Day." Probably that's all different now. They got Sky.

Disobedient daughters, not obeying their mother. The little girl was showing the littler one a stunt on the slide. Jump off the top and land on your bum halfway down. Hasn't got the confidence. In Steve's head: concentration-loss followed by subject-change. He stopped thinking about hurting Terry and started thinking about hurting Gwyn.

Of course, Gwyn had off-street parking. It was hard to do much to a man in the bay of his own house, with all its windows standing above you and looking on. Off-street parking: vital in certain circumstances to the longevity of the urban male. Not to mention the ulcer or cancer you don't get, spending two hours a day looking for somewhere to put the fucking car. Get him at the exit to the Westway Health and Fitness Center. Send Wesley or D. Gwyn comes round the corner—and D runs right through him. That would be fifteen stone of bro coming at you at fifteen miles an hour. You're going to go down. All that coming at you, through you: you're going to go down. Then, well: whatever.

He picked up his mobile and called Clasford. He said, "Clasford? Tonight, mate." And then he added, after a pause, "No. You're going to the cinema."

"Yeah?" said Clasford cautiously.

"Starring Audra Christenberry. A touching tale about a group of children sent to the country during the Blitz. You do him in the toilet."

And Clasford just said, "Jesus."

The girls went inside for their tea. Behind him somewhere a police siren started up like a homosexual comedian: Ouuuu. Steve gave one of his agonized yawns. He started the engine and engaged first gear. Just then a *nun* stepped in front of the car and, while Scozzy sat there sighing and waiting, paused to examine some stain or discoloration on her shiny white bib. She looked up at him. For a moment the two virgins stared at one another, with virgin ferocity.

"Piece of shit," said Scozzy as he drove away.

"Audra Christenberry's in it. You like her, don't you?"

"Why's she in it? I thought it was set in England."

"She's an actress," said Richard. "They can put on voices. What do you want, the usual pint?"

Gwyn said, "I'll have a campari and soda."

"No. A pint of bitter for you. That's what they drink in *Wales*, isn't it?"

"Go on then. When's it start?"

They went with the drinks to their wives. A gin-and-tonic for Gina. A mineral water for Demi. She said that alcohol disagreed with her:

Richard now knew just how violent that disagreement was. Demi was the exception in another way too, because Richard and Gwyn and Gina had spent at least a year, all told, in the Slug and Cabbage, with speechless Gilda making up the four. Nowadays the Tulls and the Barrys were seldom to be seen as a foursome. Richard had had to promise to be good.

"What's happening with your novel?" asked Gwyn. "Are you all right, love?"

Demi looked all right. It seemed to Richard that she even managed to exude the pub placidity that pubs like to see in their women. Gina, of course, knew all about pubs—their comfort and their boredom. The doors were open to the evening traffic of Notting Hill Gate. Along with the seams of cigarette smoke, the pub vapors and pub humors, the pie waft and the yeasty burp of beer, there was also the breath of cars like a gray mesh at table height. Out on the pavement, only feebly stirred by the little cyclones of rubbish, the twisters of trex, lay several cartons of half-eaten food—meals abandoned in haste or disgust or outright vomitus. Above, the creases of the sky glimmered like cellulite. Richard sat out a wave of nausea and then said,

"It's with Toby Middlebrook, at Quadrant. Gal said she found it very ambitious. Rather discouragingly."

"But it is ambitious, isn't it?"

"Is it? I don't know."

"But it's what you intended, isn't it?"

"I don't—what you write shouldn't be exactly what you want to write. You should feel *pressed*. In some way."

"The whole process feels completely natural to me. As natural . . . as childbirth."

In any metaphor that linked writing with parturition, no, Richard wouldn't come out well. What were they, his novels? Not stillborn. More like those babies whom it was thought best to spirit away: a black bag in the loading dock. But this particular maternity hospital was primitive and remote, and superstitiously spurned its dead; and you yourself carried the dead thing home, swaddled in old newspapers. Richard sat out a second wave of nausea. The first had felt fragile, and tinselly; the second felt projectile in its tacit force. Was this excitement? Was this grief? He thought not—neither. It was simple proximity to violence.

"Have you plans?" said Gina. "Is there something you're not telling us about?"

Richard (who had been staring at Gwyn's shoes) thought that Gina was talking to him. She wasn't. She was talking to Demi, who now shook her head with a flat brief smile.

Gwyn said, "Have you ever seen anything more beautiful?"

"Than what?"

"My lady . . ."

"Don't," said Demi.

"Ah, she's embarrassed! I love it when she blushes like that. Mmmm." He hummed it, thoughtfully. "Mmm. Let's *not* go to the pictures. Let's go home and make love. We go home. You go home. And make love."

Richard said, "It does you good—I already got the tickets—does you good every once in a while to come down from the palace and mingle with your people. As one of them. In disguise." This sounded like, and was, a routinely bitter reference to Gwyn's new outfit, which he had already itemized to his listeners: russety suede jacket (Milan), brown Borsalino (Florence), dove-gray brogues (Siena). "Get that down you. One more pint. Quick."

"I've hardly got going on this."

"Another half. Get it down you."

"I'll spend the whole film in the lav."

Yes. You might very well do that, thought Richard. As he helped Gina with her coat she whispered in his ear: "I *hate* him." And Richard frowned, and nodded and felt close to vindication . . .

During the first half hour in the dark, he found his mind very difficult to control. It didn't matter what the film was—who directed it, whether it was in Japanese or black and white. This had mattered earlier. The film needed to be the kind of film that Gwyn, ever obedient, if you remember, to the wanders and gambols of his maggot, was currently saying he liked. And it really was Gwyn's kind of thing: innocent, rural, questing. A sensitive historical piece about a group of intelligent and long-winded adolescents shifted out of London to Cumbria during the Blitz—it was almost a cinematic prequel to *Amelior*. Richard, if he had been watching it, would have found it excruciating. But he wasn't watching it. He wouldn't have been watching it even if it was the kind of film *he* liked: a billion-dollar bloodbath. He wasn't watching it. Seated between the two novelists, and without looking down ever, childishly, the women shared their popcorn.

Lone male figures seated in movie theaters have about them, Richard thought, a madman or mongoloid intensity of privacy. I mean what are they? Frowning cineasts? Tramps? Movie theaters were surely much too expensive, now, for tramps to come and stink up. Richard knew that when he was a tramp there would be a lot of things he needed a lot more than stinking up a movie theater. In a full house the identity of the audience would have undergone gravitational collapse, and become one being, like a mob. But the Coronet was quarter full, loosely dotted with heads on necks on shoulders, and the cinematography somber (bombed-out basements, moonless campsites), so that Richard kept thinking that everyone around him was black, or in negative; after a while he imagined that all the people in front were sitting facing him but with their heads turned half-circle like Caribbean demons; a little later it seemed to him that the backs of their heads were really their faces, hidden by hair.

Forty minutes in, and it happened. Richard experienced the complicated pleasure of standing up to allow Gwyn passage—famous Gwyn, uxorious Gwyn, his torso bent over his famously weak bladder. Down the aisle he trudged, turning right beneath the stage and following his shadow across a screen of green: curving field, rank of trees, evening sky. He went through the door marked EXIT and GENTS. No one followed. An old man followed. Richard stopped watching. He watched the film. He watched a five-minute scene about hot-pot preparation (a crofter's wife showing Audra Christenberry how you did it) with no interest whatever. But his body swarmed with affect, as if he was watching something else: the climax of a deathless tingler—*Strangers on a Train, Vertigo, Psycho.*

Time passed. There was a transitory period during which, no doubt, the women subliminally and approvingly assumed that Gwyn had set himself the stark and universal challenge of defecation. Riding on with this assumption—as it were in tandem with Demi and Gina—Richard imagined Gwyn's quest for full voidance steadily growing in complication and dolor; after fifteen minutes its dimensions approached the Augean. Next came an interlude of localized travail: Richard, having heartily matched Gwyn pint for pint, was in need of a bathroom himself. The need was sharp, sour—as sharp and sour as his curiosity.

"Excuse me," he said, and got to his feet.

It was one of those cinema toilets whose promise and scent lead you up ramps and stairways which then double back and deepen like the chutes of an ancient airport, or a city of myth—the twisted construct of embittered immortals. Richard walked on into the bowels of the building, past chained fire exits and beneath seeping ceilings, until the penultimate door, with a soft flap, like an internal valve, seemed to admit him and exclude all else, and there was the marked entrance—GENTS—at the bottom of the bending steps . . . He paused, listening. Only the eternal toilet trickle, sharp and sour, like the rumors of its odors. Slowly he leaned on the door. The room let him in and then closed again.

His first thought was that he, *Richard,* had disappeared. He faced an arrangement of toilet furniture (double rows of basins, double roller-

towels on the walls, double striplights above) so symmetrical that intuition demanded that a mirror stood at its center. But there was no mirror: only two of everything, opposed to a counterpart. Richard squeezed
his eyes shut and opened them again. No mirror, so no reflection; and he
was a vampire, momentarily, denied its natural simulacrum, and fearing
death by running water. Palpably, the Coronet toilet was the scene of a
very recent gastric catastrophe: but it was the scene of nothing else. He
moved sideways and quickly bent to look under the saloon doors of the
cubicles: no quivering flounce of brown corduroy, no tortured dove-
gray brogues. Richard was disappointed and Richard was relieved. He
moved toward the urinal and was bending forward and breathing in
(searching for purchase on his zipper toggle) when a voice said, "Nice
smell in here."

And Richard's mind, which was always looking for pain, had time to
feel hurt at this, had time to take this personally, as a sarcastic reference
to himself. To himself, and not to the incredible smell of shit everywhere. He turned.

"Wait," he said. "This isn't me."

"I just wandered out. Get some fresh air. I told Demi. Didn't you notice
I was carrying my hat? Between you and I I went back to the Slug for a
quiet pint."

"Between you and *me*. Not a quiet Campari and soda?"

"I had a pint."

"What was the matter with the film?"

"It was getting on my wick, all that stuff about the barn. And the cows.
The way they all kept on banging on."

"You're supposed to like all that. Fields. No sex. Civic-minded discussion. Nothing happening."

Outside the study window the clematis was tinged with yellow and
gold—autumn, and Richard's cigarettes. He often smoked with his head
on the block of the windowsill, facing skyward, to spare Marco's lungs.
Out there, birds still fluttered and agitated, and they sang. The uncoil-
ings, the slipping twists of sound. Say birds were just parrots and learned
their songs from what they heard: those trills and twitters were imitations of mountain rivulets, of dew simpering downwards through the
trees. Now the parrot had left its jungle and stood on a hook in a pub
shouting "Bullshit!" Now the singing thrushes and sparrows outside the
window sounded like machines. Cold out there. Now that he was forty,
he feared the cold. Now he was forty, something animal in him feared
the winter.

It was Sunday and the boys boldly roamed the flat. Marius happened to be passing. He entered the room and came up close and carefully peered at his father's face.

"Ouch," he said.

"Yeah yeah."

Richard went next door and sat at the kitchen table with a half-thawed porkchop pressed to his right eye. By crossing this small distance he passed from the monitorship of Marius to that of Marco. Through two doorways and over the width of the thin passage Marco watched his father sitting there, in shirtsleeves and plum bow tie, but still wearing his fuzzy checked slippers. As so often Marco wanted to ask, in pleading wonderment, why Richard's slippers, unlike his own, spurned the opportunity of sporting an attractive likeness of some kiddie-book character or TV superhero—or just an animal. Nor was Daddy taking the obvious and rewarding course of reading the back of the cereal packet ... Ember-lidded, his hair sparsely stirring and twitching in the cold breeze from the open window, Richard sat there in full realism: healing himself. But to Marco (gazing now, if you remember, with *his* one good eye) Richard seemed to resemble a figure in a cartoon: he had about him the faint deep buzz of electricity. If he walked off a ledge or a cliff he could get back again so long as he turned promptly and whirled his legs; if someone hit him on the head with a hammer he would grow a pointy red bump but it would soon go down again. Marco was of course wrong about all this: in both of his scenarios Daddy would have died instantly of shock. He was right, though, about the electricity. The time Richard struck Marco across the head with the flat of his hand, the time when it all started to happen—when Gwyn's book danced on the best-seller list (his career-speed reaching escape velocity), and Richard danced, and jolted—it was as if an electric cable ran from Holland Park to Calchalk Street, bringing electric pain from one man to the other.

Illness, summer days spent at home, younger-brotherdom and a consciousness that just by being who he was he caused anxiety and exasperation—and desperate fatigue—in his parents (he understood, even when times were very bad, that it was not him they hated but the things inside that made him cough and smolder and effloresce, and cry at night after dreams had left him inconsolable; he *was* inconsolable; he could not be consoled): all this had made Marco more vigilant, more sensibly watchful, than a six-year-old would normally have need or reason to be. Adults were not other to him. Not remote and massively autonomous and alive only insofar as they maintained his domes of pain and pleasure. He knew that adults, too, were small, and pushed and tugged by many forces.

Marco knew grownups. Very often he hung out with them all day and all night long . . . Now Marco conceived the idea of giving his father pleasure, or comfort. A kiss, perhaps, on the temple? A few restorative pats on the shoulder? As he got to his feet he decided instead to regale Richard with a joke.

Sensing his approach, Richard looked up from *The Proverbial Husbandman: A Life of Thomas Tusser.* The child's uplifted face, one eye wide, the lips compressed, brewing amusement.

"Knock knock."

"Who's there?"

"I dunnop."

"I dunnop who?"

"Ooh you smelly phing!"

". . . I don't happen to find that very funny, Marco."

"I *phought* it weren't him. He came on like he expected it. That was the phing."

"No, mate. You don't say it like that. Not with *thing.* You say ting."

"Yeah. That was the ting."

"What you give him?"

"Give him a smack. First I had to catch him."

"He scurried around, did he. Jesus. You say anything? Make it look . . ."

"Yeah. I said, 'You called me chief.' "

"Yeah?"

"Yeah. You know. 'You fucking chiefed me out.' "

"Anything else?"

"Yeah. After I give him the smack I said, 'Don't chief me out.' "

" 'Don't chief me out.' "

"Yeah. 'Never chief me out.' You know. 'You don't never fucking chief me out.' "

Steve was trying to imagine Richard chiefing Clasford out. "Clasford. When was the last time somebody chiefed you out?"

"I don't know. When I was about phree."

"Yeah well take care, chief."

He pocketed the mobile and parked the Cosworth. It all proved that the town was safer than the country. The trees were more dangerous than the streets. The city was like world opinion—it held you back. The fields held no one back. Why do you think people get stabbed *fifty-seven* times? Why do you think people die from *thirty-nine* blows to the head? Given the leisure (the privacy, the seclusion), you don't stop. It's the . . . reverse righteousness. Today, it wouldn't have surprised Steve to learn that Gwyn—or, as it turned out, Richard—now faced major cranial surgery and would be eating through a straw for the next nine months. You give one smack: then you begin to think that you *have* been chiefed out. The blow that came before was there to justify the blow that will come after. The blow that comes after is there to justify the blow that came before. What held him back, Clasford, wasn't his strict instructions—but the city. Be quick: the lights, the footsteps. Suddenly Steve thought about the *nun* he had seen, out Wimbledon way. Nuns wore witchy booties and no cosmetic except the no-sex cosmetic.

Now Steve Cousins walked past security camera, past doorman, past security camera and security-camera monitor; he entered the lift and went up, high up, with the building's girders and cement blocks thrumming past him; then out past the security camera and down the tubular passageway. Excluding the two penthouses and the six maisonettes and the fourteen studios (and there were other hierarchical distinctions to do with elevation and vantage), Steve's flat was just like all the other flats in the complex. A squad of architects had been told to dream the dreams of the contemporary businessman, and to give that dream the weight of concrete and steel: economy of line, public space/private space, dynamism melding into hard-won repose. Then let the individual imprint his personality upon it—if he had one. But we all have one. Don't we? Scozzy's double reception room, the main living area where the expression of his personality was supposed to occur, had four corners: a fitness corner (weights, flexers, StairMaster), a computer corner (the usual information processors), a reading corner (cushions, a low glass table stacked with various nihilistic classics), and a video corner (a depthless window-sized TV, the numb sleek blackness of the VCRs, the heap of remotes, plus a Canaveral of decoders and unscramblers). Was there a truth to this room? In a sense it was all for show, like a stage set—despite the fact that nobody ever came here. Steve removed his clothes. At home, he went naked. At home, he sniffed his food before putting it in his mouth (his mouth: he knew that his jawbones, typically, projected at the dental arcades). At home, he stood and swayed with the wind, monotonously, unbearably, for hour after hour. At home, he often thought of renouncing all speech. Did he use to do these things when he was a wild boy? Or did he just do them now: now that he had *read* about wild boys? All he seemed to remember, from his wild-boy period, was lying under some fucking hedge. In the fucking rain.

Naked, he proceeded to the video corner. Then came a series of activations. He sank into the cold leather of the great swivel chair. On screen there slowly formed the freeze-framed torso of a woman. Scozzy stared, with consent, with recognition: you could see the bruised scars on the undersides of her breasts, from the surgeon's work: seals of approval. The woman, like the man who watched her, was all alone. But he was the virgin. The wild boy had never done the wild thing (and had his theories about the jizm and the ism). When he watched pornography, he sometimes thought, he was trying to find out whom he wanted to hurt. Scozzy touched the Play. She wrenched off the remains of her muscle shirt and then reached down with inch-long fingernails and savagely juxtaposed her fixed tits.

Three days later, by which time Richard's eye had ceased its experiments with the visible spectrum, had stopped trying to be a yellow eye or a violet eye and became, unarguably, a black eye, something else resolved itself in his head: he got up from the kitchen table and crossed the passage. On the sitting room floor Marius was showing Marco a card trick, in the autumn dusk of Calchalk Street, with the furniture acquiring ghosts of poor definition and the sound of footsteps miraculously surviving their ascent from the street below . . . The card trick, Richard knew, had involved Marius in much preparation. With the deck in his hand he had disappeared into the bathroom for about fifteen minutes. But now he was ready. His aim was to tell a story. On the leading edge of card tricks, this activity being fanatically evolved, like all others, there were hour-long spectaculars with plots as complicated as *Little Dorrit* (which revolves, if you recall, on someone leaving money to his nephew's lover's guardian's brother's youngest daughter: Little Dorrit) and with interplay of theme and pattern aspiring to the architectonic, the Prousto-Joycean. Marius's card trick was old and crude and self-defeatingly famous. Marco didn't know it. It was called "The Four Jacks" and it told a simple tale of urban striving.

"There are four jacks. See?" said Marius, showing Marco the four jacks in a vertical strip—behind which the three decoy cards (a nine, a five, a three—mere commoners) despicably lurked. "And they decide to rob a house."

"Our house?"

The upper periphery of Marco's riveted vision told him that his father was in the room, standing near the door. Reassuringly and eternally, Gina sat knitting on the window seat, her legs crossed sharply in answer to the angles of the needles.

"No. *This* house," said Marius, indicating the remaining forty-five cards. "One jack goes in the basement." Marius placed the first decoy card at the bottom of the deck; and then slid in the second and third, say-ing, "One jack goes in the first floor. And one on the next floor." He paused, thinking. "And the fourth jack goes on the roof to look out for police." Reasonably skillfully he placed the four jacks, held tightly, as one card, on the top of the pack. Marco watched with drugged interest. "Then the police came! Me-mao me-mao me-mao me-mao! So the jack on the roof called to the other jacks: 'Police are here!' And they all came running up. One jack, two jacks, three jacks, four jacks."

Marius's shoulders subsided; tension absented itself from him. "Bril-liant," said Gina. Marius gave a modest smile and lifted his eyes toward Marco—and Marco's imploring stare.

Marco said: "*Then* what?"

Richard shifted his weight. He too was thinking about a story: "The Aleph," by Jorge Luis Borges. About a magical device, the aleph, that knew everything: like the Knowledge. About a terrible poet, who wins a big prize, a big requital, for his terrible poem. "Astonishingly," the nar-rator writes, "my own book, *The Cards of the Cardsharp*, received not a single vote." Richard listened to the tuneless blues that was playing in his head. None of this ever left him and everything always reminded him of it.

"Then *what*?" said Marius.

"*Then* what?" said Marco.

". . . Nothing!"

"Did the police get them? What did they steal? Where did they go?"

"Marco."

Yes. Because Marco was always like this. Mar*co*. So unlike Marius, who was so firmly placed in the world, who constantly sought and iden-tified distinctions (that was a hem, that was a fringe; that was an eave, that was a ledge; that was a scratch, that was a scrape), who had already joined in the great human venture of classification. Richard, too, knew all about classification. That afternoon, hoping to begin a single-para-graph review of a seven hundred–page biography, *L. H. Myers: The For-gotten*, he had spent an hour with his ragged thesaurus, in search of a fancy word for *big*. Halfway through this search, Gal Aplanalp tele-phoned. "You're not going to believe this," she began . . . Whereas Marco would believe anything. He longed to believe everything. He never wanted any story to end. It had been tentatively suggested, by a young neurologist, that this was why Marco cried in the night: the bro-ken narrative of dreams, or simply the fact that dreams ended.

"*Mar*co," said Richard. "I want to see you in my study. Now."

The child got straight to his feet. This had never happened before but

Marco seemed to know how you did it. Only as he left the room did he turn his head to look at his mother, his brother. His bare legs seemed to move rather faster than usual, too, not with purpose but as if he was being steadily pushed, or urged on, from behind.

I was once lying on a low bed in a room to which a child had been summoned—in which a small boy would be denounced and arraigned. So, I was on the same level as he was, down there, three feet from the ground. I have denounced children myself and seen the head of hair, both thick and fine, inclined in contrition. But when you're on their level you see that really they're staring sadly straight ahead, lifting their eyes only in dutiful reflex to confront the cathartic fire of the parent's wrath. The accusation is stated, the confession secured, the sentence imposed. Looking straight ahead, the child's teeth—milk teeth, perhaps, or higgledypiggledy, newfangled, as the big supplants the small—are bared in an undesigning sneer of misery. Children have usually done something. What had Marco done?

"Two days ago," Richard began, "the day before yesterday you said— you said something very hurtful to me. Marco?"

Marco looked up.

"And I want to know what you meant by it."

Richard was standing behind his desk. He raised his chin, and Marco could see the blotches and stipples of his throat, the misadventures with the razor, the mobile growth of the Adam's apple, the slanting sheen of his damaged eye.

"It was the most hurtful thing you've ever said to me. Ever."

Marco's ears now heard the quiet roar of shame and turpitude. He looked up, once, and then went on staring sadly straight ahead. The room was crepuscular anyway, but darker for the child, whose world was folding slowly inwards.

"You said," said Richard, inhaling, "that I was smelly."

Marco looked up, in hope. "I didn't," he said. For Daddy, in his view, *wasn't* smelly. Tobacco, seldom-laundered clothes, a certain mysterious difficulty of the body: but not *smelly*. "I didn't, Daddy."

"Oh but you did, Marco. Oh, you did. You said I smelled"—and here he raised his chin again, and the larynx squirmed—"of poo."

"I didn't."

" 'I dunnop who,' " Richard quoted. " 'Ooh you smelly thing.' "

". . . It was a *joke*. It was a *joke*, Daddy." Marco didn't appeal to the word so much as throw himself at its feet. "It was a *joke*."

Richard waited. Then he said, "Do I or do I not? Smell of poo."

"It was a joke, Daddy."

"What do I smell of?"

"Nothing. You. It was a joke, Daddy."

"I'm sorry. Don't tell Mummy. Just say you wouldn't do your home-work or something. Come and give me a kiss. Forgive me."

And Marco did so.

At about eleven-fifteen that night the twins, in their twin beds, were winding up a long, whispered and untendentious discussion (tangerines, a new supervillain, water pistols) and had started to think about calling it a day. At any rate their silences were more extended, their yawns more musical and vacant. Marius, in particular (always the more likely to close things out), lay on his side with both hands thrust down the front of his pajama bottoms. He was indulging in his nightly fantasies of rescue. His father, at that age, taking what he needed from any genre available, was shepherding adult showgirls onto gondolas from the black gurgling rock-sides of island fortresses. Marius braved lasers and particle beams, interposing himself between their fire and a succession of alien maidens wearing catsuits and pastel tunics in video-puppet dreamscapes that rushed past or through him, as the lit runway is assimilated by the cockpit monitors of the landing plane. He rolled on to his back and said,

"Why did Daddy call you?"

Marco thought for a moment. He saw Richard's face and all the troubled calculation in it. He saw him on another day, head bent, sniffing his fingertips. And on another day (by general consensus a very bad day: the rooms were hushed), with him sitting at the kitchen table over an opened letter and smoking a concussed cigarette. Marco said, "He thinks he smells of shit."

Struck but broadly satisfied, Marius turned on to his side.

Time passed.

"He cried," said Marco, and nodded suddenly in the dark.

Marius was asleep. The words stayed in the air. Marco listened to them.

That morning with Anstice—oh, man—that morning when he woke up in Anstice's arms, or at her side, or in her bed, which was a small bed, he lay on his back and stared at the world of adultery. The ceiling was a good enough figure for it, the way the stains massed and groped around its edges (the pale orange of trapped water, of rot), moving stealthily in on the center, where the cropped lightcord hung. Plasterwork saturated in solitude enclosed him, on every side. He felt fear, and grief; he longed for the *status quo ante*. Oh, the way things were . . . Richard had but one straw to clutch at—one crumb of comfort: his utter sexual failure the night before. That fiasco: how he would cling to it. Just wait until he got into the pub and told all the lads . . . Suddenly Anstice rose from the bed. Almost as suddenly as Gina did—when Marco cried. Adulterers sometimes leave beds suddenly. But nobody leaves a bed as suddenly as a mother. Richard closed his eyes. He could hear the knout of Anstice's ponytail as she crossed the room. When she returned she had a mug of tea for him, the mug murky and stippled like Cotswold stone, its crevices coated and recoated with the residue of a million lone mugfuls. One day this residue would reach to the brim, and the mug would be dead, solid with its own deposits, and Anstice would at last be ready.

Her tone, and choice of words, surprised him when she said, "You were a naughty boy last night."

". . . What *kind* of a naughty boy?"

She was gazing at him in comfortable reproach. "Were you careful?"

"Oh yes," twinkled Richard, ever the gentleman, even when being a naughty boy.

"I love you," she said.

He felt the temptation to collapse into all this—to collapse into the vastness of his error. Her head dropped as it sought his chest. And there, tickling his nostrils, was her fierce thatch of ear-whisker and rogue eyebrow. Richard was moved, in his way. He stroked her neck; beneath the coarse dressing-gown his fingers found the shoulder strap of something softer and more slippery. He looked. It was pink. Richard understood rejection slips; he understood neglect; he understood people who had nobody to keep themselves clean for. And here was Anstice: in her rejection slip. In his hand he weighed the base of her ponytail, like the joint of a sinewy limb. Anstice's syrup, atop the pink slip. For a shampoo you would go to the carwash with such a head of hair. He closed his eyes and saw a dog in a bathtub, worriedly shivering, its body mass apparently halved by the hug of the wet coat.

And Richard was moved, in his way. He was so moved that he tried to be a naughty boy again. But that didn't work out either. He tried everything he knew that might delight a woman. He tried forcing it in with his thumb. He tried bending it double. But bending *what* double? Nor was he remiss in the matter of gasping and coughing in her ear. Ten minutes of this and then he slid away and flopped on to his back. And Anstice whispered, "Everything they said about it is true."

For a moment he was surprised and even relieved by her heartless sarcasm. But as she rambled repletedly on it became clear that she had, again, fully mistaken the attempt for the deed. Could this be seen as an improvement—another way (better, gentler), for the years of one's maturity? Gina knew the difference between the word and the deed. And, yes, it would certainly be more relaxing if she didn't. Probably, toward the end of life, universally, there *wasn't* any difference.

And there wasn't any difference when it came to guilt, and culpability. If Gina found out about this, he knew what she'd do (she had warned him often enough): Gina would retaliate, in kind. Richard turned his head. On Anstice's bedside chair there was a stack of the novels she got through at a rate of two or three a day. Prewar, clothbound. Romantic, serious: written by women. Their names—all the Susans and Henriettas—never recurred. It was amateur fiction, for a vanished reading public. One novel each: the novel that everybody was supposed to have in them.

Now Anstice said, "Thank you, my darling. You've made me ready to die. Right," she added, with a responsible frown. "What's the best way to tell Gina?"

Richard sometimes tried to anthropomorphize the sun and the planets— or to solar-systematize his immediate circle. He never got very far with it.

Gina was the Earth: Mother Earth.

Venus was both Morning Star and Evening Star. The Evening Star was perhaps Belladonna. The Morning Star was Demi.

Halley's Comet you could pin on Anstice, except she made her loop at least once a day instead of once a lifetime, an apparition of soot and ice with her comet trail of madlady hair.

Was Gwyn Jupiter, the nearly star, too small to ignite in nuclear burning, or was he already the Sun?

Was Steve Cousins Mars, the planet of war, or was he simply Mercury, the messenger, bringing you information from the other side?

Try as he might, Richard could never find anything good for the boys to be. When they fought, as they often did, then the Martian satellites of Deimos and Phobos suited them fine: Fear and Dread. More usually, though, when they were being cooperative, or at least silent, and elsewhere, then they were just spots of light—the Heavenly Twins.

He knew who *he* was. He was Pluto; and Charon was his art.

Gina was Mother Earth. Bipolar, sublunar, circumsolar.

Steve Cousins strolled over to the refrigerator. It started gurgling capably at him as he swung the door open: a larder of light. He removed a plastic bottle of orange juice. Maybe he fancied a grape? No. He didn't like the look of the skin and its adhesive gloss: *noir*, viscid, like a stain from a sticky drink, like the night streets of London. Shrugging, he picked one from the bunch; he felt it and sniffed it; he ate it, and licked his fingers. And all this would have been fine if it had been his grape, his orange juice, his refrigerator—if it had been his kitchen. But it was Gwyn's kitchen. It was Demi's kitchen. He was in their house.

I said I wasn't going in there, not yet. But here I am. I can't control him. People have been trying to control him, all his life. They couldn't control him. And I can't control him. And Richard Tull won't be able to control him. Before he left the kitchen he glanced in the dustbin. Fish for dinner. Friday: Catholic.

Scozzy had entered by the front door. Ungratefully dependent, like all of us, on technologies he didn't understand, he deployed the thermal lance and then the omni-key. Hereafter the Barry security system would go next-generation: it was the same principle as the arms race. He wore a sports jacket and charcoal mohair slacks. Not a shell suit. Everyone worked in shell suits. Wearing a shell suit at three o'clock in the morning: you might as well have a swag bag over your shoulder and a stocking on your head. He left the kitchen. He sat at the foot of the main staircase and slipped off his jacket and his shoes. Get on with it. You didn't want the au pair coming down for a cocoa. Or (an increasingly likely inadvertency: it had happened to him twice) some other burglar crashing through a window in his shell suit. He left the discarded clothes in a neat pile, as if ready for school.

Out of nothing much more than a sense of professional duty he did a quick circuit of the ground floor. He never used a torch, relying, rather, on his night vision, a valued legacy from his wild-boy period. But after a while he had had enough of staggering around bumping into things, and availed himself of a candle, in its heavy holder, taken from the dining room sideboard. Like all modern burglars he knew something about antiques (13 said that at Wormword Scrubs you could hardly get into the TV room during "Curio" or "Collector's Item") and he even knew something about paintings. How to spot absolute crap, for instance: anything with dogs in them, or more than one uniformed soldier. Steve had burgled richer places than this, places that were just bank vaults on silk carpets. What he was looking at here, though, was something he hadn't seen before: femininity on a grand scale. The feminine world was a puffy world, like the padded vest of a gold boiler. In the back room ("Den," he said) there was an archwayed nook with a television in it. He was pleased, even flattered and moved, to see the television—proof of a shared humanity. Every household, be it never so mean, shared this square of dead gray. There was a little bookcase for the videos, with a whole section devoted to the appearances of Gwyn Barry, labeled by hand. Things like "Better Read: Gwyn Barry." Or "The Seven Vital Virtues, 4: Uxoriousness." He felt a strong impulse to steal these videos—or even to watch them. They were a sham. The house was a sham. He extinguished the candle and came out into the hall and mounted the stairs in utterly silent bounds.

When he intruded, in this way, there was a thing he could do with his senses: he could send them out, over the house, and they would come back and tell him whether everyone was still sleeping. Just as all women, even little girls, even old ladies, even nuns, are said to have an *interrupter* in their heads which beeps or pages them every ninety seconds or so, making them listen for a baby's cry, so the senses of Steve Cousins, when he was working, submitted their punctual reports, ever ready for the blip of a conscious mind. On the first-floor landing he hesitated, with a sudden widening of his dark-adapted eyes. Up above him a sleeping mind was searching for a change of status; but then it settled or resigned itself, and dreamed on . . . He hefted the doorknob to accommodate the carpet's extravagant nap. His mouth formed a tight white O, like the ring of a contraceptive. And with a swivel of the body he was in their room.

Of course, Scozzy was humblingly good at being silent. When it came to keeping quiet, he was world class. Because if you'd learned your trade in campsites and trailer parks, in tramp-crammed caravans, in swaying, creaking prefabs, in a world where there was no padding and absolutely no space in between things, then noiselessness became your element and your medium. He had broken and entered the homes of the *homeless:* fishing a few bob out of an appliance carton while a family of four was dozing in it: you got to know about sleep and silence and all the things in between.

Demeter lay there, alone. Well Gwyn's upstairs with the maid, thought Scozzy perfunctorily. He moved closer. She lay there, on her back, parted legs girlishly straight and hands raised on either side of her fold of fair hair, as if in surrender. Earrings on one side table, glass of water and book on the other. Demi was sleeping in the middle of the bed. Steve nodded to himself and went straight upstairs.

First he entered a pungent boxroom in whose far corner a hot sphere of black hair and brown skin lay spliced and swaddled in the linen. One word sufficed for her, the heavy dreamer he had sensed: Colombian. Next he entered a broad attic with high inward-leaning windows, decked out as a nursery or as a shrine to babyhood and infancy: crib, abacus, rocking horse. In a third room he found a young woman sleeping on a futon, naked, her face crushed into the pillow, a single white sheet bisecting her buttocks. Scornfully and cynically he loomed up on her. To him the scene looked like the aftermath of pornography. In his head he made a move for the remote, for the Rewind: have her turn over and reenact it all, backwards. Abruptly Scozzy's eyes jerked up to the ceiling and with a fierce roll he eased the tension in his neck.

Gwyn he found in a first-floor bedroom, opposite where Demeter now slept. He was familiar with the convention of the gentleman's sanctum—not from his reading but from his burgling. This would be where the gentleman normally slept, surrounded by cufflinks and hairbrushes: his launching pad for ceremonial visits to the marital couch. The room where Gwyn slept, in a twin bed, didn't feel like a dressing room. It felt like a guest room, gradually appropriated. He checked. Closets half full. Connecting bathroom scattered with male toiletries.

After a visit to Gwyn's study Scozzy looked in to say good night to Demeter. It was still sleeping on its back. A waft of hair had strayed on to its face, tickling its nose. The shoulder-puffs of the nightdress, he thought, made its arms look innocently plump. Maybe he'd reach down and straighten that strand of hair: you could do it with your breath. He moved closer. And Demi woke up. No subliminal tripwire, no burglar's bleeper was needed to tell him this. She sat up and thickly said, "Gwyn?"

But here's what you did. He'd done it a thousand times, in bum-strewn flops, in overpopulated portakabins. You closed your eyes. Demi's head and shoulders surged up toward him—"Gwyn?"—and Scozzy closed his eyes. You just wanted to stare back thinking Jesus! But you closed your eyes and listened to their gaze. Listened to your own blood, listened to your torched armpits. Waking, they were momentarily cleansed of experience, and open to the infantile illusion. You shut your eyes and they didn't see you. They saw you, but they didn't see you: your sculpted face, your saintly eyelids. They took you for another wanderer, another sufferer, a figure of sleep, like themselves.

He listened to her gaze, her swallow, her gaze again; then her fresh collapse on to the pillows; and then the recaptured rhythm of her breath

. . . As he left the house and walked across the street to the Cosworth, he kept hearing the word "Gwyn?" and the way she'd said it. *Gwyn?* She'd said it with surprise, with caution, with anxiety, with hope. With yearning, maybe. Certainly with fear.

He had been given a black eye by a black guy, but it was his nose he was going nuts in. This was the next thing.

Richard was going nuts in the nose. This was the next thing that was happening to him: nuts in the nose. He kept thinking he smelled of shit. He knew it wasn't the case—he knew he didn't smell of shit, or only very faintly—because no one had said anything about it yet (and by now he was persuaded that Marco's joke, seemingly an unanswerable *coup de théâtre* at the time, was innocent or accidental), and anyway he had taken to spending up to an hour in the bath twice daily, with some dank biography, and smothered himself in baby powder and after-shave and anything else that smelled of anything: cigarette smoke, fried food, car exhausts. Richard knew that olfactory hallucination was a symptom—neither early nor minor—of schizophrenia. There were pills you could take for olfactory hallucinations. And where, he asked, would I put these pills? Up my nose? Up my ass? If we think about it, we all know the sneak preview of schizophrenia, with the toilet paper, those strange occasions when there seems to be no good reason to stop wiping: the thought-message (enough now—that'll do) loses its point, in a pall of inanition. The next move would be to start washing your hands all day and all night, as some do. Well, Richard, just now, was getting through a toilet roll each morning; and his flesh was numb and rubbery from the tub, like something they'd hauled out of the Thames and then hosed down with Right Guard.

Was it the blow to the head that had done this? Or was it the latest from Gal Aplanalp? "You're not going to believe this," she had said. But Richard believed it. Toby Middlebrook, of the Quadrant Press, having spent fifteen minutes with *Untitled* on his lap, was admitted the same day to St. Bartholomew's Hospital with a case of vasomotor rhinitis. At present, he was in between sinus operations. Gal Aplanalp, apparently undaunted, said she was going to "spray-fire" the publishing community with photocopies of the typescript. So publishing, as we knew it, would in any case soon come to an end.

Turning to knowledge, briefly, he tried to head-doctor himself. From what he understood of these syndromes, the *copro* was closely aligned to the *necro* in its adoration of putrescence, waste and decay. Half the time, accordingly, in necromode, he thought he was smelling his own death, nosing it, getting wind of it. And the other half (this was copromode) he thought it all made perfect sense: that if you looked like shit, and felt like shit and behaved like shit, then pretty soon you were going to smell like shit. For Richard knew he was going to hell: it was just a question of which circle. Christ, he knew *that*. Just as he knew that smoking was bad for his health. Even the packet said that it killed you . . . Having gone nuts in the nose, he wondered what to do about it, but not for long. His doctor had died five years ago and Richard hadn't looked for a new one. He couldn't see himself sitting in Casualty with the Friday-night crowd, where, anyway, to gain admission, you needed an axe in your head. Nor did he expect to pay a visit to some suburban superclinic the size of a dormitory town or a major airport where you had to get into lane at least a mile or two back up the road: Richard, in the Maestro, flinching as the signs sliced by him, looking for the one that said NUTS IN THE NOSE. In the kitchen he sidled experimentally up to Gina, waiting for her to pull back with a "Yuck" or a "Phwaw." And nothing happened. The point was that he *didn't* smell of shit. So who cared?

This Saturday morning, easing himself deeper into a bath almost Mediterranean in its oil-mantle and unguent prisms (and shit smells: would it soon aspire to the plastic 7-Up bottles, the belly-up jellyfish?), Richard thought briskly but proudly of all the bits of him that weren't nuts—or not nuts yet. People were nuts in the eyes and the ears. And Richard wasn't. People were nuts in the guts and the glands. Not Richard. The complacent roll call of organs that he was not yet nuts in might have continued—but then Marius knocked.

"Daddy. Quick."

"Jesus. Go upstairs."

"I'm desperate."

He rose, and turned the difficult doorknob. On the wall the mirror held him in its steam. After the usual pause Marius wandered inward. He lowered his track-suit bottoms and underpants a few inches but made no move for the bowl. As Richard dried himself his chest was suddenly remoistened by the thought that he was—and had long been—nuts in the Johnson. If going nuts was an internal treachery (all counter-suggestibility and finesse), then he had long been nuts in the Johnson. Oh yeah. And nuts in the brain.

Marius was now seated.

Just what I need, thought Richard: more shit.

The child's gaze was leveled at him. Marius said, declaratively, "You've got a big willy, Daddy."

"Well it's very nice of you to say so, Marius."

* * *

"Guess what. We had an intruder last night."

"Really? Did she take anything?"

"We're not really sure."

"How did she get in? Was she armed, do you know?"

Gwyn closed his eyes and inclined his head, acknowledging the satire. He had a habit, in his prose, of following a neuter antecedent with a feminine pronoun. From *Amelior*: "While pruning roses, any gardener knows that if she . . ." Or, from the days when he still wrote book reviews: "No reader could finish this haunting scene without feeling the hairs on the back of her . . ." Richard clucked away to himself, but these days he often opted for an impersonal construction, or simply used the plural, seeking safety in numbers.

"Through the front door."

"She didn't turn violent, did she?"

"Come on, don't be a tit. It's very upsetting actually."

"I'm sorry. I'm sure it is. But nothing missing."

"All very odd. You know the sort of stuff the house is full of. Candlesticks, Cellini saltcellars. Fill a flight bag with that, and you're made."

Richard stopped listening. Maybe it was because he was a Londoner, but Richard didn't think that burglary was any big deal. Calchalk Street used to get itself trashed and ransacked as a matter of routine, particularly in the summer. It happened less often now. The Tulls never went away.

"Demi dreamt that he—she dreamt he was in our room. In the room *where we sleep*. In the room where we *make love* . . ."

It looked as though the maggot was about to get going on this, consigning Gwyn to many a scowl and glower; but as they passed the hedge at the corner of the bowling green a thick flock of London birds exploded out from behind or within it, sounding like an orchestra pit full of frenetic photographers—the pigeon paparazzi, snapping at them as they passed.

Entering the Warlock, the two novelists were immediately confronted by a large group of talkative but motionless figures all pointing the same way: gathered, in fact, before the Knowledge. A tremor went through them, as of wildebeest sensing rain, and they turned. Because Gwyn now mingled and bonded with the Warlock crowd, Richard had been forced to individualize their predatory presences. There was Hal and Mal, also Del, Pel, Bal, Gel, and Lol, also a younger contingent with names like Tristan and Benedict when they weren't called Burt or Mel or Harrison, and then some rather older guys with names like Clint and Yul and Marlon, and then some guys about Richard's age with names like Dave and Steve and Chris, and yet older guys (blemished, sidelined) with names like Albert, Roger, and Bob. They turned, and greeted Gwyn, and Richard felt their humorous censure.

Pel said, "Quick. Here he is."

"Here he is," said Del. "Here's Cedric."

The Knowledge posed questions, offering multiple-choice answers (buttons A, B, and C), for modest cash prizes, depending on how far you traveled along learning's trail. To do well, to advance, you needed a good-sized crew round the Knowledge, all the smatterings you could get of history, geography, etymology, mythology, astronomy, chemistry, politics, popular music—and TV. Most crucially TV: TV down through the ages. It was in TV form that the other stuff was meant to be propagated anyway; and the newer knowledge machines, Richard had noticed, in the pubs he hung out in, actually *were* TVs: they fled the written, and embraced the audiovisual. The machine at the Warlock was trade-named Wise Money, and Richard, in his head, sometimes referred to it as the Profundity Requital, or the Aleph; but everyone else called it the Knowledge.

"Here, Cedric. What's . . . 'infra dig'?"

Richard squeezed up to the screen, which said:

Q. If a task was "infra dig," you would perform it

A. Quickly
B. Slowly
C. Unwillingly

"Complete non sequitur," brayed Richard, slapping the C. "You'd be just as likely to do it quickly or slowly. Beneath one's dignity. *Infra dignitatem.*"

"That's Cedric," said Bal.

Now the screen said:

Q: D. H. Lawrence was a well-known writer. What does "D. H." stand for?
A. Donald Henley
B. David Herbert
C. Darren Henry

"Darren's good," said Richard. "Or what about Duane? Duane Lawrence."

"Do it, Cedric," said Lol. "Go for it, Cedric."

Cedric? When it came to interpersonal humor, here at the Warlock, this was how it went. This was what you did. What you did was: you took an individual and seized upon some obvious and invariably unfortunate characteristic—and talked about it the whole time, at every opportunity, all the hours there were, day in, day out. Whatever it might be: Bal was bald, Mal maladroit, Del delinquent, Gel gelatinous; Pel was plump; Hal sported an ill-advised and much-regretted tattoo on his throat (CUT HERE along the dotted line); Lol had had his right ear ripped off in an argument about zonal marking. With Richard, they really didn't know where to start or where to stop, so they called him Red Eye and Jethro and Scarecrow and Walking Dictionary and Mr. Pastry and Lord Byron . . . Often, in such quandaries, a TV tie-in can grant clarity; and usually, nowadays, they called him Cedric—after the affected old slob who presented an afternoon quiz show about words. Richard felt that he had a lot in common with the working classes (he understood hourly disaster), but he liked them better twenty years ago, when they looked worse. There was another nickname they had for him. He didn't know about it yet.

"All the way, Cedric. All the way."

And Richard was off. On the Knowledge, the questions recurred, so you needed memory. Richard had memory, a real memory, many magnitudes greater than what the million hobble by with, calling it their memory. It was open to doubt, at the Warlock, whether knowledge—the mind—counted for anything at all. But on the Knowledge, knowledge really seemed to matter, punctually rewarded by hot coins and an electric jingle. Sometimes, as now, the guys fell silent as Richard worked the machine, his face proud and nervous and aslant, giving glosses and derivations, sneering at the screen's bad grammar (for this oracle was only semiliterate, prone to danglers and pause-for-breath commas, confounded by all apostrophes) and smacking out the answers before anyone had time to read the questions. What is the collective noun given to crows? Set. Covey. Murder. "Yes, murder. They're weird, collective nouns. Always go—" What would an orologist study? Birds. Mountains. Metals. "*Oros.* Mountain. Always go for the really fanciful one. The precious one. An unkindness of ravens. A business of ferrets. "How many years ago was the last Ice Age? 10,000. 100,000. 1,000,000. "Not as long ago as you'd think. An exaltation of larks. They must have given collective nouns to some chick poet to do. *Trecheor*: a cheat. Christ, look at that *it's*. 1968. Red shift. One *t*, two *l*s. Don't ask me to spell. *You* can't spell. *Randir*: to gallop. Six. Mars. Jesus." And on he would go, 10p, 20p, 50p—until he was tripped up by some dead comic's catchphrase or rock star's cock size, and by then

Del and Pel and the others would be so lulled by his mastery, by his Knowledge know-how, that the clock would tick along its ratchet and hum warningly, and Richard would guess, furiously, and smack the wrong button, and the quest, the trail of gold, would evaporate and a new one would form. Because of course the quest for knowledge never really ended. Like the universe, it was a saga of augmentative abasement. Who was said to be the last man to have read everything? Coleridge. Hazlitt. Gibbon. Coleridge: it was Coleridge. Two hundred years on, nobody had read a millionth of everything, and the fraction was getting smaller every day. And every new book held less and less of the whole.

"Let's go," said Gwyn. "We're on."

Richard was staring at the screen—at the resumed quest. What is coprolite? Rock. Oil deposit. Fossil dung. Turning to leave, he thoughtlessly smacked A (thoughtlessly, because the opening question of any quest allowed two attempts, as was meet, as was only right). Then with impatience he smacked B. Also wrong. "Shit," he said.

"Fossil dung!" said Pel, with humorous authority, as the quest dissolved.

"Yeah, of course. *Kopros*: shit. You know, like coprophile."

"Most untypical," said Gwyn.

Richard looked at him.

"I thought you knew everything about shit."

The guys laughed, uncertainly. TV meant that everything Gwyn said was revised upwards in terms of sparkle and pertinence; but shit, the reality, the stuff itself—this was not happy ground.

"Homer nods," said Bal. "Cedric nods. 'Anosmia' nods."

Anosmia: loss of sense of smell. Although Richard had a great memory, he didn't remember that "anosmia" had once featured on the Knowledge. And he didn't know that they called him Anosmia not because he suffered from it but because he was capable of defining it. He dropped his head and ducked away from the crowd, following Gwyn on to Court One.

"Won't be able to concentrate today." Gwyn was shaking his wrists and bobbing around like a million-quid footballer arising ominously from the dugout. "I'll keep thinking about that maniac in my bedroom."

"What did she actually . . . How do you—"

"Oh our visitor left a calling card all right," said Gwyn with disgust.

"Christ, you don't mean she—"

"Enough. Please."

If, at seven in the morning, you had told Richard he was going to play tennis that same afternoon, he would have laughed in your face. No: not true. He might have *tried* to laugh in your face. In any event he wouldn't have managed it. Out on court he felt he had forgotten how to play, but his body, with its sick nose, its damaged eye, seemed to remember the way it went. His body remembered. The low sun, the sun of winter, squinted into his face. When he threw the ball up to serve, an image scored itself onto the dark shutter of his eyelids; the ball burned in the bright orbit of his rackethead, like Saturn.

He had been a slave in his own life. Now he was a ghost in his own life.

How civilized, how spacious, how decent everything must have been, when his nose wasn't nuts, when his eye wasn't black. Everyone stared at him. No one sniffed at him, but everyone stared at him.

The only place he felt any good was in the Adam and Eve. No one stared at his black eye. No one noticed his black eye. This was because everyone else had a black eye. Even the men.

Gal Aplanalp didn't call.

At the Tantalus Press he continued to look kindly on the work of Keith Horridge. With poets, he realized, he was generally lenient. When in the year before he married her Gina started sleeping with writers, Richard found his jealousy reasonably easy to manage when she slept with poets— easier, much easier, than when she slept with novelists and (especially) dramatists. He liked poets because they had no power and no money.

He wrote to Horridge, giving him advice on the stanza:

Spume retractile, the detritus
of time. Stasis is epitaph—
the syzygy of sand.

And Horridge reworked the stanza to make it more obscure. Maybe he should fuck up Keith Horridge. Maybe Keith Horridge was more his speed. But Richard wrote back, telling Horridge to justify the obscurity—telling Horridge that obscurity must be *earned.*

Horridge was twenty-nine. This sounded like a good age for a poet to be.

At *The Little Magazine* he secured favorable reviews for the paperback of *Saddle Leather,* a collection of short stories by the Boston-based poet and novelist Elsa Oughton, and for the out-of-print *Jurisprudential* by Stanwyck Mills, Sue and Ron L. Summerdale Professor of Law at the University of Denver.

He sat in the pub for three hours staring at the haywain of Anstice's dipped head while she explored what she considered to be her only alternative to suicide: moving into 49E Calchalk Street.

Early in December Richard had lunch with the Features Editor of the Sunday broadsheet which would be publishing his long profile of Gwyn Barry.

"What we want to know," said the Features Editor, "is what every reader wants to know: what's he really like. You know him as well as anyone. You know: what's he *really* like."

They would run the piece *after* Gwyn's pub date: absorb the "impact."

More generally, the Features Editor went on, Richard should examine the pressures facing the successful novelist in the late 1990s.

On the day before his trial for drunken driving Richard took a spin in the Maestro: to Wroxhall Parade. Belladonna answered the door in a black two-piece suit, a black hat and a black veil. The veil held dull gray sequins in its mesh; it resembled a spider's web complete with dead flies. In the Maestro they rode to Holland Park Avenue. He didn't feel like a pimp or a pander or an agent provocateur. He felt like a minicab driver.

Gwyn treated him as such. Unsmilingly he led Belladonna off to his study, and Richard poked around in the kitchen, failing to read a new biography but successfully drinking beer.

She was quiet, and maybe even quietly tearful behind her veil, when he drove her back to Wroxhall Parade. He asked her what had happened and she kept saying Nothing.

Richard went to court and was duly admonished and fined and banned—for a year.

Demi failed her driving test for the third time.

Crash couldn't understand it. "This is beyond my comprehension," he said, as he drove her woundedly back from Walthamstow. Not only did the driving instructor and the driving examiner originate from the West Indies. They originated from the same *island*.

As Crash approached central London he relented, and taught Demi something nice: the use of the hazard lights to express gratitude. Often, as you joined a queue of traffic from a side road, and a fellow motorist held back to admit you, there wasn't enough time to wave or flash your thanks. A brief application of the hazard lights, however, allowed you to salute the indulgence of the car behind.

* * *

Over the chessboard, the following Sunday, Richard asked Gwyn what had happened with Belladonna.

"Nothing," he said. "What did you expect? I wanted to talk about oral sex but she just wanted to talk about *Amelior*. That book is her bible. A lot of kids seem to have taken it up. It's the message of hope, I suppose."

"*J'adoube*," said Richard, sniffing his fingertips.

"You know it's on the syllabus. Not just in America, where you'd kind of expect it. But here in stuffy old England!"

"Mate in three," said Richard. "No. Mate in two."

Gal Aplanalp didn't call.

Once a day that slobbering fuckpig of an Englishman hurled and bounced himself down Calchalk Street at sixty miles an hour in his German car. Like a low-flying aircraft—like a drug rush . . .

Richard couldn't believe this fucking guy. This fucking guy: what was his *hurry*? Who did he think could want him anywhere a *second* sooner than he was going to get there already?

Somehow it always happened that Richard was out on the street when the German car ripped past—frozen with loathing, his imprecations tousled and tossed aside by the barreling backdraft. The drooling brute in his capsule of humorlessness. White shirt, with loosened tie, and the navy suit-top on the hook behind him.

What *is* it with this fucking guy? he always said out loud—driving down my street at sixty miles an hour, coming to kill my kids.

He rang Demi. "Oh I'm okay," she said. "How are you?"

"Tolerably well," he said, for this was sometimes Richard's style. His black eye had stopped being a black eye. The lid was violet, the orbit a lively—even a cheerful—yellow. "Demi, you know I'm writing this big thing on Gwyn. This means we'll have to hang out together. Lunch, for instance. A brief sea cruise, perhaps."

"On me. What are you . . . What's your—"

"My angle? The usual, I should think. What made the princess fall for the grim little Taff."

"And what's the answer?"

"I don't know."

"So you want . . .?"

"Deep background."

Then she gave him a date in mid-January and said, "I'm going home that weekend. You could come down on the Friday or the Saturday. Spend the night. It'll be very informal. Just family."

"And will Gwyn be there?"

"No. He's doing something with Sebby."

"Demi—this is good."

Gina, these days, no longer looked at Richard as if he was mad. These days Gina looked at Richard as if he was ill. And how did he look at her, these days? He watched Gina now, as she stood at the cooker, turning his chop beneath the grill. Her small shape, the curve of her bared neck . . . Someone who didn't know Gina well might assume that the tinge of burnt blood in her hair was enhanced by, if not actually derived from, the shoots and leaves of the tropical shrub we call henna. But Gina frowned on henna, and never used it. Richard could back her up: she didn't need to. How he used to sink his face into the evidence, into the information, and stare up like the sun-helmeted author of the most suicidal travel books (the slow waterfall, the dark and arching vines) and sight genuine auburn in the slobber of his jungle love. But that didn't happen anymore. And sex, to him, was everywhere and nowhere.

He told her about Demi's suggestion. She said,

"That's all right. I might go to my mother's. What will you say in your piece? How much you hate him?"

Richard looked up. No one was supposed to know about that. "I don't *hate* him."

"*I* do. You just think his stuff is shit. Are you going to say that?"

"I don't see how I can, really. Everyone'll think it's just envy."

"Have you heard from Gal?"

"Nothing new."

". . . We ought to talk."

"I know."

"Soon." Gina's elliptical face stayed low—over the bowl of bucolic cereal. From the country, where everything was good: the sack of wheat, the rubicund apple-rack. "How are we going to get through Christmas? I hope Lizzete can help out. Should be cheaper, because she won't be skipping school. A weekend in the country'll be nice for you. You need a rest."

"Not quite a rest. I'll be working."

"It's a break," said Gina. "And a break is as good as a rest."

You hear about a guy who buys a sports car on his forty-first birthday and comes roaring out of his midlife crisis behind the wheel of an MG Midget.

One whose mother died took to the cultivation of roses.

One whose oldest son left home received instruction from Father Duryea at St. Anthony's.

One whose marriage ended traveled first to Israel, then to Africa.

They all suffered from pains. These pains were informers sent by death.

One who heard mechanical noises in his ears attached a mirror to his shoe and stood in crowds where women gathered.

One who wore his hair swiped upward from his right sideburn abjured the love of women and sought the love of men.

One who could still see the bus when the bus was nice and near started responding to the propositions written on cards and left in street-corner telephone booths.

They all kept comparing what had gone to what would come.

One abstained from meat and fish, and eggs, and fruit that failed to fall to the ground of its own accord.

One grew fat and had nightly dreams of lopping.

One bought an electric juicer and came to fear the force of electricity.

They all saw what lay behind. If they looked, they could see what lay ahead. They didn't choose to look. But at three in the morning something woke them with the fizzy rush of an old flash camera, and there they all were, staring down the sights of their lives and drawing a bead on the information.

"What does it mean anyway: 'chief me out'?"

"Like you called him *chief.* Your chiefed him out."

"What's wrong with chief? Cabbies call you chief. Chief doesn't sound too bad."

"I asked him. He couldn't remember. All he knew was if you get called chief then you've been chiefed out. And it can't get around that you stood there and got chiefed out."

"*Why* would I chief him out? Why would I chief *him* out? Why would I *tell* anyone I chiefed him out?"

"There you go. Such are the ways of our colored brethren."

"I'm assuming I got my black eye free."

"Yeah," said Steve Cousins, without any sign of amusement. "That one's definitely on the house."

"Now might be a good time to talk about money."

Richard had not been discouraged by his black-eye experience. Far from it. He felt he had traveled through the visible spectrum and had at last reached the end of the rainbow. His own life, on paper (and much of it *was* on paper, written words, memos to the self, scrawled on the corners of envelopes and on the backs of credit-card slips franked by Pizza Express), seemed so hard to worsen; and yet a single blow from a muscular fist had shown it to be capable of dramatic and qualitative decline. The non-black-eye world that he was now reentering, for all its penury and hopelessness, felt like a banquet of immortality and joy. His cheekbone, this night, bore only an arid smear of yellow (not the cheerful, nursery yellow of days past but a different yellow, a dead yellow). The eye itself was no longer a tropical anemone. It had become an eye again. It had become Richard Tull again.

"Go on," he said, and sank back, and called with languor for another Zombie . . . This was the world where the body was money: the world of pornography and vassalage. Here were Gwyn Barry's organs and appendages, laid out on trays and studded with price pegs as on a butcher's shelf—or reeling and calibrating, items on the circular slide rule that an American doctor might carry in his top pocket, for instant estimates. Steve Cousins's terms, Richard thought, were staggeringly reasonable: by pledging half his fee for the Gwyn Barry profile, he could get its subject safely bedded down, in old age. Disillusionment with the literary world—that was what had brought Richard here. If Leavis had been right, if the whimpers of provincial neglect had had just cause, if the literary world was a Hong Kong of arbitrage, of graft and drink and sex: in such a world, with a ton of money and a cooling-tower of vitamin E, Richard could have attained his goal by conventional means. But the literary world wasn't like that. When it came to fucking people up, the literary world never got started. Sadness at this, and disillusionment, had brought Richard here, to the Canal Creperie, and to Steve Cousins, his familiar and his fan.

Who was telling him that he could get Gwyn killed for a *thousand*—for eight book reviews! Some trog from up north would do it. He comes down here with all the others, for a football match, completes his business, then digs his scarves and bobble hat out of his duffel bag and takes the train back to Worksop.

"Enchanting," said Richard. "This is pure witchcraft. But please. You were saying."

"What you do is—what you do is you turn their lives into fear. Everything they do. Everywhere they go. It's like the world has—"

"Turned against them."

"Like the world hates them."

"Go on," said Richard limply.

"So that by the time it happens, by then, they just—they just hang

their heads. They're ready. It's the end of the story. They've felt it coming. They're ready. They just hang their heads."

"This is magical. This is poetry."

"Well then."

Suddenly Richard found himself distracted and oppressed: by matters
of timing. If they went ahead now, then Gwyn, one trusted, would be in
no kind of shape to tour America. Which was okay: it meant, at least,
that Richard could go on saying he had never been there. But would the
Sunday broadsheet still want the profile? Yes. The pressures facing the
successful novelist? Absolutely. He could write about the pressures
exerted by that hundred-pound pulley at the end of the hospital bed, the
pressures exerted by this or that cumbrous prosthesis.

"Put it on hold for now. I'm going away for the weekend with his
wife," said Richard, examining his fingernails and experiencing real surprise at how much dirt they stored.

"They had a break-in."

"So I heard."

"You know what he did, the bloke? Tore all his books up. *His* books.
So-called *Amelior.*"

"So. A disgruntled reader."

"Yeah, or a . . ."

Now came a moment of shared disquiet. It was clear that the young
man was about to say, a "literary critic." He was sharp with words, in a
way, as he was sharp with everything else; but his coin-slot mouth was not
designed to say it. "A literary critic": his mouth was not designed to say it.

"A good critic," said Richard.

"I was talking to Mrs. Shields?"

"I know. Your brother's mum."

"She's not working there anymore, but she's a pal of that Colombian
they got. And guess what. They sleep in separate rooms."

"Who do?"

"Gwyn. And Demeter. I got something for you." He took it from his
pocket and passed it across the table under the shell of his palm. A section of glossy paper, tightly and elaborately folded, like origami. "That's
in exchange," he said, "for the smack."

The possibility of additional or parallel universes, of which there may
well be an infinity, presents the writer with something new to worry
about. Shakespeare is the universal. That is to say, he plays well enough
in *this* universe, with its sodium and cesium and helium. But how would
he go down in all the others?

Such questions were far from 13's thoughts. He was in the orange van with Lizzete. Engine on: for the warmth.

13 exhaled plangently. He was, as usual, nursing a sense of strictly local injustice. He'd had a call from the halfway house: the leader of his Probation Program, informing 13 that the Harrow Road police were going to charge him with 43 burglaries. 43! Harrow Road! The worst. They stitch you up. 43 burglaries. And he'd only done 29 of them.

Lizzete said, "We could go in the back."

He said, "Can't. Giro there. He's wrecked. Up all night driving."

She did something.

He said, "Leave it out is it."

Lizzete was 14, 13 knew. 14 at the oldest. As always when he was with her 1-on-1, 13 was struggling to keep his relationship with Lizzete on a professional footing. He still had his shirt and his sateen wind-cheater on—but his trousers were down *there*. Lizzete had taken her pants off. She had even taken her chewing gum out. And stuck it on the speedo . . . Professional footing. Pleasure doing business with her. For example, he set Lizzete to knock on doors. Anyone home at that number: "You have a girl called Mina living here? . . . Sorry to bother!" Worked well. Don't want to be going in there blind. Don't want to be doing a creeper. Tip-toe is it. Anything comes down and you have to give someone a tap: Aggravated. Statutory: you're 4-walling it for 3 years. End of story. 3 years: 24–7, 24–7. Jesus: 60–60, 24–7, 52, 52, 52. Time I come out, Lizzete be 17. No worries. Take her down the Paradox.

"Here you are," said Lizzete, though it sounded like "eeh-ah" or "E–R."

"Yat," said 13. "Ooh intense."

He had a white man in his head. At this sexual moment, his head had a white man in it: Scozzy. Who'd said he'd be out straightaway or might be some time. Covertly 13 peered over Lizzete's shoulder: Giro's body was gathered steeply in sleep, like an ancient hassock. (His other mode was all floppy and invertebrate, like a vast dog omelette or even a hunts-man's rug made from his own coat.) So, yeah, they could slide in there easy, between the dog and the gardening tools, which 13 was selling on. Ten minutes. If Minder came out he could hide her behind Giro. Bung a blanket on her. Still, you didn't want to be taking it too far with a 14-year-old that *wanted* to get pregnant. 13 knew that Lizzete was jealous of her 15-year-old sister Patrice, who was pregnant and no mistake. Who was out *here*. They thought it got them council flats, having a youth, but it didn't, not anymore. They wouldn't listen. Tories or whatever. Her mum'd kill him.

It was not the black woman that stopped him, though: it was the white man. For 13 had long sensed, very accurately, that you didn't want to be around Scozzy with anything sexual. While to the white man the thought of the black man was some kind of antic aphrodisiac, the presence of Scozzy, with his sallow stare, in 13's head definitely went the other way. You wouldn't ever want to present the man with it. Simple as.

"Tell you what," said 13. "What say we do 68."

"68?"

"68."

"What's 68?"

"You do me and I owe you 1."

"13!"

"Take it or leave it or whatever."

Lizette left it. She left altogether, after a while. Just as well, thought 13. With an unhappy expression he fussed and sighed and softly flinched over the paper tissues. Don't want to fuck that one off. Good business relationship. Adolf emerged at twelve-forty-five, with his book, silent, satisfied. Run the man home and go out looking for a laugh.

"Oi. What's this?"

Chewing gum on the speedo! 13 scraped it off and popped it between his lips. In his haste he immediately swallowed its cold gray hardness.

Maybe they all had what Richard didn't have.

13 had it. Walk down the street with him and you wouldn't be seeing any of the things he saw. He saw earners and turners and leavers and levers, he saw locks and catches, what was unguarded and what protruded, what was detachable, what was transferable. In any shop his eyes glittered with compound calculation.

Scozzy had it, though he had it the wrong way round. Animal thermovision, in the city; the night-sight of the wild boy.

Belladonna had it. In the business of reinvention, the first act is that of renaming. The novelist does this all the time, on the page. On the street, the only thing you can rename is yourself, and everyone else you know, if you like, so that everyone has two names, just as everyone on television has two names.

Even Darko had it. When he came to London, with his bag of tools, the very air over Oxford Circus was rank with pornography, the shop windows were stills in duty-free brochures, and the cars bulged and shimmied like women, the clios, the starlets, the princesses of the street.

In truth (and we must face this), Lady Demeter Barry poses difficulties of representation. She poses difficulties of representation not just because she is a pretty blonde (with a full bosom) who is related to the Queen, nor yet because she kept various ponies and was addicted to cocaine and heroin and slept with one or two black men. In the Queen's extended family, being a junkie, like keeping a pony, is standard stuff: the landscaped grounds of the higher-priced detox clinics are like lawn parties at Sandringham. Sleeping with black men, on the other hand, shows us Demi's more adventurous side. Girls of every other class do that, perhaps because, among other less elusive attractions, it's the only thing left that their mothers haven't done. But girls of the nobility, with exceptions, don't sleep with black men. I can't think why not, if it's half as much fun as everyone says it is. We noted earlier that the black man, very commonly, serves as a sexual thought-experiment for his white counterpart: he is your gifted surrogate; he is your supersub. I myself have a bro in my head—Yo!—who, after much ritual handslapping, takes over when I'm tired or can't come, or on those nights when I've got a headache or I'm washing my hair. (The polite phrase for this habit is *imaginative delegation*: whoever he is—masterfully glistening, in the fantasy, over your wife or girlfriend or pin-up or pick-up—he isn't you.) . . . Otherness is exciting. Miscegenation is exciting. So, with all this going for it, why don't the girls of the nobility do it more? Racial guilt, egalitarian guilt, is exciting: it excites compassion in the female breast. But maybe this guilt only works when it's vague—a presentment, an unease. With the nobility, maybe, the guilt is all too palpable and proximate. The De Rougemounts were famous alike for their piety and rapacity. Demi's great-granddad, with his "extensive interests" in the West Indies. Demi's granddad, with his South African diamond mines. And then the polluting, scorching, forest-razing, rubble-bouncing speculations of Demi's father, thirteenth Earl of Rieveaulx. The guilt is still real. The spell is still fast and good.

Representationally, though, this isn't the difficulty. The representational difficulty posed by Demi has to do with the way she speaks: the way she puts sentences together. For some reason it is the destiny of Richard Tull to be surrounded by idioglots. Idioglots, with their idiolects.

Demi's linguistic quirk is essentially and definingly female. It just is. Drawing in breath to denounce this proposition, women will often come out with something like "Up you!" or "Ballshit!" For I am referring to Demi's use of the conflated or mangled catchphrase—Demi's speech-bargains: she wanted two for the price of one. The result was expressive, and you usually knew what she meant, given the context. But here's the difficulty. In fictional prose the idiolect spells trouble because the novelist, subliminally trained to reveal character through action, duly contorts his narrative to provide cute walk-ons for the next spoonerism, malapropism, pleonasm. Better, in my view, just to make a list.

So Demi said "vicious snowball" and "quicksand wit" and "up gum street"; she said "worried stiff" and "beyond contempt" (though not "beneath belief"); she said "on its death legs" and "hubbub of activity" and "what's with it with her?" and "tell him no flat out"; she said "none of my luck" and "when it comes down to the crunch"; she said "greaseboat" (as opposed, presumably, to "dreamball"); she said "he lost his top" and "she blew her rag"; she said "he coughed up" (he confessed) and "she fluffed it" (she killed herself). Once, just once, she murmured, "Sorry. I was talking aloud." Demi also pronounced her *r*s as *w*s, but I don't think I'm even going to begin to attempt that.

I said at the outset that Demeter, like Gina, had no connection with literature other than marriage to one of its supposed practitioners. This isn't quite true. This is never quite true. We all have our connections with literature, wittingly or not so wittingly. How else do we explain the intensity of Richard's interest? Everybody knew that he was going down to Byland Court to spend the weekend with Lady Demeter. His wife knew; her husband knew; the Features Editor of the Sunday broadsheet knew. But nobody knew how Demi filled his mind, sometimes—how he burned across town at her.

If you could gather together all a man's past lovers (the lovers of a modern midlifer, averagely promiscuous) and line them up in chronological order, as in a *catalogue raisonné*, as in the long passage of a gallery or museum: for the retrospective . . . You would begin with shocking diversity, with the wide-sweep eclectic. Moving along the line the viewer's eye would jump up, down, start back, all heights, all weights, all colorings. Then after a while a pattern would establish itself; the repetition of certain themes would eventually situate you in one genre or another, until you came to the last woman in the show, the crystallized: and that's your wife. So things had gone, more or less, with Richard. The arrow of obsession pointed to Gina. All the girls, all the women, got bendier and coilier and craftier—until you came to Gina. Her eyes, her mouth, the turn of her waist: these were his *Collected Poems*. Whereas members of the subgenre that Demi roamed, the big round babypowder blondes, were never numerous and petered out a long way back down the line. Though he had been awfully pleased to see them at the time. Richard was forty. He paid many visits to this passage. His life was this passage. The world was this passage.

Still, aristocratic lineage, great wealth, comparative youth, an air of vulnerability, a full bosom: wouldn't that about cover it, universally? Did Demi *need* anything literary, to ignite Richard's passion?

Yes. First, the big parties she used to throw for writers. Deliriously, ravenously, Richard sent his mind back to the napkin-scarved bottles of old champagne tipped his way by tuxedoed athletes (even the help was hip, was hot) and bims in ra-ra skirts offering *canapés* made of dodo G-spots and hummingbird helmets, in the octagonal library, where he had mingled with the knowers and philosopher kings of the living word—while all the agents and editors and publishers cowered in their nimbus of pelf and preferment: men and women who shunned him; men and women whose secretaries hung up on him without blinking; men and women whose letters he opened like some Soviet janitor getting a personal summons from Stalin . . . Hoping to impress Gwyn Barry (or, more honestly, hoping to depress him), Richard had taken his friend to the salon of Lady Demeter de Rougemount. And look what happened.

Other than that, Richard had information on Demi now, and information always points to the vulnerable—the hidden. Secrets, female secrets, tend to the poetic, like the birthmark that her rumpled shirtcollar sometimes failed to conceal: Demi's port-wine stain, which rose and glowed when she was flustered or distressed. Really she was offering the world only an excerpt of the truth. Demi had gone from the grottolike chapel at Byland Court to the cash machine on the high street at midnight (making two withdrawals, at 11:59 and 12:01: this was drugs knowledge). The element that rescued her face from mere youth-dependant prettiness was the appetite, the taste for disobedience and dissolution. It put depth into her eyes and made them humorous and propitiatory; it complicated her mouth, her teeth; it meant that her hair couldn't quite conform to its sheen and bob. Her appetite was not vulpine; it was loose and shrugging. She was hurt, she was sorry. That was just how she was. Love might have expanded her. But we are not all of us going to *get* loved. We are not all of us going to get expanded. She and her husband slept in separate beds, in separate bedrooms. Richard understood. He and Gina still turned in together; but they were sleeping in separate beds. Richard understood. An I for an I.

The representational difficulty remains. My suspicion remains. Demeter's dimensions are one short of the three. It does happen. Gina, too, maybe. If writers drain life out of those around them, if writers are vampires, are nightmares . . . To be clear: I don't come at these people.

They come at me. They come at me like information formed in the night. I don't make them. They're already there.

"Where you been then?"

"Party. Office party."

"Party? Time of year. Parties. It. You do."

"Yeah."

These minicab drivers who ferried Richard about, over Christmas, to and from the diaspora of old Fleet Street—these minicab drivers were every hue of Asian brown, but they all spoke the same language. Clearly they had learned their English from small-hour conversations with their customers, people like Richard or people in similar condition.

"Nice talking to you," slurred Richard, climbing out on Calchalk Street, under a slanting moonman and a city star or two. "What's that?"

"Uh, that's. Let's. It. Call it six-fifty," slurred the minicab driver.

"Take seven."

". . . Phanks. Cunt."

The railway station had changed since he had last had call to use it. In the meantime its soot-coated, rentboy-haunted vault of tarry girders and toilet glass had become a flowing atrium of boutiques and croissant stalls and limitless cappuccino. Trains no longer dominated it with their train culture of industrial burdens dumbly and filthily borne. Trains now crept in round the back, sorry they were so late, hoping they could still be of use to the proud, strolling, cappuccino-quaffing shoppers of the mall. There was even a brand-new Dickensian pub called the Olde Curiosity Shoppe whose set was dressed with thousands of books— written not by Dickens but by that timeless band of junkshop set-dresser nobodies . . . In other words, the station had gone up in the world. And Richard didn't like it. He wanted everything to stay down in the world—with him. Envy and schadenfreude and invidiousness: they arise from poor character, but also from a fear of desertion. The entrance to the platform he stood at called itself the Gateway to East Anglia. Monolithically overweight, like a prehistoric snake that had eaten not a mastodon or a mammoth but another snake of the same dimensions, the train moved toward him with its yellow eyes satedly averted. Asian and West Indian staff stood ready with their black ten-gallon rubbish bags. Richard stiffened in his soiled bow tie.

It was over. It was all pretty much over. That morning, in the post, he had received a lustrous envelope from the offices of Gal Aplanalp. On wrenching it open he found, not a book contract for *Untitled*, but an invoice for the many photocopies made of its typescript. The sum demanded was large enough to constitute a rumor of ruin for Richard; worse, it spelled good news for another of Gal's clients, Gwyn Barry, whose physical sufferings, in consequence, might have to be modified or abridged. In front of his assembled family Richard left the kitchen table and weaved his way toward the sitting-room chaise longue. He didn't collapse on top of it. He crawled in underneath it. One by one the boys came to peer at him with their upside-down faces. It was all pretty much over . . . Richard didn't look out at the day that was now moving past him. In prefiguration of its actual death, the sun or its nimbus hung vastly expanded above the milky medium of the troposphere. You could stare at it—a necessarily rare privilege. A deity you could stare at would not be a deity. A sun you could stare at would be no good to you: it would never have given you life. Rain came. Rain made the landscape heavier, and impeded it: the sopping trees, the steeped sheep. Richard looked up. A canal was unraveling parallel to the leaning, yawing train. There was a solitary barge, moored to the reeds, its chimney smoking; presumably a tramp sat within it, under this squall just made for him. It wouldn't be too bad, thought Richard. Our thick coats, our baked beans. Pleasantly drugged by the reek of paraffin . . .

It was over. It was getting nearer to being over. He looked for clues—in the daily crucifixion of the crossword. Ten years ago it used to take him ten minutes to finish the wide-grid Tiresias: he finished it on the can. Five years ago he was usually doing about half of it. Twelve months ago he was still doing about half of it; but all his answers (he would discover the next day) were *wrong*. They interlocked all right; but they were all wrong. Nowadays things had improved: he couldn't do any of it. This morning two clues in particular taunted and traduced him. One was:

Eggy? (16)

The other was:

Going in at number eight for Zimbabwe, Gloucestershire opener joins tailender for Glamorgan (when Other unfit to play) to produce new ball with clear appeal for the philoprogenitive (3)

He pushed the thing aside and tried to sleep but just sat there with his head banging against the wall. Why trains? Why rails? Why tracks and smokestacks? Richard would go on asking himself these pointless questions for a while, presumably, as artists will. But these questions were now *altogether* pointless. He was leaving the reconstruction business. So he had no business asking them.

At his destination he was met, not by Demi, but by a plump youth in a bulbous washable jacket, son of gatekeeper or gamekeeper. No gate or game to keep, not anymore; so just this plump youth, at the wheel of his mobile gardener's hut, marooned for life among the lanes and hedges. Richard bounced along, up hill and down dale. The road might have been taking him back down his own central nervous system, to the past, to childhood and its green world, unfallen, where the lion lay down with the lamb and the rose grew without thorn. In the city you looked for this world, in Dogshit Park, in the Warlock AstroTurf, in the ravings of the wild boy, in the leaden pages of *Amelior*. The green world symbolized the triumph of summer over winter; symbolizing that triumph, though, was all the green world could do, because here was winter and the cold he feared.

"Nearly there now."

Accurately, and with the caress of social unease, Richard felt that the land was being sculpted, was becoming, in fact, a garden, but on a sickening scale. Behold a sickening gardener, one thousand feet tall, with his sickening scythe, his huge harrow, his reaping hook, his mile-long trenchworks and earthworks, the terrible topiarist: those trees pregathered on the knoll, that planned plateau, those layered gouges to make the hillside frown or sneer.

The van dropped him off in a rear courtyard and he was directed toward the kitchen—where Demi was, and where all her sisters were: Lady Amaryllis, Lady Callisto, Lady Urania, Lady Persephone. With his small but respectably battered suitcase Richard entered a room where, against all expectation, he was greeted with mandatory informality: the four sisters, the four titled dairy maids each with a titled tit out and a baby at the end of it, and six or seven additional infants with their eternal cadences of weariness and demand, plus crunchy coughs, pi-dog sneezes, hiccup pulses, hold-everything retchings and of course the many scales of infant grief. These sounds were eternal, but louder here, and richer in eructation, because of the incredible squalor, as Demi explained.

"It's not just the babies," she said. "Everyone who comes here spends most of their time in the loo."

And you could hear it, you could hear it, the *whoop* and *whoops* of baby burp, fart and gag, continuous and cartoonish, like a baby one-man band, the perpetual motion of air.

"You'll be at it too. Can't you just smell all the dead mice?"

He drank his coffee, among the staring eyes and streaming noses and dangling, bootied feet. This was olfactory forgiveness—olfactory deliverance. Richard sat there, sniffing his fingertips; but his nose, he liked to believe, was finally on the mend. He seldom thought he smelled of shit. He seldom thought, even, that he smelled of batch. What he thought he smelled of now was *spinst*. And that just couldn't be right. Spinst, he said to himself (and it was quite a riff by now). Come *on*. Spinst. How obvious has it got to get that your nose is dicking you around? Spinst: what clearer proof could there be that your nose is absolutely *full* of it?

"Richard's writing a long piece about Gwyn."

The sisters turned to him with considered expressions.

"You're not going to get a tape recorder out or anything?"

"No no. You just do what you'd do anyway. And I'll observe. Sleepily. What I'm really here for," said Richard, "is to sleep."

Though not warm or anything like that, the house they were in (itself boundless, but distinct from the stately home, which lay to their flank somewhere, like a regiment) had the internal feel of an oven or a furnace; everywhere you went you heard the parched lungs of ancient bellows, the gasp of pilot light. The floorboards hummed and tickled shod feet with the work of the hidden hypocaust. This senile apparatus was augmented, in the unheatably high-ceilinged hall, by an open log fire, before which, on the sofa, a gravid Labrador anxiously awaited the arrival of her puppies. Sour smoke hovered and idled, bringing tears to the eyes—to the eyes of the Labrador and to the eyes of the old woman who sat there stroking her . . . Damply melded heaps of wellies and anoraks, every toilet bowl gruffly splattered and tire-tracked, every surface padded with dust as thick as iron filings. In Demi's parents two Catholic dynasties had come together. It wasn't that the Earl and the Countess loved dirt and decay. They just didn't see it. When they used the barn-dark kitchen, if they ever did, piety and pride forbade awareness of the crisped gunge in the cooker and the smell of sweet damp cardboard that heaved from the opened fridge. They didn't see it or smell it—the merely worldly. But the daughters did, and laughed at it, and added to it all with their oozing young.

Unlike the nostrils of another visitor to another great Catholic seat, *Richard's* nostrils, sensitive though they were, luckily failed to flare at the sight of a "high, insolent dome." But he had had good times in big country houses, when he was younger, and more insolent. He was practiced at skulking around inside them, stealing drinks, and avoiding church; and he had crept down many a popping furlong of corridor with his shoes in his hands. Further, he had crouched in banks of reeds and blazed with shotguns at flocks of ducks (which, on undulating wings of gratitude and sincerity, were heading home to their rightful rest). He had sat crammed with huge brothers in huge cars on the way to horse-brassed pubs on Sunday mornings (Brother One, speaking of a married blonde: "I've slimed with her too." Second Brother: "Liar!" First Brother: "Test me!" Second Brother: "What color's her minge?" First Brother: "Black!"). He had quaffed sloe gin at six in the morning and engaged in bun fights and then climbed onto a horse and bobbed around in pursuit of some ferret or weasel until he fell off again. Most centrally, he had assumed the missionary position with several hefty daughters of the nobility and gentry, and bounced around until everything smelled of come and they made a joke, and told them who Chekhov was and why rain fell and how it turned out that airplanes could not stand stationary in the sky. Richard had wondered, throughout, when all this was going to end, but he went away and then went back and it just kept staggering on. This particular dynasty, in any case, awaited cancellation. Although the Earl had sired five daughters, patiently crippling his wife in quest of an heir, and although those daughters had presented their husbands with many a Jeremy and Jasper and Joseph, the estate was of course patrilinear, and would veer off elsewhere soon.

The day cleared. Its roof of cloud began to leak, like a colander, and the poles of refracted fire looked splay-legged, as if their apex lay at airplane height—nineteen thousand yards, perhaps, and not ninety million miles. Without changing his clothes, and using a wooden racket, he played tennis with Demi, Urania, and Callisto on a court so rich in excrescences and asperities that his choice of groundstroke—forehand or backhand—necessarily depended on the ball's right-angled bounce. Then, with his hands on his hips, he admired the swimming pool. Thermals of yeasty activity rose from its mantle of peat-thick green. Richard didn't want to swim in it; he wouldn't have minded drinking it, but he didn't want to swim in it. Side by side he and Demi walked down freshly dripping avenues. They visited conservatories and hothouses, grottoes and gazebos, bowers and arbors, follies and wildernesses; Richard's notebook was in and out of his pocket, signaling his professional interest, as Demi told tales of lost kittens, beloved ponies, myxomatotic marmots, rabid rabbits, and so on, and apostasies and conflagrations and wartime commandeerings and royal visits . . . Listening is good, he thought; listening is always good. They approached the kitchen, through the kitchen garden. She lost her footing on the path and he reached out to steady her. Richard was biding his time.

He found a gym-sized library that contained not a single readable book, not even any Trollope. So he went to sleep in it. The room was dark when Demi woke him with a cup of tea, and a biscuit. She remained at his side, on the tasseled sofa, holding her teacup with both hands as if it contained something sacramental like incense or holy warmth; her blue-jeaned thighs were widely and rigidly parted, her feet erectly tensed on their toes. He watched her face in its offered profile, how it wavered and resolved itself—the bitten underlip, the tremors. Of course it seemed obvious enough what the immediate trouble was. Unborn babies were swirling round her head, like flocks of *putti*.

"You're the middle sister."

"I'm an aunt twelve times over. Gwyn is very worried about the state of the world."

"Well he could have fooled me."

"He's even talked about having that operation."

"I've always thought that was a strange response—to being worried about the state of the world." Richard had just woken up, so he spoke reasonably innocently. He *did* think it was a strange response. Signs of major ferment, down the road, in the human story—and the first thing you do is go and have your cock off. Or go and have it out: a slightly more complicated (and more expensive) operation, which he felt might be necessary in the unusual case of Richard Tull.

"That's not for your piece," she said.

"Of course not."

She felt for his hand. She said, "We ought to change."

Richard felt something stir within him. The seduction of Lady Demeter: how paltry, how mean, how puerile. He hereby assigned himself a higher goal. Seducing Demi would indeed be a hollow victory. The real clincher would be to get her pregnant.

A succession of headlights now poled and peered its way through the dark and dust of this room of books. Here came the husbands, arriving in four-Porsche formation, from the City. How had they spent their Saturday? Buying and selling, Richard assumed, and sleeping with women who hadn't had any children. Car doors slammed, seeming to entrain further illumination from the courtyard lamps and lanterns. He could see them through the window. He could even see their teeth, their slablike teeth, dripping with avidity.

Dinner was unforgettable, and Richard would remember it for the rest of his life. At the table each place was furnished with a name tag and a silver salver and a drawerful of cutlery; also, in squat crystal (the size and shape of a diner ketchup-squirt), an individual carafe of red wine. Which were not to be replenished. Richard found this out early on, because he was wiggling his decanter over his glass well before the bruised avocados were served. Demi gave him hers, and that helped him through the next five minutes. Then, two hours later, after the women had left the room, he ground it out with the husbands in exchange for two thimbles of port . . . Beaming boys in beaming shirts, the husbands, so far as he could ascertain, were forthright, friendly, loudly clued-up about the workings of the world and by no means agonizingly stupid.

So: intensely sober, in a permanent panic attack of sobriety, Richard now sat on a bed with Demi, in a dark tower: a dark tower that wore a witch's pointy hat. They had crossed two frosted lawns to get there, and climbed a curling stone stairway, and had entered this spherical turret by means of a damp and heavy key. The kind of tower from which wronged princesses traditionally craved escape or rescue. One princess whom

Richard had recently read about (sitting there with a twin on either side of him) had fled such a tower by climbing down her own hair: the big-hair princess. In his own fantasies of escape, he often saw himself clambering from that bedsit in Blackfriars—that eyrie of spinst—on the rope ladder of Anstice's crackling rug . . . For some mysterious or even magical reason, their little belfry, as Demi said, was "lovely and warm." It had served as the bedroom of one of the household's fabled nannies, long deceased. They sat side by side on her narrow cot, whose springs, presumably, had never creaked in passion.

"This thing Gwyn does," said Richard, adjusting his notebook, "when he stares at things in that rapt way, like an orange or a pencil. As a child might. When did he start doing that?"

"He used to get very fed up when people said how *simple* his writing was. He said it was as if he'd written a children's book. Anyway he started doing it around then."

". . . This carpentry thing. He doesn't actually *do* carpentry, does he?"

"Never. Except he did a bit . . . He told somebody that writing was like carpentry so he thought he'd better get some carpentry stuff in case people asked if he did carpentry, and then he did a bit of carpentry just in case."

Women's foreheads, sometimes, provide the punctuation for their speech: underlinings, accents *grave* and *aigu*, the puzzled circumflex, sad umlauts, wistful cedillas.

"What made you fall for him?"

Unlike Richard, Demi had changed for dinner: a tight gray cardigan, a light gray skirt. Her shoes lay on the floor, still imitating her characteristic stance: heel-to-heel, obtuse-angled. Her legs were tucked up beneath her, but now she unfolded herself and slid up onto her knees, and turned, folding her arms on the narrow vent of the windowsill. Richard stared: the two lanes of Demi's thighs, entering the tunnel of her skirt. Where is the middle of women, he wondered; where is the center of their gravitational pull? In different places. In the color of the mouth's interior, in the breathy and gulpy laxity of the lungs. In the gap or wake between the thighs, where no flesh is, a flute of air the shape of a cocktail glass, where he sensed the invisible quicksilver of gin . . . He put down his pen and pad and moved up beside her. Their cheeks were almost touching as she said,

"I could always come up here and know everything would be just as it had always been. People think that people like me don't have to struggle. But I have struggled. Oh, I could tell you a couple of tales or two, don't you worry. I got . . . so lost for a while. I'm still lost. I still have to take it one day at a time. One day at a time."

They both swallowed. She said,

"Look."

He looked. He looked out through the arrow-slit and its web of churchy glass: the frosted field, the tall fir, the gibbous moon, the slice of cloud, the spire. The spire did indeed look like a thing that had some business pointing heavenward, unlike the berkish bulk of office block, of highrise. It pointed, with its tapered tentativeness . . .

"That's St. Bodolph's in Short Crendon. See? There's a cloud passing over it. I used to take my pony Hester there and back every evening. It was as far as they'd let me go. And I always used to think that if I got there and back before Nanny Smith laid the table for tea . . ."

"What?"

"Oh. You know. That I'd have a happy life."

This was romance but they were doing it in winter.

Richard said, "You want some coke?"

Just as there are genres of skies, and car alarms, and many other things, so there are genres of the hangover. Tragic treatments, enriched with various amounts and shades of irony. The epic frame, which finds the hero, toward evening on the second day, still sitting there wiping his eyebrows with his fingertips and still saying to himself things like dear oh dear. There are futuristic hangovers, there are chillers and tinglers, there are thrillers. There are bodice-rippers. Probably there are sex-and-shopping hangovers: there are hangovers made of junk and trash. There are hangovers as dull as rain . . . Not all genres, on the other hand, correspond to a hangover. For instance there are no Western hangovers. In life, hangovers usually cleave to a genre which literature finds hard to do and rarely attempts: tragicomedy. *Murphys* and *Metamorphosises, Third Policemans, Handful of Dusts* . . .

At first it seemed that Richard's hangover might find a relatively comfortable generic home: the country-house mystery. *Every* hangover, after all, is a mystery; every hangover is a whodunit. But as soon as he reared and swiveled from his bed, and placed a plumply quivering white sole on the lino, it was amply and dreadfully clear what genre he was in: horror. This horror was irresponsibly absolute, yet also low-budget: cheaply dubbed, ill-lit and hand-held. Outside, the courtyard, the cold stamp of the hooves' iron. A couple of centuries ago, Richard had raped the director's girlfriend. He was now the cursed painting of a staked viscount, kept in a secret attic. Or else he was the ruined stableboy, all drained and scorched and peed-on, and left for dead in the owly hovel, under a heap of old straw. Something good had happened and something bad had happened. There was a mirror, above the washbasin: Richard went and stared at the gormless ghoul who lived behind the glass. Such hair as had not fallen out overnight now stood on end, and his mouth was crinkled like a frozen chip. Nor did he not perceive that he had *another* black eye.

He came downstairs with a clicking handkerchief pressed over most of his face. Everybody was out. Denied a full and frank account of why he looked how he looked, an elderly couple, keepers of the hangover, closely monitored him in the kitchen as he put together a sustaining mixture of chicory essence and condensed milk. He took it into the hall and sat on the sofa holding his cup with both hands, just under the chin, like a woman . . . Something bad had happened and something good had happened: his internal balance told him this. Both to do with Demi, it could safely be assumed. Huddled over his nameless cupful he suddenly remembered that he had written the good thing down: committed it to paper. Let other pens dwell on guilt and misery, he thought, and even whispered, as he searched himself for his notebook. There it was on the last page, capitalized, and gloatingly underscored. It said, DEMI: "GWYN CAN'T WRITE FOR TOFFEE." He took what comfort he could from this.

For Richard knew, already, that he was in very serious physical trouble. This hangover had symptoms, remarkable symptoms, including a primal incredulity with regard to all bodily actions and accomplishments, like crossing the legs, or scratching the head, or breathing: when Richard inhaled, he wasn't quite getting there—he wasn't turning the corner, he wasn't getting there and he wasn't getting back. But what were these symptoms symptoms of? He knew: mortal fear. His only ambition, at present, was to die well. To go gently, with, perhaps, a modest but timely apothegm on his lips. Now, granting him further seclusion, both his ears abruptly gulped shut.

And so he sat there, composing himself, and asking himself who done it. He knew the who, and never mind the why (fuck the why), but how about the how? Here was how. Demi had efficiently favored either nostril with a trail of Richard's cocaine—and then gone to bed. (He remembered the preemptive *mwa* of her kiss as he bade her good-night outside her room.) Richard had then finished all of it. And this wasn't the usual seventy-five quid's worth (which always half killed him anyway). This was the cocaine Steve Cousins had given him. This was the cocaine you saw in films. Films about Colombians with private jets and ponytailed bodyguards. Next, with that achieved, he had uncomplainingly burgled the house until he found a cupboard with a few hundred Christmases of near-empty liqueur bottles in it: plum, cherry, apricot—Benedictine,

Parfait Amour. The evening had finally vanished down the long vistas of De Quinceyan visions: visions of the success that *Untitled* might yet enjoy (that coke, he now concluded, must have been some really good shit). Richard also remembered sitting in the dark dining room, his chin sticky with spiritous distillment, and listening to the Labrador as it whinnied in nightmare or labor, and hoping that no one would come down to tend her, and feeling the comfort of the community of pain . . . Richard twitched. So violently that one of his ears gulped open. He waited. He *was* feeling warmer and had even stopped shivering. The log fire fumed purposelessly, yet a gentle liquid heat seemed to be suffusing his nethers. Perhaps, if he sat there incredibly quietly, attempting in a while, say, a salubrious cigarette . . .

The great doors opened. Richard turned, with diffidence. And what did he see in the cold bright morning but life, the colors of health and youth that make the dying thing shrivel tighter in its lair. Horse haunch and hot horse breath, and the jodhpured brides and the grinning grooms and, ever onward, the caravan of prams. Demi was upon him. With the blue and white of her eyes and the white and pink of her mouth she made it clear that he had to *hurry*: Mr. Bowyer-Smith himself had agreed to give Richard the full forty-room tour. With a difficulty that knew no theoretical upper limit, he climbed to his feet. And now at last everyone—the world—was looking at him appropriately, with decorum, with pity, with terror. He followed their stares and looked down: at himself. From crotch to knee Richard's trousers were steeped in purple blood. But not to worry! No matter! It was just the Labrador's afterbirth he'd been sitting in! And so *what* if this was his only pair! Demeter led him to a side passage where she delved deep among gym shoe and windcheater until, half a minute later, he was shown into a room full of plastic tubs of laundry and quaking washing machines, there to slip into his oatmeal flares. The Labrador lay in the corner, on a raft of cardboard. She didn't notice him. She was busy with biology, licking her moley young.

He did the forty-room tour and came back and sat in the kitchen while all the children who could walk trooped past him and inspected his black eye like a file of little generals reviewing the lone squaddie— disgraced, and on kitchen patrol. And you know what the world did to him then? I can't believe they're doing this to me, he said to himself, in the van with Urania and Callisto and Persephone. He felt he was pleading—with whom? With the Labrador's puppies, blind, burrowing, and wet with their newborn varnish. Oh, Christ, how can they do this? To me, me, so lost, so reduced, and sniveling for sustenance. A soul so sick of sin, so weary of the world's shadows and figments. Jesus, they're not really going to do this, are they? They are. They're taking me to fuck-ing *church*.

In the village square the van opened up, and let him out.

"A girl called *Girl* called."

Richard reared round. "A girl *called* Girl called?"

"Someone called Girl. She called."

"Could it be *Gal*?"

"Yes. Or Gal."

His interlocutor was Benjy—husband to Amaryllis. He held in his hand a scrap of paper ripped from an exercise book, and then scrawled on, with Darko-like difficulty. Richard snatched it from him and said,

"May I see?"

"The old man took the message. Rather to his irritation. Then of course they got cut off. The telephone never works here and we're not allowed to bring our mobiles. House rules. She said she had news. What was it?"

"What's that say. What's this word say?"

"*Position*?"

"No it's an adjective."

"*Perverse*? Uh—*pervious*?"

"Could it be *positive*?"

"Yes, that's it. I think that was it. Positive news."

It was Sunday evening, and everyone was drifting away into the perennial dreadfulness of Sunday night. Into the motorway, and Mon-day. Gal had positive news. What could that mean? Everyone was posi-tive that they didn't want to publish *Untitled*? Gal was positive that *Untitled* was unpublishable? No. Positive was the opposite of negative. A positive was what two negatives made . . .

"Come on," said Demeter, and took his arm. "Time to meet the old man."

Men wear trousers all the time, even in bed, and women wear trousers about half the time they're up, but it's women who wear culottes and pantalettes and pantaloons and hot pants and knickerbock-ers and buckskins, and cycling pants when they aren't cycling and sweatpants when they aren't sweating and jodhpurs when they aren't riding and buckskins when they aren't rustling, while men just wear *trousers*—strides, jekylls—and that's that. So Richard might have taken some pleasure, really, in his oatmeal flares: rejoiced in the novelty of them. Their wrinkliness, for example. How they swung low on the hip and pranced high on the ankle. The playful way the seat kept gathering and wedging itself in his bum crack. And they itched—these old jekylls tickled and prickled, all over, but most mortifyingly in the inner thigh, beginning at the knee and burning worse and worse until they went at his groin like a riot of crabs. And, yes, the hairy rope between his buttocks also crazingly bristled. So Richard hated his trousers. He had hated them all day because they made him old. An old man staring out from the doors of the snug of the Slug, the wrinkly in his wrinklies, in his charity flares.

"Demi," he said giddily, "I was looking in my notebook this morning. And I just want to check a quote with you." She was leading him through the dark across a courtyard to the nursery wing above the coach house where (she explained) the Earl and the Countess had sequestered themselves these last seven years. "You did say, didn't you, that Gwyn can't write for toffee?"

After a pause she said, "Yes. Well he can't, can he."

"No. He can't."

"It's as clear as a pikestaff, isn't it."

"Exactly," said Richard.

"Up we go."

He now stood, finally, in the presence of the Earl of Rieveaulx. The old bloodsucker sat upright in a functional armchair before a slit-faced paraffin stove. His surroundings were characterized by wipeable surfaces, lined bins, plastic tablecloths, and an undersmell of carbolic and Sunday-best batman BO; here, geriatric praxis was still in its infancy. So the old slavedriver was making his last preparations, was shedding worldliness . . . The Countess, his junior by a lustrum or two but also his senior in mortal time, seldom left her bedroom: had good days, had bad days. He addressed his daughter with a classicist's pedantry and relish: with the three long *es*. Richard sometimes managed Demeeter; but it fell to the old tariff-hiker to manage Deemeeteer.

Demeter addressed her father by a familial diminutive that Richard had never heard before. It began with *p* and rhymed with *khazi*. The other word it rhymed with was *mbazi*, whom Demi announced her intention of looking in on.

"This is Richard *Tull*," she repeated as she left the room. "He's a very good friend of *Gwyn's*."

The old sanctions-buster sat there, his skin bricklike in hue and breadth of pore. He didn't extend a hand. There was intransigent vigor in the way he wagged his crossed right leg.

"How do you do," said Richard, and sipped on the schooner of piercingly sweet sherry that Demi had given him. The stormlit valleys of his hangover were beginning to settle and heal. Mortal fear was general, now, rather than clinical.

"What are you?"

He means my profession, Richard decided, and thought of something like, *I ply, sir, the scrivener's trade.* What he said was, "I write. I'm a writer."

Writing, like dying, wasn't worldly, wasn't quite of the world. Would that be held in its favor? The old rent-gouger was perhaps considering this question, his narrow chin upraised, his smeared and bloody blue eyes loosening in their orbits. His head, which was idling like a spool on a spindle, now tightened into a steadier quiver.

"So! You grace us with a *second* visit. We thank you for your condescension. Tell me—what keeps you away? Is it that you are happier in the town? Is it the lack of 'hygienic facilities'? Is it all the children and babies, is it the *progeny*, you abhor?"

Richard was wondering how the old kaffir-flogger had had *time* to get to dislike him. But he remembered Demi saying that her father's eyesight and hearing were not of the keenest. He didn't dislike Richard, not personally. He just thought he was Gwyn.

"Well it's as you say," said Richard, glancing over his shoulder and stepping forward. Waste not want not. Cut your coat according to your cloth. "Partly it's the dirt. The filth everywhere. And the babies too. I can't bear babies. And I'm a *writer*, do you see. I have *higher things* on my mind."

Was that enough? Would that do? No. It was coming on him again— the desire for passionate speech. This could be the chance of a lifetime: God-given. He leaned into the rockpool gaze of the Earl of Rieveaulx, saying, "Writers are sensitive types. Me, I happen to be very worried about the state of the planet. Which is all the poorer, wouldn't you say, for *your* depradations. But you don't want to think about that now. It never happened. That—that Vatican of swag you've got next door. It never happened. It's just you and God now, right?" He moved yet closer. "Tell me something I've always wanted to know. Your God: how far does his influence stretch? All across the universe, or just around here? How big are his lands? About the same size as yours? Or do they go all the way to Short Crendon and the church spire? Let's make a deal. No more grandchildren from me. And no more gamekeeper God for you. No more kids' stuff. Oh yeah. Don't you know who Persephone was the *daughter* of? Deemeeteer. Look at you. You even fucked *that* up."

After an inhalation, a sigh, a few old beats of oldster time (themselves an adventure in hatred), the old man's gaze settled—on Richard's trousers . . . It then took about half a minute for his refreshed disgust to gather, to solidify, to come to a head. In minute detestation he ran his eye from Richard's doubled-over waistband, down the wizened shank to the bobbing hems. And Richard felt by now that the Earl—in concert with these terrible jekylls—was finally winning. How the strides burned, and cringed, and miserably itched. Oh men, oh trousers, what they cover, what they hide, the tanned rump, the bush torched off behind the black bikesheds, the braggings and debaggings, the billion bullybags . . .

"Get them *off*."

Richard stopped breathing. He searched for sarcasm in that shattered visage and saw only woundedness and even the seep of bleeding tears. Was he wearing—was he stealing—the old man's old strides?

"Get them *off*," he said, on a rising scale, with that final *whoof* of dogged rage. "Get them *off*. Get them *off*."

Did he want them, did he covet them? Round about, all renounced, lay forty rooms and four hundred years of pocketed knickknacks, of trousered loot—yet did he pine for his oatmeal strides?

"Off! I said get them *off*."

Demeter reentered the room. She looked quickly around at the silence.

"I'm afraid your father," said Richard, "has been bearding me about these trousers."

She sauntered up to him, shaking her head in playful reproach, and put a hand on his shoulder. "He may be the oldest," she declared with a cock of the head, "but he's still the brightest."

". . . What?"

"I said you may be the oldest but you're still the brightest."

"The what?"

"The brightest."

"What?"

"The brightest."

"The broadest?"

"The brightest!"

"The what?"

"I said you may be the *oldest* but you're still the *brightest*."

"The widest?"

"The brightest!"

"The lightest?"

"No, the *brightest*."

"The what?"

Richard had backed off with his glass. From the courtyard below he could hear the van, revving—revving against the cold and damp. It was almost over.

He got back to Calchalk Street at six o'clock the next morning. Prominently displayed on the kitchen table was a couriered package from the offices of Gal Aplanalp. It contained a bottle of champagne and an envelope, which he opened in turn. The letter said:

> Although there has as yet been no response here in England, we have positive news from America. *Untitled* has been accepted by Bold Agenda, Inc., of New York. This is a small imprint, recently launched; they are unable to offer an advance, but the royalty percentage will be correspondingly readjusted in your favor. Roy Biv, your editor there, is very enthusiastic and hopes that we can all get behind the book. They want *Untitled* in their spring list: of course, you will be there, with Gwyn, for publication. This could turn out well for you. I hope you're pleased.

Richard did what Gina did when he asked her to marry him: he assented with a sneeze of tears. An hour later he still had his face in his hands when his wife came lightly down the stairs, and carefully approached. He looked up. A weekend in the country had reduced him to the condition of a barely usable scarecrow. Black-eyed, flare-trousered, and rigid. All night he had juddered, as if in vibrant motion, on the ice-locked rails.

"Oh, what have you done to yourself?"

Behind her, across the passage, Marius and Marco were waking. You could hear them croak and stretch.

"No it's all right, it's all right. I don't know quite how it happened. But I think everything's going to be all right."

I saw the yellow dwarf today. Not the one up there (the weather has been bad). But the one down here (the weather has been bad). A single picture said it all.

The thing was, I think she had a date. Short skirt, high heels, new hairdo. Of course, any description of her appearance and get-up immediately involves you in niceties of scale. Any skirt, on the yellow dwarf, would have been short, and any heels would have been high. Nevertheless, short was her skirt and high were her heels. And her big-hair hairdo, similarly, seemed doubly big—prodigiously, recklessly big . . .

For a moment, for that flashbulb snapshot of time, before the pathetic sepia had a chance to form on the plate—I felt usurped. Me, myself: *I* was big enough to show the yellow dwarf a big time in, say, Big Top Pizza. Now wait. She stood in a doorway, with others, a hole in the wall between the enchained off-license and the appliance emporium to which, and from which, Richard Tull sometimes staggers, furled in the tartan coils of his vacuum cleaner. The yellow dwarf, with others, was sheltering from the rain; the crowded doorway dankly steamed—with cooling vapor, with the dark breath of traffic, and with the trailing edge of one of those London mists made entirely of respiratory betrayals and the gasps of asthmatics. She looked down: her puckered shirt, her ruined shoes. She looked up, with maximum defiance, through the gap in the sodden hedge of her hair.

It so happens that I know quite a lot about dating—down at that end of the scale. As a man who stands five-feet-six-inches tall (or five-feet-six-and-one-half-inches, according to a passport I once had), I know about dating and size. In my early teens I was at least a foot shorter. My mother kept telling me I would "shoot up." I was still asking her, at the age of twenty: "What's all this about me shooting up?" (It never happened; but I grew; and I have no complaints, anymore, about five-feet-six.) Thirty years ago my very slightly older but very much taller brother would sometimes arrange foursomes for my benefit: my brother's girl-friend would be asked to bring a girlfriend along—or a sister. And I would wait, in a doorway, while he made a rendezvous and then report back, saying, "Come on. She's tiny"—or else (shaking his head), "Sorry, Mart." In which case I would perhaps follow him at a distance and watch him rejoin the two sixty-inch giantesses at the entrance to the milk bar or under the lit portals of the Essoldo or the Odeon, and then numbly make my way home in the probable rain.

But this rain, probably, almost certainly, was just ordinary rain, and not the Old Testament deluge that had engulfed and ruined the yellow dwarf. She stood in the doorway, with all the other flashflood amphibians. The makeup, the get-up—the tide-marks round her ankles, like socks; and her face in full defiance under the flattened hedge of the big hair. And I had to think: this is *awful*. But you tried to make too little go too far. You tried to make so very little go so very far.

. . . The information is telling me to stop saying *hi* and to start saying *bye*.

PART *THREE*

Of the pressures facing the successful novelist in the mid-1990s Richard Tull could not easily speak. He was too busy with the pressures facing the unsuccessful novelist in the mid-1990s—or the resurgent novelist, let's say (for now): the *unproved* novelist. Richard sat in Coach. His seat was non-aisle, non-window, and above all non-smoking. It was also non-wide and non-comfortable. Hundreds of yards and hundreds of passengers away, Gwyn Barry, practically horizontal on his crimson barge, shod in prestige stockings and celebrity slippers, assenting with a smile to the coaxing refills of Alpine creekwater and sanguinary burgundy with which his various young hostesses strove to enhance his caviar tartlet, his smoked-salmon pinwheel and asparagus barquette, his prime fillet tournedos served on a timbale of tomato and a tapenade of Castilian olives—Gwyn was in First. Richard was in Coach, drinking small beer, eating peanuts; and Coach was the world. Coach World—World Traveler. To his immediate left sat someone very young. To his immediate right sat someone very old. And there was Richard, in the middle. The child leaned and pushed and sometimes squirmed up against him in a careless way, carelessly confident that its touch would be welcome. Whereas the old guy on his right, coated in his crepe of age, remained properly withdrawn. Richard found himself inclining to his left, courting the child's thoughtless touch. After all, he was at the time of life when—sitting in a garden or a park—he was more pleased than vexed if a bee buzzed him, flattered that anything, however briefly and stupidly, could still mistake him for a flower.

Was this, then, a renovated Richard we were looking at? You might have thought so. If you had marked him in recent weeks, his black eye erased (even that whispered query of nicotine, high on the cheekbone), his nose as sane as any other nose (his nose now basked on the shores of reason), his air of pitying detachment in the offices of the Tantalus Press ("It will be a relief to return to your metrical meditations," he had written to Keith Horridge, "after the brouhaha of publication in the States"), his quite frequent renderings of *Respect* as he showered and shaved (having made love successfully, or at least undeniably, to Gina the night before—"*What* you want: baby I got"), his slurred promise to Gwyn, which helped foreclose an otherwise pleasant dinner at Holland Park, that he was going to run him *out of town*: seeing and hearing all this, you might have thought that, yes, here was a writer on a roll. He had put in a lot of time with Anstice, patiently steering her away from her latest plan (that of committing suicide *at* Calchalk Street) and encouraging her to take that brief but restorative holiday in the Isle of Mull (the Isle of Mull, in mid-March, he reckoned, would get Leibniz himself drooling over his pill jar). He had called off Steve Cousins, an exquisitely delicate operation, in which he had eaten a lot of shit, and during which he had felt great and immediate harm skittishly considering his person; calmer himself, he had glimpsed the white-capped *tormenta* in the digital grid of the young man's face; and walking home that night, from the Canal Creperie, he had sensed a kind of thunder at the back of his neck, which never broke. He had not called Belladonna. He had lunched uneventfully with Lady Demeter (and was even pretty sorry to hear about her father's pretty serious heart attack, which had hobbled him that same Sunday night—and apparently within twenty minutes of Richard's departure). But did he hate Gwyn any less? That would have been the key to it. Did he hate Gwyn any less?

In any event Richard was persisting in the belief that a rewarding experience lay ahead of him, despite his immediate discomforts, despite his adhesive doubts about Bold Agenda, Inc., and despite the pillow of crimson tissue paper that he clutched to his face. Soon after take off, while the plane was still climbing, about a period's worth of blood had burst from his right nostril. Now, as he settled down with his beer and his biography, and looked forward to the lunch that was edging ever nearer, about a period's worth of blood burst from his left nostril. Richard's nose, it seemed, was once again a reliable instrument; it just happened to contain a gallon of restless gore. He bent and squeezed himself toward the aisle, past the child, its single parent, and another, older child, and joined the queue for that most despised section of the aircraft, Toilet World—deep in the machine's rump. After his first visit there he had rested on the haunch of the emergency-exit door and looked down at the rink of London and tried to connect it with his own journey from home to airport in the silver courtesy car so affably skippered by Gwyn: that staggered sideways drift through the pale and permanent Sunday of west West London with its patches of green beneath patches of gray, past files of houses tortured by the road you drove; then the ground thinned and flattened in preparation for the netherlands of sky launch (freight, catering), while above a quivering crucifix was spearing down toward you, with its arms out to get you, and screaming at you with its machine scream. "America will kill me," he had said to Gina, on the doorstep, smiling but hot-eyed, and the fine-grained hair of his sons' heads feeling hot beneath his hands—"It's just going to kill me."

Half an hour later Richard emerged, leaving behind a toilet resembling the kitchen of a serial murderer in slapdash but hyperactive career phase; bent over the basin, he had started like a guilty thing when the PA system identified him by name and demanded that he make himself known to the cabin staff. A few last bubbly snorts into the paper towels, and then he squelched his way out of there. In the aisle he saw that a stewardess was coming toward him, looking to left and right and dutifully saying,

"A Mr. Tull? A Mr. Tull. A Mr. Tull at all?"

He watched her. He knew her. He had already singled her out for attention. And we are inclined to speculate whether anyone would really want this—Richard's attention. She was the stewardess who, before takeoff, had been obliged to demonstrate the safety procedure, standing a few feet from Richard's knees. Normally of course the task would have been assigned to a surrogate: to the electronic stewardess on the video screen. But the image had fluttered and stalled; and so, in some bewilderment, they'd all had to settle for the real thing. The stewardess, and her sign language—the hard old dame of the middle air, nearing retirement, her systems warped by the magnetosphere, and by disuse (he understood disuse), like a madam summoned out of deep retirement for the last thing she wanted, going through the motions with the hand stroke, the knee bend—the cursey curtseys of the stewardess.

"A Mr. Tull? A Mr. Tull at all."

This too was the language of the air, this was airspeak; no one on *terra firma* would ever talk like that. But to Richard's ears, still papery with blood loss, it seemed well said. A Mr. Tull. A Mr. Tull at all.

He owned up.

The stewardess escorted him down the length of Economy, and then another stewardess escorted him through Business World; he ducked under a curtain, and then another stewardess led him into First. As he made this journey, this journey within a journey, getting nearer to America, Richard looked to see what everyone was reading, and found that his progress through the plane described a diagonal of shocking decline. In Coach the laptop literature was pluralistic, liberal, and humane: *Daniel Deronda*, trigonometry, Lebanon, World War I, Homer, Diderot, *Anna Karenina*. As for Business World, it wasn't that the businessmen and businesswomen were immersing themselves in incorrigibly minor or incautiously canonized figures like Thornton Wilder or Dostoevsky, or with lightweight literary middlemen like A. L. Rowse or Lord David Cecil, or yet with teacup-storm philosophers, exploded revisionist historians, stubbornly Steady State cosmologists or pallid poets over whom the finger of sentimentality continued to waver. They were reading trex: outright junk. Fat financial thrillers, chunky chillers and tublike tinglers: escape from the pressures facing the contemporary entrepreneur. And then he pitched up in the intellectual slum of First Class, among all its drugged tycoons, and the few books lying unregarded on softly swelling stomachs were jacketed with hunting scenes or ripe young couples in mid swirl or swoon. They all lay there flattened out in the digestive torpor of midafternoon, and nobody was reading anything—except for a lone seeker who gazed, with a frown of mature skepticism, at a perfume catalogue. Jesus, what happened on the Concorde? Scouring the troposphere at the limit of life, and given a glimpse of the other side—a glimpse of what the rest of the universe almost exclusively consisted of (unpunctuated vacuum)—the Mach 2 morons would be sitting there, and staring into space. The space within. Not the space without. In the very nib of the airplane sat Gwyn Barry, who was reading his schedule.

"Hi," said Richard.

Gwyn pulled a lever which caused him to surge up from the supine to the sedentary. He pointed to a little bulkhead table. Richard sat on it, next to the vase of tulips. There were posies everywhere, here in First.

"How are you doing?" said Gwyn. And his eyes returned to his schedule: six or seven sheets, with many a box and bullet-punch, and highlit and color-coded—TV, radio, press. "Wow, they've really got me gridlocked in LA," he went on. "It's all the interest leaking down from San Francisco. Look at that. How can I do the *Chronicle* and then Pete Ellery back to back?" He turned to Richard as if he expected an answer. Then he said, "What have your people got lined up for you?"

"I told you. My editor moved on. They've given me some other Chuck or Chip." And it was true. Roy Biv, Richard's editor—so full of enthusiasm and ideas—had moved on from Bold Agenda, and every time Richard called he got shuffled around from Chip to Chuck, from Chuck to Chip. "Is Chuck there?" *You mean Chip.* "Then give me Chip." *You want Chuck.* And they were never there. Richard couldn't decide whether Chuck and Chip were the same person (like Darko and Ranko), who was permanently absent, or whether both Chip and Chuck were the inventions of a *third* person called something like Chup or Chick. The only editor he ever got through to, these days, was an inoffensive-sounding guy who went by the name of Leslie Evry.

Gwyn said, "So what have they got lined up?"

"I said. I won't know till I get there."

"But this is America, man! You got to get *out* there. You got to *go* for it." Richard waited.

"You got to come on strong. Talk big and kick ass."

"Let's get this straight. Are you trying to be funny, or is it your intention to pretend to be American while we're there?"

Gwyn sank back, and gave his schedule a careless brandish. "You know, you're lucky. This is just show business. While I'm scurrying around out there, you'll have time to absorb everything. Time to think. To ponder. Time to dream. Are you all right, mate? You look a bit pale. But it could be the light."

And the light was coming in sideways, and everything looked combustible or already white-hot, close to burnout or heat-death.

"I had a nosebleed. I haven't seen so much blood since the twins were born. I used up two whole cans' worth of tissues and towels."

"Beautiful flying weather."

"It's always sunny, you know. Above the clouds."

"I got you up here, and it took some doing, so you could see what it's like. For your piece."

Then, for Richard's further benefit, Gwyn cast his gaze round the cabin with an expression that judiciously combined embarrassment and mischief. "Who would have thought it? A boy from the valleys. Flying to America first class."

"Do you mind if I use that line?"

"It's nice, though, isn't it? Dead comfy."

"The sickbags," Richard said dully, "look no better or bigger than the ones in Coach. And they still have turbulence here. And it still takes seven hours. I'll see you on the ground."

He made his way back, past *Magenta Rhapsody* and *Of Kingly Blood*, past *Cartel* and *Avarice* and *The Usurers*, and into the multitudinousness of *Hard Times, La Peste, Amerika, Despair, The Moonstone, Labyrinths* . . . Two people—a man in Business and some dope in Coach—were reading *Amelior*: the paperback.

But as Richard shackled himself back into his seat (which itself bore the heavy indentation of *The Wouldbegood: A Life of Edith Nesbit*), he had other information to process. Gwyn, Gwyn's schedule, *Amelior*, the unfortunate defection of Roy Biv from Bold Agenda: these swayed like loose harpoons from the nucleus of his soul. But he had other information to process, the kind that only comes when life is turning, the kind you have to be there to get, because no one will ever tell you about it. And if they did—you'd never listen.

On his way back through the plane Richard had seen women crying—three women, four women. And he realized that there always were these women on planes, crying, with makeup in meltdown, folded over in the window seat or candidly hideous in the aisle, clutching Kleenex. Before, if he assumed anything, he assumed they were crying about boyfriends or husbands (partings or sunderings), or crying (who cared?) from toothache or curse pains or fear of flying. But now he was forty, and he knew.

Women on planes are crying because someone they love or loved is dead or dying. Every plane has them. The talent on the short hops, the broads on the wide-bodies, with their clutched hankies. Death can do this; death has the power to do this. Death, which sends women hurrying to the end of the street, to bus stops, which makes them run under the clocks of railway stations, which lifts them five miles high and fires them weeping through the air at the speed of death, all over the world.

While it would always be true and fair to say that Richard felt like a cigarette, it would now be doubly true and fair to say it. He felt like a cigarette. And he felt like a cigarette. His mouth was plugged with a gum called Nicoteen. And he wore circular nicotine patches, from the same product stable, on his left forearm and right bicep. Richard's blood brownly brewed, like something left overnight in the teapot. He was a cigarette; and he felt like one. And he still felt like a cigarette . . . What he was doing was practicing non-smoking. He knew how Americans treated smokers, people of smoke, people of fire and ash, with their handfuls of dust. He knew he would be asked to do an awful lot of it: non-smoking. So he felt like a cigarette, and he felt like a drink—he felt like a lot of drinks. But he didn't drink and he didn't smoke. All he had was the plastic bottle of mineral water that Gina had made him bring.

He spent his first two hours in New York wearing an expression of riveted horror. This expression of riveted horror was not a response to American violence or vulgarity, to the disposition of American wealth, the quality of American politicians, the condition of American schooling or the standard of American book reviewing (hopelessly variable but often chasteningly high, he would later conclude). No. This expression of riveted horror Richard came to know well. He looked horrified and riveted, and he knew he looked horrified and riveted, because he was staring into the riveted horror of his own face.

In the bathroom, at the hotel. It was a shaving mirror, on a retractable arm, supplementing the broad background of the regular mirror (itself implacable enough). The shaving mirror had a light above it; it also had a light *inside* it. He thought there must be a lot of people who imagined they looked okay, who fancied they could pass for normal, until they met a shaving mirror in an American hotel. Then the jig was up. Presumably, with the human face, the worst possible representation will always be the truest. This was the best mirror, and it was the worst mirror. All other mirrors were in public relations. After an audience with such a mirror, only two places to go (and maybe the hotel took its cut): the cosmetic surgery, or the church. Richard tried to tell himself that he had looked terrible in London too. And memorably terrible. A week before departure he found that his passport, disused for some while, had quietly gone out of print, or been remaindered. So he breezed along to Woolworth's in Portobello Road and slipped into the booth, expeditiously, without even pausing to arrange his hair. Three minutes later he was shredding the strip of photographs with his fingernails—photographs in which he looked, at once, incredibly old, incredibly mad and incredibly *ill*. He returned to the beauty parlor of Calchalk Street, and then tried again; and he spent another six quid before he came up with anything he could seriously present at Petty France . . . The mirror had the power to hold him in position, like a vise. His face, it was nothing. It was scorched earth.

Next door on the bed there lay a bundle of early reviews and a copy of the schedule and some bright new hardbacks and even a spray of flowers, all sent by the publisher. By Gwyn's publisher, that is to say: to help him with his piece—his piece about Gwyn. There was nothing from Bold

Agenda, no message, no word and no meaningful reply to the calls he kept making from the bathroom telephone, with his nose an inch from the glass. Richard's requests to speak to Leslie Evry got bounced round the office until they seemed to evaporate or else were pounded into submission and silence by a background cacophony of impulsive home improvement, complete with pummeled nailheads and creaking bucket handles and one-liners tossed back and forth by guys with names like Tug and Tiff and Heft. In twenty minutes he was due upstairs: to listen in on Gwyn being interviewed. Then, when that was over, he was going to arrange to interview the interviewer about what Gwyn was like to interview. Richard left the bathroom and went and sat on the bed and calmly smoked his way through a panic attack. He wanted his boys with him, Marius on this side, Marco on that side. Marius here, Marco there. The mirror was telling him that his body was close to death but his mind felt six months old.

Gwyn's suite seemed as crowded as Coach: waiters, the hotel assistant manager, two interviewers, one incoming, one outgoing, two photographers ditto, two lady high-ups from Gwyn's publishers or its parent corporation and one publicity boy. The room was additionally infested with bouquets and bowls of fruit, presumably real but impressively fake-looking, and, at some unguessable level of authenticity, the excitement of increase, of reputable profit, the kind you get when commerce meets art and finds it good. Richard sat down near the publicity boy, who, he saw, was not only on the telephone but was physically attached to it: he had a thick wire circling his chin like a pilot's mouth-mike, freeing both his hands to cope with his laptop E-mail and all the other light-speed technologies they had wired him into. He was plumply handsome, the publicity boy, his backswept hair as darkly super-lustrous as an oil stain on a blacktop.

"I really do feel," Gwyn was saying, angling his head to accommodate the photographer who crouched at his feet, "that the novelist has to find a new simplicity."

"How, Gwyn, how?"

"By *evolving* into simplicity. By deciding on the new direction and heading for it."

"To where, Gwyn, where?"

"How about if we loop the *Post* guy," called the publicity boy, "and he can just *watch* you do the radio spot?"

"To fresh fields. Okay: the guy from *EF* can listen to me do the TV spot—from the audio booth. And pastures new."

"So have the signing after the reading but before the meeting."

"Have the meeting *during* the signing. And I can get photographed while I'm getting photographed. Phyllis Widener. Richard Tull."

Richard knew from his *Amelior Regained* publicity pack that Phyllis Widener had a bold-print twice-weekly column in one of the New York tabloids: personalities, arts, local politics. Wry seniority was her thing; she was meant to be twinkly and unfoolable. That's what you got when you were old: experience. And maturity too. In person, Phyllis seemed to be the kind of American woman who had taken a couple of American ideas (niceness, warmth) and then turned up some dreadful dial, as if these qualities, like the yield of a hydrogen bomb, had no upper limit— the range had no top to it—and just went on getting bigger and better as you lashed them toward infinity. Only her colleagues and superiors knew that the pieces she wrote, over many hours and many cups of strong coffee in her small and memento-strewn apartment on Thirteenth Street, often and increasingly turned out to be unusably vicious . . . Richard found a bit of hotel notepaper and a hotel biro and dragged up a chair. He was immediately rewarded with a good bit for his piece: Gwyn pausing mid-word, actually mid-syllable (halfway through "unsophisticated"), like a machine himself, when Phyllis's tape clicked off at the end of its spool; he sat there with his mouth open, on pause, while she replaced it. Meanwhile too it became clear that the energies of the publicity boy were directed not to the further accrual of publicity opportunities but to their radical attenuation.

"Unsophisticated approach, then that's their opinion. I prefer to liken it to carpentry."

"Are you a carpenter, Gwyn?"

"With wood, a poor one, Phyllis. With words, well, I have my molds and templates, my spirit level, my trusty saw."

"I think it's so beautiful the way you say that."

"You know. Pottering away."

The interview ended, and the room thinned out, and Gwyn, who looked fresh enough to Richard, went to freshen up next door. So he was left alone with Phyllis; he sat there, rinsed in her entirely embarrassing gaze, and duly began to interview Phyllis about her interview with Gwyn. After a minute and a half he had no more questions.

Preceded by the publicity boy, Gwyn passed through the room. He was expected downstairs in the restaurant, to be interviewed.

"I have been busy," he said to Richard, "on your behalf. How's your schedule? There's a press interview in Miami and a big radio slot in Chicago. And a reading-signing in Boston. I was wondering if you could work them in."

"Why's this?"

"I'm double-dated all over the place. I offered them you. It's all fixed."

Gwyn's was a non-smoking suite, on a non-smoking floor. Over half the hotel was non-smoking. Whereas Richard had dedicated his life to the cause of non-non-smoking. He had laid it down, his life. They sat in silence until Phyllis said,

"You two are old friends."

He gave an economical nod.

"You know, he admires your work deeply. I heard him. Telling everyone on the phone what a truly marvelous writer you were. He loves you very dearly."

"No he doesn't. He might want you to think he does."

Surprisingly she said, "You think he's trying to hurt you?"

"He doesn't need to. The world will do it."

You live alone, right? This was what the greeters and credit-card ratcheters of American hospitals said to the pungent phantoms of the reception desk—to those rendered unpresentable by neglect, to those singled out and quarantined by neglect. Phyllis *looked* okay. Richard didn't understand that much about other people. But he understood neglect.

"You live alone, right?"

She made her blue eyes rounder and her closed lips wider; she gave him rich assent.

"Never any husband or anything?"

It made him despair twice over. Because he had believed, until then, that he wasn't ready for despair. Suddenly Richard thought of Anstice— but saw himself living with Phyllis: rigid among the chintz and dimity of her bedroom, in new pajamas (the pajamas, perhaps, were a key part of this fresh beginning), with Phyllis leaning over him and applying a moistened washcloth to his brow . . .

"I'm sorry," he said, and sat up straighter.

"That's okay," she said. "Now can I ask about Gwyn?"

The piece she intended to write was going to be borderline hostile anyway—before Richard even got started. As it turned out, Phyllis's editor would get no further than the end of the second sentence before deciding, with a practiced shrug, that the Barry profile had better be quietly spiked. In fairness, Richard never thought that Phyllis's piece would be influential enough to be worth contaminating. He was just getting in shape for later on.

Broadly satisfied, he left Phyllis in the lift and returned to his room. Over a club sandwich he roughed out a 550-word review of *Time's Song:*

Winthrop Praed, 1802–1839 and then curled up with *AntiLatitudinarian: The Heretical Career of Francis Atterbury*. At one in the morning, by which point his day was twenty-five hours old, he went out into New York. A brief turn, in his mack, along Central Park South.

He knew American fiction, and he knew that fiction, considered in aggregate, would not lie. For him, coming to America was like dying and going to hell or heaven and finding it all as advertised. Take hell: black fire and darkness visible, the palpable obscure—and ice, to starve your soft ethereal warmth: the anti-universe of the damned. New York was out there and he didn't have any time to think about it. But he knew, the instant he arrived on its streets, that New York was the most violent thing that men had ever done to a stretch of land, more violent, in its way, than what was visited on Hiroshima, at ground zero, on day one. He looked up. He looked up and saw no difference: the usual metropolitan sky with its six or seven stars weakly guttering. Raw land can do nothing about them but cities hate stars and don't want their denizens to be reminded of how it really goes with ourselves and the universe.

"So!" said Leslie Evry, settling back in the swivel chair with his hands interjoined behind his head. "What brings you to our fair land?"

Richard had to hear this again. This was great. The whole adventure had lasted five seconds. And here he was: wiped out.

"I beg your pardon?"

"What brings you," repeated Leslie Evry, with brio, "to our fair land?"

Richard had been asked this question several times already—by lift-men, by barmen. Now he was hearing it from Bold Agenda. He was hearing it from his own future. Of course, Richard liked to think of himself as a virtuoso of rejection; his history of humiliation was long—was long and proud. The humiliated are always looking for consideration and getting the unconsidered, the offhand and ready-made. So Richard sat there, devastated, wiped out, by a reflexive banality from Leslie Evry.

"What brings me to your fair land? I somehow ran away with the idea that I had a novel coming out in your fair land."

"You certainly do. Seen this?"

He was handed a slender flyleaf or bookmark. On it were listed ten or twelve titles. There he was, near the bottom. Richard Tull. *Untitled.* $24.95. 441pp. Richard Tull recognized Richard Tull. The other names were not familiar, were in themselves unfamiliar; even the compilers of American telephone directories, he sensed, might have been impressed by their unfamiliarity. The only thing they reminded him of was the cast list of *Amelior* and *Amelior Regained*: Gwyn's identikit hominids—Jung-Xiao, Yukio, Conchita, Arnaujumajuk.

"Have you heard anything about any reviews or anything of that kind?"

"For sure," said Leslie. Smartly he flipped open a folder on his desk. "John Two Moons had some coverage in the *Cape Codder*. He keeps a fishing boat up there or something. And Shanana Ormolu Davis had a nice mention in the *Shiny Sheet*. In Miami. She's working with the hearing-impaired down there. At the Abbé L'Epée Institute?"

Two stamp-sized clippings were passed toward him. Richard looked and nodded.

"You know how John Two Moons got his name? It's kind of a nice story. Apparently—"

"Excuse me. What about *Untitled*?"

"Excuse me?"

"*Untitled*. Twenty-four-ninety-five. Four hundred and forty-one pages."

Then Leslie Evry did a terrible thing. He said "Excuse me?" again—and then lavishly blushed. "Not thus far. Insofar as we know."

"Is there a *prospect* of any reviews?"

"A 'prospect'?"

"Is there anyone in the publicity department I should be talking to?"

"May I ask what this would be in regard to?"

In the past, Richard had often been known to be "difficult." *Difficult* was a word that applied to his person as well as his prose. Unfortunately, though, he soon failed to command much of an arena to be difficult in. There was surely no more elbow room for difficulty (difficulty was exhausted), he decided, after his yodeling stalk-out from the debating hall of the Whetstone Public Library Literary Association ("Whither the Novel?"). He stalked out because he was the only panel member who, in the cafeteria before the talk, had not been offered a biscuit with his tea. As he rode alone on the bus and, later, on the tube train, with his armpits ablaze, Richard recalled that he *had* been offered a biscuit. But not a chocolate one. Just a ginger-nut. And that same year he had to be expensively dissuaded from suing a reviewer of *Dreams Don't Mean Anything* for that dismissive filler in *The Oldie* . . . Richard considered being difficult now, and stalking out of Bold Agenda. Then what? A few plangent inhalations, on Avenue B? Like all writers, Richard wanted to live in some hut on some crag somewhere, every couple of years folding a page into a bottle and dropping it limply into the spume. Like all writers, Richard wanted, and expected,

the reverence due, say, to the Warrior Christ an hour before Armaged-
don. He said,

"Frankly, you surprise me. Roy Biv was full of ideas. As it happens
I—"

"Ah, Roy! Roy Biv!"

"As it happens I've already fixed a few things. A reading and signing in
Boston. I'm doing the Dub Traynor interview in Chicago."

"Dub Traynor? For the book?"

"For the book."

"Well that's *great*. Hey. May I introduce my co-director. Frances Ort.
Frances? Come and say hi to Richard Tull."

Bold Agenda, as an operation, was still only half constructed. Frances
Ort had not so much entered Leslie's office as wandered on to his floor-
space. Behind her, big clean guys in overalls plodded about carrying sections of white wallboard. On arrival Richard had himself plodded about
among them for a while, before finding Leslie. You could see how it was
all going to look one day—cord carpets, white cubbyholes.

"It's certainly a pleasure to meet you, sir. I'm really looking forward to
reading your novel."

"I was just telling Richard," said Leslie, "how John Two Moons got
his name."

"I love this story."

In appearance Frances Ort suggested a rainbow coalition of the chro-
mosomes. She could probably go anywhere in the five boroughs—
Harlem, Little Astoria, Chinatown—and provoke no comment other
than the usual incitements to immediate and rigorous sexual congress. In
this she resembled her colleague. Ethnically, Evry and Ort were either
everything and nothing or neither one thing nor the other. They were
just Americans.

"Well. You know how Native Americans get their names."

"I think so. It's the first thing the dad sees."

"Right. Now. The night John Two Moons was born there was this
beautiful full moon, and his father—"

"Was drunk," suggested Richard.

"Excuse me?"

"Was drunk. And saw two moons. Well they are meant to be incredible drunks, aren't they? Native Americans? I mean we're bad enough,
but they're . . ."

". . . And—and his father walked out, by the lake, and saw the full
moon reflected in the water."

"That's it?" said Richard. He was thinking about smoking, in direct defiance of the sign on the wall, which told him not to: not to think about it.

"Frances here has been working in Miami with Shanana Ormolu Davis," said Leslie, standing, and taking up position at her side, "updating—"

"How did she get *her* name? I beg your pardon. Go on."

"Updating sign language for the hearing-impaired. It's really interesting."

"African, or Afro-American," said Frances, "used to be this." She flattened her nose with her palm. "And Chinese used to be this." She tweaked her left eye slantwise with a childish fingertip. "And 'tight' or 'cheap' used to be this." She stroked her chin.

"Meaning?"

"Jewish. With a beard."

"Christ. I can see that needed some work."

"And a person of same-sex orientation," said Leslie, "used to be—"

"Queer," said Frances.

"Excuse me?"

"Queer. They're called queers now."

"Right. Queer," Leslie went on, "used to be this." He gave a languid flap of the wrist. "Can you believe?"

"And now what is it?"

"Queer?" said Leslie, turning to Frances. "What's queer now?"

"Queer? I think it's just sign language for *queer*."

"We've come a long way," said Richard.

"Too right," said Frances.

"Too right," said Leslie.

He took her hand. Or she took his. Or their hands joined. In a way nothing was expressed by this, no claim of love or friendship or even solidarity. But it still looked like sign language. Meaning the future, the next thing, meaning evolution, and *Amelior* . . .

Frances said good-bye and very soon Richard was being guided toward the stairs by Leslie, who was saying, "As hard as we're working here you can see we still have a way to go. Copies have been submitted for review. At the present time distribution is light going on minimal but if the reviews are perceived as positive then things may build from there. Can I ask you something? Are you just touring the States *anyway*?"

Now Richard paused on the stairs. He saw no way out. "I'm writing a piece about Gwyn Barry."

"Isn't it amazing the attention he's getting?"

"Yes. Consternating. How do you account for it?"

"I guess it's a book whose time has come. The Profundity Requital—that's the key for him. He's on fire. And if the Requital goes his way: abracadabra. Supernova."

Don't worry about it, he wanted to answer: the Requital will not go Gwyn's way. Richard was resolved. He owed it to Profundity. He owed it to the universe.

They moved on.

"I'm sorry we can't get out there more for *Untitled*," said Leslie. "But yet. If you so choose to do so . . ."

At the front door he veered off to the left, into a storeroom or junk room. There were sounds of mauling and tugging and dragging and his sudden and surprising "Shit!" and then more dragging, until he finally flung a lumpy brown mail sack out into the passage at Richard's feet and came stumbling in on after it.

"You're doing readings, signings," said Leslie. He looked vivid—warmed up. "I don't know. You could care less, right? I don't know. There's eighteen copies in there. You feeling strong?"

What could he do? *Untitled* was his youngest, and probably his last born. The sack looked ragged, frayed, at the end of its tether. But Richard swung it up onto his shoulder. And he had to make it clear to Evry that he could lift it: that he was man enough.

"Boston. That your first stop?"

"Last stop."

"Oh. By the way. Great book."

It wasn't until now that Richard teetered, all his weight gathering on his back foot. "Thank you," he said in a youthful voice. "That's very kind of you. I did feel I was on to something. You don't think . . . I was worried about the penultimate bridging passages. You know: where the figment narrator pretends to attempt that series of decoy refocusings."

Leslie nodded understandingly.

"Because the travesty is a counterfeit."

"Yup."

"Not that he's really a narrator."

"Mm-hm."

"Reliable or otherwise. But he had to be a surrogate if the sham refocusings were going to *seem* to work."

"Absolutely. Hey are you sure you can handle that?"

Out on Ninth and B, between Bold Agenda and the Life Café, a little bookshop (The Lazy Susan) lurked, in a half-basement, behind thick light-bending glass. Unlike most American bookshops—unlike the bookshops he had already meandered between on Fifth and on Madison (monitoring his own absence and turning *Amelior Regained* to the wall or inhuming it beneath stacks of contending trex), and unlike the book-shops he would come to know, the Muzaked and mallish, the underlit and wood-paneled and pseudo-Bodleiaic, the disco-Montparnassian—this was Richard's kind of bookshop. It looked like a garage sale thrown by the dependents of some bibliomaniacal niggard. As he ventured fur-ther, into the pleasant barnyard smell (the smell of the twins' hair), he was struck by a contrary association—the Christian Science Reading Rooms of the English high street, and their structural futility: because a Reading Room meant freedom and possibility, and (as he was often reminded on his doorstep) Christian Science, which was all there was to read in there, was a nonstarter and meant absolutely nothing. He bumped about with his mail sack, finding categories, alphabetization. Maybe this was a broader church; it offered revelation by a variety of means—crystals, heavenly configurations, numerology and, here and there, yes, poetry, fiction, criticism, philosophy. Then he saw it, on a bench, the slow staggered stacks and the sign saying BOLD AGENDA. The mail sack thudded into his spine as he quickly approached and quickly halted. *Hush Now* by Shanana Ormolu Davis, *Cowboy Boots* by John Two Moons, and, among other works by other visionaries of the Bold Agenda imprint, a brace of copies of *Untitled* by Richard Tull.

He tarried in the Lazy Susan Bookstore for over an hour. No one bought *Untitled*; no one flipped through it or weighed it in their hand; no one strayed that close to the bench enshrined to Bold Agenda—all of whose publications, it turned out, bore the same strange nimbus of fur and fuzz, as daunting to the eye as to the touch. It was certainly a pity about the look of it, the look and feel of *Untitled*. No dust jacket, for instance; and that horsehair texture. Wrenching his first copy out of its Jiffy Bag, back in Calchalk Street, Richard had caught a hangnail deep in its bristling weft. And his fingertip was little more than a blob of plasma when he eventually shook it free . . . Richard tarried for over an hour. And no one touched *Untitled*. But he paid this no mind. What was an hour? Literary time wasn't cosmic time or geological time or evolution-ary time. Still, it wasn't quotidian time. It went slower than the clock on the wall.

Which Gwyn Barry would do well to learn, thought Richard, when he got back to the hotel. Shackled and hostaged to the secular, to the tem-poral, an eager hireling of his own novel, Gwyn was still stockpiling interviews in his suite on the fourteenth floor. Richard watched and lis-tened to three or four of them (simplicity, unsophistication, carpentry), quietly mesmerized by boredom and disgust. True, *Amelior Regained* wasn't published until early next month, and *Untitled* had been out, or available, for at least a fortnight, but Richard still reckoned he was holding his own. Why? And why did he want a great deal of alcohol so much (why did he want to upend the drinks table into his mouth?), and why did he throb for Gina's touch? Waking beside her, on some recent mornings, he had felt as questingly nubile as the opening bars of *Peter and the Wolf* . . . They were flying out in the late afternoon. Somehow Richard found time to cab downtown to Avenue B, to reenter the Lazy Susan and establish that neither copy of *Untitled* had left the bookstore. On the other hand, perhaps one had been sold and his modest pile had been fondly replenished from the stockroom. Perhaps one copy had been sold. Perhaps, somewhere, a reader was frowning and smiling and scratching his hair. Perhaps one copy had been sold. Perhaps two.

We have reiterated that neither Demeter Barry nor Gina Tull enjoyed any connection with literature except by marriage. Just as Richard had no connection with Nottingham except by marriage. Just as Gwyn, at the outset, had no connection with the nobility, or with central heating, except by marriage.

This wasn't true. Demi had her literary salon for a while, after all, and had briefly served on a committee or two which championed the cause of oppressed, silenced, imprisoned and murdered writers, and the cause of the Ghost Writer himself, he who is here and yet not here, he who is among the living and yet not among them. As for Gina, she and literature went way back.

The first time Richard set eyes on her he wondered why she wasn't doing her nails in the master bedroom of a thirty-berth yacht in the Persian Gulf, or bawling out her greeters as she stepped from the scrapertop helipad, late for her little lunch with B.J. or Leon or Whitney. More than this (because her face was artistic, unhackneyed, it was original), he could see her on the parapet of the Spanish castle, long emplaced as mistress-muse of the smocked and popeyed iconeer . . . All these impressions were strongly and strangely reinforced the first time he went to bed with her, which in fact took some doing. But there she sat, unregarded, behind a desk, selling postcards and catalogs in a black-timbered Nottingham museum, and behind her, through the glass, a patch of walled garden with the sun squinting at it after the rain, and a lone crow on the grass flexing its shoulders and straightening its sooty zootsuit. The world had not found out about her. How come? Because Richard knew it couldn't just be *him*. This was genetic celebrity, which had an audience and an essential value. In other times and climes her family would have kept her in a locked room and held an auction on her sixteenth birthday. Leaning forward at her desk, counting money and sighing without weariness, she was ten years further on into womanhood—and the word, the phone calls and faxes, still had time to go out to the planet's playboys, all of them, from the pub spiv with his white-lipped salacities, up past the jodhpured joke in his jeep and right the way through to the kind of OPEC keltocrat who blew half his GNP on his own Johnson. Richard felt the ignoble excitement of a Sotheby's smoothieboy buying a Titian from a tinker. He was thirty, and Oxonian, and still handsome. He lived in London: the capital itself. He had a notorious girlfriend—the powerful Dominique-Louise. He was a freshly published novelist. But his knees were the knees seen through that bendy leaded window, seen by that brute of a crow, which was watching him and harshly purring.

He bought his seventh postcard and second catalog and said, "Do you like Lawrence?" And she looked up at him with eyes so great and clean that they were obliged to include some vapidity, some provincial vapidity, because there was room in there for everything. Gina was no English rose, dead the next day. This was subsoil: Celt-Iberian, Northern-swarthy, gypsyish. Her eyes were set in dark loops of shadow, like badger, burglar, brawler, dramatically bruised by some internal suffusion (embarrassment always deepened these shadows); her nose was a Caligulan quarter-circle; her mouth was lean— wide, but not full.

"Do you like Lawrence?"

"Eh?"

"D. H. Lawrence. Do you like him?"

How do you mean, *like*? her eyes said, then. But her mouth said, "You had me there. My boyfriend's called Lawrence. Anyroad, I can tell *you* like him."

Richard laughed sparingly, grandly. (And she really did say anyroad. Just that once. And never again.) With his ears all gummed and humming, Richard explained. This was indeed his fifth visit to the museum in two days. But his interest was professional, was shrewd, was remunerative. Around them a temporary exhibition in honor of D. H. Lawrence had been mounted (his shaving brush, his fob-watch, his manuscripts, his surprisingly well-controlled paintings), here in the author's hometown. Richard was writing a piece about it—very much the kind of piece he wrote in those days: regional, marginal, with a flat fee for expenses. Richard in a room at the bunky boardinghouse; a half-bottle of whisky and the *Selected Letters*, the poems, *Lady Chatterley, D. H. Lawrence, Novelist, A Selection from Phoenix, Women in Love*. That kind of thing made him happy then.

"It's for the *TLS*. The *Times Literary Supplement*." That was good. All those prissy syllables were good. Richard knew that words were all he had. Not the words that would appear in the *Times Literary Supplement*. Nor the words that would appear on the pages of *Dreams Don't Mean Anything*, due out in the autumn. Just the words he would use on Gina Young. In speech, and of course in letters, in notes. Because Richard knew about women and letters, women and notes. He knew about women and words.

She said, "Where are you stopping?"

Ah: a local ambiguity. Stopping meant staying. And Richard wasn't stopping anywhere. He was going all the way. He said, " 'The Savoy,' 3 Stalton Avenue. Can I ask you if you'll do something?"

"Eh?"

"Come live with me and be my love."

"Bloody hell."

"And we will all the pleasures prove . . . Wait. I'm sorry. But what does one say? I've never seen anyone like you before. Your eyes."

She was looking around. Who for? A policeman. Or a critic, to come and help with the clichés. But we like clichés, don't we, in matters of the heart? Lovers are a mob. No detail, thank you, nothing too interesting in itself, if you don't mind, where *love* is concerned. That all comes later. Our tiring and fantastical requests and provisos, our much-humored peculiarities, our exasperating attention to detail.

"Get away," she said.

"Okay then. Lunch."

"I've a boyfriend."

"Yes. Lawrence. I bet. Long time? How long?"

"Nine years."

"Of course. And you like Lawrence. And Lawrence wouldn't like it."

"No he wouldn't. What would I tell him?"

"Nothing. No, not nothing. Tell him good-bye. Good-bye, good-bye."

He turned. A lady—her tolerant swallow, her habitual beam—had formed a one-lady queue behind him. Richard glanced at the postcard in his hand: Mexico. He paid for it. How sore his throat was. And her face, pointing up at him from where she crouched at the brown table, how swollen, how infused. We must remember the particular ghost (though Gina hadn't read him, and never would) who presided over the innocent triteness of their exchange. Not Henry James. Not E. M. Forster—oh dear me no. Look at Sir Clifford Chatterley, in his wheelchair: *he* wasn't man enough to call a cunt a cunt! But now behold the hot Lawrence with a hundredweight of hot horseflesh clenched between his thighs, with the fat and frightening Frieda on the next saddle along, thundering through the spark-shower and crimson brushstrokes of Popacatapetl . . .

Gina had slept with Lawrence, he assumed. She hadn't slept with any writers. Before very long, she would sleep with many.

"Can I meet you after work?"

"No."

This is the past. And so it's true.

In Washington there was a party for Gwyn at the British Embassy, co-thrown, it seemed, by Britain and the publicity boy.

Under a ton of chandelier Richard stood with ovals of light streaming at an angle across his face. This made him look like a creature on some riverine mission or vigil: it imparted an amphibian—no, a reptilian—quality to his unvarying stare. And it was with reptilian patience, a croc-like consideration of the percentages, the rot-rates and backlash factors, that Richard watched and waited, and waited and watched. Gwyn was doing his thing on Lucy Cabretti: Lucy Cabretti, who in Richard's hearing had been referred to by the publicity boy (the publicity boy was big on game plans) as Profundity One. For the first hour or so they'd stationed Gwyn at the door, working the arrivals: a succession of sodden wayfarers (they seemed to form a subscription audience of the local sociocultural), with their snow-capped umbrellas and slithering galoshes. Effusive enough when introduced to Lucy in the hall, Gwyn was now concertedly loving her up—on a sofa beneath the mullioned window, against a galaxy of lamplit snow. She was laughing with her small head thrown back, a hand placed on Gwyn's arm to ward off further hilarity. Under the trembling chandelier Richard maintained his reptilian vigil. He wondered what Gwyn had going for him, these days, in terms of sexual charm. Gwyn never *used* to have any; but since then he'd thrown some money at his appearance (need Richard adduce the tinted contacts?), and of course he had the entree now. Success revamps you. It must keep you young. Because failure sure makes you old.

For largely accidental reasons (an international conference, plus culture week at the White House, according to the publicity boy), several American writers were present, none of Richard's outright heroes but a fair selection of middleweights, hallowed background figures, on cautious exhibit. Had they been here, their British counterparts would have been sitting in a clump, cheerfully monolithic and practically indistinguishable. Yet the carved idols of American letters kept their distance, the nuclei of their own inner circles. And Richard had circled these circles, earlier on, appreciatively sensing the repulsive force that kept them apart. Why did they hate each other? It was obvious. To exaggerate: here was a two-foot Alabaman with his face in a bucket of hooch: there was a towering Virginian belle with her mint julep and her honeysuckle vowels; here was a gnashing Jew from Dneopropetrovsk: there was the writhing moustache of the wandering Lebanese; here the granddaughter of an African slave, here a Boston brahmin, here a Swedish hippie from Duluth. America is like the world. And look at it, the world. People don't get on. And writers *should* hate each other, Richard naturally believed. If they mean business. They are competing for something there is only one of: the universal. They should *want* to go to the mat.

"Excuse me, are you Lucy Cabretti? Richard Tull. Literary Editor of *The Little Magazine*, in London. I wonder if you saw the review we ran of *Double Dating*."

"No! I didn't see that."

"I was told you'd be here so I brought along a copy of it. Look at it later. An interesting review, as well as a favorable one. *I* thought too that you found the most tenable position. You make the legal situation very clear, without losing sight of the fact that we're talking about real men and women."

She thanked him. Richard *had* skimmed *Double Dating: Yes and No*, Lucy's how-to book about not getting raped by all your friends. He had agreed with her arguments, while simultaneously wondering why anyone would need to hear them. Who could explain the fact that "My Way" was the anthem of modern America? Americans didn't want to do it their way. They wanted to do it *your* way.

"I'm actually traveling with Gwyn while he's touring here. I'm writing it up. We're *very* old pals. Yes, we shared rooms at Oxford. Scholarship boys. I came up from London, and there he was, fresh in from the Welsh valleys."

"How romantic."

"Romantic? Yes. Well."

"I'm sorry. I'm a disgusting Anglophile."

"He was from Wales, not England," said Richard, who thought it extraordinary that Anglophilia was still staggering around the place. "Imagine it as something like Puerto Rico."

"Even more romantic."

"Romantic? Well, Gwyn was certainly a ferocious . . . A 'ladies' man' is I suppose a polite way of putting it."

"Really?"

"A *very* polite way of putting it," he said, realizing that he was about to get carried away. "Let's go and sit over there. Let's get a drink. You'll need it."

Richard had not, so far, found much to do in Washington, which was only the center of the world. All afternoon he reclined on his hotel bed in a trance of cunning. While Gwyn had done four photo sessions and six interviews in a variety of mediums, while also finding time to visit the Phillips Collection, the Senate, the Library of Congress, and the United States Holocaust Memorial Museum, Richard had succeeded only in washing his hair. Oh yes. And in throwing in a call to the Lazy Susan (this *was* arduous), where he was eventually told that they had two copies of *Untitled* in stock. Washing his hair was no formality either. Again he found himself riveted to the bathroom mirror, immersed in the question of how the same human being could look so bald and so shaggy. In the end, after a visit to the pharmacy, he smothered himself in mousses and conditioners. It hadn't worked out, and, for the time being at least, Richard's hair was basically in deep shit . . . He made his own way to the party. Because of the weather, or the zone system, his cab kept picking up new passengers, all orphans of the loosening Milky Way, all starred and kissed by the six-faceted snowflakes. Richard sat zestlessly in the back while the driver idled them all over town, along the unbarricadable boulevards, through the bare snowfields of American history; the cab glass creaked to the sharp switches of the winds, but the many-eyed Capitol seemed to loom no bigger however close you got to it; they did Georgetown, the Hill, Du Pont Circle, following the city's large design which was accessible only to a higher being. He climbed out at last, in the embassy district. And Gwyn was there to greet him at the door.

"There's probably a medical term for it now," Richard was saying. "Satyromania or some such."

"Well he has a certain style," Lucy said tolerantly. "And all those pretty students . . ."

"Oh no. It wasn't with the students. All those little paragons from Somerville and St. Hilda's. With as many O-levels as freckles on their noses. No no. He'd never get the turnover he needed. It wasn't the students. No." Richard paused and said, "It was the college *servants* that friend Barry looked to for his sport."

Lucy frowned: a small frown under her dark ringlets. As a parting gesture, Richard conjured up a genuine memory from his first year at Oxford: himself, crashing in at two in the morning, after some debauch in some bedsit at the secretarial school, to find Gwyn, in his earphone sideburns, still bent over his books, inching down that long road toward his bad Second. Every other weekend Gilda would bus herself in from Swansea. She used to cower in the little bedroom. On Sunday mornings, after breakfast in Hall, Gwyn would bring a bun back for her hidden in his pocket. She liked marmalade. Anyway, marmalade was what she got.

"He was notorious for the way he went after the scullery maids. In those days, the college servants, or 'gyps' as we used to call them—unbelievable, isn't it?—were almost slave labor. They were sacked en masse at the beginning of the long vacation and hired in the autumn, after a summer of breadlines and doss houses. So if a young gentleman wanted to take advantage . . ." Richard moved his head upward and sideways, in pained recollection. "There was one particularly unfortunate incident involving a kitchen maid of barely sixteen. A touching-looking girl. Dark ringlets. Just a child, really. Some said she was a Gypsy girl—a foundling." Richard tried to pull himself together. His eyes were stinging at his own fiction. "Gwyn . . . Gwyn and one of his fellow bloods contracted a wager. I'll spare you the details. Gwyn won, but his friend—Trelawney his name was—refused to pay up. A matter of a few guineas."

"Guineas?" said Lucy Cabretti.

"A unit of currency. Favored by gamblers." He lurched on, raising his voice. "And so Gwyn forced Trelawney's hand. He nailed up her—he nailed up a section of her underwear onto the notice board of the Junior Common Room. With full details of the hazard."

"Then what? Trelawney pays up, right? Pays Gwyn the gwyn—the guineas. How much is a guinea?"

"Twenty-one shillings." He thought it had probably been a mistake about the guineas.

Lucy folded her arms and sighed. She said, "You know, your story is really hard to believe."

"Oh? Why's that?"

"He seems so nice and normal. And his books. That *Amelior* stuff. He writes like such a *whuss*."

"A what?"

"You know. A real pooch. As if all he wanted to do was not offend anybody. I mean it's pleasant enough, that stuff, but it's just dead."

Richard was happy and proud. But he could see that he didn't need to waste any more time on Lucy Cabretti. He stood up, saying, "It's been nice talking to you. And I hope you like that review."

"Thanks. You too. Wait. What happened to the girl?"

"What girl?"

"The serving girl. The foundling."

He paused. He actually had one foot in the air—about to begin its ponderous journey to the door. Pregnancy? Prison? Thrown out into the wind and the rain, naked, without a groat to her name? But she thought Gwyn's stuff was shit anyway, so all he said was, "Who knows? Once they've been used and cast aside—who knows what happens to these poor girls?"

When he got back to the hotel Richard rang home and spoke to Lizzete, Marius and Marco, Gina being elsewhere . . . Then he sat down at the desk and coerced himself into facing up to something: biography. As he had long suspected, the ring road of his reviewing schedule was all freezing fog and black ice, all sideswipe and whiplash: he faced a catastrophe of deadlines. Richard was actually reviewing more books than ever before. It remained true that he was partly resuscitated as a novelist; but novels still showed no sign of earning him any money. This had taken a while—and many reminders from Gina—to sink in. He turned in his chair. Biographies were scattered . . . No. Biographies were stolidly installed around the room, each of them as heavy as a cinder block. Richard felt dizzy and that was strange, because he'd been very good at the party and had carefully counted his drinks: he'd had seventeen. There were several more biographies in his suitcase: his suitcase, which he would never unpack; his suitcase, gravid with heavy lives.

It was ten o'clock. Lucy Cabretti was home by now. And she, too, was reading. Richard was on page five of *The Mercutio of Lincoln's Inn Fields: A Life of Thomas Betterton*. Lucy was on page 168 of *Come Be My Love*. Within minutes she would finish *Come Be My Love* and would begin *Magenta Rhapsody*. Lucy read chain-store romances at a rate of three or four a day. This had no effect on the stern probity with which she fought for the Equal Rights Amendment; it did not color her speeches and lectures on economic equity; in no wise had it vitiated her non-anecdotal and dryly legalistic best-seller on sexual mores. But she read chain-store romances at the rate of three or four a day. Lucy was in bed, alone. Her handsome and sagacious boyfriend was in Philadelphia, visiting his sister. As she read on (with his cane, his snorting mastiff, Sir William was stalking Maria through the hayricks), her eyes swelled fearfully, and her hand sought her glowing throat. Maria was a serving girl, small, pretty, with dark ringlets.

Midnight. Richard was on page seventy-three. He was also drinking from the mini-bar, which sounds comparatively prudent of him. Given a free hand, he might have been drinking from something bigger. Richard was drinking beer from the mini-bar only because there was nothing else left in the mini-bar, except for mixers and snacks. Slowly Richard's head jerked back. He stared at his drink with indignation. The softly humming liquid seemed disturbingly bland to his tongue. The suspicion formed that it contained no alcohol. Under the light he peered closely at the bottle until he found some small print warning that its contents might fuck up pregnant women. And so he drank on, calmly nodding, mightily reassured.

The next day they were flying south.

Clearly there was a spiritual bond—a covenant, a solemn sympathy—between airports and junk novels. Or so it seemed to him.

Junk novels were sold in airports. People in airports bought and read junk novels. Junk novels were about people in airports, inasmuch as junk novels needed airports to shift their characters round the planet, and airports served, in junk novels, as the backdrop to their partings, chance encounters, reunions and trysts.

Some junk novels were *all* about airports. Some junk novels were even *called* things like *Airport*. Why, then, you might ask, was there no airport called Junk Novel? Movies based on junk novels were, of course, heavily reliant on the setting of the airport. So why wasn't one always seeing, at airports, junk novels being made into movies? Perhaps there really was a whole other airport, called, perhaps, Junk Novel Airport, or with a fancier name like Manderley International Junk Novel Airport, where they did them all. This wouldn't be a real airport but a mock-up on a soundstage somewhere, with everything two-dimensional and made of plastic and tinfoil and other junk.

Even when they found themselves in airports, characters in junk novels didn't read junk novels. Unlike everyone else in airports. They read wills and pre-nups. If they were intellectuals, connoisseurs, great minds, they were sometimes allowed to read non-junk novels. Whereas real-life people who read non-junk novels, even people who wrote non-junk novels, read junk novels if, and only if, they were in airports.

Junk novels have been around for at least as long as non-junk novels, and airports haven't been around for very long at all. But they both really took off at the same time. Readers of junk novels and people in airports wanted the same thing: escape, and quick transfer from one junk novel to another junk novel and from one airport to another airport.

Richard, as he made his way through all these airports, toting his mail sack of *Untitled*s and his burden of biographies, wouldn't have minded trying the odd junk novel, but he was too busy reading all this crap about third-class poets and seventh-rate novelists and eleventh-eleven dramatists—biographies of essayists, polemicists, editors, publishers. Would the day dawn when he reviewed a book about a book reviewer? Or a paper-clip salesman or a typewriter repairer. You didn't have to do much in the literary field, he thought, to merit a biography. So long as you knew how to read and write . . . Quite a few of the amblers and hurriers and sprawlers in these airports were sporting copies of *Amelior Regained*. This puzzled him. In Richard's view, certainly, *Amelior Regained* was junk. But it wasn't a junk novel. It was a trex novel. But it wasn't a junk novel. The heroes and heroines of junk novels, even when they were car-

dinals or novitiates, remained ravenously secular. And look at Gwyn's little troupe of trundling dreamers, none of whom had any money or sex or
facelifts or cool cars, and never went anywhere near airports.

Whatever junk novels were, however they worked, they were close to
therapy, and airports were close to therapy. They both belonged to the
culture of the waiting room. Piped music, the language of calming sua-
sion. Come this way—yes, the flight attendant will see you now. Airports, junk novels: they were taking your mind off mortal fear.

Now, wearing woolen jacket, and bow tie, and two nicotine patches, and chewing (or sucking) nicotine gum, and smoking a cigarette, and feeling like something in a ten-gallon bag behind a nuclear power plant, humbly awaiting its next dreadful atomic declension, Richard lounged on a lounger: before him idled the uninviting Atlantic, in bayside calm; on either side the raked and watered sands of South Beach, Miami, stretched far away . . . Gwyn and the publicity boy were staying in a five-star citadel farther up the shore, whereas Richard was more informally lodged down here on South. And that was okay. Richard's snobbery was sincere snobbery; he didn't just pretend to be a snob because he thought it looked upper class. All right, he hadn't made it as a contemporary guy. He was a modern. But he wasn't a postmodern. So he really didn't want to be wallowing and languishing, with Gwyn, in that twenty-first-century nautilus, that regency spaceship of fish tanks and startling energy bills, where every room had three televisions and five telephones (American luxury having much to do with the irreducible proximity of televisions and telephones), and in which money flew off you every minute whatever you did. Solacing himself, too (as always), with the fixtures of neglect, he liked his flaking medium-rise on South Beach, with its shot early-morning smell of damp plaster and India. Kafka's beetle didn't just pretend to like lying around on unswept floors beneath items of disused and disregarded furniture. To paraphrase a critic who also knew about beetles and what they liked, Kafka's beetle took a beetle pleasure, a beetle solace, in all the darkness and the dust and the discards.

Behind him, between the beach and the main drag, where resort commerce convulsed itself against an innocuous proscenium of art deco, lay a halfheartedly vegetated area, bounded by low brick walls, in which Gwyn Barry, and others, were making a rock video. Gwyn's role was more or less a passive one, it had to be allowed. He wasn't dancing in it or singing in it. He was just sitting in it—at the request of the featured band's lead singer, an *Amelior* enthusiast. All Gwyn had to do was place himself at a table that had a globe and a book on it; behind him they had positioned a flapping tapestry where bent sheep grazed, wisely watched over by white-haired pards holding crooks and lyres, aeolian harps. A squad of young black dancers were then to move past him, dipping and straightening, like cookie cutouts. Richard had stayed to monitor an edifying conversation, duly recorded in his notebook, between Gwyn and the sleek publicity boy. Something like:

"Trust me. This'll help *Regained*. It'll groundbreak it."

"Maybe," said Gwyn. "But it might hurt the Profundity thing."

"We have their guarantee that it won't screen until *after* the Profundity thing."

". . . How much will it help *Regained*?"

"Major. Come *on*. Just think who it'll reach."

After that Richard had fled, down toward the sand and the sea, the eye-hurting metal of the sky. It was not the spectacle of vulgarity or venality that hastened his departure. The reason lay inward, as everything, now, lay increasingly and irreversibly inward. Richard fled the black dancers and their grip and torque of life, their raised temperature of youth and health. These little black stars, teenagers, every inch of their bodies primed and juiced, were nonetheless the opposite of artists in that they did what other people told them to, and unreservedly accepted the time and place they were living in. They were still enslaved. Richard could claim as his forebears only free men and women, but he was a slave and a ghost in his own life; the only bit of him that acted freely was the bit that planned and typed his fiction. Then, too, the dancers were at the top of the chattels business, cosseted calves, priceless specimens, skittish and exquisite. Whereas Richard . . . Still, it wasn't his thoughts that had driven him over the wall and onto the beach, where the sky glistened and pulsed more heavily than the sea, his head down, one forearm bent beneath the two big books he carried, the other raised to soothe or steady his flinching face. It was the burn of their brownness, and the colder clarity of their eyes and teeth, the pulp salmon of their tongues—which made him feel that from now on all life and love would be harbored elsewhere. It seemed as if the atrocious doses of powerful medications that he soon must surely take were already in dour operation, bringing down a thick and wobbling penumbra of turbulent air, the kind which, in larger quantities, makes big jets quake, secluding him, roping him off from life and love. Before him on the beach Americans exercised, and played games. American health got everyone where it hurt, in the pocket, and had things so arranged that each disaster for the body was a multiple disaster for you and everyone around you in your life. Loved ones, and so on. But those with the money were clearly getting a lot out of it, the health deal here, and Miami, with all the robot methuselahs of Miami Beach, was the holy city of its miracles. On the faces of those who leapt and limped and hollered and panted in front of him Richard was seeing something that he had heard about only in discussions of American foreign policy (and then not recently): American resolve. Visible on the face of the fattest jogger. American resolve, which is like no other resolve, not the steeliest, quite, but always saying that their right to it need never be examined. Seriously considering the removal of his bow tie, Richard lit another cigarette.

He was heating up, and not just in his person. Also, apparently, as a commodity. Even the publicity boy, surveying Richard's situation, might have said without irony that all his prospectives were zeroing in. Once or perhaps twice every day Richard had called the Lazy Susan, deploying one or other of his strikingly talentless American accents (he was no better than the twins, who, when imitating Americans, pronounced *yes* as a trisyllable and put three *n*s in *banana*); and it seemed that *Untitled* was suddenly and unaccountably taking fire. Instead of having two copies in stock, the Lazy Susan now had one copy in stock. With his enhanced royalty deal, that meant he was a clear $2.50 to the good. More than this, much more than this, he now had something resembling a publicity schedule. He would be interviewed, the following afternoon, by Pete Sahl of the *Miami Herald*; in Chicago he would be the subject of the hour-long Dub Traynor interview; and in Boston he would give a reading-signing at the Founder Theater. All fixed or facilitated by Gwyn. The publicity boy had sent over a sheet of paper with all the details typed out on it.

"Hi."

Richard looked up. A young woman was standing over him. She wore cutoffs, tattoos, a plastic money pouch like a belt with a beer-gut.

"That'll be three bucks."

"What'll be three bucks?"

"The lounger you're lying on."

"I haven't got any money on me."

"Sorry, *sir*."

It was a nice idea, Americans calling everyone *sir*, addressing everyone—waiters, cabbies, toilet attendants, serial murders—as *sir*. The consequence was, though, that they made *sir* sound like *Mac* or *bub* or *scumbag*.

"Okay. I might just have it."

Bearing his two crumpled bills and a handful of his brown and silver change, she climbed back into her caddycart and whirred softly off on it, looking for other people who were lying on loungers. "Great job you got," said Richard quietly. Said Richard to himself. He lay back on his padded rack, and yawned, and briefly nursed his bubonic jet lag. Anyway, that was what he hoped it was: merely jet lag, rather than a no-surprises, by-the-book expiration from advanced old age.

His one concession to his surroundings was a Day-Glo yellow flexi-grip highlighting pen (found beneath the bedside table in his hotel room), with which he was marking passages of especial interest in *The Character of Sir Thomas Overbury (1581–1613)*. But really he was reading two books at once, with one drooping and one auspicious eye. The book on his lap was a literary biography. The book in his head was his own, *Untitled*, from whose pages he would read in Boston, Massachusetts. Which bits? The description of the escort-agency advertisement done as a chapter-long parody of *The Romance of the Rose*? That miraculously sustained tour de force in which five unreliable narrators converse on crossed mobile-phone lines while stuck in the same revolving door? Gwyn had given him confirmation of the engagement that lunchtime, backstage at the Miami Book Festival, as the seconds ticked away before "An Hour with Gwyn Barry." Touched by his friend's words, Richard hung around for the event, hoping it would simply be a severe disappointment as opposed to an unqualified flop. Annoyingly, about a thousand people showed up for it. Why? In Miami, for pity's sake, where there was so much *else* on offer. Why not the mall, the pool, the casino, the crack house? Didn't they have anything *better* to do? The only good bit came as Gwyn was leaving the auditorium, lingeringly, accepting congratulations and handshakes, and giving previews of his book-signing skills—soon to be deployed in greater earnest at the Gwyn Barry stand out on the mezzanine. Abruptly and with such marked address that the publicity boy interposed himself between them, a burly woman in jeans and tank top stepped up to Gwyn and said, "Nothing personal, but I think your books are shit." With corporate calm and erectness the publicity boy steered Gwyn past this bejeaned embarrassment, this tank-topped glitch. And she called out after them, "Not everyone thinks you're wonderful!" Gwyn hesitated; he hesitated, half turning, half smiling, as if grateful for this salutary reminder—that America still contained one or two holdouts. The woman turned, and communicated with her companion, in sign language. She didn't pinch her nose with her fingers or anything, but it was clear that she was telling her deaf friend that Gwyn's books were shit. With pride and solidarity, Richard had already intuited who this must be: Shanana Ormolu Davis, of Bold Agenda. He watched Shanana shoulder her way out of there, content to admire her from afar.

The haze above South Beach was evaporating under its share of the sun's heat. Under that fraction of energy which our terrestrial star—a star on the main sequence but heavier than ninety percent of its peers, and just entering early middle age—radiated with such moronic munificence, not only earthward: in every other direction too. Every second,

640,000 tons of mass were *lost* in the solar reactor and were multiplied, in (inefficient) obedience to the Einsteinian equation, by the speed of light squared: $186,282 \times 186,282$. Richard took off his jacket—a taxing task. He had never given a reading before. But he had spoken in public often enough. If you defined *public* freely enough. Dollis Hill tube, then 198B. Follow the walkway. You will be met near the ticket machines. What Price Modern Poetry? All welc. The invitations came in every other year. He always accepted. He could see himself, one day, being stretchered out of his deathbed to go and discuss the death of the novel. Would the novel have any last words? With a harsh groan he leaned forward and started unlacing his shoes.

Over the ocean was where Gina was. Now, when he thought about his wife, he was sorry to find that he always pictured her in flagrante delicto, in blazing crime, and he had to stand there with a towel over his wrist, like a waiter, while she hauled herself out from under . . . He didn't know. But he had strong suspicions. In a few minutes Richard would go back to the bar at the hotel and write postcards—to Marius and Marco, to Anstice, to Keith Horridge. And he would write a letter to Gina. Containing no news. A letter of love. That song he'd sung, those mornings, in the face of February:

> *What* you want:
> Baby I got.
> What you need:
> D'you know I got it . . .

And then the second verse, rendered at the very limit of female rapture and practicality:

> I ain't gonna do you no wrong
> While you're gone.
> I ain't gonna do you no wrong
> Because I don't wanna . . .

He refastened his clothes and gathered his things and went back up the beach.

"Nothing. No, not nothing. Tell Lawrence good-bye. Tell him good-bye, good-bye."

Gina told *Richard* good-bye, that time. Good-bye, good-bye. And he kept coming back. He didn't get the lunch or the early-evening drink.

He certainly didn't get the glazed and heavy-blooded hour in his room at the Savoy. But when he rode the train back to London he had her home address in his waistcoat pocket; and after that, sexually, the when was in doubt but not the what. The why? Because in skilled and determined hands the pen and paper are near equivalents of the ravisher's doctored drink, the rapist's spit-steeped balaclava. Like the fists of the martial artist, written words, hereabouts, can be classed as weapons of deadly force, usable only in the ring or on the mat—for display. If men knew about women and letters, women and notes. If they *believed* it. Thus the veteran husband, before setting off for work, scribbles something like GASMAN SAYS HELL CALL LATER or WERE OUT OF BUT-TER *AGAIN*, and that evening returns to find his wife in a bikini and high heels and with a chilled cocktail glass in either hand; after dinner (his favorite dish), she softens the lights still further and engages the tape of swoony music and puts another log on the fire and settles him there in the marmalade light on the rug with the cushions and the creme de menthe. And retires from the room. So he can have a hand job. Wait. That comes later. Where was he?

Here. Richard Tull, leaning over a bottle of Valpolicella at the kitchen table of his flat in Shepherd's Bush, late at night, with the telephone's cries smothered under a pillow (Dominique-Louise), writing to Gina Young. The letters were confetti, like apple blossom in the accelerator of the April streets. By every post they came. He was sending her formulas and borrowings—truisms, the disposables of love. Her replies were like thank-you notes to an excitable and ultimately goonish godfather. He barely glanced at them. Every other weekend, persistently, long after D. H. Lawrence had been supplanted by local pottery and crafts, by antique typewriters, by imperial loot, he journeyed up there, his facial flesh jud-dering to the jolts of strip light and rail track, his cheeks urban pale but for the dabs of color where Dominique-Louise had scratched or elbowed him; slowly he would raise his chin in stern romantic pride. Half hours in the High Street coffee bars, strolls through the municipal gardens in rain too light to fall. Feed the ducks. Her hand, when at last he took it, was elegantly nervous and long-fingered. He said so. He said more. Back in London he made an important correction to the final proof of *Dreams Don't Mean Anything*, on the dedication page, where he put a line through Dominique-Louise and went for something simpler. In the sod-den pastoral of Victoria Gardens he leaned against her under the drip-ping birch. She sadly kissed him. Her lips were lean and there were raindrops on her hair. He knew it was in the bag when, one Saturday night, round the rear of the Station Hotel, he was lugubriously beaten up

by Lawrence, the outgoing boyfriend, who was accompanied by an older
brother and a cousin—who were not needed. Richard wasn't much good
at fighting. He was good at writing. Book reviews. Love letters. Richard,
in his bow tie, went down and stayed down. His body more bent than
curled, one open hand slackly resting on his knee. Even when
Lawrence's boot started coming in, and Richard resignedly sat there on
the concrete, against the wall, giving a quiet yelp or a loud hiccup every
time the leather met his ribs, he didn't feel picked on or hard done by.
He took it for granted that Lawrence would do what Lawrence would
do, with his body. So Lawrence nutted and loafed, then kneed, then
kicked (the head-butt was his first move: pain began at this instant with
their brows crushed together, their noses interwedged, their lips a kiss
away). He swore: "Cunt!" He also wept. Richard had taken Gina back to
his room at the Savoy that afternoon for the first time. Inconclusively.
But he went down very quickly, in his bow tie and his paisley waistcoat,
and just sat there on the wet stone. He knew Lawrence couldn't be that
bad. Lawrence must be okay, or must have become okay, after nine years
with Gina.

Two and a half months after Gina moved down to London (she was surprisingly well organized and unterrified, and without his seeming to do
much about it she soon had a tube-map and a duplicate of his door key and
a diary/address book and a job and—no, she insisted—a studio flat nice
and near to his place with white curtains and a white sofa that at midnight
she transformed into an aromatic bed infested with embroidered pillows
and cuddly animals where he too was cuddled and canoodled and regularly
rendered speechless by her ultrametropolitan diligence and ingenuity on
top of all the primitive ardor), Richard left her and went back to
Dominique-Louise, to his bulimic vamp, who screamed at him all night
long and never got the curse. He had a whole sequence of girlfriends, at
that time, who never got the curse. He didn't have anything against the
curse, so far as he knew. It was just that none of his girlfriends ever seemed
to get it. He drew no conclusions; but it remained the case that several
years had gone by without him glimpsing a tampon or a drop of blood that
wasn't his own. Until Gina, whom he left anyway. She didn't cry.

Richard hoped and even expected that she would go back—to Nottingham, and to Lawrence. The day he left her he noticed, as he
undressed that night, under Dominique-Louise's unadmiring gaze, that
all vestiges of Lawrence's beating had at last been absorbed by his body:
the tenacious bruises on his hip bone, the scrape on his forearm, the
eventful spectrum of yellows and purples that had looped his right eye,

to which, that night in Nottingham, Gina had herself held the lump of raw meat. This coincidence seemed to Richard to demarcate the affair as an episode of reckless *nostalgie*: class, blood, the provinces, D. H. Lawrence, uncomplicated love. Five nights later he went back to Gina, or at least he went back to her flat. The same right eye had been adventitiously reblackened by Dominique-Louise. Once again Gina flew to the fridge. The meat she returned with came out of polyethylthene packet. This was London; that was Nottingham. "Are you going to *stop*?" she said. But she didn't mean *stop*. She meant *stay*. Oh, stay! Richard went back to Dominique-Louise. He left the cuddly animals, the morning tea and toast, the birds fussing trustingly on the windowsill, round-eyed Gina with her baby-doll nightdress and her puffy slippers and her clutched hanky (there were two or three tears this time, silent, welling), and fought his way back to Dominique-Louise. Dominique-Louise's bedroom, by the way, was painted black and had no windows. Its darkness, at night, was classical, mythological. She would be lying in it cradling the twenty-pound ashtray she sometimes threw at him (she had found out about the changed dedication), smoking and waiting and not getting the curse.

He thought Gina would return to Nottingham. But it didn't seem to occur to her. Richard assimilated this, and found it to be good: he could just show up and sleep with her whenever he liked. He could continue to do this, he projected, even after she had secured some sympathetic simp with a regular job. Because she loved him. Girls, in those days, couldn't do anything to you (they couldn't call the lawyers, the tabloids, the cops) except kill themselves or get pregnant. All they had was life: they could augment it, they could bear it away. They could subtract from it or they could add to it; and that was all. Richard had two additional certainties. Gina would never kill herself. And Dominique-Louise would never get pregnant. What Gina did was this. She took up contemporary literature, systematically. It was her idea of night school. Gina started sleeping with writers.

The next afternoon Richard was back on the beach. He had just done the interview with Pete Sahl of the *Miami Herald*. And it hadn't worked out. Nothing disastrous; nothing apposite either; nothing embarrassing or even interesting. It just hadn't worked out.

Personally they had hit it off well enough. Richard had liked and fancied the *Miami Herald's* Pete Sahl—for she was a woman. Shockingly well preserved, Pete came right out and told you she was fifty-three, with grown-up children. Pete's dad had wanted boys. So he went ahead and gave boys' names to all his five daughters. Pete had stuck with Pete, and never tried to pretty things up with Petranella or Petula or Petunia. Just Pete: Pete Sahl.

It wasn't that she talked about Gwyn the whole time or anything. Encouragingly, in a way, Pete seemed unclear about who he was either. The interview consisted entirely of her recommendations: recommendations of other novels, of books of poetry, of films, of plays, of shows. "I'll write it down for you," Pete kept saying. But she couldn't quite remember what anything was called. She was just spaced out, like everyone else in Miami. By the time the half hour was up, Pete was recommending restaurants.

"Okay. Gino's," she said. "It's a twenty-minute cab ride. If you can't get a table, tell them Pete Sahl. Gino's. I'll write it down for you. Go for the veal. Tell them Pete Sahl."

"That's what I'll do, when I get in through the door. I'll tell them Pete Sahl."

"I'll write it down for you. The veal *alla picante*. They do it with a lemon sauce. Go for it. Nice talking to you. Remember: tell them Pete Sahl."

"Write it down for me."

The Earl of Rieveaulx had wanted boys. And he was an old brute too. But he had called his daughters Urania, Callisto, Demeter, Amaryllis, and Persephone. He hadn't called them Lady Jeff, Lady Mike, Lady Pete, Lady Brad, and Lady Butch.

Richard twisted in his lounger as he heard the whir of the caddycart. The little witch was steering her way toward him on her electric motor, with jinking money pouch. A light aircraft was flying laterally across the strand. It seemed to be trailing a long rope ladder—reminding him of the black dancers: the cookie-cutout men. He tried to focus against the hot pulse of the sky. The rope ladder was saying something: it was made of words. It said simply, in small caps, GWYN BARRY AMELIOR REGAINED. The plane fired a bolt of light at him and then deliquesced in the sun. Richard picked up his book. They themselves were flying out in an hour. He had seen this plane before, trailing a different banner, selling some other piece of shit. What was it? *Bloodbath*, by someone called Chuck Pfister. So that was okay.

But for a moment there the sky seemed to like Gwyn Barry—the sun slapping palms with the plane's wing. For a moment there the solar system seemed to like Gwyn Barry.

Chicago was the only city that really frightened him.

It frightened him because it was there, in Chicago, that he would—or would not—be the subject of the Dub Traynor Interview. Radio: hour-long, one-on-one. This was now in doubt. But it frightened him for other reasons too. The severity of its naked steel frightened him. Chicago, he knew, was the cradle, or the ancient assembly point, of the American political machine. What goes around comes around. I'm okay: you're okay. We don't take nobody nobody sent. Chicago, he knew, was the eighth biggest city on earth. Cities are machines. No other city he had ever been to said to you, as Chicago said to you, This is a machine. I am a machine.

There was a traffic jam all the way in from the airport, and dark rain. The mist was as thick as clouds and the clouds were as thick as smoke and the smoke was as thick as chalk. Chilling Chicago awaited them in its vapors and gray medium, deeply massed and square-shouldered on the vague horizon. They heaved on, five yards per heave, along Kennedy Expressway. The five lanes coming into the city were all blocked and the five lanes going out of the city were all blocked; between these two great metal Mississippis of steam and suffering, of spiritual durance, there lay a railtrack on which brightly lit and entirely empty trains sped past in both directions. No one ever used the trains. They had to be in the cars. Americans were martyrs to the motors; autos were their *autos-da-fé*. Never mind what cars have in store for us globally, biospherically; cars— our cars—hate us and humiliate us, at every turn, they humiliate us. Types of car drivers (timid, pushy) are also types of sufferers: the silent, the permanently enraged, the apparently equable, those who persuade themselves that *they* are running the show (known as "motorists"), the snarl-prone, the oath-casting, the sullen, the erased . . . They drove on. Their driver—a woman, affiliated with Gwyn's publishers—who was seated beside the plump-necked publicity boy, pointed out where the first, third, and fifth tallest buildings on earth might be seen, on a clear day. They drove on: the shell of Shell, yellow on red like a hand raised against the sun. LEE'S LUMBER and WAYNE'S WINDOWS. Zero Willpower Meets Zero Fat, a billboard slogan in praise of a product that at least *tasted* fattening, struck a brief chord in Richard, who wasn't particularly fat, yet. A sodden flag. And then at last they were in the city or under the city, with its halls and chutes and stanchions of steel, and you were a lab-rat in the rat-trap of steel Chicago. Richard suddenly felt that American cities were the half-mouths of lower jawbones and held a monstrous acreage of wedged dentition; with those big teeth they have, no wonder their gums whine with permanent maintenance and repair, all the deep scaling and root-canal work, the cappings, bridgings, excruciating extractions. Now they were engulfed by the sounds of this desperate periodonture, and for a moment Richard's teeth felt like claws, seized in his gums.

They dropped him off first. For the second city running Richard was to be lodged in a separate and of course much worse hotel, and he didn't mind . . . He took the long walk down the long passage, follow-ing the lively stride of the big black porter. With an easy swing of his right arm the porter was carrying Richard's unliftably heavy suitcase; but authorial pride dictated that the fabler himself should tote his own mail sack which, he knew, had warped his spine forever before they even left Washington. They turned a corner: before them lay a fresh infinity of corridor. To the porter this journey was utterly and indeed miserably familiar. The corridor could hold no surprises for him. Not to mention or admit the much older guy, the quivering white stiff coming past the other way, struggling and rattling with some super-awkward and overrated and probably obsolete contraption like a triple tureen on wheels. Forty years ago this old guy might have been happy to return Richard's gasped good evening. But he had no use on God's earth for it now.

In the Spinnaker Room he dined alone—the Spinnaker Room with its stags' heads and bearskins, the walls studded, for some reason, with locally kilned plates and the ceiling hung with locally loomed bolts of cloth in carpet-booklet colors and textures, reminding him, oppres-sively, of the jacket of *Untitled*. He felt as if he was wedged between the covers of his own novel. As Richard was simultaneously finishing his porkchop and *The House of Fame: A Life of Thomas Tyrwhitt*, a telephone was brought to his table, not a cordless or cellular device but an ancient white dialer on a long, squirming lead.

"Yeah well it's all fixed," said Gwyn. Behind his voice you could hear drowsy self-approbation—also the murmur and tinkle of festivity: dis-creet, corporate.

"How did you do it?"

"I told him I'd got a TV crew flying in from Detroit, which turns out to be true. And offered him you."

"Was he . . . How did he take it?"

"Okay in the end. I told him I'd do him when I tour with the paperback."

At about 11:00 P.M. the hotel bars of big American cities fill up with men who don't necessarily spend much time in big cities: conventioneers, business trippers. You are therefore at liberty to observe what the big city does to them. Not that much, really. The big city turns up their volume dial; it floods faces with heat; it makes them young and bad and lewd (how the waitresses roll their eyes). The metropolis makes them overdrink, of course; the Smoke makes them smoke, too, some of them: they light up with a flourish and tell everyone how long ago they quit . . . Richard sat smoking and drinking in the corner: the corner he had painted himself into, with his smoking and drinking. Smoking and drinking were what he liked to do. He was approaching the point where smoking and drinking were *all* he liked to do. Beyond that point lay the place where smoking and drinking would be all he *could* do, anyway, stupefied, entirely immobilized, by smoking and drinking. Nevertheless, he felt good (he was smoking and drinking), and if he stayed up late enough he could call Gina and tell her that things weren't going at all badly, what with the Lazy Susan sale, and now the Dub Traynor Interview and this further dissemination of *Untitled*.

With so many biographies down him Richard knew what America was capable of doing to British writers. Timid rubes who crossed the Atlantic, timidly blinking, were immediately swept up in the indigenous panic of make-or-break. They twirled right out of control, like Dylan Thomas and Malcolm Lowry, done in by dread and drink. This appeared to be Richard's strategy. Or else (this was Gwyn's) they rigged themselves up with temporary personalities, new smiles, new laughs, so it felt okay to walk the streets all night waiting for the reviews in the papers, like Broadway impresarios. Then the fever of transformation ends, and they go back where they came from and become reasonable again. And so what? But the question is: who are they leaving behind? If America can do that to frowning bookworms from middle England, what was America doing to Americans—who, on the whole, hadn't spent three years at twelfth-century universities with *Paradise Lost* on their laps, and who had no Home Counties to come from or go home to. They never had a lifetime elsewhere to protect them from it, from America and the fever of possible change. Lie awake in the big city and you can hear it like the beady scrape of cricket wings in the Miami night—the nasal insect drill of need and neurosis.

Insects are what neurosis would sound like, if neurosis could make a noise with its nose.

* * *

It looked like another garage sale—thrown, this time, by a troglodytic kindred of petty thieves and welfare hustlers. The old car seat to sit on, the old cardboard box to put your paper cup on, the grunge-drenched carpet, the leprous wallpaper . . . it could only mean one thing: a radio station. Or, much more specifically, RPT4456 4534, and "The Dub Traynor Show." Richard was undisquieted. The BBC, where he sometimes went, for something like £11.37, and talked about book reviewing or biographies or anything at all to do with little magazines, was just as rough, in its way. Cruelly lowering surroundings: this was the thing about radio. Radio knew it would always be heard and not seen and could let itself go; it was okay—people understood; radio would never have to cringe in apology and pain, under the general gaze. So Richard accepted the atmosphere, but not without internal comment. If the imperfect—the half-made, the failed, the let-gone—is what you sympathize with, then you will find much with which to sympathize. He was given a cup of unbelievable coffee. Dub would be with him soon. Dub, who, according to Gwyn's publicity boy, was a very serious guy and a great reader: he *loved* modern prose. The night before Richard had extracted a copy of *Untitled* from his mail sack and, feeling briefly stratospheric, cabbed it round to Dub's West Side address. Probably Dub wouldn't have had time to read it all, but Richard was looking forward to what he got so little of: a response. Furthermore, his mail sack felt appreciably lighter. Experimentally hoisting it onto his shoulder that morning, Richard thought that his retch of pain was, in retrospect, detectably quieter: appreciably more subdued.

The girl who had provided him with his coffee came through and told Richard that there was, of all things, a problem: the local baseball team, that very hour, was announcing its intention of changing sponsors.

Richard looked at her expectantly.

"It's a big story here. Dub will be having to deal with it. Just bear with us."

In came Dub, with his chinos and his bearded preoccupation and his strictly localized charisma. He nodded and shook hands and then led Richard into the gloom of his booth, which consisted of an Okie kitchen table under the usual mess of radiobiotics. Dub had the copy of *Untitled* in front of him, under a heap of press releases and folders and legal pads. He kept touching his eyes, with thumb and forefinger, and then blinking glutinously.

Settling himself, Dub flicked a switch, and murmured, "We're having to take all this . . ."

"What Max has done here," a voice was saying, dully, dutifully, "for the ball club, from a business standpoint, has been from our . . . standpoint . . . has been real good business—for the ball club."

"Sorry," said Dub, "but it's a big deal here. Have you been to Wrigley Field?"

"No. Should I? What is it?"

"It's the ball park. It's sixty years older than any other ballpark in America. The slopes, the hardboard. It's sad there, as it should be. Even the best teams lose fifty games a year. That sadness gives the game its poetry. Like no other. Look at the writers it attracts. Lardner, Malamud . . ."

He flicked the switch again. Another voice was saying, "We like to think that Coherent is tops in our product category. And that that success will be reflected back on to the ball club." Then the original voice was saying, "And so what's good for Coherent will hopefully, for the ball club, also be . . . be good."

With a nod to Richard, Dub said briskly, "That was Coherent VP Terry Eliot and Fizz Jenkerson talking at Wrigley Field. We'll have more on the sponsorship switch, after some messages, and I'll be talking with the British cult writer Richard Tull. I was going to be talking with another British writer, Gwyn Barry, but we've been switching too, and now it's Richard Tull. Say," he said, "do you like great musicals? All—"

"No," said Richard.

Dub looked up from his mike.

"I don't like any musicals."

". . . Well, if you did, all this week there's a sweet brunch-and-matinee deal at the Ashbery. For just twenty-five dollars you get the hit show *and* an all-you-can-eat *grande bouffe* right across the street at the Carvery, extras and service charge not included. Now doesn't *that* sound good?"

"But I don't like musicals."

"It's not—it's a *message*."

"What?"

Once more Dub fell to touching his eyelids as a voice was saying, "The problem was not any problem with Ultrason, who've been real good for the ball club. The problem . . . well it's not a problem, because it's good, is Coherent, is the Coherent deal, which is more . . . which is better. For the ball club."

"Don't you wish sometimes," said Dub, "that writing were just like sports? That you could just go out there and see who'd win? See who's better. Measurably. With all the stats."

Richard thought about it. "Yeah," he said.

"And I hear," said Dub to his mike, "that the ball club's transfer play is already being reenergized in the trading pits of La Salle Street. Do you have a little doggy?"

"No," said Richard.

Dub looked up, apparently appalled by this admission. He raised a palm, saying, "Well if you did I'd really recommend the Fenceless Fence from Perter Pets at forty-nine-ninety-five. This way you put pooch on a non-tangle leash with a range limit set by you. He'll like it. And so will the neighbors."

"My two boys keep pleading with me to get one—a dog," said Richard. "But we live in a flat and you know how the . . ."

"I don't believe this guy." Dub coughed, and continued, "You know what Berryman said when they told him Frost was dead? He said, 'It's *scary*. Who's number one?' "

"The answer being Lowell. I suppose."

"Right . . . Right. There was a witness to Berryman's suicide. Washington Avenue Bridge. Into the Mississippi. The rocks along the bank. The witness said, 'He jumped up on the railing, sat down and quickly leaned forward. He never looked back at all.' The witness's name was Art Hitman. University carpenter. Art Hitman. Don't you love it?"

"I do. I do. Berryman said he always felt 'comfortable' about being number two to Lowell. Oh sure."

"Wait." Dub was nursing his eyes again, even more intently, as if Richard wasn't there. He started to do parallax exercises with his thumbs, focusing and refocusing and jerking his head back affrontedly. Meanwhile they went live to the media conference at Wrigley Field, and stayed there.

At three minutes to twelve Dub freed up his copy of *Untitled*. It sprang open on page five. Dub's hand groped for his eyelids as he said, "It's the weirdest shit. I was just getting into your book last night and I— I thought you know like something had gotten in under my contacts. Then I . . . That was Fizz and Terry Eliot, wrapping it up at Wrigley Field. We're almost fresh out of time here, and we were going to be talking to Gwyn Barry about his vision of a new direction for our troubled species, but here we have another British writer, Richard Tull, whose new novel has just appeared. Richard Tull. We know from the *Amelior* novels of your friend and colleague where *he* would have us go. How about you? What's your novel trying to say?"

Richard thought for a moment. The contemporary idea seemed to be that the first thing you did, as a communicator, was come up with some kind of slogan, and either you put it on a coffee mug or a T-shirt or a bumper sticker—or else you wrote a novel about it. Even Dub clearly thought you did it this way round. And now that writers spent as much time telling everyone what they were doing as they spent actually doing it, then they would start doing it that way round too, eventually. Richard thought on. Dub tapped his watch.

"It's not trying to say anything. It's saying it."

"But *what* is it saying?"

"It's saying itself. For a hundred and fifty thousand words. I couldn't put it any other way."

"Richard Tull? Thank you very much."

Before he left he offered to sign Dub's copy of *Untitled*. Bent over in his chair, with his hands semaphoring in front of his face, Dub abstractedly declined. In fact he insisted on returning the book to its author. Making quite a thing of it; pressing it on him, so to speak. Richard tried to give it to the girl who had brought him coffee.

"Thank you, sir," she said. "But I believe not."

There was a traffic jam all the way to the airport, and dark rain. The five lanes going out of the city were all blocked and the five lanes coming into the city were all blocked. On the central divide the empty trains, rigidly balanced, cruised by. You could sense the shape and mass of blackened smokestacks. You could see lights, and the reflections of lights, car lights, murkily glistening—the filthy jewelry of Kennedy Expressway. They heaved on, flanked and tailed by mustang, bronco, pinto, colt, by bluebird and thunderbird and ladybird and lark, by panda and cobra, by jaguar, by cougar: the filthy menagerie of Kennedy Expressway.

Alone for many hours in the backs of planes, drinking, reading, looking out the window, with his being in a process of steady diminution, he had a chance to get things straight about the sky. He saw clouds all day, from above and from below.

From above. Imagine clouds as you would be seeing them for the first time: *on your way in.* Clouds would be telling you about the earth. About its cliffs, its mountains and plateaus, its pastures and snowfields. Clouds would be telling you about its sandbars and sandflats, and insistently telling you (seven-tenths of the time) about its oceans and their postures of turbulence and calm. From above, even though the beauty of the clouds had lost some of their innocence, their pristine aura of eternal unregardedness, because nearly everyone from below had seen them now, the sky was telling outsiders about the earth.

From below, the sky was telling *you* about the outside—about the universe. Richard was back on the ground, in Colorado, on the tarmac, and then with his mail sack in the flatland of the car park . . . The sky was getting bigger as he moved west; the sky would have much to say. Most commonly the sky imitated vacuum: vacuum laced with impermanent matter. Next most commonly, interstellar gas, tufts of dust and nebulae. Next, the characteristic shapes of galaxies—disc, corkscrew, spiral, cigar, sombrero. It could do other imitations. It had a supernova imitation and a quasar imitation. Richard was destined soon to discover, with horror, that it could do black holes. It was working on its pulsar imitation. The sky was there to provide the artistic comment on the day, the weather, the light it was screening for you, but it was also there to tell you about the universe, the gentlest pointers and reminders for the most part, with no hard lessons about where you stood in it and where this left you.

"I'm dying here," said the publicity boy, all that night in Denver. "I'm dying here."

In Denver, which was also a Profundity stop, they were coming in at the end of a national booksellers' convention, or works outing, and gimmick parties were the thing: parties in gymnasiums, parties in precinct stations, parties in mineshafts. The party they threw for Gwyn Barry and *Amelior Regained* was in a circus, small scale and itinerant but under a medium-big top and so on, with sawdust, animals, jugglers, tumblers. It was meant to be good because the performers were all Hispanics and Gypsies and Amerindians—just finishing a tour of male-pride Sweat Lodges and Reservation casinos. In fact the circus was a squalid disgrace and everyone was completely grossed out by it. With his plastic glass on its paper napkin, the publicity boy pounded the sawdust saying, "I'm dying here." He also threatened to call the fire department, the sanitation people and the company lawyer. But what he kept saying was: "I'm dying here." He was like, "I'm dying here." Considering how ill and old he felt, Richard had the time of his life.

The animals were all wrecks, and the troupers all looked stupid and cruel, and none of them seemed to be any good at anything. It was cold out and hot in, and there was a nightsweat crossfire from the laboring generators and the Alaskan drafts through the ragged canvas and the slow-moving gusts of beast-warmed gas ... Gwyn's countenance, on arrival (Richard noted), was obviously geared up for a whole evening of childlike wonder; but he soon forgot about that and fell in with all the flat smiles and crinkled lips and the earnest concern with animals' rights and animals' germs.

"Who's *funding* these clowns?" asked the publicity boy, rhetorically.

But there were no clowns.

Cringing off-white dogs were being urged with many menaces to attempt bedraggled diagonal leaps through hand-held hoops as Richard identified Professor Stanwyck Mills, standing near the spread of crates and trunks where the performers stored their juggling batons, their sequined capes, their bolts of damp finery. He was talking and being talked to by Gwyn Barry; Gwyn had his head cocked at a sympathetic angle, and was frowning and nodding as if assenting (on TV) to a proposition both beautiful and true. And there in the ring, after his stunts with the dogs, the matador, arms raised, had gone into his tense-buttocked appeal for recognition and praise.

There followed a collective high-pitched groan—almost a hoot—as a putrescent little elephant waddled out into the glare. Was this an elderly dwarf elephant, or just an afflicted infant elephant, already rotting at the age of one? Its well-intentioned wanderings and blunderings were somehow meant to be combined with the fierce determination of a piebald pony, running in its tight circle with a kind of traumatized invariance, apparently prepared to keep doing that forever while the elephant plodded helplessly about, so anxious to please, black rheum thrown off from its eyes like sweat, its damp-damaged hide lightly coated with the kind of hair that sprouts out near a healing wound, gingery and brittle, like the weft of baklava. Dressed in overalls, the elephant could have passed for a London builder: cheerful, not very dishonest, complete with beer-paunch and bony coccyx—prominent on its fleshless, winded rump.

Richard saw his chance. "Professor Mills?" he said, and introduced himself at length. "I wonder if you were ever sent a copy of our review of the reprint of *Jurisprudential*? I brought a copy along. Hoped you might be here. An interesting review, as well as a favorable one."

"Why thank you," he said. "I'll look forward to that."

The reviews, thought Richard, had definitely been a good idea. Americans couldn't know—couldn't possibly imagine—just how little *The Little Magazine* really was.

"I'm particularly interested in your ideas on penal reform," Richard went on. "I like what I might call your humanely utilitarian slant. In a field so full of humbug. As you say, the question is: 'Does it work?' "

They talked on, or Richard did. Mills had an air of troubled and shaky preoccupation. Glancing at the animals, the runts and curs and strays bobbing round the ring, Richard was struck by Mills's inches: for an Irish-American he seemed fabulously tall. So maybe this tremulous fatigue was what the tall ended up with, after a lifetime of lugging that sack of height. Round his neck he wore a light surgical brace like an aerodynamic yoke.

"It's amazing how hidebound we are in England. Still the old ideas. Deterrence. Sequestration. There's a lot of talk but no will to bring about change. Even our most liberal public figures say one thing and . . ." Richard appeared to hesitate, as if considering the etiquette or equity of simply seizing on the nearest example. "Well. Take Gwyn Barry. Thoroughly liberal in all his pronouncements. But deep down . . ."

"You surprise me. In his writing he seems—irreproachably liberal on such matters."

"Gwyn? Oh, you've no idea the kind of things he'll say in private. He actually favors a return to more public forms of punishment."

As Mills leaned backward on his plinth Richard went through the formality of telling himself not to get carried away.

"With paying spectators. Retributive and exemplary. But with a vengeance. So to speak. Stocks and pillories. Ceremonial scourgings. Ducking-stools. Tarring and feathering. Impalements and flayings. You see, he thinks the mob has had a poor deal in recent years. Public stonings, even lynchings—"

He was interrupted, not by the professor, but by the publishing and bookselling community and its fresh consensus of exhausted forbearance: a pair of midget camels or lumpy llamas were now trotting anx-

iously about, to so little purpose that the ringmaster was now giving
them the taste of his lash. A modest instrument—a black cord on a black
stick. Nothing like the deafening bullwhips that Richard had in mind.
He said,

"You're an Irishman, Professor. You must have followed that case—
the bomb in the shopping center. Here's what Gwyn said. He said: round
up all known IRA members and shackle them to the gates of the Tower
of London. With a big sign, with pictures, saying what they did and
inviting the public to go ahead and vent their anger. And then, after a
couple of months of that, when their arms and their legs and their 'cocks'
have been ripped off (do excuse me), string them up for the ravens. *Oh*
yes. That's friend Barry for you."

Richard might have said more; but now a steel-hooped tunnel was
being hastily and noisily pounded together, leading through the crowd
toward a square cage in the ring. There was talk of a tiger . . . The two
men found themselves pushed together in the press, Richard taking care
to shield the professor, who seemed fearful for the upholstery supporting his neck. They stood side by side, enjoying what Richard felt to be a
just and wordless solidarity. Earlier that winter (the case was still *sub
judice*), Mills had Christmased with his wife at their holiday home on
Lake Tahoe; forcing entry on Christmas Eve, a crew of nomad joy-
raiders had then subjected the Millses to a two-hundred-hour ordeal of
abuse, battery, bondage and arson. The professor was of course aware
that a personal experience, however dire, should carry only statistical
weight in the settlement of one's intellectual positions. But he was
doing a lot of rethinking, which he was going to have to do a lot of anyway, because the many scores of texts he had studied and annotated in
preparation for his next book (a lifetime effort provisionally entitled
The Lenient Hand) had been mockingly torched by the intruders, along
with the rest of his work station and, it seemed, everything else he had
ever cared about. His wife, Marietta, still in deep therapy, hadn't uttered
a word since New Year's Day.

The tiger was coming. Richard dumped Stanwyck and managed to
dispatch another tray of drinks before sidling his way ringside. Along its
tube of bars the tiger moved silently in the hush, with almost inorganic
smoothness, like the contents of a hypodermic responding to the pressure of the surgeon's thumb. Richard looked up suddenly: Gwyn was
nearby, part of the inner circle, but he kept on slackly turning to the man
who leaned over his shoulder, a suited sophomore intent on finishing his
joke or his pitch or his ramble. It was then that Richard knew, for at least
the thousandth time, that Gwyn was not an artist. If it was a woman he'd

been talking to—then okay. But to be only half engaged, attending to some bloke, when you could be looking at a *tiger* . . . Equally but not quite equivalently remiss, Richard now tried to assimilate the animal as an artist ought to, and he greeted it first with fear, which was surely right; even Steve Cousins you greeted this way, with the thought of what the wilder thing could do to you if you two were really alone. Of course the tiger in question was no glittering savage of the rain forest or the tundra: it seemed detoxed or pre-tamed, displaced from its very phylum, and burdened with its camouflage gear—its worn sun-and-dust yellow, ridged with shadow. Even the essential severity of its stare felt disorganized. Richard feared for its teeth but they were intact, the feline's dirk-like canines revealed in its fixed yawns of hatred, hatred of the handler and the handler's stool. Hatred of the drug that dried its mouth, imparting desperate struggle, desperate servitude, to the tiger's yawns.

Soon it was gone and all the other animals gathered to take their curtain call—for the publicity boy was breaking everything up. One of the dogs started gagging and retching, either from delayed stage fright or from unimaginable wolfings before the show, and another dog inclined its trembling snout to sniff and lick the flesh-pink stew, and the publishers and booksellers of America all groaned, then gagged and so it went on, in relays of disgust.

At Denver's Stapleton International Airport, at five o'clock in the morning, nobody wanted to work. So they had a robot doing it. A computer, with a robot voice: female. Richard thought that the robot, considering it was a robot and every inch a slave, didn't take any shit, always telling him to move on, to unload quickly and move on, to deposit bags quickly and move on. He let his suitcase and his mail sack splash down onto the carousel, where he inadvertently but briefly joined them, and then while Gwyn went on ahead he picked himself up and retraced his steps to the door and the cold blue yonder, planning on a quiet cigarette. The cigarette was a cigarette—but not a quiet one. He coughed his heart out behind a baggage trolley and ralphed his ring out behind a soft-drinks machine and finally cried his eyes out leaning backwards against the glass and smoking another, quieter cigarette. These tears incorporated an element of relief, and of grateful mortality, under the big western sky, which happened to be practicing its quasar imitation: a multitude of clouds had been foregathered, bright and compact and in cluster-galaxy posture, surrounding and obscuring something strange and grand—the sun. The sun, as he watched, went from early-morning tumescence to full-face pallor, from red giant to white dwarf. When the sun was white you had no trouble at all believing in black holes, in singularities. Because this ordinary star already looked half blistered out of space-time.

Mandated to hang around and deal with all the fallout from the circus thing, the publicity boy was catching a later flight. Therefore Richard would be traveling first class, up there with Gwyn. With Gwyn, who had to make some early interviews at the next city along.

"We're all a little discombooberated here," said the stewardess.

Richard told her that he was all right.

"Ah," said Gwyn, "an English breakfast."

"Coffee for you, sir? Coffee for you?"

"Have you got any brandy?"

"Any?"

"Brandy?"

Finding out how many kinds of skin and hair the world had, Richard looked out of his porthole all the way to the Pacific, while Gwyn capably slept. All the way, over the waffle fields and hanks of french toast sprinkled with confectioner's sugar, over salt lake, pious plain, desert, more desert, mountain, valley, and then the coniferous ridges of the continent's edge, all the way from tundra to taiga.

He thought the circus crowds in the Kafka story were probably right, to turn away from the hunger artist, from *Der Hungerkunstler*, who just lay there half buried by the straw in his cage, fasting, plangently not eating; the crowds were probably right to favor the panther which replaced him. Because the panther had no sense of servitude or even captivity, and carried freedom around inside its own body (somewhere in the jaws it seemed to lurk). In the photographs Kafka always looked so amazing, so amazed, perpetually spooked, as if he kept seeing his own ghost in the mirror.

When they landed they were given an additional hour, enplaned, on the ground. A technical matter, or a slave revolt; not even Gwyn could find out which—Gwyn, whose interviews were being stacked above him in the sky like tiers of jets . . . Richard had come to know the landscapes of airports—which were landscapes of the incomplete. Not the interiors, with their popcorn smell and cheerful yellow popcorn light, which were landscapes of incessant addition. The tacked-on *B*s and *C*s and *D*s, the proliferating lego of elbow and kneejoint; and for every sundered couple there was another kissing thirstily at six in the morning, and for every weeping granny there were familial burgeonings elsewhere—feasts of cousins. Planes moved at the same speed but the human travelers had different rhythms, hurrying, ambling, sprinting, sprawling. Outside, though, the landscape insisted on incompletion. The empty crew buses and stationary forklifts, the prefabricated portakabins. And then headless trucks and cabless wheel sets, staircases pointing upwards but leading nowhere, the joints of amputated corridors, stranded on the tarmac, both ends leading nowhere, insisting on the incomplete.

"We're just going to be thinking out loud here."

"Bear with us. Okay? Okay. Amelior . . ."

"Now. For us to care about this community, what we need is for it to be . . . threatened from outside."

"So we care."

"So we care."

"The community is threatened, if we're going to go with the eco thing, by . . . I don't know. Okay. Shoot me. Killer rats. *Mutant* rats."

"Please. Keep it human. The community is threatened . . ."

"By Nazi bikers. The Klan. I don't know."

"Way-wait. Solomon—Solomon's up on the hill, tilling it or whatever. With Padma and Jung-Xiao. Baruwaluwu shouts out! And Solomon sees . . ."

"The dust trail."

"The dust trail?"

"Of the Nazi bikers."

"Way-wait. A construction company plans to . . ."

"Build a highway through . . ."

"Wants to turn the community into a . . ."

"A chemical warfare facility."

"A casino."

"A bioengineering plant. Which gives us the eco thing. Do we *want* the eco thing?"

"Where they make mutant cattle."

"Mutant cattle?"

"Mutant . . . pigs. You know, like a block long with no head. Or mutant rats."

"For the military. And Solomon . . ."

"Figures out . . ."

"How to fuck them up. Way-wait."

Not even in his sweatiest dengues and beri-beris of facetious loathing had Richard ever seriously considered that he would one day be asked to face the prospect of a Gwyn Barry movie sale. But there they sat, Richard and Gwyn, on a sofa in a luxurious prefab within the Millennium precinct of Endo Studios, Culver City, in Greater Los Angeles. So

L.A. had brought fresh horror, and in the form of a double bill. *Amelior Regained* had been optioned. But *Amelior* was a firm sale.

"Yeah," Gwyn had said the previous evening in the hotel. "Millennium are doing it. Hey," he added to the publicity boy, newly arrived, and emerging plumply from the shower, "I don't want this to break until the Profundity thing is all straightened out."

The publicity boy looked at him.

"People will think I don't need it," said Gwyn in a wronged voice. "You know. Rich wife related to the Queen. Back-to-back best-sellers. Movie deals."

"Rock videos."

"Rock videos. They're bound to ask me about movie deals here. I've already been asked about *nine times*."

"Just say there's been movie interest."

"Okay. Yeah, that's good. Movie interest is good."

Richard still couldn't figure it. No matter how degraded or talentless, every work of art belonged to a genre. And the Amelior books belonged to the literary utopias. There had been plenty of movies about failed utopias and anti-utopias, but there had never been a movie about a nice utopia, where everyone was happy all the time. Whole movies about nudist colonies, early *Kulturfilmen*, the iron jawlines of socialist realism: utopia, in the cinema, belonged to propaganda and pornography. Besides, the big thing about Amelior, as a joint, was that it was cleansed of all incident—cleansed, too, of sex, violence, conflict and drama.

Such thoughts had evidently occurred to the three-person development team gathered there in the wheeled bungalow to toss ideas around in Gwyn's presence. The two guys wore complicated sports gear—reversible wetsuits. The woman wore a plaid skirt and a white blouse; and she smoked.

"Wouldn't it be better," said Gwyn, who, in this pre-Profundity period, had yet to commit to writing the screenplay, "if you made the conflict internal?" Gwyn opened his hands and fell silent again.

"Let's run with it. Like Gupta's one of *them*."

"A Nazi biker."

"No. A bioengineer."

"Gupta? Way-wait. Solomon . . ."

"Why always Solomon?"

"Okay. Abdelrazak . . ."

"Can you imagine the shit we'll have to sit through if it's Abdelrazak?"

"Okay. Jung-Xiao . . . tricks Gupta—"

"Not Gupta. How about Yukio?"

"Tricks *Yukio*? Are you kidding?"

"Okay. Piotr . . ."

"Yeah. Piotr."

"Jung-Xiao tricks *Abdelrazak* into revealing that Piotr . . . is one of *them*."

"A bioengineer."

"Or a Fed."

"Way-wait. Gupta hates Solomon, right?"

"Right. And so does Abdelrazak. And Yukio hates Jung-Xiao. And Eagle Woman hates Conchita. And Padma hates Masha."

"And Baruwaluwu hates Arnaujumajuk."

". . . Why in Christ's name would Baruwaluwu hate Arnaujumajuk?"

"Because they're always going after the same *funding*."

"Way-wait . . . Conchita is spreading a mutant *disease* through Amelior."

". . . Which she got from the bioengineer: Piotr."

". . . Who's also having a thing with Jung-Xiao."

". . . Who's putting out for Yukio."

". . . Who's feeding it to Abdelrazak."

". . . Who's deep in the jeep with Eagle Woman . . ."

Asked to comment, after an unusually long silence, Gwyn said,

"There's no love and no hate in Amelior."

"That's true, Gwyn. We wondered about that. And everyone has these diseases anyway."

"The hardback is in its eleventh printing," said Gwyn, who went on to list the hemispherical achievements of *Amelior*. "All this without love and hate. Perhaps you should think about that."

"There has to be love and hate, Gwyn. Even if it means hazing the ethnic distinctions—and making them all Americans."

"And losing the diseases. There has to be love and hate. So we care."

"So we care."

"So we care."

"While we're on the subject of caring," said Richard, who was about to take his leave (Gwyn would be lunching with the team), "can I ask a question? There's a big dump bin in reception, where we came in. It's got a little stenciled sign on it which says 'Caring Barrel.' What's a Caring Barrel? It looks like a big trash can."

"Ah yes. That's the Caring Barrel. The Caring Barrel was placed there after the earthquake for—"

"After the riots."

"After the riots. The Caring Barrel is for concerned employees to . . . deposit food or warm clothes for . . ."

"Those who might be in need."

"Thanks," said Richard. On his way to the door he passed the third executive, who was frowning and massaging his eyebrows and saying,

"Is *that* what it is? I thought it was just a big trash can."

While the lady in reception called him a cab Richard had a good look at the Caring Barrel. It did indeed contain an old scarf and a pair of socks and a couple of packets of cookies and cereal, half hidden by all the regular trash tossed in there by employees who didn't know it was a Caring Barrel. Richard cared. Caring was what Richard was all about. If caring was wrong, then—yes—Richard was wrong. But he didn't know he cared so much. In later years, he supposed, he might have to spend a lot of time peering into Caring Barrels and caring about what they contained.

Back at the hotel he threw in a call to the Lazy Susan. Sure enough, sales were holding firm at one copy.

During the tour Richard had been solicitous of his own health, careful, for instance, to stop drinking every night when he was still a good milliliter clear of liver collapse; he quite often remembered to take his Vitamin C, until it ran out; and of course his smoking had been much reduced, or much rearranged. The confinement and immobility and canned air of modern travel, and the effects of at least three huge and ill-chosen meals a day, he offset with his frequent sprints to the bathroom and with his roilingly aerobic insomnias. But in Los Angeles he definitely started to let himself go. The thing seemed to be that he was making a superhuman effort to avoid thinking about the future, and it was taking a lot out of him.

Everyone said that Gwyn was meant to be taking it easy—secluding himself from the pressures ranged against the successful novelist. But he looked and behaved like a walking power surge, and continued to indulge and even embolden the publicity boy. When he wasn't being interviewed elsewhere, Gwyn Barry, wearing white tennis shorts and black espadrilles, was being interviewed out by the pool. Sometimes Gwyn would be accompanied by the publicity boy; sometimes (there were at least two occasions Richard knew about), the publicity boy's place was taken by Audra Christenberry, the young screen actress, and *her* publicity boy, or agent, or agent's agent: this young man was in any case Audra's reality-handler, just as Gwyn's reality was handled by *his* publicity boy. Audra, who claimed to be a great admirer of Gwyn's material, was up for the role of Conchita in *Amelior*. Richard had to say that

Audra didn't look the part. She was no longer the fresh-faced tomboy from Montana. After six months in Hollywood, Audra was now a corny phantasm of man-pleasing artifice—whereas Conchita, in the book, was just another fresh-faced tomboy in straw hat and coarse dungarees with green fingers and a chest condition.

But this was Hollywood, and Audra was heady effluvia from the dream factory. And Richard stood alone, he felt, in the real world. Stood before the mirror, in fact, where he auditioned or screen-tested himself in his swimming trunks, and decided *no*. There wasn't a publicity boy good enough to handle the reality that faced him. It was decidedly inopportune that his reading-and-signing engagement was scheduled for the end of the tour, in Boston. Had he read and signed in Washington, in Chicago, Richard thought, his mail sack might by now have been lightened, or even emptied. And then there were the biographies, which habit forbade him to discard. And anyway his suitcase, with its appalling tonnage, seemed to provide a chiropractic counterbalance to the sadistic burden of his mail sack.

The mirror said it was reality. He felt convinced that he had lost at least three inches in height since leaving London. He stood there, in the wizened trunks; his polyplike pallor was relieved only by the loud rash or broad abrasion that swathed his right shoulder. There was also a kind of bedsore in the corner of his clavicle. The right arm itself felt okay if it wasn't being asked to do anything but when he sobbed himself awake at night it felt numb and blood-logged and inflexibly swollen. When he could distinguish his hand, in the dawn, he expected it to look like a boxing glove. His one pair of shoes bore testimony to what gravity was doing to him: there they wallowed on the carpet, like cowpats indented by unfortunate footprints.

So he never went out. Except when the maid came, he never went out. He developed a liking for *The Simpsons*, a cartoon sitcom about an average American family, awkward-bodied, totem-faced; they bickered a lot. He was also intrigued, as they say, by all the pornography. The television in his room went about its transmissions nonjudgmentally, but to Richard the set itself often seemed scandalized and even persecuted by these gladiatorial displays—this modern marriage of window-shopping and blood sport. Or this post-modern marriage: pornography tried to occupy the basements of other genres (sex Westerns, sex space operas, sex murder mysteries), but it looked to be increasingly preoccupied by pornography: by "adult," as the industry called itself. Pseudo-documentaries about adult; rivalries between adult stars; the ups and downs of an adult director. There was also many a talentless parody of other small-screen entertainments. There was even a loose parody of *The Simpsons*—called *The Limpsons*. All this footage had been bowdlerized, on the set, for hotel use, with a strategic lampshade here, a fruit bowl there. You saw faces, not bodies. The men perspired and bared their teeth, as if under torture. The women snarled and whinnied, as if giving birth. So: *The Simpsons, The Limpsons*, and room service.

Usually, around midmorning, propping up the mini-bar in a pair of black socks, Richard thought about calling home. It was his boys he wanted to talk to, for selfish reasons. Marco. Or Marius would be better. Marius had a telephone manner, he listened and paused (you could hear his warm young breath), whereas Marco just grabbed the receiver and babbled about whatever had happened to him in the last ten seconds. So Marco'd be no fucking good. And it all cost too much. When they checked out of these hotels, all these monuments of inflation and entropy, Gwyn strolled straight to the cab or the courtesy car while Richard queued at the desk and then weepily tallied his traveler's checks against his Extras: telephone calls, service charge, beverages, bed rental. Richard went over to the desk and resumed another long letter to Gina. As he wrote, three related anxieties competed for his attention. Letters were made of paper and had no bulk, no mass, to deflect or impede her; something on the doormat would be hopelessly outweighed by someone on the doorstep, ringing the doorbell: who? He felt, also, that his marriage and even the existence of the twins represented not a cleaner parallel to his mortal career but were simply more of the same—the product of literary envy, and literary neglect. Finally he imagined that all his letters to his wife would just be opened and skimmed and then filed or thrown away, and would remain unread like everything else he wrote. Or not even. Just trampled into the downstairs doormat along with all the other junk.

When Richard went back to Dominique-Louise that time, and Gina, instead of going back to Nottingham and to Lawrence, stayed in London and took up contemporary literature, she started—of course—with the poets.

With the poets: the pastoral, the lyrical, the satirical. Richard had always found stimulation and unaffected good cheer in the company of poets because they were the only living writers who were lowlier than he was. And who would stay lowlier, he then thought. Richard had shown Gina off in the forsaken pubs where the poets gathered. She was not daunted by them: they weren't from London either. They understood her and where she was coming from. As soon as Richard left Gina and started regroping his way around the blackened bedroom of Dominique-Louise, the poets, their scavenging instincts of necessity highly evolved, moved in, with their metrical love letters, their crying jags, their bottles of *Sangre de Toro*. For a time, when Richard went round to her flatlet, which he was allowed to keep on doing, the hallway was like the common room of the Poetry Society on an average weekday evening. At the door he would edge past some Proinnsias or Clearghill; in the stairwell some Angaoas or Iaiain would be bent over his bicycle clips or patting the pockets of his donkey jacket. There were symbolists and dadaists and acmeists. But Gina was a realist. Did she actually sleep with them, or did they all just talk about the heart, as poets will? Maybe she just heard them out about the heart. Promiscuity among the poets simply wasn't practical; it placed you in a disadvantageous retelling of *The Beauty and the Beast*—wandering the municipal gardens, going down on down-and-outs, giving blow jobs to bullfrogs, and hoping for a prince. Princeliness, here, was a long shot. Did she further sense that contemporary circumstances were demoting or declassing the poets, reducing their size, reducing their reach? And none of them drove cars. Soon, anyway, Gina was having parallel flirtations with a literary editor and a literary agent. Then she moved on to the novelists. Even now, nearly ten years later, poems still appeared in magazines and slim volumes, with titles like "Stop and Stay" or "Trent River" or even "For Miss Young," eight-liners paralyzed with romantic nostalgia, or longer and looser and murkier efforts full of sexual playback or thought-experiment. You could never be sure (and Gina wouldn't tell him). Poets got women. They didn't get anything else, and women sensed this; so they got women.

Gina's novelist period was unquestionably the toughest time for Richard. He assumed that she *must* be sleeping with at least one or two of them, or must be seeming to be about to. Why else were they going round there? She wasn't an aristocrat or a psychopath. She was touching (she was a flower from out of town); proletarian-exotic, and still largely speechless, she was perfect for the poets. But that wouldn't hold the novelists. Those marathon men, those grinders of the desk hours, those human sandglasses: they would want diversion at the end of the day. Later, when Gina and Richard were married, two or three novels appeared in which Gina could be firmly identified (largely by her association with an uppity book reviewer who had a sharp tongue and a line in paisley waistcoats); and certain descriptions of her sexual gifts rang tinkly, tinselly little bells of nausea, deep in Richard's middle ear . . . Where did it come from, then, the talent? He was her second lover; and he couldn't imagine Lawrence as an erotic exquisite, not Lawrence, with his tears and his smearing fists. It seemed that Gina was a sexual discovery: she stood *revealed*. Like the Wesleyan district nurse who has her first drink at the age of forty and wakes up five days—or five years—later in a puddle of hair tonic and skin-bracer. Now, happening to walk down her street, he would exchange wary leers with magical realists, with urban brutalists. Now, standing on her doorstep at dawn, all mauled and blood-shot after a night with Dominique-Louise, he would encounter a brilliant anatomist of contemporary culture or a meticulous dissecter of post-modern mores or (more simply) a strangely compelling new voice. He was a strangely compelling new voice himself, at that juncture, with one book out and another imminent. It seemed that Gina's novelists were becoming richer (and older); he thought she must keep a master best-seller list in the drawer of her dressing table, and intended to work her way up. Although Gina wasn't literary (Gina was literal), she stuck to the literary novel, and did not experiment with the genres—or with the kind of novelist who was famous, but famous for doing something else. Richard wouldn't have minded so much, probably, if she was wintering in Bali with some golfer who wrote novels about computer fraud. Or about golfers. But Gina had chosen to operate within what was approximately—and temporarily—his peer group.

There is a beautiful literary law, slightly scuffed and foxed, yet still beautiful, which decrees that the easier a thing is to write then the more the writer gets paid for writing it. (And vice versa: ask the poets at the bus stop.) So there was a sense of sighing inevitably when, via an arts editor and a theater critic, Gina made her switch to the dramatists. Here too Richard bade farewell to his reveries of arm's-length coquetry and provincial restraint. She moved: and her new flat, in a modern block off Marble Arch, was soon established in his mind as the locus of the most humorless carnality. Visiting her now (nodding to the porter, waiting for the lift), Richard was obliged to review, one after the other, the fiery mediocrities of the London stage. No famished bard, no myopic story-teller. Instead, an elaborately quenched Marxist in black leather trousers. Richard had hated all the poets and novelists too, but the playwrights, the playwrights . . . With Nabokov, and others, Richard regarded the drama as a primitive and long-exhausted form. The drama boasted Shakespeare (which was an excellent cosmic joke), and Chekhov, and a couple of sepulchral Scandinavians. Then where were you? Deep in the second division. As for the dramatists of today: town criers, toting leper bells, they gauged the sickness of society by the number of unsold seats at their subsidized Globes. They were soul doctors demanding applause for the pitilessness of their prognoses. And also, presumably, and crucially, they made a lot of money and splashed their way through all the actresses. Richard could stand it no longer, and he made his move.

Afterwards, he often used to wonder how far Gina would have gone. And he had no trouble visualizing her poolside with the five-million-a-pop screenplay writer, walking the chateau grounds with the belly-worshipping Francophile—or holed up in the safe-house of the Ghost Writer (he who is with us, and not with us), or piously following the electric wheelchair of the afflicted astrophysicist. Really he should have married her the day she came down from Nottingham. What held him back—the feeling that she was insufficiently literary, and would never give him enough to write about? There'd been an evening, early on, at Gwyn's. Gwyn and Gilda. Richard and Gina. Pasta, and a family-sized bottle of red wine. Gwyn was still a failed book reviewer then, back in those golden days. The humble meal, the whispering girls with their wavering vowels. Richard, in his soiled cravat, somehow thought he deserved better. He left Gina's cuddly animals for the stygian boudoir of Dominique-Louise. But he kept coming back. Her thing with all the writers—it looked like a stratagem but maybe it was just despair. It seemed to say, Look what you've made me do. Why not? Why not? it seemed to say. It also gave him a chance to leapfrog over the entire opposition. Which he took.

So one morning he lingered at the hospital long enough to see the IV tube attached to Dominique-Louise's wasted bicep and jogged straight over to Gina's and stood there with his arms folded while one of Britain's more outspoken young scenarists put his electric toothbrush in his metal briefcase and went out of the door forever, with Richard saying, "Let's get married," and Gina assenting with a sneeze of tears.

That sneeze of tears: he thought it belonged to the female repertoire. Yet he had done it too, when his book was accepted by Bold Agenda . . . This had nothing to do with the dramatists, but Richard still wondered about female theatricality. Women did all this feeling, and seemed to need guidance from the theater. Still, men were theatrical too, insomuch as they needed to be, feeling less. As with the styles of trousers they wore, women liked variety. And men attended only one school of acting (the method), that of the cool. That's men. That's men for you: hams of cool.

"Is Audra Christenberry going to be Conchita?"

"She's a very talented actress. Such radiance. And vivacity." Gwyn nodded to himself, considering this. "Yeah, I think she'd be good."

"She'll have to have her tits back out," said Richard, who wasn't cool, who had failed at cool. He was decreasingly a cool guy, and was abandoning cool. But was there anywhere else to go?

"Back out?"

"Yeah, back out. You know. Off again."

"Off again? I don't get you."

"In the book Conchita is flat-chested, right? She has a rather masculine chest."

"Not masculine. Just not pronounced."

"Flat."

"On the small side, I suppose."

"So what are you going to do about them?"

"About what?"

"About those two windsocks of silicone she's got now?"

"It's a different medium. Christ, the way you talk. How do you know they're false?"

"We've seen her in films before. We saw her in that film where I got my black eye. She didn't have any tits then. She had two backs. Perfect for *Amelior*."

"Maybe she's a late developer."

"Oh sure. When she turns a corner, she goes one way and they go the other. She goes indoors for a club sandwich, and they're still poolside, soaking up the rays."

"Jesus."

"She's like the girl in *The Limpsons*."

"What's that?"

"Pornography."

"I would never watch that stuff."

"Because?"

". . . Well, for one thing it objectifies women. It turns them into objects."

"It'd be a handy way for you to check on changing sexual styles. Whither fellatio, and so on. Actually you can never see anything because there's always some wine bottle or flower bowl in the way. It turns women into objects. Such as silicone."

"What's the matter with you?"

"I'm dying here."

"You're drunk. What's the matter with your voice? You sound like a farmer with adenoids. You better get your voice fixed by Boston. No one's going to understand a word you say."

Thus, occasionally, in the afternoons, Richard was venturing out, hopelessly dazzled, to the dazzled courtyard, in his antique T-shirt and long khaki shorts. Usually he sat at a diffident distance from Gwyn and whoever Gwyn was with—and watched the bathers. By no means all of the women were as high-gloss and high-tech as Audra Christenberry. Many were as matte and as mottled as he, though no doubt at least twice his age. They did their laps, with that bent-arm crawl favored by women, especially American women, and with that expression, not pinched, but set—that expression of American resolve. This particular Hamlet, and physical ruin, felt no urge to mock American resolve. Unprecedentedly overweight, Richard was still pretty slim compared to the Texan couple with whom he had rode down to the mezzanine: a couple so fat that they had you rereading the installers' guarantee that the elevator could carry eighteen people. The men out here on the deck—these wonderful providers—swam and ate and telephoned; confidently occupying the sun beds, they sprawled on their sides with one leg crooked and one hand flat on the tensed belly, and talking provider talk with fellow providers, fellow prime-of-lifers. Richard felt, in Los Angeles, that he wasn't hard currency; he was a zloty, a despicable kopek. Nearby, Gwyn would be sampling a plain omelette, an iced tea, and answering questions. Writing is like carpentry. It's speculative, but there has been movie interest. I use a simple word processor, more like a typewriter with added functions. From breakfast until lunch, and a bit more in the late afternoons . . . Five feet away, the stress-equations of Audra Christenberry's swimsuit. Or else the hundred-percent expressionlessness of the publicity boy.

With his Iberian blood, Gwyn grew dark and sparkling in the sun. Richard's brief visits to the pool, in his nontransferable English flesh, gave him first-degree burns on his arms, thighs, neck, nose and forehead. When clothed he looked like a bit player in a cheap video, or in pornography, the repulsive patsy of slapdash makeup and deathwatch lighting. Naked, he felt he had the distinctive markings of a London pigeon. Even the skinny pigeon redness of his legs contributed to his homesickness. Other things were going wrong with him here in the Pacific city. He couldn't get his mouth wet, no matter what he drank. His tongue was curling up at the edges. Beads of information were traveling along his gum lines, information about the immediate future. In two locations (upper left, lower right) the pain fairies were already breaking little fairy eggs of fairy pain, at every second's throb. Then it would go away again. At night he reviewed biographies in his room, and marked up *Untitled* for the reading in Boston, which was the end of the line.

Other things were going wrong with him here in the Pacific city, the city that went on being a city as far as the eye could see in every direction, forever and ever. A couple of times he accumulated the energy to be driven out into it, when Gwyn did radio or TV, and he attended Gwyn's reading, in a mall somewhere. The city was like a city doing remarkably well so soon after that unfortunate all-out nuclear attack, after that Everest of a meteorite, that mile-high tidal wave; there were blips and glitches, square miles of them, but sun and enterprise and multicultural synergy were always getting the place back on stream. As Gwyn had truckingly told his audience, during the warmup at the reading, Los Angeles was Amelior . . . With differences. Nikita Khrushchev, flying in over the West's last stop and seeing all the swimming pools innocently open to the sky, knew at once that Communism had failed. And Richard's body knew that whatever it was Richard stood for—the not-so-worldly, the contorted, the difficult—had failed. Los Angeles sought transcendence everywhere you looked, through astrology or crystal or body-worship or templegoing, but these were stabs at worldly divination, tips and forecasts about how to do better in the here and now. What mattered was to prepare for the future. And Richard was not prepared for the future. Bodily knowledge of this seemed to pass in through his sinuses; knowledge of this presented itself not in the mind but in the ears and nose and throat.

Women, he thought, understood about time. (Gina understood about time.) Women could send their imaginations out over the future and situate themselves at certain points within it. Time is a dimension, not a force. But women felt it as a force, because they could feel its violence, every hour. They knew they would be half dead at forty-five. This information did not fall in the path of men. Men, at forty-five, were in "the prime of life." The prime? *Prima (hora)*: first (hour)? They get the Change. We get the Prime. And this is the reason why our bodies weep and seep in the night, because we're half dead too, and don't know how or why.

"Wow," said the publicity boy. "Too bad about your face. Does it hurt a lot?"

Richard said, "Not as much as you'd think."

"Pardon me?"

"Not as much as you'd think."

"Pardon me?"

He shook his head no. *That* hurt a lot. Just before dawn Richard had got out of bed and moved toward the bathroom mirror with unusually intense disquiet. Sure enough, his face was the shape of a television. He looked like one of the Simpsons. He looked like Bart Simpson. In profile Richard resembled the joke figure in a newspaper cartoon about a dentist's waiting room. Full face, though, he looked like Bart Simpson. Because he had two joke toothaches: lower right, upper left.

At the airport he sat with Gwyn while the publicity boy banged his head against the wall of a nearby phone booth, rearranging interviews. Their flight to Boston was delayed, and there were further complications. Following the mid-afternoon reading they were to make a short hop to Provincetown, over the bay, in Cape Cod, there to attend a party at the holiday home of the toiletry tycoon or burger king who owned Gwyn's publishers. The publicity boy returned, saying,

"The *Globe* guy and the *Herald* lady will meet us at Logan and we can do a double interview in the cab."

"Did you get Elsa Oughton?"

"I keep getting this jig who just bawls me out and won't take a message."

The publicity boy sat down heavily.

Gwyn was staring at him. "Try again. What is this? She's Profundity Three for Christ's sake."

On the afternoon of Gwyn's Los Angeles reading the publicity boy had pointed to the lone cloud in the sky—pink-fringed, chef's-hat-shaped, utterly lost—and predicted, drolly, and wrongly, that no one would show up, this being Los Angeles. In Los Angeles the sky had only one imitation it could do: that of the interstellar void. As for telling Los Angeles about the kind of day it was having, the sky, like Gwyn Barry when they asked him about the Millennium deal on *Amelior,* had no comment. The sky above Los Angeles was a no-comment sky.

The simultaneous or parallel reading was to be given in a converted theater in Boston's commercial midtown. Richard took it as auspicious when he saw the crowd outside, and the crowd in the entrance hall, and the crowd lining the passage, and the crowd in the bar where the simultaneous or parallel signing session would later take place. Gwyn's table was ready, hardly visible beneath the earthworks and palisades of his fiction: the stacks of *Amelior Regained*, the stacks of *Amelior*, and (Jesus) the stacks of *Summertown* in a bright new paperback original. Richard approached his own table, which was of course entirely bare, and started unloading his mail sack. Lifting out the first copy of *Untitled*, and catching the usual hangnail in the rough loom of its jacket, Richard watched Gwyn and tried to imitate his expression, benign, bemused, unsurprisable. He was also endeavoring to take heart from the rampant and (by definition) laughably undiscriminating enthusiasm on display. In England, if your favorite living author who also happened to be your long-lost twin brother was giving a reading in the next house along, it would never occur to you even to stick your head round the door. But Americans clearly went out and did things.

For the next fifteen minutes the two writers were to occupy a sectioned area of the bar, where a group of journalists and academics had been gathered for them to hobnob with. Elsa Oughton stood among them. Richard was startled by her appearance. She was no longer the angular, Gina-like dryad of her jacket photograph: he wouldn't have identified her if she hadn't had both Gwyn's shoes sticking out of the back of her skirt. On the happenstance/coincidence/enemy-action principle, Richard had decided against any further defamation of his friend. But after Gwyn was done with her (in parting he gave Elsa the full PR handshake, two palms enfolding hers as if in joint prayer), she came over to where he was standing with his swollen face and his plastic beaker of white wine and Richard thought what the hey and said,

"Elsa Oughton? Richard Tull. I wonder if you saw our review of *Saddle Leather* in *The Little Magazine*. A favorable and also a very interesting piece. I'll make sure you get sent a copy."

"Thanks. Good. How was your tour?"

What Richard was looking at here was a narrative of fat. The whole story: how she'd got that way, how she'd tried to get back. How much she hated it. He wondered whether it was in him to dream up something about Gwyn hating fat people—a taunt directed at a small child with gland problems, perhaps. But he didn't see how the subject of fat people could be smoothly raised. For a moment he felt pride in the shaming bloat of his own face. The only other stuff he knew about Elsa was that she wrote twangingly sensitive short stories about hikes and sleepouts and mingling with animals. And that she had recently married Viswanathan Singh, the Harvard economist.

He sucked in his chest and stuck out his gut and said, "Rather shocking, actually."

"How so?"

"Well. I've known Gwyn for twenty years." Richard didn't even bother to tell himself not to get carried away. "I know his foibles. Or I thought I did. Outrageous looks-snob. Loves his creature comforts. Hates animals. So what? Who cares? But I had no idea he was such an unreconstructed racist. Really. I'm flabbergasted."

"Racist?"

"Of course he did grow up in Wales, which is racially very homogeneous. And in London he and his wife—that's Lady Demeter to you—move in very select circles. But over here, in the great 'melting pot' . . ."

"What kind of thing?"

"For two weeks now I've had to endure a constant stream of snide remarks about geeks and slopes and wops and wogs and boogies and pakkis. Send them back to the hellholes they came from. You know the kind of thing." What next? Gwyn punching eye-slits in his hotel pillow slips? Gwyn with his blazing cross, thundering over . . . No. No horses. Richard made a serious effort and managed to mutter in his clogged new voice, "I tried reading him Dickens on the American South. No earthly use, of course. Oh no. Not with friend Barry."

"But his work's so bland. *So* bland."

"Yes, well this is often the way, isn't it."

"I can't stay for the reading. I . . . can't stay."

Elsa Oughton couldn't stay for the reading because a curtain-hanger was expected at the house, and Viswanathan refused to deal with tradespeople. The Singhs had moved, not so long ago, and something like this happened almost every day. Viswanathan would call and tell her to come home because there was a man outside trying to deliver a parcel. Late the night before he had caught her crouched over the icebox in the dark and announced his intention of moving into a separate bedroom. And a separate bathroom. That morning: another fight. She had crossed the room in front of his desk. In future she was to cross the room *behind* his desk. Even as things stood it seemed that she was only allowed to look his way every other Tuesday.

"At the airport just now," said Richard, "our porter was an elderly Asian gentleman and he accidentally dropped Gwyn's shooting-stick. And Gwyn called him a fucking monkey! I'm sorry. But can you believe that? I mean *I* don't care whether people are green or blue or polka-dotted . . ."

Oh sure, she thought. Come back to my place and try handling *my* fucking monkey. "Nice talking to you. I'll look again at his work."

"Do that."

It was time. The lady organizer took his arm and with an indecipherable smile drew him away, ahead of Gwyn. As he was led down passages, and up stairways like fireman's drops with steps curled round the pole, Richard began to suspect that a disaster awaited him: not a literary humiliation but a disaster, with body counts. First a young woman on a stretcher came flowing past, borne by two health-industry freelancers in orange salopettes. There followed a policeman, another medic, and a genuine fireman, with an axe, and then a young couple seemingly brought together and sustained by deep shared sorrow. He turned a corner. The walls were lined on either side by leaning figures in attitudes of distress and exhaustion and qualified recovery. This was the entrance to Theater A, where Gwyn would be reading. Richard glanced inside and saw human congestion on a scale no longer imaginable in the civilized world. Perhaps in Japanese commuter trains, in crushed crowds in news footage, watched over by the sneer of calamity . . . He thought of deportations, slave-packing, the cages of Calcutta. The room gave off the thick insect buzz of coagulated youth—a hive of hormones. Richard's escort paused to reassure the two firemen who doubtfully flanked the doorway, and then turned to him and said, with ominous tenderness,

"I'm sure you're a beautiful writer too."

They walked on, to Theater B. Theater A sat 750 people, Theater B 725. Richard had agreed altogether readily, with much astute nodding of the head, in an airport somewhere, in a flickering coffeenook, on a cab chute of a hotel forecourt, that Gwyn belonged in Theater A. With a last nasal drool into his handkerchief, Richard stepped into the space and silence of Theater B.

Later, he would tell himself that the reading was the clear high-point of the afternoon. His audience might not have been large. But it was varied. One was female, one was black, one was Native American, and one was fat. And that was that. But wait. The fat man was fabulously fat—how his folds seemed to slur and slobber over two seats, over three! And the black man was as black as the bedroom of Dominique-Louise: as black as Adam. And the Amerindian wore cowboy boots, and had one leg up over the aisle armrest with the spur lolling in pluralistic suspension. And the woman, beneath the quilted lodge-skins of her smock, was all woman, Richard was sure. Fat man, black man, cowboy and Indian, womankind . . . He took the lectern to a Krakatoa of applause: from next door. It sounded like an espresso machine going off an inch away from his clogged right ear. Instead of fainting, he started reading, from the early pages of chapter eleven: the description of the coven of tramps, rendered as a burlesque of *The Idylls of the King*. Immediately he lost a quarter of his audience when, with a primitive ululation, the Native American got to his feet and started walking backwards up the steps. Richard raised his head. Their eyes met. The Native American was severe and vain and stupidly lissome in his cowboy boots. *Cowboy* boots? The boots of your slaughterer? With a rush of hurt and hate Richard knew that this was his comrade from Bold Agenda: John Two Moons. Three listeners remained. As he got going again Richard found he was becoming increasingly and then entirely absorbed by the question of their tenuous equanimity, their whims and mood swings. What he was reading was no use at all: he needed paragraphs that praised fat people, black people, smocked women. Causing intolerable suspense, the fat man was now making successively enfeebled attempts to get out of his seat. He flailed, and failed, and eventually subsided into a troubled sleep. The African American, too, was providing conflict and drama: ever more energized by his private agenda, he began to mouth, mumble, intone and holler, louder than the man at the mike. Only the woman—thickly made-up, unblinking, flatly smiling, his age—maintained an undivided composure: the dream audience of one.

And the reading was the clear high point of the afternoon. After that it was all downhill.

During one of the many intermissions, caused by the stridor from Theater A, Richard fell to the perusal of his handkerchief. A handkerchief the likes of which no American had set eyes on since the invention of paper tissues. (The publicity boy, Richard knew, just couldn't believe this handkerchief.) Some bits bunched, infinitely parched and crackling to the touch; others as glutinous as the white of a half-boiled egg: the whole seeking a strange shape—definitive asymmetry. He moistened his nose with it. Yeah, a real old snot-rag. Such as the schoolboy he once was might have found in his blazer pocket, after a term of flu. The shape and color of London skies.

* * *

Boston was burning behind them in its brick-red dusk as they walked out of the gate and headed for the plane—the light aircraft. Richard turned. The rust and dust of the Logan evening contained something lurid, something brothelly and lewd. And you could hear the primal moan over and above the ordinary wind.

Gwyn said, "Reassure me."

"It's a hop," said the publicity boy. "Like a half hour. We'll beat the storm. They guarantee we'll beat it."

"We're not going up in *that*. Jesus. It's the Wright brothers."

"Orville and Wilbur," said Richard ramblingly. "The *Kitty Hawk*."

"I've done it like a thousand times. It's a breeze."

"It's not a breeze. It's a hurricane."

"Don't worry about it."

Richard unyoked his mail sack from his shoulder and lowered it to the ground. His mail sack was fractionally heavier than it had been before the Boston signing session. As if to prove and memorialize this fact, as if to give it chapter and verse, his mailsack was now going to be *weighed*. Weight, hereabouts, was much in the air. All the passengers, at check-in, were asked what their weight was, Gwyn disclosing a game 140, Richard an overparticular and outdated 167, the publicity boy eventually coming up with a regrettable 215. Tensing her legs, a young woman in a blue pants suit now hoisted Richard's mail sack on to the broad bucket of the platform scale. If his suitcase had raised eyebrows, his mail sack was the theme of candid debate. To get them through this debate, Richard had to smile. And if it hurts when you smile, you realize how often you smile when you don't want to—how often your smiles are smiles of pain. He knew from mirrors how his smiles made him look. They made him look as if he was recovering from a stroke. So these smiles, performed on behalf of his mail sack, in front of Gwyn, in front of the publicity boy, these smiles took from him everything he had. These smiles removed the change from his pockets. These smiles just cleaned him out . . . A couple of hundred feet away the light aircraft crouched self-consciously in its bay, spindly-legged but plump-girdled, and eloquent of aerodynamic ingenuousness. Looking at it, Richard thought not of the goggled smiles of Orville and Wilbur but of the spastic wrigglings of moustachioed hobbyists—riding off cliffs on buttressed bicycles and flapping their pantomime wings. His mail sack was skeptically returned to him, as hand baggage. He shouldered it once more, and turned to Gwyn.

"Christ. Will you look at that."

"Where?" he said, and looked to the south.

Night was ready to arrive, to roll over, but the day was not accepting this. Light was being displaced by dark, because the earth turned; but light was not accepting this. Light and day hadn't gone to bed. They were up after dark. In the core of the advancing darkness, light—talent, passion—feverishly struggled and would then rear up madly bright: hysterical day.

He wasn't worried because he was already dead. It was over. He went off with his mail sack and sat down on it, behind a staircase pointing upward but leading nowhere, and stuck a cigarette into the unfamiliar tautness of his lips, and let his death go slowly by.

It was the signing that had killed him. Keats was killed by a review. Richard was killed by a signing. Of the *reading* you could at least say that there weren't many people there to see it. But his audience for the signing was biblically vast. Submitting to demand, Gwyn had given a shortened reading—in three sittings. And everyone stuck around.

So while his friend and rival exhausted four whole ballpoints, signing *Amelior Regained, Amelior, Summertown*, signing programs, flyers, press photographs, signing autograph books, plaster casts, girls' forearms, girls' inner thighs, Richard sat at the other table for two hours doing nothing . . . In the past, and in various capacities, none of them exalted, he had hung around at fairs and festivals and studied, with casual enmity, the signing queues of writers. Each queue, like each book and each writer, had a genre it belonged to. The countercultural, the contentedly pedagogic, the straggly, the ramrod orderly, the playful, the earnest, as well as all the other emphases of class, age, sex and race. And Gwyn's queue, it had to be admitted, looked like the universal. Here they came, stepping up the gangway to the ark of the future.

While queueing (and where did this queue end? Where did it end?), the queuers had Richard to look at and wonder about—they had Richard to delectate. They didn't know it, but they were actors at his funeral, they were mourners, weepers, moving slowly past the corpse of his calling, the tinpot jackboot, numb and luminous in his death wax.

The ghost went on sitting there, at the table heaped with unsigned *Untitleds*. About forty minutes in, an old man wearing pressed jeans approached, his face archangelic with integrity: the ghost of Tom Paine. He produced a copy of Richard's novel from under his arm and smacked it down on the tabletop. *Untitled* snapped open on pages eight and nine, both of which were unmistakably stained and warped by dried blood; in the interface lay the distinctive bookmark of the Lazy Susan; the top corner of page nine had been forcefully turned down and bore the perfect contours of a gory thumbprint. He didn't want it signed. He didn't want it . . . His only other visitor was a woman: the woman who had attended his reading. At the time, she had seemed to him to be the only person present who had paid the slightest attention to his words. With kittenish timidity she approached his table. Richard bade her welcome, and meant it, and went on meaning it as she extracted from her shoulder pouch a copy of a novel written not by Richard Tull but by Fyodor Dostoevsky. *The Idiot.* Standing beside him, leaning over him, her face awfully warm and near, she began to leaf through its pages, explaining. This book too was stained, not by gouts of blood but by the vying colors of two highlighting pens, one blue, one pink. And not just two pages but the whole six hundred. Every time the letter *h* and *e* appeared together, as in *the, then, there*, as in *forehead, Pashlishtchev, sheepskin*, they were shaded in blue. Every time the letters *s, h*, and *e* appeared together, as in *she, sheer, ashen, sheepskin*, etc., they were shaded in pink. And since every *she* contained a *he*, the predominance was unarguably and unsurprisingly masculine. Which was exactly her point. "You see?" she said with her hot breath, breath redolent of metallic medications, of batteries and printing-plates. "You see?" . . . The organizers knew all about this woman—this unfortunate recurrence, this indefatigable drag—and kept coming over to try and coax her away. Richard wouldn't hear of it. Never had he found another's company so gorgeous. Never had he lived so deliciously. Never would he stray from her side. Together, in their dwindling years, with no kids of course but with new twin sets of highlighting pens, they would tackle the great texts, one by one. If he should falter, she would take up the blue. Should she grow weary, he would wield the pink. But life is short and art is long: would they ever exhaust the great Russians? Side by side, him with his pint jug and his painkillers, her with her zinc and her manganese.

Lady with Lapdog and Other Stories. The Greatcoat. Father and Son. A Hero of Our Time.

The Death of Ivan Ilych. The Gentleman from San Francisco. The Master and Margarita.

The Devil. The Double.

We.

Richard raised a palm to the spongey cladding of his face. He thought he could probably work it out, now—where his stuff stood, and where Gwyn's stuff stood, in relation to the universe. The publicity boy was calling. Up above, the sky was showing that it could do black holes. This imitation (the event horizon only roughly circular, with the standard drug-squeezed pupil at the eye's center—the kind of puckered blob you would find in one of the twins' astronomy booklets) needed more work.

* * *

They rolled forward, soon to go. The seven passengers sat with their necks bent almost sideways, in postures of tortured compression. It wasn't just the low ceiling: it was also the embarrassing proximity of the tarmac, only a few feet beneath the soles of their shoes. Richard assumed that the engine was so loud that it was off the human scale altogether, and all you felt was vibration, in your every atom. More or less engulfed by his mail sack, he sat jammed into the rearmost row, next to Gwyn. They were both assessing the pilot—a figure of unusually enhanced interest: tall, fleshy, ginger-blond, a big man with a light step, he deployed a feminine delicacy in the arrangement of his peaked cap, his flightbox, his earphones. Turning sideways in his seat, comfortingly perfunctory, he had run through the safety instructions in a voice perhaps incapable of modulation anyway, and then attended to his controls—the sort of dashboard appropriate to a prewar spaceship or a glue-and-balsa nuclear sub, dials, graphs, metal switches coated in worn paint. Richard realized that the dash contained no plastic. Was that good, he wondered, and tried to lose himself in silent tribute to durable and horny-handed craftsmanship and skills, now, alas, long vanished. The pilot wore a white shirt and lumpy cream trousers the texture of flock wallpaper. It was easy, somehow, to lose yourself in the expanse of his cream rump: firmly framed in the lower aperture of his seat, it filled its space solidly and proudly, soft-cornered, like a TV—like the shape of Richard's face.

So the little plane queued for take off. The little plane was a little plane, among all these big ones, and hoped it wasn't in the way. But it was. The passenger jets, dog-nosed (their noses black and damp in the dew or sweat of the coming storm), waited in line behind them like rigid pointers cocked for the hunt. Richard looked out through the propeller blades, which were moving invisibly fast, seeming to smudge the air or bruise it. Ahead of them, round the turn, were the tensed haunches of the important shuttles—to New York, to Washington—waiting to take Americans where they needed to go: around America. Over and above the compound anguish of the checked planes, all screaming at each other to get out of the way, you could hear the sky and the epic groan of the middle air. Darkness, night, was wheeling in from the north. But from the defiant south came a negligent and unanswerable demonstration of light, the electromagnetic: god's whips, knouts and sjamboks of solder and copper.

No one spoke. Gwyn suddenly leaned forward and engaged the publicity boy. His inquiries were muffled by the headrest, and when the publicity boy replied he seemed to be talking or shouting to himself, like a bum or a wacko, like American fever. *Come on, you seen what's behind us . . . They do this like nine times a day . . . No way is it a hurricane. It's a storm . . . You mean like a hurricane with a name?*

"Hurricanes used to be all girls," said Richard. He had spoken, really, to make the publicity boy seem saner. It made *him* seem saner too, though, and he continued ramblingly, "Now they alternate them. Girl, boy. Boy, girl. I think that's better, I don't know. Hurricane Demi. Hurricane Gwyn. Hurricane Gina. Hurricane Marius. Hurricane Anstice. Hurricane Scozzy."

"Hurricane who?"

"Nothing."

"Listen to this one," said Gwyn. "He's already flipped. Jesus. All this for a *party*."

The pilot put his face into profile and monotonously informed them that it would be a whole lot cooler in here when they were off the ground. This was good news. Because the passengers were finding out what happened to the air on planes and what would happen to the air on jets unless they doctored and gimmicked it. How soon it was exhausted, and went blood-heat and pungent. How soon you were all breathing each other's yawn. On the jets you could wait at the can door for half an hour and step right in after some exploding nonagenarian had dragged himself out of there: that's how good these guys were. But on the little plane the air was already critically delicate. You wouldn't even want to worry it with speech . . . Now all the passengers were silent, giving themselves up to that strange modern activity, fancy-priced suffering, in which America leads the world; but when the plane rounded the last corner and found nothing ahead of it except sea and sky, and made its rattling gallop for the bruised yonder, and was up, away, exchanging one medium for a new and better one, and was immediately sent skidding sideways, windmilling its arms, then all eight of them moaned in harmony, answering the moan above their heads.

They steadied, and climbed. Over car park, over graveyard, over the harbor, over the bay. Soon the patchy whitecaps were no more than flecks of dandruff on the broad shoulder of the sea. Richard looked casually out of his porthole, to the south. And he couldn't believe it. The storm was there, like a gothic cathedral, with all its glaring gargoyles . . . Diurnal time was a figure for the human span: waking, innocent morning, full midday and the pomp of the afternoon, then loss of color, then weariness, then mortal weariness and the certainty of sleep, then nightmare, then dreamlessness. Outside, day was gone but it wouldn't go to bed. The day was dead and gone but wouldn't believe it and wouldn't accept it, the day and its sick comeback, trying to return and saying, *I'm still day. Don't you* see me? *Don't you like me* more? *I'm still day,* and not letting go, jerkily reanimated, hot-wired, and pulsing under the jump-leads. And the rain: the rain was wanting to lubricate this desperate tension between day and night, wanting to soothe and cleanse. But the rain was panicking and completely overdoing it and sounding like psychopathic applause.

"That red switch," said Gwyn. "What's he doing with that red switch?"

Next to the digital clock on the dashboard, which recorded their flighttime (nine minutes elapsed), there was a red switch and a flashing and beeping red light which did seem to be exercising the pilot in an unencouraging way. He kept twiddling it, as if hoping that the light would go off, or change color, or stop beeping. But his movements were perhaps more curious than agitated. The stiff cream carapace of his backside was still stalwartly ensconced in its chair.

"We're losing height. I think we're losing height."

"He'd tell us if something was up. Wouldn't he? Or wouldn't he?"

Without turning round the pilot said, "We're having a weight problem. Hopefully it won't be a . . . a problem. It'll keep us under this weather here." And now he did swivel round, eyeing each passenger in turn with reasonable suspicion, as if searching for a superfat stowaway.

"I'm not going to worry," said Gwyn, "until *he* starts to worry."

The pilot didn't seem worried. He had even started to whistle.

"That sounds wise," said Richard, and turned to his porthole. And the sea looked as close as the tarmac had looked ten minutes ago, and the plane suddenly seemed to be traveling not through the air but through the churned water. The dip, the climb, the crest, the fall. The wave, the wait, the wave, the wait, the wave, the wait, the wave.

"Oh man," said Gwyn.

"He's stopped fucking with that red switch."

"Has he? Good."

Above their heads the cabin lights dimmed and flickered and dimmed again.

It was when the patch of shit appeared on the pilot's cream rump that Richard knew for certain that all was not well. This patch of shit started life as an islet, a Martha's Vineyard that soon became a Cuba, then a Madagascar, then a dreadful Australia of brown. But that was five minutes ago, and no one gave a shit about it now. Not a single passenger, true, had interpreted the state of the pilot's pants as a favorable sign, but that was five minutes ago, that was history, and no one gave a shit about it now, not even the pilot, who was hollering into the microphone, hollering into a world of neighing metal and squawking rivets, hollering into the very language of the storm—its fricatives, its atrocious plosives. The gods had put aside their bullwhips and their elemental rodeo and were now at play with their bowling balls clattering down the gutters of space-time. Within were the mortals, starfished from white knuckle to white toe-joint, stretched like Christs, like Joans in her fire. Richard looked and now felt love for the publicity boy, his sleek, shaking, tear-washed face.

This would end. He reached for Gwyn's hand and said, loudly, in his ear, "Death is good."

"What?"

"Death is good." Here in America he had noticed how much less he cared, every time, whether the plane he was in stayed up. There was so much less, every time, to come down to. "Death is good."

"Oh *yeah*?"

Richard felt he had won. Because of his boys—because of Marius and Marco. Gwyn had a wife. And Richard had a wife. But who *was* your wife? She was just the one you ended up with who had your kids. And you were just the one she had them *with*. Childhood was the universal. *Everyone* had been there. He said,

"I'll survive."

"We'll survive. We'll survive."

No, not you, he thought. But he said, "The world liked what you wrote."

"Who fucking cares? No. Thanks. I'm sorry your . . . Gina loves you. She just . . ."

"What? She just what?"

Now came a thousand camera flashes through every porthole. The parting shots of the paparazzi of the storm. With rolling deliberation the sky gathered them into its slingshot, wound and stretched them back ("Death is good," he said again) and fired them out into silent night.

You could sense the presence of the peninsula, and see the lights of the airport. Some lights were fixed. Others moved.

"Avoidance apron," sobbed the pilot into his mike. "Avoidance apron . . ."

The passengers unwrapped their voices and sank back, harshly purring. Richard offered his handkerchief to the publicity boy, who accepted it.

"*Avoidance* apron. *Avoidance* apron!"

"What's he mean?" said Gwyn, jerking around in his seat. "What's the avoidance apron? Where you crash-land? Is the landing gear down? Is it gone?"

It didn't seem to matter and no one else seemed to care. They were getting nearer to their own thing, the ground, the earth. Not scored and seared by another thing, the fire, not covered and swallowed by another thing, the water, not plucked apart by another thing, the air.

Provincetown Airport was a baby airport, meant for baby planes, and it was shy about the fuss. With his case and his mail sack Richard had plonked himself down on a patch of grass—over on the civilian side of the airport's main bungalow. He patiently chain-smoked, and from a plastic bottle with a plastic tube patiently drank the brandy given to him by a sympathetic medic. On the airfield a scene of human and mechanical confusion was approaching its completion and dispersal point. There was a handsome fire engine, and two blue-cross station wagons on the lookout for custom (into one of which an elderly passenger had been levered, clutching his pacemaker) and a couple of cops creaking about . . . The pilot had left the plane last, attended by ground staff. He was wearing a shiny black mid-length skirt or pinafore. Two other passengers, slumped on chairs in the airport building, attempted to give him a cheer; but he shuffled on through, with marked modesty. Gwyn was in there now, with the publicity boy and a gesticulating young journalist from *The Cape Codder*.

He closed his eyes for a while. Someone took the cigarette from between his fingers and drew on it with audible hunger. He looked up: it occurred to him that they were both in a state that had a medical designation, because Gwyn resembled no one he had ever seen before. And maybe *he* didn't look that hot or that cool, sitting with his shoulders shaking on the frosted grass, and steam coming up all around him—animal vapors. But he laughed his tight laugh and said, not ramblingly anymore,

"I worked it out. You know the pilot? We thought he was shouting *avoidance* apron. But he wasn't. I heard one of the ladies here. He wanted a—*voidance* apron. She called it a shit-wrap." Richard laughed stealthily, under the cover of his shaking shoulders. He did think it was kind of great. You wouldn't want to radio ahead for a shit-wrap. That would offend the passengers. So you radioed ahead for a "voidance apron." And the passengers can remain unoffended as they prepare to crash-land or mass-eject onto the airport latrine. "A voidance apron," he said. "It's kind of great, I think. You were saying? About Gina?"

Gwyn stood over him.

"She loves me?"

"Despite everything. Which is saying something. Oh, you know. Despite you being a failed book reviewer who comes on like Dr. Johnson. I can see why *you* think death is good. Because then you and I are the same. But I'm alive. And I'm going to go on doing what every man would do if he thought he could get away with it. Everything's changed." Gwyn knelt, his hands folded on his thigh, as if for a knighthood. "Let me tell you the interesting thing about the star system. It works. You want to know what silicone feels like? It feels good. It feels better. Because of what it says. Whither fellatio? you ask. Well that's changed too. I'll tell you whither. I can sum it up for you in one word. It's *noisier*." He straightened up again. With a sudden apprehension of disgust he flicked the cigarette away and said, "You know what bloody near killed us up there? Killed you, killed me?"

Now he stepped forward and gave the mail sack a careless kick—and Richard was holding it close, like a boxing coach with a punchbag, feeling the force of the contender's right.

"Your lousy book."

The publicity boy came out of the building with his mobile phone and told them that they had three choices. They could go straight to the hotel and rest up. Or they could go to P-town General or wherever for checkups and the usual post-trauma bullshit. Or they could go to the party.

They went to the party.

At dawn the next morning the two writers checked out of the Founding Fathers and, traveling by limousine, made the six-hour journey to New York in unpunctuated silence. When the chauffeur was pulling off FDR Drive, Gwyn said,

"While you're here . . ."

From his briefcase he took out the copy of *Untitled* that Richard had given him, back in London, a month ago. They both looked at it. Just as *Amelior*, in Richard's judgment, could be thought remarkable only if Gwyn had written it with his foot, so *Untitled*, as an object, could be thought passable only if its maker had fashioned it with his nose.

"You might as well sign it for me."

"I've already signed it."

"Ah. So you have," said Gwyn. "So you have."

Whereas Boston had been trussed in its green-studded rustbelts, Manhattan, as they neared it from the north, looked like a coda to the urban-erotic, the garter and stocking-top patterning of its loops and bridges now doing service as spinal supports and braces, hernia frames. Above it all, the poised hypodermic of the Empire State.

There wasn't much time. Richard parked his suitcase with the porter at Gwyn's hotel, and, accompanied by his mail sack, his fat face, his handkerchief, and his hangover, walked the sixty-odd blocks to Avenue B and Bold Agenda. He arrived unannounced at the desk of Leslie Evry, who climbed cautiously to his feet. Silence fell over the entire workspace as Richard said, in his loudest and reediest voice,

"In what sense, if any, are you publishing *Untitled*?"

Leslie looked at him in the way that so many Americans had looked at him: as if they wanted to call Security. Americans, it transpired, were disappointed in Richard. Not because he wasn't a duke or a beefeater but because of the clear imperfections, the reparable tarnishings of body and mind, that he chose to live with. Frances Ort was there, hesitant in his peripheral vision, but undaunted.

"In what sense, if any, are you publishing *Untitled*?"

"Excuse me?"

"Well let's go through this one step at a time. Are you distributing it?"

"Not directly."

"Have you sent out copies for review?"

"We have sent a number of copies out to certain . . . outlets."

"*What* number? I know. One! Zero! How many did you print?"

"There's a run on reserve. They're not bound, not as yet."

"How many did you *print*?"

Regretfully Leslie indicated the mail sack that Richard still wore on his shoulder. "That's it."

"Who made the decision to publish my novel—to print the typescript and bind it between hard covers? Where's Chip? Where's Chuck? Where's Roy Biv?"

"Ah, Roy," said Evry, shaking his head. "Roy Biv! Tell me. Did he ever sign himself Roy *G*. Biv? . . . He changed his name to that. If you were American, you'd understand. It's a mnemonic. The rainbow. Red, orange, yellow, green. Blue, indigo, violet. He wanted to please every-one. That's Roy. Poor Roy."

"*Someone* published it. On what criteria? Please tell me the truth. This is a literary life. Of a kind. Tell me the truth. On what criteria?"

He felt Frances Ort's young hand on his arm. He turned. The friendly spaces of Bold Agenda were still taking shape for future use, whatever was necessary, kindergarten, rape hotline, health-crisis center. Its cubbyholes and cord carpets—its pro-bono feel, like a clinic. And he could of course see himself there, sitting quietly on a low sofa, awaiting counsel for all his pains and his ills.

"Basically," said Leslie Evry, "basically to balance the list. We felt the mix was wrong and may look badly. We felt it might imperil our funding."

"Because," said Richard, "everyone else was called Doo Wah Diddy Diddy or Two Dogs Fucking. And you needed . . ." On the wall, he noticed, was a framed poster of the Bold Agenda flyleaf or bookmark. With recognition, with love, Richard saw that one of his fellow authors was called Unsöld—Unsöld Inukuluk. "Christ," he said. "A token honky—not even *Gwyn* bothered with that. Why me? Why not some-one from Boston?"

"It's our policy to represent the most authentic possible—"

"Did anyone read it? Did anyone? Did Roy?"

"*Roy?* Roy never read *anything*. *I* read it."

"You read it all?"

"Not exactly. I had a—I'd just gotten into it when I had a . . ."

"Leslie was hospitalized with suspected meningitis," said Frances Ort.

"Okay. Okay. Well, I'm going to leave this here, if I may. I'll just take—no. Here." Richard looked from face to face. And he remem-bered. He said, "Richard Of York Gains Battles In Vain. That's it. That's it. That's the difference between the cultures. Between the new and the old. Between you and me. Richard Of York meets Roy G. Biv. It's no contest. It's no contest."

"We're sorry," said Frances Ort.

"I'll find my own way out. So long."

So long, and no longer. He stood on the sidewalk, outside the Lazy Susan. Whose windows . . . Even the windows of the Lazy Susan were telling him, with American emphasis, that if you do the arts, if you try the delirious profession, then don't be a flake, and offer people some-thing—tell them something they might reasonably want to hear. He felt light. He felt light because there was nothing to carry, nothing to grip and tote, nothing to heave and buckle under.

The first bar he hit was selling vodka and milk to old black men for $1.25.

By the time he reached Central Park South he had driven this up to ten bucks a pop, and came out of the Plaza, where they wouldn't serve him, in some disarray. As he staggered about, among shoeshine and fountain spray, a phalanx of civilians streamed past him in distinct amateur-military style, and on their faces—well, he took his last look at it: American resolve. Their mission was simple. They intended to embarrass the horse-and-carriage trade of Central Park South. Across the road they surged, raising their daubed placards, all of which had something pithy or rhyming to say about the incompatibility of beast and city: how the two didn't mix. The horsemen, slaves of tourists, dressed in low-caste colors (and there was a horsewoman too, not that old but her face grimly lined, wearing what looked like an entire tepee over a body as thin as a ridgepole): the horsepeople watched their advancing adversaries with a loathing that lay at the limit of human fatigue. Swept along, Richard now disengaged himself and pushed his way toward the railings. A horse halted his progress—a horse and its sightless stare. The animal, the blinkered clipclop, cause of all the fuss, raised its head in pompous indifference, and then dropped it again, wholly preoccupied, it seemed, by the task of wiping shit from its shoe (not dog shit but horse shit—in a class of its own, really, as shit went), and doing this not as humans do it, heel-first and backwards, but as horses do it, toe-first and forwards. So the charioteers in the ethnic heft of their patchwork and motley, in their gypsy jackets, averted their gypsy chancer's eyes, and the horse scraped its shoe, not minding. Agony, of which there was much in the air, found expression only through the cars: the delivery vans, the Plaza limousines, the yellow cabs. Deliberately obstructed for now, until the police showed up and cleared the scene, the beasts of burden, made of metal and serving the concrete city, twisted and shuddered, blaring blue murder with smoke coming out of their ears. Beyond, exhaustively deconsecrated, lay the enchanted glade of Central Park.

Making his last move he sideswiped his way east, across Fifth and Madison, on to the avenue of sun and gold. To the north the prospect was seized in the city's grid, locked and channelled by the buildings on either side and their stiff-chested measure. The vista looked infinite, and entirely unknown, like the open sea to the first traversers of the Atlantic (when gods and terrors were still young and strong), ever ready to become the end of the world, where water became waterfall, oceanfall. Richard realized that he would have to stop saying he had never been to America. To that distinction—his main accomplishment and claim to fame—he could no longer pretend. He had been to America.

He had been to America.

PART FOUR

Gwyn awoke. He had slept, as always, now, in what Demi called not the spare room or the guest room but the visitors' room, which faced the master suite on the first floor—where Demi slept. With a brisk clearance of the throat he turned over onto his back, and then over onto his side. The nearer pillow of the other twin bed was evenly scratched with strands of straight black hair: hair belonging to Pamela, his research assistant. A section of her sharp-shouldered back was visible, and even through the curtained blur of early morning he could see the fine indentations her hair had made on her impressionable flesh. For half a minute or so he tried to think of a good way of describing this sight. Other men, other writers, might have started off with—who knows?—map contours or shallow estuaries; but Gwyn had decided some time ago that there weren't going to be any descriptions of women's bodies, or anyone else's, in what he wrote, because some bodies were "better" than others (and Pamela's body, as it happened, was better than most), and although Gwyn felt the way everyone did about bodies (always complaining to Demi about her body and telling her to get it fixed), he knew that comparisons were odious (and nearly always unflattering)—so why waste valuable time? Gwyn sat up and drank a tumbler of bottled water. The water was called Elixir and its ads promised you eternal youth.

Probably there is no word in contemporary usage delicate enough, *nice* enough, to describe Gwyn's feeling-tone as he crossed the few feet of carpeted floor and slipped into Pamela's bed. "Condescension," in the eighteenth- and nineteenth-century sense, would perhaps come closest. When the Rev. Mr. Collins dines with Lady Catherine de Bourgh and, the next day, his voice weak with gratitude, praises her extraordinary "condescension"—that comes close. The willing, the indulgent dilution of one's own superlative being, for the delight and enrichment of simpler lives. Considering how wonderful he was, it seemed wonderful of him to behave so wonderfully when he could justifiably behave so badly, if he felt like it. Lady Catherine was a snob and a toady. Mr. Collins was a snob and a toady. And Gwyn Barry, like Jane Austen, was a *writer*.

"Good morning," he said indulgently.

"Mm," said Pamela. Or was it "Hmm"?

Women do adore to be cuddled and babied in the morning. It really was universal. There weren't any that didn't like it. All the more reason not to say so, in writing: an offensive commonplace is what you'd end up with. Gwyn had a great deal to attempt and achieve that day (What is this life of the mind? what asketh men to have?), so he came as quickly as he could.

Where was his simple dressing gown? There.

He got out of bed and crossed the room and opened the door and crossed the landing and, most symmetrically, opened the door and crossed the room and got into bed. Demi was awake. He reached for her hand and gave it a benevolent squeeze.

"Time to get the tea, love," he told her.

It was all laid out on a tray, of course—laid out by Sherilee or Paquita. All Demi had to do was go and get it. Yes, and his mail.

"Come on, love. Tick tock goes the clock."

Demi moved very lazily sometimes. Gwyn's green eyes leniently twinkled.

"Pam's having a little lie-in. A little snooze," he whispered, remembering—as he quite often remembered—that Demi disliked running into Pam first thing in the morning. Or any time at all. But especially first thing. He occasionally found it depressing, the spiritlessness with which Demi rolled from the bed. Now he could establish himself in her vacated warmth, unfastidiously, loving all that lived.

"As I think I've gone to the trouble of pointing out before, you are at liberty, you know, to adjust the present arrangement any time you like. As I think I've gone to the trouble of pointing out before. Listen to this: 'The attractive simplicity of Mr. Barry's fable may sometimes tend towards the simplistic.' This, anyway, is the belief of Mr. Aaron E. Wurlitzer of the *Milwaukee Herald*. Don't they know how hard it is to make the complicated *look* simple? At your say-so, Demi, the present arrangement could also be submitted for review. Or modification. I am a man, in his manly noon. I am a man. Take me for all in all. As a man, I have certain needs. To satisfy these needs, Demi, I have to stray less far and less perilously than most men would. I see by your pinched expression and throbbing port-wine stain that you would wish me to stray farther than across the landing to the visitors' room. But would you, Demi? Would you really? Ah. This is good. This is excellent. Marion Treadwell, of the *Midland Examiner*: 'It would seem that Barry has somehow tapped a deep collective yearning. This explains the book's success. Nothing on the page explains it.' " Gwyn paused stoically. "Why are women fractionally less keen on my work than men? You might ponder that, Demi. I would be grateful for your 'feminine intuition.' "

Demi watched her husband, who was now contemplating his halved grapefruit, and with suspicion: not with rapt and childlike curiosity, the way he used to, as if he'd never seen one before. He had stopped doing that to grapefruits after a certain grapefruit, responding to Gwyn's rapt and childlike prod with the tined spoon, had squirted him in the eye. Then he'd had her running around for half an hour with moistened washclothes and bottles of Optrex.

"Again. Let's see if you've got it right at last. I have a duty to follow my impulses. To catch after my impulses, wherever they may lead. Because what am I *really* doing?"

"Research."

"Research. When I'm playing snooker with Richard, or tennis, or chess, when I'm—"

"I wish you wouldn't."

"Wouldn't what?"

"Play games with Richard. You always lose and it puts you in a *vile* mood."

Gwyn paused stoically. "When I'm out playing snooker, I'm doing research. When I'm asleep, I'm doing research. When I go out hunting or gambling with Sebby, I'm doing research. When I'm having sex next door with Pamela, I'm doing research."

"She's your research assistant."

"Demi, that's rather good. We research in the missionary position. We research in the doggy style. We research with her on top: the cowgirl."

"But there isn't any sex in your novels."

"You may or may not have noticed," said Gwyn, letting his head drop (so might Richard let his head drop when, for the thirtieth time in fifteen minutes, Marco mistook a *d* for a *b*, or a *q* for a *g*) but also realizing, in that instant, that he could never leave Demeter, because only with her did he wield this thrilling and frightening eloquence, this drolly rolling periodicity, "that there isn't any snooker in my novels either. It doesn't work like that. It works like this. The prose is given tautness and burnish precisely by what it deliberately excludes. Picasso's abstracts gain their force from the . . . from the representational mastery he holds in check. Something held back. Or held in harness. Just as the coachman, with the reins in one hand and the—"

"Or the carpenter."

"What *about* the carpenter?"

"There aren't any children in your novels either. Half the men have had vasectomies. Shouldn't that mean that we ought to have children? So you can deliberately exclude them?"

"Don't try to be clever, love. It doesn't suit you. Well. I see we have returned to base. And I say unto you: Go on the pill, Demi. Get a coil fixed, Demi. Get a cap. This is 'against your religion,' you will say. Unlike taking cocaine and fucking black pushers. Or is all that *for* your religion? God moves in mysterious ways. Thou shalt take cocaine. To get more cocaine, thou shalt . . ."

Demi got out of bed and went toward the bathroom, saying, "There was only one black pusher."

"Congratulations. Were there pushers of other creeds and hues? White, say, and Church of England?" He raised his voice, to make himself heard; but his tone did not change. "Richard rang. He's preparing his major piece about yours truly. Something tells me it's going to be very hostile. I wouldn't be surprised if he puts all that in."

She came back to the doorway. Her arms were folded. "All what in?"

"About you fucking black pushers."

". . . He can't. What can I do about it?"

"I don't know. Perhaps you'd better go round and fuck *him*."

At ten-thirty or thereabouts Gwyn stepped into his study: the three tall windows, the inlaid bookcases, the heavy wealth. His great work station—mahogany dining tables, French desks—formed a broad arc in the center of the room, slabbed with the thick shapes of processor, printer, copier. Here the two cultures, Gwyn believed, were attractively reconciled: the bright flame of human inquiry, plus lots of gadgets. Give Gwyn a palatinate smoking jacket, as opposed to a pair of tailored jeans and a lumberjack shirt, and he could be Captain Nemo, taking his seat at the futuristic bridge of the sumptuous *Nautilus*.

His morning coffee was there, laid out by Paquita. His morning newsprint was there, laid out by Pamela: all the non-tabloid dailies, three weeklies, one fortnightly, two monthlies, and a quarterly. On the French desk lay an Italian notebook, open on the front page, where Gwyn had written, in longhand, *The Road from Amelior? The Road to Amelior? Beyond Amelior?* The house was utterly silent: a silence of tiptoe, and finger to the lips. Like the house of his grandfather, who worked all night and slept all day.

Gwyn relied on two different agencies for his press clippings. His publishers used an agency, and they sent him stuff. And he'd made do with that, for a while. But he kept coming across extra references to himself, over and above what they sent him. And he didn't like that. So now he employed a rival outfit, giving them the broadest possible brief; and still he would encounter stray mentions of his own name, unduplicated in the agency envelopes. Now he sat himself down.

In the early days he had confined himself to reviews of his contemporaries, in which the example of Gwyn Barry might reasonably be invoked. Then he branched out, reading reviews of the novels of younger, and indeed older, novelists. Before he knew it, he was reading all fiction reviews. Reviews of Panamanian allegories, Japanese thrillers; reviews of reissues of *Don Quixote, Humphrey Clinker.* It was the same with literary criticism. Reading all reviews of books about modern writing quickly developed into the habit of reading all reviews about any writing whatever (poetry, drama and travel had long since climbed on board). Pliny, Nostradamus, Elizabeth David, Izaak Walton, Bede. The besetting interest in contemporary fiction expanded not only upward but also sideways. He started reading reviews about contemporary art, and then non-contemporary art; contemporary sociology, architecture, economics, jurisprudence, and then non-contemporary ditto. And then again: it seemed natural enough that reports on contemporary agriculture would eventually contain some lighthearted reference to the pages in *Amelior* that dealt with, say, crop rotation. And this happened, it came to pass; and from that day forth Gwyn found himself helplessly committed to agriculture, as something to follow, plus hydroponics and so on, all in the same sheep-dip and turnip-swagging prose. Now, new interests struck him suddenly, and at tangents. One morning he was reading a piece (idly, almost disinterestedly, with no secure hope of seeing fresh news about Gwyn Barry) on the property page by a guest writer who had experienced supposedly comical difficulties in selling his small flat; the flat was small and the writer, evidently, was big, which made the small flat seem even smaller. "Better to be a titch like Gwyn Barry," he wrote, "rather than a—" And here he cited a playwright of celebrated obesity. After that, Gwyn was reading everything he could find about property and, a little later, everything he could find about size: cars, holiday accommodation, clothes, prison cells. Pretty soon—and you could see this coming—he was reading everything about everything. Not in itself a bad idea, if information was what you sought. But we see accidents, everywhere, on the information highway. We see hazard lights and freezing fog. We see jackknife and whiplash.

There was a time, about fifteen years ago, when Richard Tull was so worried by alcohol, so worried that he might be an alcoholic, that he became almost as interested in alcoholism as he was interested in alcohol, which was plenty interested. And, when *he* read, his eyes would mutiny. He was of course transfixed by any incidence of the word *alcohol*, and all its cognates and synonyms and homonyms; and innocent words, innocently used, came to rivet him: words like *stout* and *punch* and *sack* and *hock* and *mild* and *bitter*; "high spirits," "small beer," "in the drink." He knew he had gone about as far as he could go with this when one day he veered in on the word *it*. He was thinking, he realized, of gin-and-it, or gin-and-Italian vermouth. So even *it*, not to mention Italy, was all fucked up for him. *Alcohol*, naturally, retained its suzerainty. And any word that looked anything like it. Anabolic. Laconic. Interpol. Uncool. School. Any word that had an *l* and a *c* in it, or a *c* and an *h*, or an *o*, or an *a*. Richard was less interested in *alcohol* now, largely because he was an alcoholic . . . Analogously, Gwyn Barry's scannings and skimmings (and what was his mood when he read? Puzzlement, mainly: a desert of patient disgust, with infrequent oases) were Gwyn Barry–seeking. All that kept him from lecteurial chaos were those two capital letters, *G* and *B*, the twin sentinels of his sanity. How many times had his eyes bumped into George Berkeley and George Balanchine, into George Bush and George Brown, into Guy Burgess and Geoff Boycott, Gerald Brenan and Grigori Baklanov, George Brummell and Georges Braque, Geoffrey Biddulph and Gertude Bell, into Giovanni Barbirolli and Giovanni Boccaccio and Gianlorenzo Bernini and Giambattista Bodoni. Into Granville Barker and Gaudier-Brzeska. Into Guinea-Bissau. Gladstone Bag. Gutenberg Bible. Grolsch Beer. Great Bear. Great Britain.

Soon he would have to go out into it: into Great Britain, and *its* capital, London, which had suddenly—or was it gradually? . . . Which had suddenly turned, and shaped itself against his peace. It was now two-forty-five. Lunch had already been brought to him; he didn't even know who had borne the tray, such was the tact, discretion, and awe with which she had slipped in and out of the room—Demi? Pam? Paqui? Sheri? As if he was a whispering visionary, a couturier of the cosmos, on the brink of discovering . . . the universal. Actually he had got through all the Saturday supplements, and the weeklies, and the fortnightly; but the *PMLA* and (Christ) *The Little Magazine* remained unprobed. Today he found three mentions: one in a piece about parking meters; one in a piece about the limitations of multicultural street theater; and one in a piece about the Profundity Requital (this made it all seem worthwhile, and even rational), in which he learned that he had bounced back into consideration, though he still lagged behind the Bosnian poetess who also ran a thousand-bed children's hospital in Gorazde—among others. On top of this he had also managed to cross the room occasionally and write something like *Onwards from Amelior?* in his notebook. Now he stood with his fists leaning on the long table (once more Nemo over his charts); he was staring at a loose pile of mail, non-urgent, second-echelon, which he would soon spare an hour on with Pam and a few yeses and nos and thank-yous and maybes. You don't know me but. I have recently been appointed as the. I am a student in my. This is the first time I have ever written to a. Despite recent triple heart-bypass surgery I felt I. You're probably fed up with. Here is a photograph of me in my. We at. I don't usually. What's it like being . . .

Gwyn advanced to the central window and looked down at the street and its ballroom of cherry blossom—the dance partners in their ball gowns, swelling and jostling and bristling, all the way to the bottom of the hill. How could the street not like him? The universe, the world, the hemisphere liked him. But the street didn't like him, and the city didn't like him. He would have to be going out into it for important and expensive meetings (things with Richard were not yet over): audiences at the feet of the great Buttruguena, the great Abdumomunov, the great O'Flaherty. Before, the city had never paid him any mind, except in theater crush bars or high-visibility restaurants and, yes, every now and then out there when people stopped and stared in that fixed, gratified way, or frowned forgetfully as if trying to place him among their acquaintances . . . But now the city behaved as if it wanted to break his face. The city wanted to break his face.

Cognitive dissonance was what he was dealing with. Nothing rhymed.

Whereas applause and praise were gathering, circumambiently, in response to the new thing he had brought into the world, his novel, his gift, the world itself—the streets, which stretched away, in folds and folds—had begun to hate his being. Not *qua* novelist, he assumed. But personally. It wasn't that the streets were giving him a bad review. The streets didn't read. Newsprint often told him that he was the spokesman for the next generation, and even Gwyn could imagine the next generation minding *that*—looking around, and seeing how very few he spoke for, and how quietly. But, again, the next generation didn't know he spoke for them, or that newsprint thought he did. This was personal. The compact Celt in his expensive yet essentially democratic chinos and leather jacket, under his silvery blacktop of hair (lightly cropped, at present, against baldness): this creation was no longer invisible and monochrome in its A-to-B, pavement-using, pause-for-thought and taxi-hailing functions, but floridly motley. Was it fame? He had become part of the landscape. And the landscape didn't want him there. Gwyn stood by the window, looking out, wondering what he'd done.

It started happening almost the instant he got back from America. Did America do it? Was it the Californian tan, the money-color, the aurora of American fever?

Maybe it wasn't anything. Maybe it was nothing.

Take the day before yesterday. The talented fabulist—his prose as clear as a mountain creek—is walking along Kensington Park Road, through the spring rain, after a visit to the local bookshop, when out of the flow of the street an oncoming figure distinguishes itself, by retardation, by arrest, and stands there, awaiting his approach. And as the modern myth-maker nears, this figure starts to retreat in front of him, as if, by following, Gwyn was being followed—preceded, but followed. There is no alternative: the standard-bearer of the near future must raise his eyes and confront those of his follower. A sodden youth in a track suit. Who says simply, keeping step, "Don't look at my face. Don't look at my face. Look at my hands. Look at the paint on these hands. Look at the blood on these fucking hands."

Maybe it was nothing. Maybe it wasn't anything.

Take yesterday. That rarest of literary phenomena—a cult writer with a mass audience—is walking home up Holland Park Avenue with his plastic bagful of coffee. He looks down for a second and walks into a slab of black. Loose change scatters all around them. The resonant allegorist takes three steps backwards, looks down, looks up again. The dark face in dark glasses is simply saying, "You dumb cunt. Pick it up. Pick it up, you dumb cunt." And there is the one-man paradigm-shift, down on his haunches, prizing pennies from the sticky street. He offers up the gathered change and it is dashed from his hand and he's down there again, and again. "Come on, man. It was an accident." And the mouth, as vivid as fruit pulp, just said, "Yeah? I ain't your brother. You ain't my brother. Yeah?" Until he let him go.

Maybe nothing. He stood by the window, looking out, wondering what he'd done.

Gwyn had a new hobby, now, in his head. He was writing, or para-
phrasing, his own biography—in his head. Not his autobiography: by no
means. His biography, written by someone else. It was the *official* biography. Gwyn liked his new hobby so much that even he could tell that it
might have deleterious—possibly disastrous—effects on his mental
health. Solitary gratification didn't come much more solitary than this:
even his own body was excluded from it. Here, biography was pornography. But he had managed to reach the (counterintuitive) conclusion that
his new hobby somehow kept him sane. Anyway, he was hooked. He
couldn't put it down.

Of course, the biography was insufficiently *finished.* It had no title, for
instance. Yes, it needed work. Now he left his study and went across the
passage to the visitors' room, to change.

Although Barry was no. A keen. While no jock or gym rat, Barry
responded to the heightened life of fierce competition. He loved games
and sports. (But he hated games and sports. Because he always lost.)
With his old sparring. With his old friend Richard Tull he enjoyed a
healthy rivalry—on the tennis court, over the snooker table, and across
the chessboard. (And he always lost. He never won.) As a novelist Tull
was no. Unfavored by the muses, Tull was nevertheless. In hand-eye
coordination and spatial awareness, if not in imaginative fiction, Tull was
Barry's . . .

Superior? T-shirt, shorts, jockey pants, socks: all laid out for him. As
usual, hereabouts, Gwyn moved on to a better chapter.

He had a reputation as a. He made no secret of his love of. To him, the
fairer. In every sense he was enamored of womankind. Demeter, who
would continue to love him dearly, eventually resigned herself to the fact
that. Some men, she came to realize, carry with them such intensity of.
In him, the lifeblood. Now that Lady Demeter, in the words of W. B.
Yeats, is old and gray and full of sleep, it is with a rueful smile that she . . .

Wearing his new black track suit he came down into the hall and
browsed about the sideboard, reviewing the invitations and looking for his
car keys. He was meeting Richard at the Warlock. Things had changed:
they just said hello, and played, and said good-bye. The Warlock was good
because he could drive straight into the car park, eschewing all real contact
with the city and the streets that suddenly hated his life.

Gwyn was looking forward to reading the Richard Tull profile: five
thousand words. At least it was going to be all about Gwyn. And while he
was reading it he wouldn't be reading about soil erosion or Norman
architecture or curtain rails or Keir Hardie or deck chairs or treetops, or
any of the other stuff he read about, just in case.

p. 1   GWYN BARRY   R. Tull

Gilda Paul sits in Room 213 on the East Wing of the Gwynneth Littlejohn Care Center—or "the mental home," as they call it, down Swansea way. As in a naive poem of sorrow and rejection, the gulls of the Gower Peninsula, their famished cries weakly audible, drift and turn above the bay. Gilda is thirty-nine. Her psychological being unraveled four years ago, on an anonymous London railway platform, the day Gwyn Barry dispatched her to the past, and went his own way: to the future. He writes to Gilda—to the past—every now and then. But he hasn't been back.

Richard was sitting at his desk. His life was desks. Life had changed. But life was still desks. Always desks, there in front of him. First, school, and twenty years of that. And then jobs, and twenty years of that. And always, in the early mornings and the late evenings, more desks. Homework: forty years of that.

The horrendous surface was now strewn with sheets of foolscap, themselves strewn with his doodled dry-runs. His eye dodged over them. A useful idiot of cultural forces he only dimly. Love of fame, which Milton called the last infirmity of noble. The actress Audra Christenberry, glimpsed at the poolside, presents a redoubtable tribute to the surgeon's. Perhaps Lady Demeter puts it best: "Gwyn," she says, "can't write for." Equipped with a voluptuous wife, a huge readership, a big house, and no talent, the author of. In the annals of philandery, hucksterism, and opulent hypocrisy . . .

"Daddy?"

"Yes?"

"Daddy? I don't want to be called Marco anymore. I want to change my name."

"What to, Marco?"

"Nothing."

"What, you don't *want* a name? Or you want to be *called* 'Nothing'?"

The child raised his blunt but shapely eyebrows and nodded once.

Richard waited until Marco was on his way to the door, and then said, " 'Nothing'?"

The child paused disaffectedly—nihilistically—and said, ". . . Yeah?"

"Bath time."

He got to his feet and began doing the boys . . . When you've been away, and you come home again, your life re-enfolds you. And not lovingly. He had come home. Manually and very doubtfully assisted onto the aircraft at Kennedy, Richard had been at first wheelchaired and then eventually stretchered off it again at Heathrow. He was still amazed and impressed by this. The wheelchair, it transpired (after a confused and even quite humorous interlude on the tarmac), had been inadequate to his needs. So he came home again and his life re-enfolded him. And not lovingly. For a few days after his return, when he looked back on his torments in America, he saw himself up there among the big-league sufferers, with Job, with Griselda, with Milton's Adam, with Milton's Eve. But by now he had demoted himself to one of the squawking hopefuls on some Japanese endurance show, grinningly abasing his being in the quest for immediate gain. He also wondered if *Untitled*, so clearly and entirely hopeless as a novel, might have its uses as something else. A military application, perhaps. The army might like to have *Untitled* up its sleeve. Marie Curie's notebooks, even today, a century on, were still carcinogenic. He could imagine a copy of his novel preserved in a lab behind foot-thick glass, and occasionally leafed through by jolting robots. With that book Richard had so far earned himself, worldwide, a readership of one: Steve Cousins. He had sent him a proof in February, and the response came back almost by return post. "You're good, man," Cousins wrote (typed, touched: justified margins), and went on to make intelligent, or anyway intelligible, comparisons between the new novel and its predecessors. Between *Untitled* and *Dreams Don't Mean Anything* and *Aforethought*. You're good, man: the words often breathed in his ear when he sat around wondering why he *wasn't* good. And he knew why, now. He wasn't good because he wasn't innocent enough. Writers are innocent. Not guiltless—just innocent. Tolstoy was certainly innocent. Even Proust was innocent. Even *Joyce* was innocent. And another thing: he didn't love his readers, as you need to do. Although he had nothing against them personally, he didn't love them; and you must love them. So, to conclude. Richard *was* innocent (look where he was heading), but in the wrong way. He *did* love his readers (how he yearned for them), but in the wrong way. Look what he would put them through . . . He should have held a knife to Gwyn's throat and made him read aloud from *Untitled* until he reached page eleven. Some fantastic brain tumor would have done the rest. Gwyn wasn't good either; but Gwyn was a special case.

"Hands," said Richard. And then after a while, "Bums." Then after a while, "Necks." And so on.

Richard in America, old Richard, in the new world. It was like pulling over on the six-lane highway, that time, and clambering out of the . . . no, not the Maestro but its predecessor, the thirdhand off-white Prelude:

clambering out to change a tire, to secure a slewing roofrack, to open the hood and assess (or contemplate) its soiled and steaming innards. Out there, in the breakdown lane (Gina rigid in the passenger seat, the tiny twins in the pantaloons of their carseats), it struck Richard that he was the only organic figure in that landscape of remorseless purpose, which sounded—Christ—like a million Band-aids being ripped off a million sections of fuzzy flesh (with accompanying whines of pain and surprise). And he thought: I'm a joke. And an old one. This place belongs not to the bare and dithering human creature but to the intent hundredweights, to the leaning machines and the howl of their anathemas.

"Teeth," said Richard. And then after a while, "Socks." Then after a while, "Slippers." And so on.

When the boys were done he squelched into the kitchen and unplugged his bottle of Norwegian Cabernet, to go with whatever bit of whatever animal he would eventually flip onto the grill. Gina would be in and out, wearing a dressing gown, a hair cap even, a mask of cream. It was all right. She was working four days a week now; they would have more money; she was resolved on a full family vacation this summer, and was already staring critically at burnished brochures. It was all right. Gina was no longer a writer's wife because he was no longer a writer. He didn't think she was going to leave him: yet. Together they had joined the great community of the exhausted.

"The boys' lips," he said. "Children's lips. They always look just a little bit sore. Like the lips of trumpeters. Halfway through the second set. They toughen up later, I suppose."

It was all right—and do you know how he could tell? Sometimes, later on, when he had finished his chump chop and she had finished her bowl of porridge or village-idiot cereal, he would go on reading *Man of his Words: The Life and Times of Ingram Bywater* and she would go on reading *Budgeting for Belgium*, as the tap dripped and the strip-light fizzed like a fat fly—and they would yawn together. Nothing too sensual or explicit, three or four each, a transient contagion of yawns. From his private culture, from his stock of inherited information (Unless The Kettle Boiling Be), Richard knew that you couldn't catch a yawn from someone you didn't like. He caught hers. She caught his. At present, this was the extent of their physical life. A shudder in the jawline answered by a widening of the nostrils; a slow gasp answered by a moan of mild surprise. Nothing too candid or throat-baring. But a definite exchange of yawns. A little epiphany of yawns.

Gina went to bed, and Richard headed for his study, availing himself of this facility, because he knew she had other plans for the room.

GWYN BARRY: R. Tull. He reread the first paragraph, his eyes itching with melancholy and pride. There'd been a bad moment that morning, when Richard had called the madhouse to fact-check the status of Gilda Paul—and been told that she was no longer a patient. But it was cool (whew): she had merely been upgraded to some kind of trusty. Gilda was still sectioned. And still considered nuts. The only other good news to come Richard's way since his return from America was that Anstice, his devoted secretary at *The Little Magazine*, had not taken a welcome break, alone, in the Isle of Mull, as everyone thought, but, instead, had gone home and killed herself.

Oh, this profile would tax his journalistic skills to their very limit! Let's be honest: he would be ducking and weaving all the way to the deadline. Now Richard lit a cigarette and fed a fresh piece of paper into the barrel. With a sense of afflatus, of pregnant illumination, he wristily typed—

p1.   GWYN BARRY   R. Tull

The airway is open—the breathing unimpaired. The patient can now squeeze the examiner's hand and resist passive motion of the extremities. Retrograde amnesia at first suggested major closed-head injury, but the patient can now maintain a consistent level of consciousness. His voice is weak, yet clear. Gone are the drips and feeding-tubes of the Emergency Room. Signs of trauma are painfully apparent—but Gwyn Barry is out of Intensive Care.

———————

Here's what struck Steve Cousins about pornography: at last he had found something that was as interested in sex as he was.

He had found something that was all about sex. And nothing else. The bits in between were just breathers: breathers for the breathers. Pornography sometimes tried to be about other things, or to happen in other settings. But all it could ever tell you about these other things, these other settings, was that *they* were all about sex too. And nothing else. Freud thought that everything was about sex. That was his *theory*. Pornography, though, was demonstrably all about sex. Sex as a spectacle, of course. And nothing else.

Steve Cousins didn't *read* pornography (words were no use here), but he read everything he could find that was about pornography—that was all about the thing that was all about sex. His ludicrously eclectic library (Freud, comic books, Nietzsche, the complete works of Richard Tull) contained several yards of books that were all about pornography. Patriarchy and the Limits of. Just Push My. Commission on Obscenity and. The Traffic in. Visual Anthropology and the. I Was a. Many times he had read that many of the actors and almost all of the actresses on the pornographic screen had been abused as children. That meant that he and they formed . . . not a happy family. But a big one.

He watched them aging, the terrible stars in their terrible galaxies. The anti-stars, in their anti-galaxy. Without exception the men seemed imperishable (stupid, tireless, ever-thrusting, ever-wincing), but the women, with their limited screen-lives . . . Tenderly, in every sense, he monitored their facelifts and breast-implants, their tattoos, pubic hair-dos, the bodies in question increasingly encrusted with cellulite and jewelry, chokers, anklets, bracelets, nipple-rings, navel-studs, tongue-clasps—heavy brooches, carbuncles, pierced into the tongue. See them in something ten years old and they looked ten years old themselves, bucktoothed with inbreeding. And wall-eyed with incest. Then they passed through a kind of lab or clinic, which reinvented them for male desire. Where did they come from? Where did they go? Some made it into mid-career, with frequent recalls to the drawing board—permanent outpatients. Others fell apart right there, in the ponderous beam of your ponderous gaze (Scozzy's gaze, with its slow-pulse blink rate, in the darkness he owned, which held the brightness of the TV screen like something precious in its hand—like the charm or amulet on the tarnished tongue). Identifying, with difficulty, a familiar veteran in her third or fourth incarnation—looser, frecklier, and above all suddenly and seriously older—Steve would say things like "For it now, darling" or "Downhill now, darling," or sometimes, just as typically but in a lower and slower voice, "Oh my dear . . . what have they done to you?" Toward career end, it looked to be a rite of passage: the mature Adult actress, subjected to abuse. You know. After her hours, belly-up on the bar, three speckle-faced hardhats bearing down on her. You know. As if in reenactment or commemoration of what brought her there.

So they were all children. They were all children together, in this—this big family. All children, until they weren't. Pornography was the story of his life.

He was out, now, down Wimbledon way. Not in the Cosworth, with its low racing skirt, but in the hulk of the orange van. With an occasional flinch he registered the scattered presence of 13's tabloids and Ting tins. Proof of his vigils, his time-killings. There was also less palpable evidence (a hairpin, a tissue) that with one or two flinches of its own the aged van had served as a setting for the act of love—as bedroom, as bower. Scozzy had some trouble imagining this, 13 and Lizzete being too young to have their equivalents in Adult. He supposed, anyway, that it didn't last that long. 13 wouldn't want to hang about. Giving Lizzete one was illegal all right, but there was no money in it.

Apparently the wind had to blow that bit harder every year. Whatever it was the wind thought it was doing, blowing the dust off, getting the smells out—this was becoming a bigger job, every year. Each spring. Nice to think that it did have a function. Other than driving you out of your mind. Scozzy knew wind (country wind, mate): in some hut somewhere, in some field, as a wild boy he had waited out the wind, moaning to it, swaying to it, with unbearable monotony, for hour after hour. Even light, as it traveled, grew tired. But wind never tired. It had blown *him* clean. He was as light as air. He had told 13 and 13 had said . . . Oh yeah. He remembered. Early retirement is it.

Again, he was watching Terryterry's women, the two little girls with their stunts on the slide and the swing, the mum in the kitchen tapping on the glass above the sink, like any mum anywhere, which was probably how she saw herself, no babymamma, no hired box or Quacko test tube. He realized he had become addicted to this spectacle (the girls were called something like Diandra and Desirée); anyway he came here for no earthly professional reason, on nice days. One thing about being inside the van: you weren't outside the van, and looking at it. That unforgivable orange, an orange you could never associate with any living fruit, an orange that belonged to plastic, kitchen dustbins, and the beaks of certain black London birds. He found the suburbs exotic and innocuous, not wild, like the country, not wild, like the city. What *was* this, going on around him? The leaves, the broken sunlight, the child-molester calm and fixity of the male passersby, the single craven car inching down the street on its brothel-creepers, the windswept cries of the girls in their stripes and dots.

In for their tea now. He thought: only time it gets lively round here is when the tennis. Scozz could see but not hear the girls being summoned, the mum's voice failing at the windbreak of the garden wall. The three of them now at the kitchen table. He used his binoculars: yack yack yack. Diandra was holding up a comic. Mum giving Desirée the wagging finger . . . He knew exactly how quickly and radically he could transform this scene. Scozzy had a chaos organized in his mind, and ready to go. You're coming into their place but really you're taking them to your place: which is the world of fear. Which you know like the back of your hand. And they've never been there before, even though it's home. This wouldn't be business. Business was over. It wouldn't be business. It would be the other thing. Still, Scozzy had no intention; the option was duly waived. And they were *that close* to what he wanted to hurt. Wrong size? Wrong color? He didn't know. But something was wrong with them.

He reached for the keys, staring out through the glass, itself alive with the riotous reflections of maddened foliage. Here came that *nun* again. Jesus, he thought: look at the state of her boat—the ridged mouth, the mineral eyes. Nuns, in his personal utopia, wouldn't be allowed out unless they daubed themselves an inch thick. Then at least you could tell they were meant to be women. And not runty results in cross-dress mourning gear. "Don't look at me that way," he whispered. "You think I don't have time for you? Look at me that way, and I'll have time for you. I know nuns. Brides of Christ." Steve Cousins: Barnardo boy. "God wants *me* for a sunbeam too."

The orange van came noisily and dirtily to life. Scozzy pulled out (piece of shit) and, after a couple of lefts, joined the chain-gang of the traffic, back London way.

"D mate," he said into the phone. "Tomorrow, mate." He listened, seeming to stare over his own cheek, top teeth bared, eyes dimmed. "Gimme . . . Gimme Styx."

If you wanted someone picked up off the street, say, if you wanted them quelled with a stare, a hand on the shoulder, you'd opt for a couple of schwartzers every time. D and Styx. Big Dread and Wisely. Thelonius. Netharius. It wasn't just their blackness, their density and mass. It was their otherness and the severity with which they imposed it. You stepped into a new etiquette, into unreadable conventions.

A minute later he got D again and said he'd changed his mind. He didn't want a bro on next. It might create a false impression. So put Styx on hold and give him . . . Gimlet. "Yeah," said Scozzy. "Gimme Gimlet."

And then he called Agnes Trounce.

Gwyn was in the octagonal library, reading—or vetting—a piece about Etruscan pottery in *The Little Magazine*. Demi came in and served him his drink (a dry sherry) in its crystal *copita*. And she lingered, arms folded, with her long glass of Perrier. He had stopped being nice to Demi. On account of information conveyed to him by Richard, he hadn't looked at her for two days. And for two mornings he had taken his breakfast in the visitors' room, with Pamela.

"How was your lesson?"

"Good," said Gwyn. "Positive."

"Maybe I'll go to him. He could teach me a few tricks or two."

". . . What?" It was quite an effort, asking a question without looking up.

"Just a thought."

"Teach you *what*?"

"Some tricks."

"You said 'a few tricks or two.' It's 'a few tricks.' Or 'a trick or two.' Not 'a few tricks or two.' "

Demi shrugged and said, "Um—'Pamela' told me about your incident. How very unpleasant. Are you sure you're all right?"

His face formed the expression that meant: work. Research. Demi apologized and left the room. Gwyn started reading—or vetting—a piece from the recruitment methods of Albrecht Wallenstein (1583–1634). This piece fell into the (by now capacious) category where it was the very distance of the subject from his own concerns that claimed his interest. Things were either pleasant or unpleasant, after all, and, if pleasant, they might be compared to the world of Amelior, and, if unpleasant, they might be contrasted with it.

* * *

Three hours earlier: Gwyn, hunkered down courtside with the great Buttruguena, in the vast fridge of the Oerlich.

The great man looked even older than he looked on TV—when they picked him out in the royal box or the celebrity enclosure, or when he stepped forward, as he did every year, to congratulate the champion at Roland Garros. Older, and less benign. In fact he looked almost as savage and stupid as some carnivorous ray or eel of the deep—after a more or less satisfactory kill (no poisons—yet; no impenetrable carapaces). Gwyn didn't feel any of this. He was a busy man with an immediate purpose. And if, in the mind of Richard Tull, there was always a kind of blues playing, with Gwyn the signature tune was much more upbeat; it was usually easy listening. The two men were introduced by affable Gavin in the bar, and had then walked slowly and silently down a long bunker of a passage whose walls were studded with framed photographs of famous tennis players and of famous people playing tennis, newscasters, soap stars, mountaineers, royals (Gwyn spent much of his time at the Oerlich wondering when Gavin was going to get out his camera. But maybe there wasn't any room). When he walked, the sole of the great Buttruguena's right gym shoe was almost fully exposed to the air. His right foot seemed to be upside down.

"We'll hit," he said. And they began.

In terms of trajectory and weight, there was no difference between the forehand and the backhand of the great man, the forehand hit flat, the backhand with a slice that made the ball hum as it crossed the net. Without apology or embarrassment Gwyn skipped and twirled around the baseline, his game a disastrous miscellany. Steadily the great man reduced the power and the depth of his drives. After ten minutes he pointed to the bench and limped toward it shaking his head.

"I don't understand," he said, staring at the net post. "You have no talent."

"I know there's a long way to go."

Using his forehead only, the great Buttruguena shrugged: traduced, trifled with. "It's quite hopeless."

"I know there's a lot to do."

"What you want? Spend a fortune to be one percent better?"

Buttruguena sat there, fierce, old, handsome, sour. He had won the French on clay and the Australian on grass. He had been a star in the days before the star system. Now he taught nineteen-year-olds who had their own airplanes.

"The thing is, there's only this one player I want to beat. I thought you might be able to— —you know, give me a few tips."

Buttruguena showed interest.

"He's not a whole league better. He beats me 6–3, 6–4. His backhand is pretty weak but it's—"

Buttruguena erased all this with his hand. "Okay. We can do it in five minutes right here and then we walk off the court. Okay?"

"Perfect."

"Are you richer than him? Who buys the balls?"

Afterwards, with his hair still wet from the shower, Gwyn had a Danish and a cup of espresso, more out of a sense of duty (duty to the expensive amenities) than hunger or delectation. Next he went and pretended to look around the pro shop: here you got a good view of the girls who policed Reception, shell-suited blondes from Sweden and South Africa, their tans growing lusterless under the striplight of public relations. He moved past them with his smile, his jerked nods, his colossal sports bag.

Outside he turned right, under the tube track where members such as himself were allowed to park. There was the builders' yard, there was the dead pub (peer through the glass: it looked as though it had been wiped out by some criminal knees-up, thirty years ago). He walked on. He hesitated, and walked on. A big black guy in a big black leather coat was leaning on the driver's door of Gwyn's Saab. Now what? Gwyn approached briskly, producing his keys: a busy man with an immediate purpose.

"Excuse me. My car."

They smiled at each other. The black guy didn't move. He announced: "Tennis."

"That's right," said Gwyn. "Just had a lesson."

"No you ain't."

"Excuse me?"

He unfurled his leather coat. There was a pouch sewn into the lining which contained a baseball bat. He lifted it out between finger and thumb and lowered it to the ground.

Gwyn felt the impulse to run, but the impulse was youthless; it wouldn't get him anywhere.

"You want a baseball lesson?"

"No thanks," he whispered.

The black guy stepped aside saying, "Nah. You don't want any of this. You don't want *any* of this . . ."

He had to step forward. He could feel the back of his own head, the hair cringing, or trying to grow—to pad and cover the helpless egg of his skull. As he beeped the lock-release and opened the door he could hear the swathes cut by the bat through the surprisingly heavy resistance of the air.

———————————

The time had come for him to share the good news with Gina.

"Bad news," he said. "You know Anstice? Brace yourself. She's dead. Sleeping pills. She just went home and did it."

Of course, it wasn't *all* good news, and Richard had been wretched at first. Say she'd fingered him in some suicide note and Gina found out about it. Say the police came round—with the diary he knew she kept. But he seemed to have got away with it okay. And that was that. It was done. And nothing would ever persuade him that Anstice was having a worse time dead. On the other hand, he was free to wonder why so many writers' women killed themselves, or went insane. And he concluded: because writers are nightmares. Writers are nightmares from which you cannot awake. Most alive when alone, they make living hard to do for those around them. He knew this now—now that he wasn't a writer. Now that he was just a nightmare.

"*Good* news," corrected Gina. "Good."

"Gina!"

"So at least that's all over."

"What?"

"*You* know."

"*You* know. How?"

"She told me."

"Who?"

"Who do you think? It happened while I was at my mother's, right? When I came back there was a *nine*-page letter waiting for me. With all the details."

"Nothing happened. I was impotent, I swear."

"Well I can believe that . . . But it isn't what *she* said."

Gina made it clear that Anstice, in her letter, and on the telephone, and in person, one Friday, over coffee here in Calchalk Street, had consistently portrayed Richard as a Lionheart, a Tamburlaine, a veritable Xerxes in the sack.

"Oh sure. So likely. It was a one-night fiasco." Yeah: just one of those crazy things. "One night. Instantly regretted."

"Still. You tried."

"I tried . . . What did you do? You know. In the way of counter-measures."

"Ask me no questions," said Gina, "and I'll tell you no lies."

"It's the Town Crier, isn't it? Dermott. Or did you revive one of your poets? Is it Angaoas? Is it Clearghill?"

"Ask me no questions," said Gina, "and I'll tell you no lies. We're quits. How could you? I mean. What a dog. And what a *drag*, too. Bloody hell. She used to call me twice a day until I told her to bugger off. Now go and do the boys."

Doing the boys—something he did plenty of—was nothing like as bad, moment for moment, as it used to be even a year ago. Their status was no longer that of royal exiles, of imperial prisoners under house arrest. Now they were treated like extravagantly distinguished, headstrong, and senile VIPs in, say, a Stalin-era sanatorium or retirement home (from their window they could glimpse a scrapyard full of twisted excavators and, beyond, an envenomed canal the color of a green traffic light). Their beds were made, their towels warmed; the badges and medals of high office were laid out before them and cleared away after them; their many mishaps, breakages, and self-soilings were tactfully and skillfully smoothed over. At the sanatorium, these days, the inmates might detect in their more lucid intervals the symptoms of a new laxity: the result of forced economies, or ideological revision, or merely the male meanness of the male nurse. For example it was no longer thought necessary to carry them down to breakfast or even lead them there by the hand; the simple provender would be ready on the table but they were now expected to feed themselves (though of course they could continue to be as messy as they liked). Privilege loss was something the inmates were forgetfully growing accustomed to. Occasionally it seemed that they remembered how it used to be, and they struggled weakly, fitfully—and they wept for shame . . . But the male nurse sits at the kitchen table, hearing their cries. His singlet, his newspaper, his coffee mug, his idle toothpick . . .

One thing about being a househusband: it gave you plenty of time to search your wife's bedroom. You could go up there with a cup of tea and make an afternoon of it. Richard had the leisure. The children were at school all day. Soon it would be half term, and the children would be at home all day. He kept thinking there were other things he ought to be doing. Reading a biography, talking to Anstice, writing modern prose. But Richard had the leisure.

He found: a shoebox containing all the letters he had ever written her, chronologically arranged, all of them opened, all of them read. They bore traces of her body scent, he believed.

He found: a polaroid of Gina and Lawrence, sitting on a wooden bench in some seaside pub. His arm round her shoulders, the pale mid-morning sunlight, the dusty wash of pubs.

He found: in a gray plastic zip-up folder, letters written to her by other writers, and poems written to her by the poets: none of them recent.

He found: under the floorboards, in her closet, four soot-coated brown envelopes each containing twenty fifty-pound notes. He thought he might have to borrow some of this and give it to Steve Cousins, depending on when he got paid for the Profile.

With the savaging of Gwyn's physical being now well entrained, Richard's mind could soar free and contemplate something higher: the savaging of Gwyn's literary reputation.

The way he figured it, in his soaring insomnias (with Gina breathing steadily and neglectedly at his side), there were only three ways that writers could get into serious trouble—on the page. Obscenity was one, and blasphemy was another; and both afforded little hope. There wasn't any love or sex or swearing in Amelior. As for blasphemy, Gwyn's stuff was incapable of giving offense even to the people who were all wired up and hair-triggered to receive it—the people who *lived* to take offense. But there was, he believed, a different way. The whole thing came to him like this.

Richard stood over his desk at the Tantalus Press. He was smoking. He exhaled fatalistically. A week ago he had resigned as Books and Arts Editor of *The Little Magazine*. Now he did an extra day and an extra morning a week for Balfour Cohen, and also took work home. Furthermore, he was turning down book reviews. Assistant Literary Editors all over town were left staring into their telephones—as Richard turned down book reviews. Would he like to write three hundred words on a three-volume life of Isaac Bickerstaffe? No. The definitive critical biography, perhaps, of Ralph Cudworth, of Richard Fitzralph, of William Courthope? No. In terms of time and motion, in terms of money, it would work out in his favor. Correcting the trex of the talentless, for private publication: this was better paid, was more highly prized by the world, than the disinterested perusal of on the whole passionately conscientious studies of minor poets, novelists, and playwrights. Books about duds, and written by duds: but not trivial. With book reviewing, Richard strolled the temperate climes of mediocrity. At the Tantalus Press he entered the Wirral of florid psychosis. Given a two-word account of how things had gone in America, Balfour had taken him off fiction and put him on nonfiction—more specifically, the Study of Man. From which Richard learned that there were crazed old wrecks crouched in attics all over England, revolutionizing twentieth-century thought.

They saw off Marx. They turned Darwin on his head. They yanked the carpet out from under Sigmund Freud.

"Jesus," said Richard, at his desk. He said it all day long. That morning Richard had agreed to let his name appear on the letterhead and in the literature of the Tantalus Press . . . He exhaled fatalistically. His teeth were grinding their way to the end of yet another five-hundred-page fool's errand by yet another pompous (and vicious) old dunce (and arsehole) who, in this case, and without much apparent effort, had found the missing link between genetics and General Relativity. Richard wrote ENDS under the author's final exclamation mark and tossed the typescript into his Out tray.

Balfour Cohen stirred tolerantly in the background and said, "Ah. Here's your poet."

"Horridge?"

"Horridge."

"Ah."

The distinctive manila envelope favored by Keith Horridge; the distinctive paperclip; the distinctive bite of his manual typewriter. Richard was trying to persuade himself that it might be reasonably satisfying: to find a poet. To seek out the pleasures, if any, of the literary middleman. Horridge's envelope contained a note and three poems. The first, "Ever," began:

> In the Gnostic cosmogonies
> The demiurgi knead and mold
> A red Adam who cannot stand
> Alone.

Now wait a minute. It was overcompressed, maybe, but wasn't that kind of *good*? Like Yeats at his grandest and raciest?

> To be immortal
> Is commonplace, except for man.
> All creatures are immortal, being
> Ignorant of death.

Wasn't that something that the heart assented to—already knew? At this point "Ever" became obscure, or more obscure; but it seemed to end strongly. Richard lit a cigarette. He could see himself, twenty-odd years from now, on the TV screen (unimaginably old and, of course, rollickingly hideous), saying, in a senescent singsong, *Yes, well it was clear to me at once—one always knows, do you see—that Keith Horridge was something rather . . .* The second poem, "Disappointment," was Horridge at his most compressed ("Glue, gluten, gum / Just half-made always, / Soup-sup and ooze-thaw . . ."): what you would do was steer him away from the opacity of the sprung rhythm, toward the—

"I've got a feeling," he said, "that Horridge just might be the real thing."

Balfour's swivel chair gave its squeak. "Really? The question is whether he's got enough for a first collection."

"Enough poems or enough money?"

"Enough poems," said Balfour. "And enough money."

"You know, I think he's too good for us. I think he could walk into any list. Why don't we just *publish* him? Five hundred copies. It's only poetry. He'd only expect about seventy-five quid."

Richard was reading Horridge's covering letter (and reminding himself to keep it somewhere safe). "How was America? Welcome back." Enclosed, wrote Horridge, were three "newborns": "Ever," "Disappointment," and "Woman." " 'Woman,' " Horridge went on, "is a departure for me, and possibly a breakthrough. Here for the first time I cast off all influences and speak in my own voice."

And here it was—"Woman":

Yesterday my woman, this girl I care about more
Than anyone else on the face of this earth, said
That
She
No
Longer
Wants
To
See
Me
Again.

There was more. The lines got longer again, as Horridge licked his wounds, and then got shorter, as Horridge girded himself to "Try/To/Win/Her/Back/Once/More." Richard looked around for his wastepaper basket. But of course you didn't do that here. You didn't reject stuff—you didn't stomp it into the trash. What you did was publish it. You held it in front of you and with your red pen you wrote, *center title* and *set as verse*.

"It's something to think about," said Balfour.

"No it's not. Forget Horridge. Let's just take all his money and never talk about him again."

If literature was the universal, then all you'd ever get in here was space trash. A slowly twirling door panel from some old Telstar. A scorched waste-chute from some old Sputnik. "Woman" was what Horridge sounded like when he cast off all influences and spoke in his own voice. And "Disappointment" was what he sounded like when he was fucking around with his thesaurus. And "Ever" . . . The authors published by the Tantalus Press were in the habit of giving themselves credit for things, but most people weren't, and Richard wasn't. Otherwise he might have been gratified by the way his memory now went to work—the way its tumblers swiftly recombinated. In the Gnostic cosmogonies the demiurgi knead and mold a red Adam who cannot stand alone. To be immortal is commonplace, except for man. Jorge Luis Borges—and from something impregnably famous like "The Library of Babel" or "The Circular Ruins." He looked at Horridge's shining margins and saw all the thumb prints and palm sweat. And it came to him.

It came to him. Obscenity, blasphemy: Gwyn Barry's novels had survived any such booby trap. But there was a third hazard, one that could sneak up on you, at whatever time. Richard reached for his desktop dictionary and read: "L. *plagarius* a kidnapper; a seducer; also, a literary thief." *Plagiary*: it was an ugly word.

"Balfour. There's something I want you to help me with."

Having heard him out, Balfour said, "You're not planning to do anything rash, I hope."

"How long will it take? And how much will it cost?"

He waited at the school gates for his sons in the rain.

Thence to the video shop, whose windows were as thick with steam as the windows of Mick's Fish Bar across the street. The damp dogs had to wait outside in the wet but the damp dogs were what the video shop smelled of. At this hour the place was full of other adults and other children. Richard thought that the adults looked like child-murderers, and so did the children, with their hairdos and earrings and their shallow, violent eyes. Marius and Marco were crouched under HORROR, in pious supplication, but they would eventually have to settle for CHILDRENS with no apostrophe. Then he took them across the road (don't tell Mummy) to Mick's Fish Bar for their fries.

When he got home he installed the boys in front of *Tom and Jerry*. Two or three years ago they used to watch *Tom and Jerry* with full attention but with no amusement, as if it was a simplified and stylized but essentially truthful representation of how an average cat got on with an average mouse. Nowadays, though, they found it funny. And Richard found it funny. He found everything funny. Listening to their laughter, he sat at his desk, a room away. He wasn't writing. He was typing—typing *Amelior.* And not word for word. But making little changes (sometimes for the worse if he could contrive it, sometimes unavoidably for the better) as he went along.

———————

"Now, son," said the great O'Flaherty, "how old would you be?"

"I'll be forty-one next month," said Gwyn, as if expecting this news to cause considerable surprise.

"Now you won't be giving up your day job, I hope. I fear you'll starve!" O'Flaherty shrugged—so lightly, so gently. "You see, it's your *cueing*. And your eye, son. Your eye."

For the second time O'Flaherty talked, at some length, about snooker being a game of visual imagination. Earlier, Gwyn had perked up, thinking he ought to be pretty good at that. But the experiments O'Flaherty had had him conduct (with an additional white ball placed against the object ball at various set angles and then removed) seemed to make the game no easier.

Gwyn interrupted him, saying, "The thing is, there's only this one player I want to beat. And he's no good either."

Soft-faced, still, at sixty, but with a protuberant ironic prow to his upper lip, the great O'Flaherty patiently inclined his head. "Now if I was to take your cueing apart," he said, "you'd lose for a long time before you won."

"Yeah and I can't have that."

"But think. In a while you'd be knocking in breaks of thirty. Thirty-five!"

"No I want to beat this guy now. What I'm here for are some tips. About how to win."

O'Flaherty inclined his head, not sadly, but with professional docility. To him, the game stood for temperance and fair dealing; it stood for civilization. He had twice been runner-up in the World Championship in the days when you got ten bob for winning it. And he'd got five bob for losing it. In contrast, though, to the great Buttruguena, who spent every waking moment wondering why he wasn't a resident of Monte Carlo, the great O'Flaherty did not mourn the Marbellan holiday home—did not mourn the personalized number plate.

"If it was down to me I'd advise you not to bother. But I am in your employ . . ."

"That's true," said Gwyn with emphasis.

He straightened up. "Now you both have your own sticks?"

"Yes. But mine's much more expensive."

"The purchase of a chamois cloth is usually worth a couple of blacks, initially. Then you could go further. The cue extensions, the half-butt, and so on. The little rest-extension gadget."

"So you're saying that just getting more equipment helps?"

O'Flaherty inclined his head. "Initially. For a little while."

Gwyn offered a suggestion.

With a twist of the wrists the great O'Flaherty sundered the two sections of his cue. "That probably ought to do it."

It was not a snooker hall, nor a cave of pool, that Gwyn had now to take his leave of; and Gwyn was glad about that. Snooker halls, with their darkness, their pyramids of light over the green-decked slabs of lead—snooker halls were places where violence might traditionally lurk. But no. The lesson had taken place in one of the public rooms of the Gordon Hotel on Park Lane. It was here that O'Flaherty gave his trick-shot displays for the instruction and delight of corporate gatherings (it was Sebby, in fact, who had put Gwyn in touch with the Irish magician). Now he took out his wallet and asked what the damage was, but it had all been taken care of at the other end, and O'Flaherty didn't even want Gwyn's tip.

The Boy from the Valleys: A Life of Gwyn Barry was no good because Barry chimed with Valley and he wanted to *stop* reminding people he came from Wales. *Allegorist* was quite nice and more modest than *Visionary*. *Gwyn Barry: Troubled Utopian* was far from ideal, and too gloomy, though he liked the notion that being utopian wasn't as easy as it looked. *A Better Way: Gwyn Barry and the Quest for* . . . Really he would prefer plain old *Gwyn Barry* or even, simply, *Barry*. American writers had those good surnames—gruff, rasping, unassimilated. You didn't seem to get that here. *Pym. Powell. Greene.*

Gwyn with his cue case strolled up from the depths of the Gordon Hotel, through hallways, arcades—like a tube station that served an unknown plutopolis. At one point he paused and looked to his left over the gallery rail and saw a ballroom with a boxing-ring at its center with laid dining tables clustered around it. A placard on an easel told of the Amateur Finals: spectators were to wear black tie. Gwyn began noticing shell-suited youths here and there on the staircases and in the ground-floor reception zones. Dressed in shiny shorts they would perform, tonight, in a termitary of dinner jackets. He moved past them, tidily, meekly. The faces of these teenage fighters forbade inspection; these faces were warrior-caste, with everything unnecessary shorn away—just two dimensions of defiance and dawning brain damage. They had their names on their backs: Clint, Keith, Natwar, Godspower. Godspower must have been teased about his name: but not recently. One of them swiveled in his direction and Gwyn almost fell over sideways—onto the lap of *another* boxer, who was just sitting there stupidly on a sofa, waiting for tonight. "Sorry," said Gwyn, into the depthless young face. He felt ashamed, not of his fear but of the dislike he seemed ready to inspire, almost universally . . . How would he break this to his biographer? Gwyn crept outside, through the swing doors, between the pillars. It was his intention to look in on the publicity department of his publishers' offices in Holborn. There was the ten-laned street, and Speakers' Corner, and the Park. Miles and miles of enemy lines.

As it happened he had a great time in Publicity. It was as if, on his way up in the lift, he had dropped a tab of C: that drug called Condescension. People in publicity are committed to making you feel good about yourself, even or especially when you have no reason to feel good about yourself, and they are good at that, and Gwyn felt good about himself already, so it all worked out. He thought they thought he was wonderful because he was wonderful but also because he made their jobs seem wonderful. Forget the cookbooks and the diet plans, the decrepit poets, the Hebridean novelists. He did it all for them: a serious writer who could comb publicity out of his hair. Only once did he lose his temper, and that was enjoyable too, in its way (he increasingly found). The new girl, Marietta, started talking about the Profundity Requital—completely failing to realize that Gwyn didn't *want* to talk about the Profundity Requital. Such talk tempted fate. And made him nervous. Anyway, they got her out of the toilet in the end, with her red nose, and Gwyn produced his wallet with a humorous flourish and sent her out for champagne.

Ninety minutes later he rode the elevator earthward, leaving the team working late. He said hi to the young black porter, thereby making his day. That was what Gwyn was doing all the hours there were: making people's days. Whew, that C was really good shit! In the early darkness Holborn was still yellowly illumined by its shop windows, and abandoned. That was the modern city: worked in, but not lived in. He was letting the door close behind him and buttoning his coat and had just started forward into the wind . . . It hit him like a solid tumbleweed of sweat and freckles and bare busy flesh: there was an instant of extreme facial proximity—yeast and loose saliva and ginger eyebrows—and then the two men were staggering quickly in each other's arms and Gwyn fell carefully, lumberingly, lowering himself on to the speckled sheen of the flagstones at no greater rate, really, than Richard had hit the car-park deck ten years ago in Nottingham, there to receive Lawrence's talentless and essentially unenthusiastic right boot.

A young man stood over him, stripped to the waist—and giving off steam. Sticky, coppery, he appeared to be mantled in a galaxy of hormones and youth. And evening steam.

"Sorry." This was Gwyn, offering it from the floor.

Steadying himself, the young man said, "They sending me this now? Let me tell you something. I got a little . . ." But he was moved! He was desperately moved. And his voice cracked and deepened, saying, almost with tears of pride, "My mum's got a little son. He's only twelve years old. And he'd fucking murder you."

Then the evening sky was empty and the street was as it had been before. Momentum reengaged the young man and he was gone, down the street and swiftly slantwise across it toward the stalled traffic of Kingsway. Gwyn was sitting there. Now he got up. He ran a damage check, first from the inside outward, then with his palms and his fingertips. For the moment he felt unnaturally healthy, and unnaturally safe, because that was that for today, and he need expect no further encounter.

No encounter, for instance, with the young man's younger brother, or half-brother, or kid bastard. The twelve-year-old capable of murder. Whose acquaintance one was naturally impatient to make.

Clearing out his desk at *The Little Magazine*, Richard found—to his alarm, but not to his surprise—a keepsake from Anstice. Upstairs his farewell party was already under way: a concentration of raised voices and blundering footsteps. He was working on his speech. They were going to present him with a bound set of *The Little Magazine*, sixty volumes, going back to 1935. Richard had asked Gina along to the party, and Gwyn, and Demi.

Anstice's memento was a book, with an inscription. *Love's Counterfeit*, by someone called Eleanor Tregear. She used to read many such books, at least one a day, all the Dorothys and Susans, bought and sold by the boxful. Noncoincidentally, no doubt, *Love's Counterfeit* was the sample novel he had once borrowed from her (and read about half of), curious, as always, about any prose work that found a publisher. Richard remembered now. It was about a country girl who comes to London and falls in love with a great artist, an opera singer or somebody. No, a conductor. No: a composer. Anstice's inscription said:

You were no counterfeit. That night we shared bore love's very imprimatur. Ah, but you were wed, with your two bonny boys!

Now I venture into another night, alone, without your hugeness inside me. No regrets, my love. Adieu.

Richard put his speech aside and looked at his watch and lit a cigarette. Upstairs the rumor of carousal was now diversified by sounds of breakage. Self-injury, dissolution, in the name of love: so innocent, so period. And literary, as opposed to televisual. TV trained women not to be victims. I mean (he thought), with Gilda you could kind of understand it: years of contiguity, in tiny beds, in tiny rooms. But Anstice. Anstice, who topped herself for a no-show . . . It took him ten minutes to speed-read the second half of *Love's Counterfeit*. Beautiful provincial (Meg) comes to London, to work as secretary to fiery composer (Karl). He smolders, and attempts to seduce. She smolders, and resists. For Karl is an emotional tyrant, devoted to his art; he also has a wife, a volcanic diva based in Salzburg. No kids. Smitten, desolate, Meg does a deal: one night of love. She would give Karl her body and then go back to Cumbria—to the hills, the valleys, the healing sheep-dips . . . Their big night got a chapter to itself and was rendered entirely in terms of metaphor—musical metaphor. Richard lit a cigarette. He was prepared for a muted performance. Say a *scherzo* for second piccolo. But this was a power symphony, with full jingoist hysterics from brass and strings and with buffalo stampedes from the kettledrums. On the last page Meg is standing in a puddle in Cumbria when Karl's cream sedan appears at the end of the lane. Happy ever after. The volcanic diva has killed herself—about something else.

There was a knock at the door and R. C. Squires entered the room. For the second time in half an hour Richard felt alarm unqualified by surprise: one or two other distinguished ex-occupants of Richard's chair had already arrived. R. C. Squires entered his old office with a misleading swagger. He doffed his hunting hat with the tweed earflaps and brandished his stained umbrella and shouted,

"Any advance on seventy thousand pounds?"

People who made big entrances, Richard had decided (now that he sometimes thought of making them himself)—people who made big entrances did so as a diversionary measure: to distract you from how terrible they looked, how old, how ill. R. C. Squires: his shattered visage, the color of Parma ham, his hair as soft as winebar sawdust. For fifteen years, unbelievably, he had written judicious and elegant "middles," on Courtly Love, on Shakespeare's women, on Rosicrucianism and Pantisocracy, on Donne, on Keats, on Elizabeth Barrett Browning. It was possible, presumably, to think of looking to R. C. Squires for mentorship.

He showed Richard the future and the past: his own available future, and the marginal literary past. Something could presumably be learned, at the Hush-Puppied feet of R. C. Squires.

"Seventy thousand pounds! Or do I hear eighty?"

It turned out that he was referring to the debts bequeathed by Horace Manderville (another distinguished predecessor), whose liver had finally exploded that spring. Richard had seen the filler-sized obituaries.

"How did he get people to lend him all that money?"

"Banks! He had rich wives."

R. C. Squires turned to the bookshelves. You could tell that he was translating their merchandise into gin-and-tonics. His eyes were gin-and-tonics, pleading for more gin-and-tonics. Earlier in the year Richard had come across R. C. Squires leaning on a broken jukebox in some barnsized pub loud with canned rock. Contemplating Richard with the stalest disgust, R. C. Squires inflated himself with several lungfuls of air, and began. The attempted denunciation sounded almost pre-verbal. Just a few glottal stops here and there.

"Why don't you go on up? You can hear them up there. I'll be along in a minute."

"Sorry about—Anstice. Anstice! Poor girl. Later we'll talk. I want a word with you."

"What about?"

"About your destiny."

Left alone, Richard reread his farewell speech, which seemed much too long. It wasn't often he had an audience—one that couldn't get away. For the last time he left his chair, the chair that had cupped the buttocks of Horace Manderville, of John Beresford-Knox, of R. C. Squires . . .

As he passed the outer office he saw a figure leaning over the book table (her hat, her scarf like a rope of hair, her angle of dutiful inquiry)—and death brushed past him. Death with its nostril hairs, its nicked and narrowed lips concealing a skeleton staff of teeth. But it wasn't Anstice. Anstice was dead.

"Demi. How sweet of you to come. No Gwyn, I see."

"No Gina?"

"It's Friday. Gina likes to have Fridays to herself."

He helped her off with her coat and when she turned to face him he thought for a moment that both her eyes had been blackened or bruised. But now her eyes widened, contradicting him, and she said abruptly,

"Gwyn seems to think you're going to say something about me in your piece. Something mean. Are you?"

"No. I don't think so. I'm just going to say what you said about his stuff. That he can't write for toffee."

"Well that's a relief. He shouldn't mind that."

And Richard wondered for the first time how Demi could *tell* that Gwyn couldn't write for toffee. But all he said was, "Let's go on up. I've got a speech to make. Wish me luck."

They went up the stairs to where all the noise was coming from. Except there wasn't any noise, not anymore. Side by side they moved down the corridor to the conference room. He reached for the handle and pushed. The door gave an inch or two. He leaned on it but it gave no further. All he could hear was a single anguished sigh. All he could see was a single sandy suede shoe, which quivered for an instant, then twitched, then stretched and straightened in death or repose: the olden Hush-Puppy of R. C. Squires.

Meanwhile, Richard had "finished" *Amelior*—in the novelist's sense. He hadn't finished reading it. He had finished writing it. Had he *become* Gwyn Barry? Was *this* the information?

Having written it, Richard was now obliged to christen it. What he really wanted to call it was *Dogshit Park*. Another possibility was *Idylland*—his rather slapdash substitute for that sylvan utopia, that newer, better world. In the end he settled on a nice plump phrase from Andrew Marvell's "The Garden." *Stumbling on Melons*.

Having named the book, he now had to name the writer. It might be cute, he thought, to anagrammatize "Andrew Marvell." And make it a woman. With his crossword skills, it shouldn't . . . Ella something looked promising. Ella Rumwarden. Ravella Drew, M.D. No. Velma . . . Jesus. Drew la Malvern. Wanda Merverl. Leandra Wrelmv. This is pathetic. Marvella Drewn . . .

Having tried and failed to anagrammatize "Andrew Marvell," he now tried to anagrammatize "The Garden." And make it a man. There was no sex in *Amelior*, and there was no gender either. Gwyn didn't write like a man. Gwyn didn't write like a woman. It wasn't personal: he wrote like something in between. "The Garden" . . . Gren Death? Grant Heed? Garth Dene?

Stumbling on Melons. By Thad Green. *Yes*.

The business of writing *Amelior* had of course involved reading it, again, and with rare attention. It was, in Richard's view, without merit. A straightforward armpit-igniter. You could come home, after a full day at the Tantalus Press, and *Amelior* could still gnarl your toes. But at last he thought he knew what Gwyn had done and how he had done it.

Plagiarism was good. Plagiarism was just punishment. Richard Tull was going to make it look as though Gwyn Barry had stolen *Amelior*. And Gwyn *had* stolen it. Not from Thad Green. From Richard Tull. And Richard, as he typed, had been stealing it back.

There were witnesses. It all originated, as so much literature originated, from an incident featuring conversation and alcohol. It all originated from a symposium, which means "drinking party": *sym* (with, together), plus *potes* (drinker). It all went back to a pub. Present also were Gina and Gilda. Richard was summarizing his latest project, a big bold book he never wrote called *The History of Increasing Humiliation*. In that same evening they spent almost half the advance.

"Literature," Richard said (and it would be nice to write something like "wiping the foam from his lips with his sleeve as the company fell silent." But he was drinking cheap red wine and eating pork scratchings and Gina and Gilda were talking about something else)—literature, Richard said, describes a descent. First, gods. Then demigods. Then epic became tragedy: failed kings, failed heroes. Then the gentry. Then the middle class and its mercantile dreams. Then it was about *you*—Gina, Gilda: social realism. Then it was about *them*: lowlife. Villains. The ironic age. And he was saying, Richard was saying: Now what? Literature, for a while, can be about *us* (nodding resignedly at Gwyn): about writers. But that won't last long. How do we burst clear of all this? And he asked them: Whither the novel?

This was already more than enough, surely. Oh, it was pitifully plain what Gwyn had done. He had gone back to his bedsit and gathered his Brit.-Con. textbooks and his gardening manuals and sat down and written *Amelior*. But it went further. That wasn't really the key . . .

Supposing, Richard went on, flown with cheap red wine and an audience of three—supposing that the progress of literature (downward) was forced in that direction by the progress of cosmology (upward—up, up). For human beings, the history of cosmology is the history of increasing humiliation. Always hysterically but less and less fiercely resisted, as one illusion after another fell away. You can say this for increasing humiliation: at least it was *gradual*.

Homer thought the starry heavens were made of bronze—a shield or dome, supported by pillars. Homer was over long before the first suggestion that the world was anything but flat.

Virgil knew the earth was round. But he thought it was the center of the universe, and that the sun and the stars revolved around it. And he thought it was *fixed*.

Dante did too. Virgil was his guide, in purgatory, in hell: because nothing had changed. Dante knew about eclipses and epicycles and retrogradation. But he had no idea where he was and how fast he was moving.

Shakespeare thought that the sun was the center of the universe.

Wordsworth did too, and thought it was made of coal.

Eliot knew that the sun was not at the center of the universe; that it was not at the center of the galaxy; and that the galaxy was not at the center of the universe.

From geocentric to heliocentric to galactocentric to plain *eccentric*. And getting bigger all the time: not at its steady rate of expansion but with sickening leaps of the human mind.

And prepare yourself for another blow, another facer: the multiplicity—the infinity, perhaps—of *other* universes.

So that's what you'd have to do. That's what you'd have to do, to make it all new again. You'd have to make the universe *feel smaller.*

Which is what Gwyn had done, Richard realized, as he typed out *Amelior.* Quietly, uninsistently, reassuringly. It provided the novel's only memorable phrase: "the naked-eye universe." That's what Amelior was the center of: the naked-eye universe.

Of course, in Gwyn's novels, there wasn't much talk of astronomy. There was talk of astrology. And what was astrology? Astrology was the *consecration* of the homocentric universe. Astrology went further than saying that the stars were all about *us.* Astrology said that the stars were all about *me.*

Richard wanted to know how Gwyn was feeling these days. He called him and said, "How's your elbow?"

––––––––––––––

"Still bad," said Gwyn.

"So no tennis. And no snooker, I suppose. But why no chess? I know. It's that nagging brain injury of yours. That niggle in the brain. Better rest it. Rub some Deep Heat into your hair when you go to bed."

"Hang on a minute."

Gwyn was sitting on the armchair near the window in his study. He was between interviews. He had fixed it with Publicity that they all came to him now. All he needed was a tennis court in the basement, and a couple of restaurants, and he'd never have to go out. Pamela knocked and entered. She named a monthly magazine and said that its people were here.

"Photographer?" he asked.

"Photographer."

"They're early. Have them wait ... Interviews," he explained. "Where were we?"

Richard said, "We were talking about your brain."

"Look, I'd better tell you that I've been deceiving you these past couple of years."

"In what way?"

"I'm actually much better than you at games. Much better than you at tennis and snooker. Even chess. This sometimes happens, you know, after a great worldly success. There's a power rush. It overflows. Particularly into the, into the sexual and competitive spheres."

"But you always lose."

"That's right. I didn't want to win. I thought, you know, what with everything else, it might be more than you could handle. Losing at all games too."

"Oh dear. It's happened. I always knew you had a rogue maggot loose in your brain. Twanging its way from chamber to chamber. Well. It's happened."

"What's happened?"

"The maggot's had kids. Demi said you weren't yourself anymore. Not yourself. Whatever *that* might have been."

"Listen. Clear a day for it. We'll have a triathlon. Bring a change of clothes. We'll play tennis. Then go and play snooker. Then I'll give you dinner here and we'll finish up with a couple of games of chess."

"I can't wait. No excuses now. No checking into Intensive Care."

"Listen. What was it *exactly* Demi said to you? About my work?"

"I've got it written down. On my typewriter. Gwyn can't write for toffee comma you know full stop."

"You're sure she was talking about me."

"I ran it by her the next morning. She said, 'Well he can't, can he?' And I said—"

"Clear a day."

Gwyn stood up and walked toward the window and stared out. The world loved him, but the world loved him not. Poor Gwyn, and all this cognitive *dis*.

Outside, now, he didn't know where or how to look. The world *said* it loved him. So why was it stinging him in the corners of his eyes? He was the unrequited. The pink lips of the cherry blossoms were kissing him and mouthing his name, and whispering, and showing him the papillae of their tongues. Mother Earth was blowing hot and cold, as hot as Venus with its trapped gas and ceaseless lightning, as cold as Pluto and its frozen rock.

In truth, Gwyn's interests didn't extend very far above ground level. Up to the troposphere, because weather came from it, and even as far as the stratosphere, sometimes, if he happened to be flying in it. He knew the earth went round the sun—he knew this twice a year, when he adjusted his watch because of it. The cosmology of *Amelior* owed nothing to Richard Tull. What Gwyn had been trying to provide, as usual, in that book and its successor, was the reassurance of honest practicality. He sought to represent the universe only to the extent that a sensible person (himself, for instance) had any use for it. There was a sun, made of whatever it was made of, which went in and went out, which rose and set, which helped grow things and gave you a tan if you lay in it. There was a moon with a man in it. There was a backdrop of stars, if you looked at it, which could guide you at sea, if you needed it. And beyond all that—don't worry about it.

He lingered by the window while the new photographer deployed his lights, his tripods, his white umbrellas. The new interviewer was a girl (unattractive). With nonspecific hostility Gwyn noticed that Pamela had at some point deposited a fresh stack of weeklies onto the round table by his armchair. Next to last week's weeklies. And he hadn't even . . . An avid reader, Barry always. He felt it was his duty to keep up with as many. Here as elsewhere, Barry was committed to the spirit of serendipity: everything was grist to his—

"Do you mind if I use a tape? . . . Could you say something? What you had for breakfast?"

"Let me think. I had half a grapefruit. And some tea."

"You once said, 'Nobody seems to like my books. Except the public.' Would you still say that?"

Beyond the window the cherry blossoms rolled. London went on from there, spreading out in all directions.

"How, then, do you account for your universal appeal?"

London went on from there, spreading out in all directions. The world was like a lover that loved you only sometimes. Sometimes, when you touched her, she went *mmmm* and enveloped you with all her warmth.

"Is Amelior a kind of promised land? Does it play on that myth and on that appeal?"

Sometimes when you touched her she went *mmmm* and enveloped you with all her warmth. But sometimes she was hair-trigger, was fingertip, in her hate. And she twisted to your touch.

"Are the two books formal utopias?"

She twisted to your touch. And this you could live with, could even understand. Only: all her brothers were out there.

"Could they be described as pastorals?"

All her brothers were out there. All her brothers were out there, waiting to break your face.

"Do you see the reinvention of society as one of the novelist's responsibilities?"

One last interview after this interview. He hoped the last interview would be easier than this interview. He wanted an interview with more questions like Did he set himself a time to write every day? or Did he use a word processor? or (come to think of it) How much money did he earn? or Who was he fucking? These days he was being taken far more seriously. Because it worked the other way round now: the literature-and-society people came in through the back door, to investigate an incidence of mass appeal. Gwyn liked being taken seriously and wanted—and expected—much much more of it. He felt strongly attracted to the idea that his work was *deceptively* simple. But he wished they'd make their questions easier. Now, as he traipsed through his answers, Gwyn checked the schedule to see who was coming next. Someone from the in-flight magazine of a charter firm based in Liverpool. Good.

After that, the great Abdumomunov was expected: to teach him chess. Gwyn used to go to the great Abdumomunov (up on some crag in Kensal Green) but now the great Abdumomunov came to him. He supposed that the old grandmaster must relish these visits. And he was wrong. These visits pained the great Abdumomunov; they pained him in the chess sense, which was more or less the only sense he had. He was used to teaching pampered but owlish ten-year-olds in whom you encountered a riotously burgeoning vocabulary of the thirty-two pieces and the sixty-four squares. Gwyn was hospitable enough, and paid the carfare, and his house was pornographically luxurious; but he never learned anything. It was like teaching poetics to someone who could only say *bus*, *hot* and *floor*. Currently they were working on stonewall openings where a pawn-infested center gave drawing chances to Black.

It seemed to the great Abdumomunov that Gwyn wanted to learn how to cheat at chess. Cheating at chess, or wanting to cheat at chess, had a long and illustrious history. *Seat your opponent with the sun in his eyes* was a maxim that went back to the indolent nawabs and the reclining caliphs of sixth-century Asia. Of course, you *couldn't* cheat at chess: with cheating, all you could do, at the chessboard, was think you were being cheated. Like many old grandmasters the great Abdumomunov could still teach the game but he couldn't bear playing it. Forced stalemates

gave him some pleasure. Agreed draws left him more or less undisquieted. He couldn't bear losing. He couldn't bear winning.

Gal Aplanalp said, "Wait. You're not asking me to *fire* him."

Gwyn was out of the house. This was his weekly meeting with his
agent, something he didn't want to skip, so near to publication day.
He said,

"He's fired himself. He has cast his staff into the cold waters. His wife
goes out to work. He stays home and minds the kids."

"I'm going to go to hell for placing him with Bold Agenda. Who knew
they were *that* Mickey Mouse? He didn't even call me and bawl me out.
Why?"

"Shame," said Gwyn.

". . . It *is* sad. Kind of."

"Kind of. Anyway. Now: foreign rights. I see from my statement that
I'm paying one and sometimes two extra chunks of five percent to various intermediaries. These intermediaries are probably very good at
sending and receiving faxes. But what other services do they do me? And
why is it *twenty* percent in Japan?"

Gal told Gwyn that this was how it had always been. Gwyn told Gal to
find a new and better way. Then he said,

"What time is it?"

"Uh-oh."

He got out of bed and began the business of locating the socks and Y-
fronts he had hurled here and there forty minutes earlier—in an imitation of heedlessness which he now found overdone. Then, too, Gal's
bedroom was disappointingly unkempt. From somewhere in his digestive tract came a cluck of quiet confirmation: the impeccable career-
woman led you from her impeccable office, and you followed her
stocking seams and their impeccable perpendiculars, upstairs—into an
arena of neurotic disarray . . . Actually, Gwyn felt wonderful. Nothing
had happened to him on his way to St. James's. And he had a hunch that
nothing would happen to him on his way back to Holland Park. It was
like being back on C after a month of the sweats. Wishing to express his
confidence, wishing to give that confidence expression, Gwyn turned
and said,

"Don't fire Richard. He lends a kind of respectability to your client
list. Otherwise it's pretty cheesy stuff, isn't it. Novels by weather fore-
casters. And darts players and royal chauffeurs . . . You ought to go on a
diet, love."

Gal waited. She then said, "You think I'm not on a diet already?"

"Seriously though, love. I don't see myself with a fat agent. It wouldn't do. I'd have to go elsewhere: to Mercedes Soroya at IPT. Can you believe those eyes? And those ankles!"

Patiently Gwyn went on standing there with his Y-fronts hanging from his hand. Gal, who was half out of bed, now rolled back into it, saying,

"It's not fair. You're a world-famous novelist. And you have the body of a young boy."

"Thanks, love."

For a moment he stopped thinking about Mercedes Soroya and started thinking about Audra Christenberry, who would shortly be in town. Then he thought about Demeter: indulgently.

"About next week. Demi's dad has taken a turn for the worse. Yeah. She wants us to go up there for a few days. So I can't make it next week."

"Boo-hoo," said Gal.

"Now what was *that* look all about?"

"Nothing. You know I always smile when I watch you getting dressed."

He stood upright, in his socks, his Y-fronts, beneath the inlets—the lagoon—of his male-pattern baldness, and said,

"Thanks, love."

This time it was like walking into a lamppost. He always dipped his eyes, discreetly, as he came out of Gal's and took a sapless little hop off the last step to generate a turn of speed . . . "You're ready, mate." The black guy cast out of black iron flattened him up against the railings and leant forward holding the pads of his thumbs—so warm, so firm, so aromatic even, like a doctor's touch—over Gwyn's closed lids, saying, "What can I tell you. We've all heard it all on the TV. I'm your worst nightmare. I'm going to put your lights out. We've all heard it all. On the TV. You're ready, mate. Look at the way you drop your head. You're ready."

Now came half term, and Richard's week of Sole Charge.

It was a time of great revelations. It was a time of ceaseless discovery. Who would have thought it? In a scant five days, while he went about his simple tasks in the company of those two young souls, more genuine illumination came his way than in as many years of cloistered endeavor, bent over his books and all their fust and dust . . .

By midmorning on Tuesday Richard knew why women never did anything and were no good at anything and never amounted to anything and never contributed anything to anything. To anything *permanent*, that is to say. It wasn't *having* children that did it, necessarily. It was hanging out with children that did it. Whatever you thought of this arrangement, it had something to be said in its favor: it demanded no further inquiry. And it wouldn't be getting any—not from him. Why waste valuable time when you could be untangling a shoelace or picking up crumbs or tripping over a squeaky toy or slapping some slice of trex onto a frying pan or going down on your hands and knees to search for a weapon component under the sofa or the bunk bed or the oven? Gina came home at six. Richard went into his study and began his review of a new Life of Warwick Deeping. After forty minutes he had something like—

This is a long book. This book has pictures. I like pictures. Pictures are good. There is a picture of a man. There is a picture of a house. There is a picture of a lady. You have to read pages but you don't have to read pictures. I like pictures because pictures are good.

On Wednesday morning, first thing, he escorted the twins to the video store and the three of them returned with a sack of cartoons. Marius boycotted these, and pleaded for stronger fare. By Thursday the boys were watching anything they liked so long as the movie wasn't actually called *Snuff*. By Friday they would both have thick and fluent American accents, spurning strawberry jam at breakfast, for example, and inflexibly insisting on *peanud budder*. With the children parked in front of some ghoul or Nazi Richard made progress with his review, managing to add that the book contained a picture of a dog and that he liked pictures of dogs because pictures of dogs were good. He seriously considered typing this out and biking it in. Because he knew that even his book-reviewing days were numbered. A slow contamination would be seeping out from the Tantalus Press. The appearance of his name on its letterhead, and in its ads (the Tantalus howled to the talentless: the talentless howled back), this would be seeping out . . . And Richard accepted it. Here there was no cognitive dissonance. He felt fully contaminated. He thought of clear liquids, of saline solutions. He wanted people in white to gather round him and wash his blood . . . On Thursday afternoon he came out of his study, drawn by a squall of salvos and screams. Eating jellybabies, the boys were engrossed in a billion-dollar bloodbath called *Decimator*.

"I could practically go to jail for this. Jesus. Don't tell Mummy. Why can't you watch something *nice*?"

"Like?" said Marius.

"I don't know. *Bambi*."

"*Bambi*'s quap."

"How can you say that?"

"There's *one* good bit in *Bambi*."

"What bit's that?"

"When Bambi's mother gets killed."

"Let's go to Dogshit. Marco? Marco's asleep."

"No he's not. He's pretending. He's scared of violence but he won't admit it."

"Come on. Let's hide the videos."

"Marco! Dogshit!"

Dogshit—that verdant world, that ghost of Eden, so late our happy seat . . . From a distance the grass had a layer of silver or pewter in it: the promise or the memory of dew. Up close, its green was as municipal as paint. And then there were the formal flowers, the pudding blooms, the gladioli in their thin old-lady overcoats; the flower bed was Dogshit's flower hat. People, park wanderers, provided other colors, from other countries: spice and betel.

Suddenly he knew what London children looked like. London children, those of London raising—they looked like crisps. They looked like Wotsits. Which wasn't to say that they all looked the same. There were genres, even here. This one looked like cheese-and-onion. This one looked like beef-and-mustard. This one looked like salt-and-vinegar.

Three black women moved through them, across the playground. The two grown girls with their African height and verticality, and behind them the old lady, in a white smock and a dark sash, round, rolling, like a pool ball waddling to the end of its spin.

It seemed to him that all the time he used to spend writing he now spent dying. His mind was freer now. Alas. He no longer did his "middles" for *The Little Magazine*—where he got his hands on the first-echelon talents, great men, great and childless women. He no longer solaced the childless Anstice by telephone for hour after hour. He no longer wrote. Boredom and sordor used to be asked to be seen as interesting and beautiful, and you could do it, with your energy. Transformation would occur. It seemed to him that all the time he used to spend writing he now spent dying. This was the truth. And it shocked him. It shocked him to see it, naked. Literature wasn't about living. Literature was about not dying.

Suddenly he knew that writing was about denial.

Suddenly he knew that denial was great. Denial was so great. Denial was the best thing. Denial was even better than *smoking*.

He came to think of denial as a fashionable resort, a playground for the rich, in a prose borrowed from Gina's brochures.

On Friday, she was home. So they had to be out. Colossally girding himself, Richard promised the children a trip to the zoo. On the bus he took his head out of his hands and said,

"Where shall we go first? The reptile house?"

Marius shrugged. He was working on this shrug, palms loosely outthrust from tight elbows. Five years ago he was practicing his reflexes. Now he was practicing his gestures—his shrugs.

Richard said, "The aquarium?"

"The gift shop," said Marius.

"You're very quiet, Marco. What are you sitting there thinking about?"

And Marco came alive and said, "My secred idendidy!"

In the zoo there were many kinds of animals for the people to look at. But there were only two kinds of people for the animals to look at. Children. And divorcees.

He was not a divorcee, he knew. At night, in the arid fever and miserable magic of the dark, he would whimper up to his wife, and hold on. He wasn't seeking warmth. He was trying to stop her going away. Which she wouldn't do, so long as he held on. More than this: in the depleted menagerie of their bed he could sense certain rumors of beasthood, not the beast of old, which was a young beast, but a new beast, which was an old beast. Something patched together, something inexpensively revamped. In the mornings, too, especially at weekends: watching her as she showered and dressed, and then looking up through the skylight at the clouds, their paunches, their ashen love-handles . . . I will arise and go now, with a suitcase, to the callbox. He thought of the fame-ruined lines from "The Second Coming," about the rough beast, its hour come round at last, slouching towards Bethlehem to be born. What would it look like, this beast of his? Yeah. Rough. Now he was impotent again but without his excuses. And what is a man, without his excuses? There was nothing for Gina to stick around with. There was nothing for Gina to leave. Richard no longer cried in the night. He thrashed, and gnashed—but he no longer wept. Because he did all that in the day. The day, and the dusk. He wasn't crying in front of anyone yet, as women do. Crying in front of people was part of their catharsis. He was determined never to cry in front of the boys, as he had that one time, in front of Marco, long ago.

At the zoo he felt the end of all childish promises.

I will stay with you for ninety-nine billion nine million nine thousand nine hundred and ninety-nine thousand million billion—

I will love you forever and ever and ever and ever and ever and ever and ever and ever and—

She wouldn't leave him. She would never leave him. What she would do was ask him to go.

And I will go, with a suitcase, to the callbox.

The children will have to come to love us separately.

Saturday morning Richard rose late. Around noon Gina said,

"Why don't you go out for a newspaper? Look in at the pub. Do the crossword."

"I might well."

"Pop in and get the Hoover on your way back. This afternoon if they're very good you can take them to choose a video. Something nice, mind. Disney. *The Jungle Book* or *Beauty and the Beast*. None of that *Tom and Jerry*."

Who are the girls in the backs of police cars? He stepped through the pigeons and their truckdriver tans.

London pubs always lag ten years behind the stretch of city they serve. If, ten years ago, Calchalk Street had made that upward lurch it was gearing itself for, then the Adam and Eve, starting today, would call itself the Tick and Maggot and would offer you quiche and cheesecake in a pavilion of striped parasols. But Calchalk Street had stayed where it was, and the Adam and Eve had stayed where it was—ten years behind. The same donkey-jacketed Irishmen drank the same black beer. The same black dog was still dying in the cardboard box beneath the pie-warmer. Richard found his usual seat. A pale girl moved past him, powdered and tinted like a bride of Dracula. As he started flinching and mumbling over his crossword Richard thought, quite unconstructively:

always give the devil the best tits. Such thoughts, thoughts of unknown provenance, came often to him now.

"Charisma bypass," said a voice in his ear.

He looked up, wondering if this, or something like it, was the answer to 3 down, and said, ". . . My dear Darko. Or is it Ranko?"

"Darko," said Darko.

Or was it Ranko? One or other of them, at any rate, had lost all his hair, or given it away. What remained was gathered in little fungal patches here and there, above a face essentially and now irreducibly his own—the purple orbits, the purple lips. And Richard, who had had some bad haircuts in his time, found himself thinking: Samson and Delilah. Oh, what a haircut was that! Ah, what syrup work was there . . . The Adam and Eve was ten years behind. Darko, somehow, was ten years ahead. No, twenty. He asked him,

"How's the writing?"

"That's Ranko. I don't do that shit."

"How *is* Ranko? And how's Belladonna?"

"They're both fucked."

"Now this is kind of great, you know, because you're the very man I need to talk to. Let me ask you something."

In his Profile, Richard was arriving, with a show of regret, at the first of his paragraphs about Gwyn's sexual delinquencies; and he was doing all he could with Audra Christenberry. But there was another paragraph he wanted to write. Quite recently I. Doubtful privilege to introduce. Barely sixteen, this young student was keen to. Of their two-hour encounter, she. The child, whom I shall call Theresa, had this to . . .

"Did anything happen between Gwyn and Belladonna? I need to know because I'm doing a long piece about him. For the papers."

"Oh yeah."

Richard thought it might look good if he wrote this down. He produced his checkbook—all scrolled and furled.

"I get it," said Darko. "Checkbook journalism."

". . . Do you want a drink? At last. We can have that 'jar.' "

"I'm out of here. And you're a piece of shit. She did his favorite, right? She's way out there. She wanted them to die together."

"What? In the poetic sense?"

"What? She ain't mega-well. She's *positive*, man."

It took a moment. But Richard's body was quicker than his mind. His body was walking past a dry cleaners' on a warm day: it breathed its false breath on him, and a hot damp gathered in every crevice of his clothes.

"Jesus. What about you? Are you all right?"

"Ranko—he's got it. But I'm clean."

"Stay well, Darko. Stay well."

Left alone, he sat for half an hour with the crossword on his lap. He still had his pen out but he wasn't called upon to use it. The only clue he was sure about was 13 across (eight letters). There was only one possible answer: *shithead*. And that couldn't be right.

He thought: the lion will lie down with the lamb. The lion can and must lie down with the lamb. But he doesn't have to fuck it. Unless they both say it's cool.

Come to Denial.

Denial. For that "holiday of a lifetime." Or just to "get away from it all" and take a well earned "break."

Your room, ideally designed for comfort, offers a panoramic view of the ocean setting. In the restaurant you may sample typical local cuisine or delicacies from our international menu. Before your meal, why not enjoy a "cocktail" in the "Crow's Nest" bar?

In Denial, amenities abound. There is a wide variety of activities and the finest entertainment. Hunt for "bargains" in the bustling market town. Or simply recline by the pool and "relax."

Whilst we reserve the right to increase our prices at any time, once you pay your deposit the price of your holiday as shown on your invoice will not be increased unless you amend your booking. No refunds will be made for cancellations, exchange rate movements, or cost adjustments that would otherwise decrease the holiday price.

So book now for the sun and fun of Denial. Denial: the true "never never" land of all your dreams . . .

But the information comes at night. The communications technology it picks is not the phone or the fax or the E-mail. It is the telex—so its teeth can chatter in your head. The information makes sleep interdisciplinary, syllabus disciplines, and then disciplines unknown or not yet devised: eschatoscopy, synchrodesics, thermodonture.

The information is advertising a symposium of pain. Pains of all faiths and all denominations. These are your little ones, these are your pretty ones. Become accustomed to their voices. They will grow louder, and more persistent, and more persuasive, until they're all there is.

It is ordinary and everyday. On the beach the waves do it ceaselessly, gathering mass and body, climbing until they break and are then resummoned into the generality with a sound like breath sucked in between the teeth.

Weakness will get you where you are weakest. Weakness will be strong and bold, and make for your weak spot. If in the head, then in the head. If in the heart, then in the heart. If in the loins, then in the loins. If in the eyes, then in the eyes. If in the mouth, then in the mouth.

The information is nothing. Nothing: the answer is so many of our questions. What will happen to me when I die? What *is* death anyway? Is there anything I can do about that? Of what does the universe primarily consist? What is the measure of our influence within it? What is our span, in cosmic time? What will our world eventually become? What mark will we leave—to remember us by?

"Door," said Richard. "The door. I—"

"What is it?"

"Just sad dreams. It isn't anything."

"Hush now," said Gina. "Hush . . ."

It was seven o'clock and Gwyn Barry was driving westward into a low sun: into the bloodbath of sunset. The one-way street fled through the tunnel of his rearview mirror; and above his head a ragged and sclerotic cloud dangled from the sky, an outcast from a superior system: it looked like an unforgivable deepsea fish whose bad radar had taken it where it should not go—a disgrace to the bright-ringleted shallows. Thus the ambience was briefly painterly and Parisian: clarity on which a shadow is soon to fall. Had he been younger (say seventeen), or a different kind of person, he might have marked it, its queasy numinousness. But he was Gwyn Barry, and he was coming back from his hour with the pro at the Warlock, and he was having drinks and dinner with Mercedes Soroya, who had a proposal for him, and the Profundity thing would be announced that night at 2200 hours—and he was driving, in a city, which takes part of the mind and plugs it in somewhere else, into the city and the city's sticky streets.

Up ahead an orange van stood athwart the narrow entrance to Sutherland Avenue. Gwyn's car slowed and, at a respectful distance, rolled to a halt. He could see through the dusk-lit slot of the van's side windows: empty, like something brain-dead. He looked around, expecting to see the nearby berk who would shortly climb into it and drive it away or at least open its bonnet and stand there staring at it with his hands on his hips. There was hardly enough time for impatience to gather (he wasn't Richard after all, who would have been impatient already, whatever was happening), hardly enough time to give his horn a coaxing toot . . . When Gwyn felt the car jolt he was less surprised by the impact, which was not severe, than by the affront to his spatial awareness: a second ago the rearview mirror had been clear, the street bare, the evening light still and heavy. He turned. An old wood-ribbed Morris Minor occupied the breadth of his tinted back window. At its wheel, an old lady in a rimless fruitbowl hat and a white shawl, and also wearing the pleading look that old ladies wear. Sumptuously reassured, Gwyn felt love for the old lady, for the white shawl, for the wooden ribs of the innocuous Morris. Yes—wait—she was climbing out. Gwyn unclipped his seatbelt. He would be wonderful about it. He didn't know the old lady's name. The old lady was called Agnes Trounce.

He stepped into the rosy light, under the gut-colored cloud. He veered round affrontedly as the orange van gave a neigh out of nowhere and reeled off at speed down the open avenue. He turned again: the old lady, her figure bent, was walking away too fast between the parked cars, and the second door of the ribbed Morris was opening. They came out low, and then they straightened. One had hair of pale ginger and invisible eyebrows. The other was thin, with black hat pulled down and black scarf pulled up and black glasses looping the central strip of his face. Gwyn was entirely ready. He was without reflexes, without gestures. All he felt was apology and panic and relief.

"What you call my mum?"

"What?"

"Nobody," said Steve Cousins, coming forward and reaching under his coat for the car tool, "and I mean *nobody*, calls my mother a cunt."

The sun was looking down on this, but not quite sincerely. The sun is very old, but the sun has *always* lied about its age. The sun is older than it looks: eight minutes older. The sun, to us, is always as it was eight minutes ago, when its light began the journey across the eight light-minutes. As Steve Cousins and Paul Limb (backup) moved in on Gwyn Barry, the sun was really eight minutes older than it looked, eight minutes redder, eight minutes deeper in the sky. This opened up a gap in time.

Eight minutes ago Crash was behind the wheel of the blue Metro (under its roof rack of ads and L-signs), half a mile to the east, showing Demeter Barry how you negotiated speed bumps at fifty miles per hour.

Six minutes ago Crash was 400 yards to the northeast, showing Demi how you reversed over a mini-roundabout.

Four minutes ago Crash was 450 yards to the north-northeast, showing Demi how you did a hand-brake turn on a zebra crossing.

Two minutes ago Crash was 200 yards due north, showing Demi how you jumped a red light with your eyes shut.

No minutes ago, intending to show Demi how you careened in the wrong direction up a one-way street, Crash performed an emergency stop, smacked his palm on the horn, and slid with massive case through the opening door (his belt lay in a coiled pool on the floor mat, despised, disdained, dull with disuse). By the time Demi climbed out and fixed her fragile vision on the scene, she saw the Morris Minor reversing at speed down the one-way street (she was momentarily impressed), and Crash standing by her husband's car with her husband.

The sun liked him. The universe still liked him. Either that, or the universe was through with Richard Tull.

———————

Shortly after noon the next day Richard was to be found in the snug bar of the Warlock Sports Club. He was drinking brandy and smoking cigarettes and staring at his shoe. A broadsheet newspaper, uncomfortably perched on the round table nearby, carried a front-page photograph of Gwyn and his wife, and described him, in its caption, as the Inaugural Laureate of the Cairns–Du Plessis Profundity Requital. Richard went on drinking and smoking and staring, with some show of serenity, at his shoe. The snug bar was often called the squash bar, and it was certainly very cramped and airless, but it never contained any Squash Members, or Tennis Members, or any exponents of snooker, darts, or bowls. It contained Social Members. Who were all sociopaths. So around Richard were arrayed a few tattoo-bespattered warthogs and authentic thirty-year-old methuselahs fingering their earrings as they applied themselves to their tabloids, and the odd clutch of regulars whispering into the foam of their pints, shrugging, and warily rolling their necks, and marked by that air of watchful cruelty which traditionally attends the criminal twilight. The barmaid, She, moved from table to table noisily collecting empties. Richard was still recovering from *another* bad moment, on the Knowledge. Having taken the trouble to stagger over to put a quid in it, he was almost at once confronted with:

Who wrote the novel *Decimator*, on which the film was based?

A. Chuck Pfister
B. Gwyn Barry
C. Dermott Blake

Dermott Blake was the fiery playwright whom Gina used to go to bed with—and continued to go to bed with (in Richard's view), every Friday. Paralyzed, and soon in time trouble, Richard distractedly and ridiculously punched the C. Whereas *Decimator*, of course, was the handiwork of Chuck Pfister . . . He staggered back to his newspaper and reread Stanwyck Mills's Profundity address: "Initially we felt that the optimism of the Amelior novels was altogether too frictionless. We had to ask ourselves whether that optimism was the result of struggle—whether it was earned. We decided it was. And we chose to honor that struggle." Richard drank brandy and stared at his shoe.

Something happened to the snug when Steve Cousins walked into it. An outsider might have identified him as a force for good, for order— the relay of minute straightenings and self-corrections that his presence entrained. Here, the graffitied young reined in the sprawl and slobber of their sports pages, their TV pullouts; there, the cardiganed elderly sniffed briskly and lifted their chins: everyone seemed to grow an inch or two in their chairs.

"Ah. Mr. Cousins," said a swampy old voice.

Richard looked up. His eyes and Scozzy's eyes dully encountered each other. Richard said, "You're late."

"Mr. Cousins, sir. The very man."

Now Richard looked sideways. At a nearby table sat two speckle-faced and ash-haired gents whom he had come across pretty often. They weren't like the other older guys, the arthritic artists of the bowling green who, as they aged still further, appeared to be fading into sweet-jar colors of caramel and nougat, into drip-dry and ready-to-wear. No, they retained a halo of dwindled charisma, of robberies and readies—these old thrusters, with the complexions of crumpled tenners. Laconic and discreet inquiry would have revealed that they were long-retired target burglars whose deeds had made a few headlines in past decades: the round-eyed actress relieved of her jewelry box while she slept in the West End hotel; the emptied stockroom of the Mayfair furrier; the rueful viscount pointing to the yawing drainpipe, the scrabbled-at first-floor window frame . . .

"Mr. Cousins, we desire your assistance. The very man we need. A man of parts."

"Ben," said Scozzy, with formality. And then: "Den."

"Vermin," said Den.

Slowly twisting in his seat, Richard absorbed the fact that Ben and Den were poring over something that both gripped and galled them. It was a newspaper, folded a good sixteen times, almost to the density of a pack of cards. They were doing the crossword.

"We're almost there," said Ben. "It's the top right-hand corner. Just can't get it."

"Vermin," said Den. "Four letters."

This wasn't the kind of crossword that Richard used to complete. This wasn't a grid of winsome quibbles, of little winks at Restoration drama, at Greek mythology, at Cartesian philosophy, where the poet, Noyes, can never make up his mind.

"Vermin," said Ben. "Blank, blank, C. Blank."

This was a crossword of bald synonyms, where neat equaled tidy and tidy equaled neat, where big meant large and not small meant big.

Scozzy faced the old men, in his tan leather mack. Once again his glance moved past Richard's eyes. After a long interval of subjective time he said, "Mice."

Den said, "That's what Ben said. But then you got . . . 7 across."

Ben said, "Messenger. Six. Say it *is* mice. Then you got . . . M, blank, G, blank, T, blank."

"Maggot," said Den.

"Midget," said Ben.

Even the fucking tabloids had run the Gwyn Barry story: the guru from Gower, married to Lady Demeter, and his mini-Nobel: the romping zeros of the annuity, granted for life, forever and ever and ever . . .

"*Mes*senger," said Scozzy.

"Jesus," said Richard. He climbed to his feet. And he did mean *climbed*. It took him up the rungs of all his years. "Legate," he said.

Den said, "Leg it?"

"Legate" he repeated. "L-e-g-a-t-e. Christ, well what can you expect around here, where all Aristotle is is slang for *arse*. *Legate*. It's not maggot. It's not midget. And it's not mice. It's legate. Messenger. Jesus." Scozzy had turned to him and Richard stood there, resolutely swaying, and saying, "You think you're a frightener. Yeah, you're really terrifying. All you've got to do is fuck someone up. And you even fuck *that* up. You think you're a frightener and you don't even frighten me. And what do I do? I review *books*."

The room was attentive to him and his voice. His voice was right out there on its own. The voice of half a ton of opera singer, abysmally deep—the voice of Baron Ochs.

"You think you're some kind of wild boy. Some kind of wolf child. Instead," said Richard, "instead of a fucking dog who, for a while, stopped being a tramp in the city and started being a tramp in the country. Yeah, *The Wild Boy of Aveyron*. I've read it, mate. I reviewed it! They thought he was going to tell them everything they didn't know. Nature and nurture. Civilization. *Nobody* calls your mum a cunt? *Everybody* calls your mum a cunt. *I* call your mum a cunt."

"Leave it, he's pissed," said Ben. Or Den. Because there was no way, no day, that Scozzy was going to speak. Not now or here.

"But he couldn't *talk*. The poor boy couldn't talk. Wild boys never can. And what have *you* got to say? What have you got to tell us. Give me my money back. Give me my money back."

"Oi," said Den. Or Ben.

Richard turned to them with a leaning flourish. As he moved past

Scozzy's face he said, "And it's not *mice*. It's *lice*. You got that, you dumb shit? It's *lice*."

———————

Gwyn was in the financial district, in the City, in a skyscraper, in a bucket chair, thinking about certain changes it might be good to make to his being-interviewed style now that the Profundity thing had gone his way. When they asked him difficult questions, perhaps expecting him to be Profound, he would in future say something like, "I just write what comes to me" or "It is for others to draw conclusions" or "I'm a writer, not a literary critic."

His friend Sebby would be there in a minute. Then, after their chat, they would go through to lunch. Once every couple of months he came in to lunch here anyway. Sometimes he would make a little speech. Gwyn often said that Sebby knew some very interesting people. He got up and walked to the window: this was one of Sebby's many chambers of the upper air. It was like Gal's old office in Cheapside, only higher and better. You could look down past the birds over many miles of the sweated city and see what new shapes people like Sebby were molding it into.

At last Sebby entered. Rubbing his hands together, he offered apologies and then congratulations.

"Thanks," said Gwyn. "Listen."

He said he wanted to present Sebby with a hypothetical situation. Sebby was used to being presented with hypothetical situations. Beginning every sentence with the word *supposing*, Gwyn gave Sebby a digest of recent events and an account of the incident the previous evening.

"Supposing all this happened," he said. "I mean, I know when you get well-known—things like this are going to happen. But I've talked to a couple of people who are on TV more than I am, and they say these things happen to them about once a year. Not once a day. So. Suppose it isn't random. Suppose all this. What would I do?"

And Sebby said, "You'd come to me."

At once Gwyn felt a part of his mind freeing up: "I'm a writer, not a literary critic" sounded too dry and lordly. One should be humble, but also secretive: twinkly. Why do I write? Why does the spider spin its web? Why does the bee store its honey? That sounded a bit—

Sebby wanted something from him.

"Oh, right," said Gwyn. He searched his wallet for the piece of paper with the registration number of the Morris Minor written on it. No: it was in his diary. Another jacket. "It's in another jacket," he said. "You might start with the driving instructor. He denied it to me, but Demi says he knows one of the men in the car. They call him Crash but his real name's Gary."

Sebby wanted something else from him. But there was a problem here because Gwyn would be a Labour man until the day he died.

"Let me think about it. On this other matter, what exactly are you going to do?"

"You don't want to know."

And they went through to lunch.

On the whole, Richard was delighted with *Stumbling on Melons*—the feel of it, the heft of it. He compared it to *Love's Counterfeit* and it looked just as antique and marginal and forgotten—though much newer, of course. He booted it round his study for a few hours, and wet it, and used it as an ashtray, and scrabbled at it with his chewed nails. The main difference between *Stumbling on Melons* and *Love's Counterfeit* was that *Love's Counterfeit* looked *read*. So he put in a lot of time, not exactly reading it (he did read it, twice, savoring his own interpolations), but skimming it. With unwashed hands. With city fingers. Balfour had been quiet and tactful, and hadn't asked any more questions. He seemed to know. He certainly knew about the Profundity Requital, and offered his commiserations. He more or less came out and said that he wouldn't be expecting too much from Richard over the next few weeks. In effect he was giving him a Profundity Sabbatical from the Tantalus Press.

Richard called Rory Plantagenet and arranged to meet him that Friday. "No," he said. "It's too sensitive to discuss on the phone. I want to do some checking first. It could be a hoax. Or it could be a big, big story."

Annoyingly, there were now three Barry Profiles under construction on Richard's desk. Three Profiles: the original, the original alternative, and the alternative alternative. The original was, in Richard's estimation, a work of the flintiest integrity, a noble example of that ancient literary genre called "flyting." Flyting stood at the polar opposite of panegyric, which is to say that it consisted of personal abuse. Freakishly well written, and fantastically hostile, the original could take its shameless place alongside certain passages of Swift, of Jonson, of William Dunbar. But nearly all of it would have to go. The original alternative and the alternative alternative, by comparison, were just workmanlike character assassinations of the kind you might see pretty often, he imagined, in the newspapers of certain totalitarian states, when a pressured editor was softening up some internal enemy for obliteration. Still, Richard believed that the alternative alternative needn't be as namby-pamby as the original alternative, which would have appeared when Gwyn (his condition, like Richard's prose, serious but stable) was deep in Intensive Care. And of course all that would have to go too.

Okay, he thought. Plagiarism was better. With plagiarism, decorum would be observed. Those who live by the pen must die by the— etcetera. Richard still felt that violence was a better and simpler way (give him the sword every time) but violence was an alien from another genre. Look how it inhibited his prose . . . Perhaps that was what violence, all violence, really was: a category mistake. Violence was both fabulous and banal. Anyway, it would have to go. It was gone. He knew that Gwyn had finally put one and one together and was now taking the appropriate precautions. And Cousins was gone. Steve Cousins had what it took to get through *Untitled* without his head falling off, but that was the extent of his merits. Cousins: his reader. Richard's readership.

The alternative alternative. Richard would of course begin with the scandal he was about to create, saying at once, with a disingenuousness as pure and rarefied as celestial music, that he had "no wish to add to" the tumult surrounding "this unfortunate affair." He would then go on to talk generally about plagiarism and the self, how its roots lay in masochism and despair, in dreams of self-injury and self-defeat; and how, uniquely, it seemed to linger as a smear, infecting both the raptor and the raped. Next, if he could summon the gall for it, he would demand the reader's sympathy for Thad Green, that tender and neglected seeker who lived and died without knowing that his work, his vision, albeit in the form of a mercenary travesty, would eventually bring (false and transient) consolation to an entire hemisphere . . .

Plagiary meant *kidnapper, seducer*—which meant he could get the girls back in. Gilda, Audra Christenberry, maybe Belladonna. It was a shame that Audra wasn't married and that Belladonna was presumably over sixteen. Richard needed to keep telling himself that there was another test the Profile had to pass (one that the original, he now saw, would certainly have failed): it had to be publishable. No kill-fee, thank you: he was already a kill-fee down on the deal . . . Demi could stay, and the shape of the piece seemed to demand that she be treated gently. Richard had never been completely happy with the extended digression about her sleeping with black guys for free cocaine, but he was definitely going to keep, and enlarge, the passage where she said that Gwyn's stuff—or Thad's stuff—was shit.

With his thumb and forefinger Richard massaged his right elbow, in the joint there: pestle and mortar. Belladonna: what did one believe? A thin sweat of confusion formed a join-the-dots puzzle on his unreliable upper lip. His plan, he knew, had certain flaws.

"Rank beggar, ostir dregar," he incanted, "foule fleggar in the flet. Baird rehator, theif of natour, fals tratour, feyindis gett . . ."

Thief of nature. One of the birds lodging in the nicotined greenery outside his window seemed to have learned how to imitate a car alarm: a looping lasso of sound. Various car alarms belonged to various types, various genres: the nagging, the hysterical, the scandalized. There was even a postmodern car alarm, which trilled out a fruity compendium of all other car alarms. This was the car alarm that all the birds of London would eventually know how to do.

He had liked Steve Cousins because he was the hero of a novel from the future. In literature as in life everything would go on getting less and less innocent. The rapists of the eighteenth century were the romantic leads of the nineteenth; the anarchic Lucifers of the nineteenth were the existential Lancelots of the twentieth. And so it went on, until . . . Darko: famished poet. Belladonna: damaged waif. Cousins: free spirit and scourge of hubris. Richard Tull: the good guy, down on his luck, and misunderstood.

Demi was leaning on the sideboard with her arms straightened, her arms locked—near where the telephone was. She had her rounded back to the room but Gwyn could see her in the mirror as he approached: her head unemotionally bowed (over a desk diary), the skewed collar of her shirt, the inevitable glimpse of tinged brassiere. And she could see him, now: in yet another new track suit, black, hugging, frogmanlike.

"No lesson," she announced.

"What? Oh. No *driving* lesson."

"Crash has had an accident."

"A road accident by any chance?"

"He fell down. He had a fall. The reason he has accidents sometimes is he's always trying to do something really difficult in cars. Really challenging. I think it must be quite serious. They offered me Jeff. But I want Crash."

Gwyn surveyed her with marked indulgence. In fact he was yearning to go into the kitchen and hobnob with his favorite bodyguard: Phil. But he lingered, wonderfully, with his wife. Wonderfully, he was being wonderful to Demi. Watch. He even took her in his arms. Why? Because things were rather different now. But what had she done to deserve it?

The night before, over dinner, here at home, Gwyn, at considerable cost to his own sensitivity, finally goaded Demi into saying, "You hate me. Why?"

"What is a man . . . How is a man meant to feel? When his wife, when his own wife . . . sneers at his very essence. At his lifeblood. At the thing that gives his life meaning. When she sneers at his *soul*."

"I honestly have no idea what you're talking about."

A moment ago, Gwyn had felt close to tears—close to bottomless self-pity. And it was a reasonably pleasurable state, he found: loose, sensual, oozily calorific. Now he leaned back, raised his chin, slowly closed his eyes, and said,

"You told Richard I couldn't write for toffee."

"Well you can't."

"Okay. That's it."

"Well you can't!"

"Okay. That's it."

"Well you *can't*."

"I suppose the next stage—is separation."

"But you can't. It just seemed so obvious."

"This now passes into the hands of my lawyers."

"If it was wrong to say it in public then I'm sorry."

"It'll take me a day or two to move out. I trust you will do me the common courtesy—"

"Wait. I honestly don't understand why you're so cross. Let me think." And again the commentary, the punctuation, provided by Demi's forehead: bracketings, underlinings. "We were talking about how much you got paid. Not just novels but magazine pieces. You know, so much a word. And Richard said it was a lot. And I said you couldn't write for toffee. Was that so wrong?"

". . . Come and give me a kiss. Mwa. Mmm. You mean peanuts, love. Not toffee. Mwa. Peanuts."

Within seconds he was huskily promising that one day soon he would fill her with their sons. And he spent the night in the master bedroom, and might even have made love to her, tenderly, tearfully, absolvingly, if he hadn't been feeling so fucked out—and worried about getting her pregnant. Demi also told him something else about that weekend at Byland Court with Richard: something he was awfully pleased to hear. Like all writers, Barry was often at the mercy of his. Seeing that light in her husband's eyes, she would know that the. Hypersensitive, but quick to forgive, he could never . . .

Now Gwyn said, "Crash can't drive for toffee. Eh, love?"

"Well his rates are quite high."

"Ah. Here he comes."

A minute later Richard was standing in the hall, in his shorts, in his mack, cruelly encumbered, with his racket, his cue case; he was carrying his street clothes in a cheap new sports bag which was clearly made out of plastic (if that). Demi kissed him. He looked lost.

"A lamb to the slaughter," said Gwyn.

"We're not going to do this, are we?"

Richard took his place in the back of Gwyn's Saab.

Up front, riding shotgun, was the bodyguard, Phil. It might have been pleasant, Richard supposed, to claim and savor responsibility for all this anxiety, expense, inconvenience, and preposterous exoticism. But the author of *Amelior* and *Amelior Regained*, dependably and adaptably insufferable, as ever, had too clearly thrown himself into bodyguard culture: here, in Phil, Gwyn had found another reality-softener—a publicity boy who pumped iron. It emerged that he even went to the gym and worked out with Phil's co-bodyguards: Simon, Jake. Gruffly, malely, Gwyn swore as he drove. He even wound his window down to holler at some affront to his territoriality. Another category mistake. Silence, please! We may think we are swearing at others, at traffic. But who *is* the traffic? The soliloquy is the appropriate form for such language, because what we are doing is swearing at ourselves. Richard didn't miss driving; he didn't miss being plugged into the city. But he missed swearing. He missed being yet another chump in yet another reeking ton of metal in yet another bronchitic defile, swearing at himself.

As they queued for Marble Arch, Gwyn jerked his head back and told Richard that Phil had been thrown out of the SAS for being too vicious. Phil grunted leniently. Phil? Lamp-tanned, rubbery, big-lipped, with capped teeth and clear eyes—their age. Phil's full name was Phil Smoker. Richard thought it might save a lot of trouble to be called Richard Smoker, particularly when you were in America. Or Richard Smoking. Phil smoked—so Richard smoked. Gwyn was now filling Phil in about their years of rivalry—on the tennis court, the snooker table, the chessboard.

"And today's the day I clean his clock."

"He's never beaten me at *anything*," said Richard.

"Sport," said Gwyn, "provides release. There aren't many areas of transcendence left to us now. Sports. Sex. Art."

"You're forgetting the miseries of others," said Richard. "The languid contemplation of the miseries of others. Don't forget that."

Their destination was not the Warlock but the Oerlich. "I'm paying for all this," said Gwyn. "And I'll have to pay your guest fee. You can get the balls at least." Phil, who had done a lot of staring on their way in from the car park, now did some more staring before settling down with the newspaper. Staring, Richard decided, was what bodyguards were really good at. He bought the balls: they were Swedish, and internally pressurized, and cost a bewildering amount of money. On the way down the cold green tube to their court Gwyn came to a halt and said, "Look. I've arrived." There on the wall was a framed photograph of Gwyn in his whites (together with his semiliterate signature). Nearby there were framed photographs of a dress designer, a golfer, a boxer, and the great Buttruguena.

"How long have you been a member here? What's it cost?"

"Thousands. Quite a while. This is where I play all my *real* tennis."

After the first changeover Richard said, "What happened to the fourth ball?" They searched for it, and failed to find it. This was an indoor court, and there was of course nowhere for the ball to go. But there were plenty of places for the ball to hide. And tennis balls long to be lost. It's their life; they long to be lost . . . After the second changeover Richard said, "Where'd the *third* ball go?" They searched for it, and didn't find it. Gwyn, in the keel of whose leather sports bag the two balls now nestled, asked Richard if he wanted to go and buy some more. But Richard shrugged, and played on.

He didn't understand how it was happening. Was it possible to hate too much? At all times he hated Gwyn on the tennis court, even when he was winning easily: even when he sent him from corner to corner like a lab rat (and then put him on his backside with a simple wrong-foot); even when, after a long alternation of lobs and dropshots, he had him gaping over the net, and, with big windup and loud puppy-yelp of racket on ball, drove a topspin forehand straight into his mouth. Hatred was part of his game but something had gone wrong with it—wrong with his hatred, wresting it beyond all focus and all utility. There were reasons for this.

Usually pretty matter-of-fact on court, Gwyn seemed to have converted himself, for the occasion, into a one-man band of affectations and tics—all of them hopelessly and inexpiably repulsive. Every time he won a point he clenched his fist and hissed "*Yes*" or, even more unbearably, gulped "Yup." Yes, the yup was very much worse than the yes. When they changed ends he could be heard to deploy a deep-breathing exercise: he sounded (Richard thought) like a pre-fire caveman warding off hypothermia. If Gwyn's first serve hit the net and plopped to the ground or rolled unobjectionably into the tramlines, he would reshape, as if to continue, then hesitate, then stand there for a couple of beats with his hands on his hips before trudging forward to retrieve it—while Richard said, for example, "What is this? The Princess and the Pea?" And Gwyn never knew the score. He kept asking what the score was: that tedious shibboleth—fit for hackers and literalists—called the score. "What's the score?" he would say. Or, "Where are we?" Or, "What's that now?" Or, more simply, "Score?" Finally and self-fulfillingly Gwyn was doing something else he had never done. He was winning.

After half an hour Gwyn had set point. Then, toddling forward on a typical piece of junk, he got an inch of racket handle onto Richard's skittish pass. The ball hit the tape, and climbed over it, and died.

"How's your thumb?" said Richard as they sat down. "Thumb all right?"

"It was an angled drop volley. And I was aiming for the tape."

"Don't worry about that thumb. Over the coming weeks that thumb will start to heal. Jesus, how could we lose *two balls*?"

Gwyn didn't answer. He had placed a towel over his head—as they do at the Australian Open when the courtside temperature reaches 140 degrees. Richard lit his customary cigarette. Gwyn peered out of his tepee and told him that the Oerlich was no-smoking. Then he added,

"You can't play for peanuts."

"How do you mean?"

"Or for toffee." Gwyn explained. "By the way, did you ever wonder how you got that black eye, at Byland? Or are black eyes just a matter of routine?"

"I did wonder. But given my condition . . ." And given the locale: an adventure playground for those in need of a black eye. If you were tumbling around it in the dark, on your hands and knees.

"You tried to get into bed with Demi at three in the morning. It was a right hook, I think she said."

"This is disappointing news."

"She doesn't hold it against you. And I think it turned out rather well."

Halfway through the second set the wall telephone rang. Gwyn answered it: Gavin, as arranged, calling to confirm the date of a pro-celebrity doubles tournament. For charity. And for Sebby.

"That was the manager," Gwyn said. "He said you've got to stop screaming and swearing or they're going to sling you out on your ear. And I must say I think he's got a point."

Ten minutes later Gwyn said, "Score?"

"Forty-love,"said Richard, coming to the net so that he wouldn't have to shout. "To you. Forty-love, and five-one. First set: six-two. To you. That means triple match-point. To you. That means that if you win this point or the next point or the point after, you will win the set and the match. Which you've never done before. Okay? That's the score."

"Gosh. Only asking," said Gwyn, who made that point too.

Richard took it like a man. "Well played," he said as they shook hands over the net post. "You're fucking useless and if I don't win love and love next time I'm giving up the game. Who'd you pay to teach you all that crap anyway?"

"Ask me no questions," he said, "and I'll tell you no lies."

The second set, like the first, had concluded with a dead net cord. Yellow ball hit the white tape: Richard had already forgotten who sent it there. Which didn't matter. The ball teetered on the high-wire of the net and even spun laterally across it for several suspended centimeters before it fell. In tennis, with the dead net cord, you want the ball to come down on the other side. Not your side. You are always wishing it away. But the ball fell toward him, and died. The ball never liked him. The world of the seamed and fuzzy ball never liked him anyway.

———

They drove back to Holland Park. Richard's tennis wear fumed softly of detergent and family wash, in opposition to the humid tang of Gwyn's cologne—and Phil's Man-Tan and Right Guard. Demi was out. "She's at Byland," said Gwyn. "Dad's dying." After a brief bonding ritual with his charge, Phil disappeared. Richard was shown into a basement toilet which had a shower in it somewhere, as well as various padded boilers and bouncing clothes-dryers. Then for a while, in his wet hair, he inspected the carpentry corner beneath the staircase. Nothing seemed to be under construction, but there was an antique bookrest whose varnish had been mostly scraped off with sandpaper: Gwyn, evidently, was trying to make it look like his own work. Richard went on up.

"Got your cue? Let's go."

"Won't we be needing Phil?"

In recent months Gwyn's wardrobe had been tending toward the softer and more capacious feminine fabrics, smocklike colored shirts, faux-naif knitwear, windblown scarves: the Will Ladislaw of W11. Now he confronted Richard in a charcoal three-piece suit of tubular severity, plus rigid bow tie. He was adjusting his cufflinks and saying,

"This won't take a second. I want to show you something before we go."

On the way to the top floor they passed Pamela, who withdrew with valedictory silence into the shadows of a distant doorway.

"You've been up here, haven't you?"

Richard had been up there, conducted by Demi, on a recent Profile-related tour. They were approaching the garden-site attic, which Demi had called the "childhood room." Painfully obviously, it was intended as a nursery: narrative wallpaper, Victorian toys (a rockinghorse with madamic eyelashes), Georgian cuddly animals, a Jacobean crib. Gwyn opened the door and stood aside.

The childhood room was no longer the childhood room. It was the snooker room. Cue trees, scoring rails, and a curved bar in the corner with four steel-and-leather stools for you to roost on.

"Amazing business. That thing weighs a third of a ton. They had to reinforce the floor. They came through the skylight—we had *cranes* outside. But the real challenge," Gwyn concluded, "was getting Demi to get rid of all her shit."

Richard lost 0-3.

They had a candlelit supper of smoked salmon, quail's eggs, and potted shrimp, prepared, or unwrapped, by Pamela and served to them in the dining room. Incapable of being struck by much, at this stage, Richard was nonetheless struck by her manner. You could not but be struck by it. Richard she served with cordiality; Gwyn, with melodramatic unceremoniousness.

"What's wrong with her? I mean apart from being your girlfriend. Is anything else the matter?"

"Not really. It's just that I'm getting on wonderfully well with Demi these days. And Audra Christenberry's in town." A door slammed somewhere. Gwyn flicked his napkin onto the table. "I suppose I'd better go and sort it out."

This took fifty-five minutes. Richard passed the time smoking and drinking. He had his hands full with that: with drinking and with smoking. When Gwyn reappeared in the doorway and made a gesture with his head, Richard said ordinarily,

"What about this?"

He opened his hands over the dining table. He meant the soiled plates, the leftovers, the inevitable decomposition . . .

"Pamela'll get it."

But before she did that she brought them coffee and brandy—in the octagonal library, as they settled over the board—and lingered to plump Gwyn's cushions and assist him in the ignition of his cigar. All this she did with an air both secretive and devout. Richard kept his eyes on the pieces he was assembling. These pieces, with their divine heaviness. Even the pawns responded greedily to gravity; and you could feel their affinity with the center of the earth.

The door closed. They were alone. Gwyn said:

"Adolescence is the best. I'm glad I left it this late. It's the tops. Can you remember—all that sexual loneliness? Lying in a single bed, thinking: there must be a million women out there, feeling like me. Sexually lonely. Nothing really changes. Even *Tolstoy* thought that. Time happens to your body. But not to your head. You're still looking out of a window watching them all go by. I'm still fifteen. But there are differences. They aren't out there anymore. They're in here. Or they're on the preselect of my mobile phone. Audra Christenberry. Gal Aplanalp. Hey, I've switched. I'm with Mercedes Soroya. You were right. Gal's list is *so* tacky. Novels by couturiers. Novels by synchronized swimmers. And Mercedes. Man. You could just drown in those eyes. Guess what. Gal had a crush on you, way back. When we were kids. You know, I really lucked out, marrying a Catholic. They can't get away. Ah. E4. Wait. *J'adoube.*"

"Resign," sighed Richard, for the second time in half an hour.

He went on staring at the board. It wasn't anything Gwyn had done, particularly. The chess just followed from everything else.

This was his last shot. "You remember that weird little sister I brought round to see you—Belladonna?" He waited, with his head down. "What happened?"

"That would be telling now, wouldn't it."

"Naturally." He waited. "You didn't fuck *her*, did you?"

"Are you out of your mind? Or do you just think *I* am? A little spook like that. And someone of my visibility. All she's got to do is drop ten pee into a phone box. And tell Reuter's I raped her or got her pregnant. I need that. Not to mention the risk of disease."

On the whole Richard felt quite impressed by himself. His disappointment was mild.

"Come *on*," said Gwyn.

"Yeah. Well."

"No. I just let her give me a blow job."

Gwyn's face was open, was declarative: the face of a man keen to transmit information clearly. He said, "After she'd taken her clothes off and done a little dance. She asked me what my favorite was. And I told her. It was pretty amazing actually. You know when they're actually down there—one thing it does is shut them up. For the time being. But not her. She took it out every ten seconds to *say* something. Me on TV. *Her* on TV. Holding it there, like a mike. It was kind of brilliant because it meant it lasted about two hours. Very skilled she was. Very noisy all round. I bet you think you're going to put all this in your piece. But you won't. You won't."

"Not Belladonna. I'm not sure but I think . . . Deadly nightshade. I think she's got it."

"It?" Gwyn considered. "I'm not surprised. Going round doing everyone's favorite all day."

. . . The way the white pieces were configured, like a hairline, and the squares drifting in his milky gaze: the board resembled the image of a face, on TV; the smeared cubes of some wrongdoer, some child-murderer, pixelated—the face of Steve Cousins. As in the first game the position was far from conclusive. But the chess just followed from everything else.

"It's late."

They stood up. Suddenly and startlingly Gwyn turned and seized Richard by the shoulders. What was this? More adolescence? With an expression of primitive alarm, Gwyn said,

"*You* didn't fuck her, did you?"

"Who? No."

And they sagged together, over the chessboard.

Richard said, "I'm touched . . . It's strange. Whatever happens, we balance each other out. We're like Henchard and Farfrae. You're part of me and I'm part of you."

"You know something? I understand exactly what you're saying. And I couldn't disagree more."

With a gesture at the chessmen Richard said, "It's a blip." And he meant the whole day. "I'll be back. I'll get you next time."

"I think not. I think there just *won't be* a next time. I think we've got to the end of one another. This'll do me. It's a wrap."

He walked home. In Calchalk Street, as he approached, he looked toward the rooftop. Two of the half-dozen stars that still shine on London (sufficiently fat or proximate) were burning; but no lights were burning at 49E. He went up the stairs, past the bikes. In the kitchen he drank a glass of water, a glass of milk, and a glass of sweet vermouth. With his head sticking out of his study window he smoked a final cigarette. Then he sat there, listening: no noises you could go ahead and locate. But the place was subtly unsilent.

He went out into the passage . . . Nothing. Just the boys. He could hear them writhing and whispering away in there. And this was very bad: Marco was supposed to be ill. Richard entered, and told them what time it was. They countered with a demand for a story—the new kind of story he had, he thought, unwisely introduced them to. Twins stories: stories in which the twins personally appeared—and invariably distinguished themselves for their ingenuity and valor. He felt uneasy as he told these tales (Marius suddenly realized. It was Marco who), while the boys lay on their backs, clutching their boyhoods, with drugged eyes. No story, he said. But he told them one anyway. In which they bravely rescued their daddy—rescued him, then tended to his wounds.

He leaned back against the cold outer wall and the window frame. And he thought: the Man in the Moon looks younger every year. It used to be a joke face he wore: a clown face. No longer. He looks pretty mainstream now, like a contemporary: I know people as fat-cheeked, people as pale, people as bald. He looks like me. His face used to smile. Now it pleads. He's sorry—about how he looks. When I'm old, that face will pout. And the Man in the Moon will look like a baby—like the god of babies.

Why cars? Why stars? Why pounds and pence? Why fog, why clouds? Why cold and gold, why dust and rust? Why tramps and vamps and dukes and nukes, why fucks and fights? Why planes? Why trains? Why jobs? Why nickel and dime? Why time? Why mire? Why fire?

I will arise . . . I will arise and go now, to the callbox, with a suitcase. A phonecall will I make there. Who to? Balfour? R. C. Squires? Keith Horridge? Gwyn, his oldest—his only—friend: Gwyn had never been a candidate. Ever. Richard realized that it had always been Anstice at the end of the line (waiting, in her urban bird's nest with its dust and trinkets, and ever eggless), but Anstice was already dead.

He turned away from the window. The twins were asleep. More than asleep. They looked like figures on a battlefield, arrested, abandoned. They too looked already dead . . . Richard didn't want to be telling them these stories; these stories about themselves. They were bad for the boys. They reminded him of pornography.

But pornography was surveillance on the act of love.

If he had climbed into his weepship and reared up over Calchalk Street, over Westway and its speed checks and electric eyes, and come on down over Windsor Court, and moved past night porter and night camera and tracked the cable to the apartment—to the Club World—of Steve Cousins . . .

"I have no words for him," said Steve. "As for him, I have no words."

He sat naked in his black leather chair, finding out what he wanted to hurt. He was conducing surveillance on pornography, which was itself surveillance on the act of love. He was watching others watching others. And it was all up in the air: because if what you were seeing didn't *remind* you of something, then you really shouldn't be watching it. You really shouldn't be watching.

Pornography, which could wear down the brake linings, releasing you forward . . .

This was so important to him: that he *chose* to do what he did. Others *thought* they had chosen—chosen, for instance, a life of crime—just by the hangdog repetition of a hangdog cliché. "You're on your own in this world." "Nobody's going to look out for you in this life"—in this life of crime. But they didn't choose it. It chose them.

What you never wanted to do was fit the profile. You never wanted to be put together like that. No, he wasn't abused by his father. Yes, he had tortured animals as a child. No, he was not in the habit of recording his illicit actions on camera or camcorder. Lifelong hypochondriac: yes. Latent homosexual: no. Stay clear of the profile and work from left field. Left field: the obstetrics nurse who takes to smothering newborns; the millionaire who sends his daughter's ear to the house of the known kidnapper.

Although he believed it contained the information he sought, Steve hadn't found it in pornography. Pornography of the visible spectrum: the red, orange, yellow, the green, the blue, indigo, violet. Boy-and-girl or girl-and-girl and boy-and-boy: this hadn't told him what he wanted to hurt. But tonight he found it. He was ready.

And it came from nowhere—from left field. He wasn't one of those people who watched things and then went out and did them.

Steve sat there naked on the black armchair. Unfolding before his eyes was something completely average. American, hard-core but heavily and vandalously edited. Called? . . . Called *Test Tube Babes*. According to the story, the women in it were one minute old. Made by the men, scientists: to their own specifications. They mixed the DNA in a test tube. Then under the microwave or whatever. And then they were born. With big hair and big jewelry, tattooed and tit-jobbed, ankle-chained and nipple-ringed—and one minute old. The inter-sex sections were meant to be funny. Reminding whoever was watching that the people in pornography had no sense of humor. It was a necessary condition. Absolutely everyone in pornography was absolutely humorless. Steve never quite got this.

Test Tube Babes. He was about four fucks in when it happened. Scientists and scientist's creation: they're on the lab floor, just finishing up. And a *kitten* wanders in. They're on the floor, covered in sweat, and a *kitten* wanders in. Actor smiled, and actress smiled back: the kind of smiles that expressed full confidence of mutual forgiveness. And the kitten (ginger. Do they call it tortoiseshell?) just tiptoes in between them, curiously, with one back paw raised in exquisite tentativeness—having no idea, being an animal, of the prevailing reality. The ergonomic reality. And Steve knew what he wanted to hurt.

It made him do something he couldn't remember having done before—maybe he'd done it long ago, when he was one minute old. He tried to cry. Kittens taken from the newborn litter and kept all alone are immune to the pain of fire and will stand there with their whiskers crackling as the flames come ever nearer. He didn't have the lungs, he didn't have the ducts; the cobbled muscles of his naked belly—each of them hardened and bulged. But it didn't work out.

What he wanted to hurt had something to do with himself. Not himself *now*. But himself. Himself *then*.

He raised a hand to his eyes. "They're doing me all over the gaff," he said, just to delay it a moment or two. "They're doing me all over the gaff," he said, just to buy a little time.

———————

It was spring: the season of comedy.

In comedy, in the end, all is forgiven. All obstacles are surmounted, all misunderstandings resolved. Everyone is gathered into the festive conclusion. Warped schemers, incorrigible pedants: they are banished. And everyone attends the nuptials of hope.

But we haven't had much luck with our seasons. Not yet, anyway. We did satire in summer, and comedy in autumn, and romance in winter.

And this was spring. The season of comedy.

But comedy has two opposites; and tragedy, fortunately, is only one of them. Never fear. You are in safe hands. Decorum will be strictly observed.

Marco Tull hurried down the Portobello Road, hand in hand with Lizzete. Unless he was being directly entertained, Marco, on the street, always wore a leer of settled skepticism. You could see his two-sized upper teeth, anxiously yet resignedly bared. He didn't seem frightened so much as overloaded: too many lines of inquiry, too many sense impressions, too many narratives to pursue and complete. Today was Friday: the end of a week of mild illness. Lizzete's pace was brisk. To keep up, Marco didn't jog or trot but walked and ran, walked and ran.

They approached PriceSlash. This was the first shop Lizzete aimed to visit. Gina had called her up the night before. Friday was her day off and she wanted a little peace: a working mum. She offered Lizzete the usual truancy bonus as well as the flat rate for three hours with Marco. But Lizzete was planning to play hooky anyhow, and get some shopping done. The truancy bonus she had fair-mindedly waived.

She looked down at him. He looked up at her. She said,

"All right? You've got a Megabar coming your way."

13 was watching them from the confines of the orange van, which was currently impeding access to Lancaster Road. He looked completely sick. Not like he looked after a night at the Paradox or on the M25. Being black, he couldn't look green, or gray, or white as a ghost. He just looked completely sick.

"PriceSlash is it."

Steve Cousins said, "There's this mouse driving through the jungle in his Porsche. Hears this cry of Help! and pulls up by this pit. Gets out of the Porsche, looks down—there's this fucking great gorilla. Trapped in this pit. 'I'm trapped, mate. Can you help me out?'

"So the mouse grabs a—grabs this vine. He slings one end down the pit and ties the other to the tow-hook on his Porsche. 'Hold on tight.' He jumps in the Porsche and starts revving. And sure enough. Bit by bit . . . Hello? I said hello? Are you with me?"

"With the Porsche or whatever," said 13. He looked completely sick.

" 'Thanks a million, mate,' says the gorilla. 'I'll do the same for you one day. Shake.' . . . Five years later the gorilla is walking through the—through the prairie. And he hears this little cry, Help! Help! There's this pit. He looks down. It's the mouse! 'Where's the Porsche? Don't worry. We'll soon have you out of there.' And the mouse goes, 'How, mate? There's no vines round here.' And the gorilla says, 'It's okay. I'll use me cock.' So he slings his cock down the pit and the mouse scampers up it. And he's free."

Steve waited. He said, "Don't you want to hear the moral?"

"Uh?"

"And the moral of the story is: If you've got a big cock, you don't need a Porsche. Park in Basing Street. In the garage that went bust. Do it."

Marco's father was fifty yards away, in Kensington Park Road. He shook his glass like a maraca at the waiter and said, to Rory Plantagenet,

"*Stumbling on Melons*, by Thad Green. It came in a plain brown envelope. London postmark. No covering letter. Copyright 1954. I didn't even look at it for a couple of days. And when I did I just thought *wow*."

"I can't understand," said Rory, "why they put us downstairs."

"Plot, characters, location. He's changed some of the names of course. There are whole pages that are word for word."

"It's too dark down here. And there's a kind of pissoir smell. Can you smell it? Sorry. Go on. Waiter!"

Rory Plantagenet wasn't his pen name. It was his real name. And it suited him. He looked cornily patrician. And altogether vestigial. A generation ago he would have been living in Cap d'Antibes with a mature ladyfriend called something like Christabel Cambridgeshire. He and Richard were schoolfriends, or schoolfellows. For several years they had simultaneously attended the worst and most paranoid public school in the British Isles.

"The thing with plagiarism is," said Richard, "—it *always* comes out. It's just a matter of time. And that's why I came to you. You know what a novel is. And how much a novel can matter."

This was news to Rory Plantagenet. Agreeable news, on the whole. He was Richard's age. After nights out during which he had attended three or more parties, Rory often found himself wondering about his place in the larger scheme of things.

Richard said, "I want to control all this. Damage limitation. The one *I* feel sorry for," he added, briefly pondering the wisdom of that third gin-and-tonic, "is Lady Demi. Considering everything else she has to put up with."

"Women?"

"Don't ask me. Ask Audra Christenberry. Ask Mercedes Soroya. You know he even has a . . . But that's another story. Look. The last thing I want to do is make this any worse for Gwyn than it has to be. He's my oldest friend for Christ's sake. I fucking love the guy."

Marco's godfather, and the object of Richard's love, was also but a block distant. Gwyn was walking west up Ladbroke Grove. He had not informed Phil of this excursion. Actually, it wouldn't have been Phil anyway, so early in the afternoon. It would have been Simon. Boldly he walked on, past the tube station, past Mick's Fish Bar, past Westway. If anything was going to happen, it would surely happen under Westway. That black cavity, where the very walls and pillars were drenched in eel juice and snake's hiss, and tattooed with graffiti. If something was going to happen, it would surely happen under Westway. But nothing was going to happen. Gwyn was clear.

The night before, Phil had told him, in the kitchen (Simon and Jake were also present, tacit, collusive, sloped over their Gold Blends), that all this "nonsense," all this recent "rubbish," all this "silly-buggers," would presently be "sorted." Presently: like tomorrow. "Who is he?" said Gwyn. "What are you going to do about him?" From Phil, a quick shake of the head and a downward glance; but Jake, without raising his crushed, Rugby League face from his coffee mug, simply said, "You don't want to know." And Gywn *didn't* want to know. Gwyn was clear. The universe loved him again. He was clear. He walked on.

When he reached the turning into Calchalk Street he paused and then entered the Adam and Eve. His expression was timid, tolerant, with anthropologist's protuberance of eye. And his voice sounded more Welsh than usual when he ordered his drink . . . Barry would often stroll the streets and sit in simple. Sit in rude. Sit in simple. Sit in unpretentious pubs enjoying a "jar" with the common. With ordinary. With the. Just like anybody else . . .

Gwyn confirmed the presence of his wallet with the inside of his wrist and then glanced masterfully at his watch.

In PriceSlash children on tautened reins pressed ahead of their guardians: little rickshaw runners, leading the way to the millennium.

To save money, or because the shops had all sold out, many parents had improvised with washing-line cord and roof-rack grapplewire. These children had enemies and these enemies were everywhere and everyone. Marco was not on reins. Lizzete usually kept a hand lightly resting on his hair. And Marco liked to grip you: by the waistband, by the jacket pocket.

Lizzete was singing a song as they moved up and down the strip-lit canyons of PriceSlash. At present they were in the domestic-hygiene section with its plastic and polythene and all the colors associated with the spick and span.

---

13 was across the street, in Ultraverse. Ultraverse sold second-hand comics: X-Man and She-Hulk, Count Zero and RoboBabe. Donnamatrix meets Dr. Strange.

"I'm dead," he whispered, and steadied himself against a comic rack. Aquavixen v. Animalman. "I'm dead."

He reckoned he was dead ten times over. Crash would kill him for this but not today and not tomorrow. Crash wouldn't kill him today because Crash was in bed eating hospital food. Even as things stood, Crash wouldn't speak to 13 or even glance his way. All 13 knew was that three men had done his brother, wanting information. It was Grievous Bodily Harm, no argument, as opposed to Actual. In his bed at St. Mary's, Crash seemed to be contemplating the letter G. Grief was what he seemed to be full of. His eyes didn't blink. They stared inward with childish and narcotic melancholy—staring at the grief of his wounds.

On top of everything else 13 had parked Giro in Crash's flat in Keith Grove. Pining, and scratching the doors.

Grendel and Cerebus, Venom and Magma. 13 looked through the dark glass of Ultraverse, across the market street: PriceSlash. As instructed, he had left the orange van in the yard of the dead garage in Basing Street.

"Who is this Tad Green?" said Rory Plantagenet.

"Thad Green. Thaddeus, presumably: American. I can't find any record of him anywhere. The publisher's long defunct. Which all figures. Oh I think we can trust friend Barry to have thought this through pretty thoroughly. He's not going to claim he wrote *Hamlet*."

"It seems so out of character. From what I know."

"Taffy was a Welshman, Taffy was a thief. Taffy came to my house—"

"This isn't some kind of hoax, is it? I've got a sixth sense about these things. When I'm being used."

"I swear on my wife and kids. Come *on*. Don't you see how hard this is—for me? We shared rooms at Oxford. I love that fucking guy."

"Well the more I think about it, the more I think that Smatt will want to whale on this," said Rory—Smatt being the office nickname for his editor (a Cumberland cruiserweight called Sir Matthew Druitt). "It's perfect for him."

"Why, particularly?"

"Because Gwyn's Labour. And Welsh. Let's get on to the women."

When the bill had been called for Richard left the table and made for the pay phone. Rory wanted to inspect *Stumbling on Melons* and take it away for the weekend; he would read it, alongside *Amelior*; and, if everything panned out, he would splash on Monday—the same morning, the same bright dawn that would see the publication of *Amelior Regained*. Richard had his head bowed over a palmful of change. It was his intention to warn Gina that he would be stopping by. That afternoon he was due—was overdue—at the Tantalus Press.

He dialed his own number.

At 49 Calchalk Street, Flat E, Gina was sitting naked in the bath, her hair all gray and greased with some glutinous unguent or elixir. She stopped her ears with her forefingertips, and lay back. Only her breasts and her caligulan nose were visible in the steam.

Next door, the telephone started ringing. It rang and rang and rang. It stopped ringing.

Gina's head and torso surged up from the water.

Space-time was not on Richard's side. The universe was definitely through with him.

———————

Gwyn came out of the Adam and Eve and walked down Calchalk Street.

Although his work conjured up an idealized vision of humankind, he himself remained. Robustly individual, he went about things in his own. No one could accuse. He always . . .

On the steps of Number 49 he rang the bell marked Tull. He waited. He looked at his watch, and at his fingernails.

"Hello?"

"It's me."

There was a silence. The buzz sounded and he went on up.

Gina was waiting by the door at the top of the stairs in her pink towel dressing gown. She said,

"Are you going to stop?"

Lizzete released Marco's hand as she stood on the street checking her change.

"Hey."

It was 13. Marco was pleased. He liked 13. And he sensed the cool of black. Lizzete was black, but she was a girl. 13 was black, but he was a boy.

"Where've *you* been, man?" said Lizzete.

"Angela wants you." He pointed with a bent finger, meaning: round the corner. "In the Black Cross."

Marco backed off as Lizzete flusteredly shifted her weight: Angela was her oldest sister. She transferred the shopping bag from her right hand and reached out for Marco.

"You can't take a kid in a pub. We'll wait here."

Lizzete looked hard at 13.

13 said, "Give us him."

"Now here, Gina, we encounter an ambiguity. You being from Nottingham. Am I going to stop. I love it when you say that. Am I going to stay? Or am I going to desist?"

"Well which?"

"Both. I'll stay this time, if I may. And then I'll desist. So I'll stop—and then I'll stop."

"You say that but you keep coming back. Please—desist, and don't stay. Go."

Gwyn sighed. He said, "Fine. So you don't mind me telling Richard. I wonder how I'll break it to him. Will it make it easier or harder for him, do you think, that you did it for the money?"

"I didn't do it for money. I did it for revenge."

"Oh yes. Poor Anstice. I met her once. Unbelievable."

"I'm surprised he hasn't guessed already. I always told him I'd do the worst thing."

"Ah but he thinks you don't like me."

"I don't."

He turned his head away. And he actually said it. He said: "Women!" He sighed again. Then he reached for his wallet and produced four notes of high denomination. "Nevertheless money was involved. I like to think of myself as Richard's patron. Keeping his family struggling along while he completed his last and, some say, his greatest novel. What was it called?"

"Enough. Stop. Desist."

"Why do *you* stop? Meaning *stay*. I must say, these days I find his presence . . . entirely soiling. But of course you have this wonderful love life, don't you. This raging sea of hysterical sex. Why don't you just chuck him out? He'd go."

And he would go. With a suitcase, to the callbox . . . He would go *quietly*. One thing about Richard. She sensed all the violence, all the verbal violence, he contained. But he had never turned it on her. And she knew he never would.

"One last time," said Gwyn. "And just beauty and the beast."

It was naturally the phenomena of his own eye-level that claimed the lion's share of Marco's attention. For example, the cavernous murk beneath the stalls where an apple or a turnip might have rolled: between the gutter and the shadow-edge. The inner glisten of things under there, where he could easily go, bending in under there, where the small was better than the tall.

He looked up. He turned a full circle. 13 was gone. Immediately Marco's ears started humming at him. He wheeled and his vision wheeled, wheeled for a face to form out of the swings and roundabouts, the costumed impostors, the taffetaed dissemblers—the kings and the queens and the jacks.

A bus stood at the crossroads. Behind it, Marco's father, accompanied by his friend, walked past, continuing down Westbourne Park Road to Ladbroke Grove.

"There was this novelist," Richard was saying, "who taught a creative-writing course at Brixton Prison. He went away for six months and when he came back all the lags had written a novel each. Or transcribed a novel each. But there were only about five novels in the prison library for them to plagiarize. *Three* of them had done *The Cruel Sea*."

Rory frowned. They walked on.

"Jesus. I'd better pick up the vacuum cleaner. Do you mind? It's been there for weeks and I get hell at home."

Three days of weather were stacked in the sky. Here was today. And there was tomorrow. And over there, the day after.

"Beauty and the beast," said Gina. "And that's it. For ever."

"Amazing that women find that *less* intimate. Particularly when they're swallowers, like you. It always seems *more* intimate to me."

"Except it's got nothing to do with babies. Why don't you and Demi have a baby? It would suit you. It would shut her up."

"But it wouldn't shut the baby up."

"But it might shut *you* up. You need a change."

"Well I might get one whether I want it or not. Demi's changed since her dad popped off. She's chucking Pamela out. She's talking of chucking *me* out. She's really changed. She's dead flash. Take your dressing gown off at least."

"Quick now. I don't want you running into Lizzete on the stairs."

Gwyn stood up and took his jacket off and said, not altogether truthfully, that he would be as quick as he possibly could.

A figure stepped out between the market stalls—instantly dismissed by Marco as playing no part in Marco's world. But then Marco's world was already falling away, falling, falling through the curved heavens. That was what he could hear in his ears: the friction of the falling world.

Persisting in their address, the face and the figure came nearer.

"Marco. It's Steve, remember? I know your dad."

The face held out its hand toward him. Marco declined it. But he went on standing there, abjectly, with his neck bent. A modern child, he knew the kinds of things the world could contain: local—personal—disasters. It was like a shadow falling, but a shadow made of uneasy light. Storm light, and summer thunder.

"Marius is waiting round the corner. I want to tell you a story. Come on. I got some kittens in the back of the van."

A hand was offered again, and declined again. They started off. To keep up with his minder, and his minder's brisk stride, Marco didn't jog or trot but walked and ran, walked and ran.

"Need any help with that?"

"It's easier if one person carries it. Funnily enough."

They had drunk more wine than they were young enough to drink; and then there was the large brandy that Richard had successfully consumed while Rory settled the bill. After the thousand-yard hike through the human and mechanical effluvia of Ladbroke Grove, Richard, at least, felt intoxicated to a sordid degree. He paced up the three double flights of stairs, giving stertorous voice to his opinion that there was probably a sequel to *Stumbling on Melons* and Gwyn had got that off the back of Thad's lorry too . . . He fell sideways, and righted himself. The bikes on the walls, on the ceiling, seemed to strike up an assonance with the oil and metal at the back of his throat. Richard opened the clapboard door: more stairs.

"Everest," said Rory.

Richard pressed on, bouncing from wall to wall with the Hoover tube tightening its grip round his neck; and he was already thinking that suicide had much to be said for it, because life was too much fucking fetching and carrying and too much scrabbling for keys in pockets and too much going from this place to that place and then to some other fucking place . . .

"It'll come out," he said. "It always comes out."

And the shoe will squeak, and the door will creak.

Gwyn heard him. His body stiffened; but his body was stiffening anyway. And do you know what he did? He pressed his hands over Gina's bath-brightened ears. He pressed them good and tight.

———————

What happens when galaxies collide? Most frequently, nothing. Stars are sparser than the conglomerations they form. Galaxy moves through galaxy. Anti-galaxy moves through anti-galaxy. There is plenty of room.

Richard is back on the street. And this story, his story, endeth here. On the street, with its opposed houses, its ranked cars—and the anti-comedy of the apple blossom loosening in the wind.

He turned. He knew that nothing in his past or his future could ever be as inimitably contemptible as the smile he had managed to rig up for Rory Plantagenet: to rig up, among the moonspots and boneshadows of his youthless face. The memory of this smile would be with him until he died; thirty years from now he would be standing there with his hands over his ears, raising his voice in a mortified yodel, trying to batten down the memory of this smile.

How much had Rory seen? He didn't know. How much had *Richard* seen? He didn't know. The gulping flurry of pink toweling. They had seen enough. Oh, *basta* . . .

"Well, as you've probably guessed," he said, "we've been leading you down the garden path."

"I don't follow you."

"Yes. Pulling the wool over your eyes." Richard shrugged and opened his hands. A negative hilarity was possessing him. The English language offered him no help—offered him nothing. "It was just a little stunt we hatched. The three of us, you see. To see how far it would go. We wasted your time. There's no story here. I'm sorry. Please forget it, Rory. Forget it. Please, Rory."

Now Gwyn chose to make his exit from 49 Calchalk Street, drooping loosely down the steps with his hands in his pockets: the feminine colors of his clothes. To Richard's eyes he looked cynically and even satanically handsome. Unforgettable, again, was the complicit rictus that Richard now laid at his feet.

"Going my way?" said Gwyn.

And Rory fell into step beside him. And Richard was alone.

As he looked down the vista into which they would soon disappear, toward Ladbroke Grove and its circus horses of traffic, Richard saw his son Marco—Marco a long way away, and on the far side of the street, but with Marco's unmistakably brittle and defeatist stride. There was something terribly wrong with Marco: there was nobody at his side. And yet the child's solitude, his isolation, unlike his father's, was due to an unforgivable error not his own. There was always somebody at Marco's side. In all his seven years there had always been somebody at his side.

A drama, thought Richard. And a diversion: at least this will get me up the goddamned stairs. He realized that he still had the vacuum cleaner: in his arms, across his body, round his neck. Richard was still Laocoön, engulfed in coils and loops. That too he would have to tote, all the way up to 49E. That too.

Father and son started hurrying toward each other. Marco wasn't crying, but Richard had never seen him looking so unhappy: the unhappiness that was always made for Marco; the unhappiness that was all his own. Richard knelt, like a knight, and held him.

"Who was with you?"

Marco told him: Lizzete.

"And you were lost?"

There was a man.

"Then what happened?"

He took me to a car: for kittens.

"Then what?"

Three men came. And took him away.

"Took him where? Were they police?"

Marco shrugged.

"Did he go willingly or unwillingly?"

Marco shrugged—with out-turned palms.

"What did they say? Did anyone say anything?"

Yes. The man said, "I'm a child."

"The man said *you're* a child?" And Richard went back four or five years, to the natural confusions of early speech. "How are you?" he would ask him; and Marco would say, logically enough, "You're fine." And Marco would reach out to him with his arms and say, "Carry you." And Richard would pick him up and carry him . . .

No. He said *I'm* a child.

"But he *wasn't* a child."

No. He was a man.

Richard stood up. A definitive misery, having to do with unintended consequences, moved past him, tousling his hair like the backdraft of a speeding car. He turned; and now Lizzete, too, was running down Calchalk Street toward them, running stockily with her waist held low. Jesus: and here came the swine in his German car, ripping down my road at sixty miles an hour to kill my kids. What is this guy's *hurry*? Who could want him anywhere sooner than he would get there already? The cone of air with the pig in its nose—it ripped past. A snapshot of profile: the thick skin (two-layered, like the vest beneath his shirt), the pale eyebrows, the plump slobber of the underlip. Richard stood wavering, his hair roughly tousled by the backdraft of the German car.

In its wake, also, crept the tublike orange van, with its limp cream curtains, and 13 slumped flaccid at its wheel. "*Yes*," he managed to say (it was pure sibilant: *Sssss*) when he saw the three of them standing there. Relief and even rapture were shoving their way through a sepsis of distress. It had hit him as he stared through the gap in the back gate of the dead garage: *Them was the same fucking blokes that did Crash.* Telling little Marco to run along or piss off. And Adolf saying, What's this then? What's this then, lads? Adolf knew what it was: it was a lesson. Compared to you lot—compared to you, I'm a child. I'm a child . . . 13 was free. He crept past in the orange van. He didn't want them to see him. He never wanted their fire of eyes.

Marco wasn't crying. But Lizzete was. And so was Richard. In the peripheries of his mind he was already rewriting his Profile (It's not often. Clash the, roll out the, raise high the. Hats off to) and working on a way of forgiving Gina. A form of words. Because if he forgave her, she could never leave him now. Who was he? Who had he been throughout? Who would he always be? He was Abel Janszoon Tasman (1603–59): the Dutch explorer who discovered Tasmania without noticing Australia . . .

All the rumors of wind, which had until then been anarchic, like all the backdrafts of London come together, like all the car alarms of London (the Blitz which each of us suffers alone)—all the rumors of wind now gathered themselves, in riptide. More a breath sucked in than a breath expelled, up the street it hastened, shaking the trees until their teeth rattled and their pretty hair fell out. Soon the apple blossoms were everywhere, as an element.

And that was the blossoms gone for another year. But for a little while longer they flew in festive and hysterical profusion, as if all the trees were suddenly getting married.

The Man in the Moon is getting younger every year. Your watch knows exactly what time is doing to you: *tsk, tsk*, it says, every second of every day. Every morning we leave more in the bed, more of ourselves, as our bodies make their own preparations for reunion with the cosmos.

Beware the aged critic with his hair of winebar sawdust. Beware the nun and the witchy buckles of her shoes. Beware the man at the callbox, with the suitcase: this man is you. The planesaw whines, whining for its planesaw mummy. And then there is the information, which is nothing, and comes at night.